PENNY'S TALE

Pe in
au

Wi e
up d
romantic Penny, born the youngest of a large and impoverished family.

Driven by innocent ideals and ambition, through hardship and heartache, success and sadness, loyalty and love, life turns full circle for Penny.

PENNY'S TALE

PAMELA ST. CLAIR

P. JONES, 3 WYEDEAN RISE, BELMONT, HEREFORD, HR2 7XZ, UK

First published in Great Britain in 2003 by:
P. Jones, 3 Wyedean Rise, Belmont, Hereford, HR2 7XZ, UK

British Library Cataloguing-in-Publication Data.
A catalogue record for this book is available
from the British Library.

ISBN: 0-9544547-0-7

All characters in this publication are fictitious and
any resemblance to real persons, living or dead, is purely coincidental.

Printed by *Manuscript ReSearch Printing,* P.O. Box 33, Bicester, OX26 4ZZ, U.K.
Tel: 01869 323447/322552 Fax: 01869 324096

ACKNOWLEDGEMENTS

My thanks go to the following:

My husband, George, for loving me.
My family and friends, for the background.
Jenna, Jill and Julie, for the typing.
Mike, for the memories and the proof reading.
Jeff, for the back cover portrait.
Michael, for the cover design.
Ann, for the front cover illustration.

CONTENTS

PART ONE

INNOCENCE

CHAPTER ONE
1935

Lavinia gave the last, final push, and felt the baby slip between her legs. It had been a relatively easy birth this time, but she still felt exhausted. She waited ... no cry yet ... had it all been in vain this time? Thoughts rushed through her head. Was it dead? They couldn't really manage another baby. No, no, she wanted this baby! She lifted her head, trying to discern the glistening shape and heard a little squeak, and suddenly the midwife was lifting and smacking the tiny form. She held her breath and then, at last, out burst a little cry.

"A lovely little girl for you, Mrs. Saunders. A bit skinny but she'll do."

Later, relaxing in the hospital bed, nursing the tiny baby, only 5lbs 4ozs in weight, Lavinia's thoughts turned to how they were going to manage ... yet again. This was their tenth child, although two were now dead. They had lost their eldest, dear Edith, at only eight years of age, when the family were struck down with diphtheria. She tearfully remembered how, on returning from the isolation hospital, where she too had spent several weeks with her own life in the balance, she was told that Edith had been buried a week earlier. Gazing down at the new baby, she examined the little mite's face. Was this Edith returned? And then she remembered tiny Theresa, the poor sickly child they lost aged just six months. She remembered also how the midwife had said at the birth, "Looks like a pretty little doll. Too pretty to live," as she placed the lifeless form at the foot of the bed, while she went back to dealing with the mother. But Lavinia's own mother was in the room, and she noticed a slight movement in the child. And then they were shaking and slapping until a weak cry finally squeaked out. But she was always sickly, and it was a credit to Lavinia that she survived the six months. As baby Theresa finally faded away, Lavinia remembered those words, 'She was too pretty to live.' This baby looked pretty too, very pale and so tiny and frail.

This was their tenth child - eight still living. Every two years a baby had materialized, but there had been a gap of four years between Rosamund and… and … a name, what would they call this poor soul? Things were so hard at home. Harry had lost their business in the slump of '26. Things had been quite hard, even when they still had the grocer's store in East London, but since then, it had been even harder, moving from one rented property to another, usually because they were in arrears with the rent, and the family increasing all the time. Harry was taking any job he could find and very often there was nothing available, and when he did get something, he was often drinking far too much of the meagre wages. Of late, the two older boys had been doing odd jobs and errands to earn a few shillings to help out. They really did not have a penny between them all. Not a penny! A penny ... Penny ... that's what they would call her ... Penny ... Penelope Saunders ... yes, that was it, no middle name, just Penelope Saunders, plain and simple, and hopefully the end of the line.

Back home from the hospital, the house in North London, where they had managed to keep up the rent for a few years, Lavinia sat up in bed, waiting to introduce the rest of the family to the new arrival. They filed into the bedroom to peep. First, Rosamund, now over four years old, a tall girl for her age, with long dark hair which Lavinia loved to plait. Then came Annie, just six, slimmer than her younger sister and with golden hair which was kept in a bob. Behind them both came Robert, poking the girls' bottoms as he pushed them in. He was a pale-faced boy with medium brown, straight hair, and he was always teasing the younger girls. He had turned eight the day before the baby was born.

"This is Penny. So now we have four boys and four girls," Lavinia said to the waiting brood. "She nearly arrived on your birthday, Robert."

"But it's another girl," Robert remarked.

Then in came Dorothy, ten years old, and 'Little Mother' to the younger children. She was a quiet, serious girl, with dark bobbed hair, quite short in stature, but already well-developed. She would have to help around the house, while her mother had to spend the customary weeks in bed after giving birth. There should be six weeks of no heavy lifting. Lavinia's own mother would also be around doing what she could, and her older sister, Mabel, who lived not too far away, would call with some home cooking for them all. But Lavinia knew that she would have to be up and doing long before she should.

Last one through the door was Lenny. In he rushed, broad cheeky grin on his face, as per usual, rushing to kiss his mother, and gently poking the baby. He was always smiling and laughing, and telling jokes to them all. He was twelve years old, very slight in build, with wavy hair, and the only one with a hint of red in it, like their mother.

The two older boys were not yet home from their jobs. Neville was sixteen. The baby who had died had been between him and Lenny. He was the tallest in the family at the moment, and had tight, curly brown hair, a blemish of facial hair, and was certainly growing into a handsome lad. But he was not strong, suffering badly from asthma. He had left school at fourteen and was now working for the local grocer, delivering orders on his bike. He had always been a mischievous boy, playing truant from school, and playing tricks on the family and neighbours. But he was not malicious and was well-liked.

The eldest of them all was Graham, turned eighteen the previous month. He had worked hard in school, and now had an apprenticeship in tool-making, and was trying to obtain a similar opportunity for his brother, Neville. He was the serious one of the family, blonde and handsome, but in a different way from his brother. He had been a very clinging child and had been deeply shocked when his older sister died. They had been very close. He now seemed to put all his energy into his new work, becoming worried about the hardship in the family and detaching himself from them when at home. When Lavinia had first told him there was another baby on the way, he had rounded on her, shouting, "We can't afford another baby!" He still seemed an innocent young man and Lavinia wondered if he meant they couldn't afford the upkeep of another baby, or did he think that babies were bought? Neither she, nor Harry, had ever discussed the facts of life with their children, but she imagined that out of them all, Neville was the most street-wise.

So there they were, all very different in appearance and character. But there was one common denominator - they all had blue eyes like their father. Lavinia's eyes were more of a pale hazel. As she looked at the new baby, she wondered what her colouring would be. It was too early to tell. The little hair that she had, was on the light side. Her eyes had not yet developed their true colour, but she imagined they too would be light. As it eventually turned out, she had fair, straight hair, and green eyes.

CHAPTER TWO

1939

The family moved house yet again, and now, more than a year later, the financial situation had improved slightly, with Neville getting an apprenticeship as a toolmaker, like his older brother. A larger house had become vacant to rent, in a very pleasant residential area, not far from Lavinia's own home, and where her parents still lived. In fact, it was just a fifteen-minute walk away.

Lenny had started work as a messenger boy for a large communications firm in the city, and Dorothy was coming up to school-leaving age. When the time came, she took a job serving in the local newsagent, tobacconist and confectioner shop just around the corner from their street. Robert had passed the scholarship to the Grammar school, which was a ten-minute walk from the new house. Annie followed him two years later. Rosamund continued to go to the original primary school, but it now entailed a much longer walk than that from their previous home. But hopefully she would soon follow her brother and sister to the Grammar School.

Penny enjoyed living in the new house. There were lots of interesting corners in which to hide and play. The small front bedroom over the porch had an enclosed balcony with full-length doors opening out on to it. This was a special place where they put the injured birds that they so often had to rescue from the cat. The bird would be put in an old shoebox, with grass and some breadcrumbs and water, in the hope that it would fully recover and fly away, or, if it was a youngster, that the parent bird would find it. Penny thought it a wonderful place where the injured got better. Invariably, they had flown away by the next day when she went back to check. Little did she know that, invariably, the poor creature died, and one of her siblings had removed the cold body before her inspection.

Lavinia thought Penny a lovely child. She had been a contented baby, and was, on the whole, well-behaved. Her main relief was that it now appeared there would be no more babies on the way. She had been forty-one when she had Penny, but had had no more menstrual cycle since. Harry was twelve years older than she, so he was now approaching his sixties.

Her own parents had become more infirm, and she had to help out with shopping, cleaning and cooking for them in their own home, several times a week. Her sister Mabel went at other times. It meant a lot of extra work for Lavinia, and she would visit them two or three times a week, taking Penny with her, doing what she could, then rushing back to catch up on her own chores and to prepare a meal for the family. The biggest job was the continual washing which a family of ten entailed. Her hands were rubbed raw, and then there was always the worry of getting it all dried and aired. Coal was a major weekly expenditure, and it was needed not only for the fires in the kitchen and living room, but to give hot water for all the washing and bathing. All the bedrooms had small fire grates, but none were ever lit. Going to bed in winter was a very cold exercise.

Penny's memories of her grandparents' house and visits there were a mixture of good and bad. While her mother worked, she would have to amuse herself, very quietly. Her grandfather was very strict. He was tall and had a moustache, which he forever tweaked. For most of the day, he would sit in the back lounge, playing Patience, of which he recorded every result in an old, leather diary. Her grandmother was a warm person, and she usually tried to find something for Penny to look at. Sometimes it would be a button box, which Penny enjoyed sorting out all the colours and then choosing the one she liked best. Or she may get out a box of old Christmas cards. Penny liked to spread them all over the large wooden kitchen table and play 'Dip, Dip, Dip'; reducing one from each round until the winner was left. One particular day, she was down to the last two or three and her mother said she would have to pack up as she wanted to set the table for the grandparents' dinner.

"In a minute," Penny replied, just as her grandfather came into the room.

"You do it now, girl, when your mother tells you," he stormed at her. Penny gathered the remaining few up very quickly, but she thought it so unfair, as she had so few left, and she had started with more than sixty, and the game had taken a long while.

At some time during the visit, her mother and grandmother would have a glass of stout each. The work would stop, and they would chat. Penny watched as they poured the stout, and a thick creamy head appeared at the top of each glass. She would sit patiently, and inevitably her mother would say, "come on then," and Penny would be allowed to sup the froth. Then she would patiently wait again until her grandmother would say, "Get the tin out, girl." Penny loved this part. There was a tin of cheese biscuits kept in the huge pantry on the lower shelf, just where she could reach. She would lift them out to the table, and open the lid and take a few. The smell of the cheese would puff out, so that she could taste them before even eating them.

But there was a scary side to visiting her grandparents. Her grandmother was a spiritualist, and when she and her mother, and sometimes her aunt too, were sitting chatting, she would often talk about whom she had spoken to one night, or whom she had seen. They never seemed to be bothered that Penny was listening. One day she was talking about someone called Helen whom she had seen that night standing at the bottom of the stairs. Soon after, Penny and her mother had to stay overnight at the grandparents' house. Penny never knew why. She was terrified when her mother took her upstairs to a huge bed, and said she would join her later. Penny dived under the covers, hardly being able to breathe, and imagining that that Helen would appear any moment. Next morning she couldn't wait to get back to the safety of their own home.

And then the war came. Everything changed. Graham joined the R.A.F, training to become a pilot. Neville wanted to join the army, but he never passed the medical, due to his history of asthma. Lenny joined the navy, and was positively excited at the prospect of seeing the world. He went off with his usual smile! With so many young men going into the forces, some jobs became vacant, and Harry managed to get a temporary civil service job. At least that gave a regular income, although with the rent, rates and upkeep of a large house and family, there was never any spare. He and Neville were enlisted into the Home Guard to do their bit for their country. At this time, Harry's elderly mother, who had previously lived alone in an

East London flat, moved in with the Saunders family. This meant them losing the use of one of their bedrooms, which Granny Saunders took over as a small bed-sitter, cooking for herself on a small, oil stove. But with the two older boys away for most of the time, the house was not too crowded, as they rarely seemed to get leave at the same time.

Penny enjoyed the war years. Not realizing its implications, she found it very exciting. Most nights when the siren would sound, all the family gathered together downstairs, huddled up, usually in Mum and Dad's bedroom. There were ack-ack guns positioned not far away, in the local park, and these would boom and vibrate through the house, planes droned, and bombs exploded all around. One night incendiary bombs were dropped all along the street. Fortunately, they were soon put out, but it involved so much activity, that Penny thought it an extra-special night. The daytimes, after raids, saw the children out searching for shrapnel pieces. They compared and contrasted their finds, and those of them at school would take them to show their friends or to swap.

Penny still slept in her parents' bedroom, and every night, after being put to bed, she prayed that there would be an air-raid, so that all the family would join them and the fun would start. In contrast, Lavinia worried herself sick. They would all huddle together on the floor behind the bed, sheltered from the windows. Harry, who had seen action in the trenches during the Great War, refused to get out of bed. Very often, Neville stayed upstairs, and sometimes, Granny Saunders did not turn up either. She was very deaf, and once asleep did not always hear the activity.

Penny was now of school-age, but Lavinia could not face sending her to school. Now that Annie was in the Grammar school, Rosamund had to make the long trek alone to the Primary school. Lavinia had noticed that Penny seemed to get very breathless after running around a lot, and when they had to hurry round to Granny and Grandpa Dale. She worried over all the children, especially when there were daylight raids and they were at school. So she clung to Penny as long as she could, teaching her to read and write whenever she could find a moment, which was not very often. But the older children took over whenever they could. Due to the war, the age for compulsory schooling was delayed until six years, and so in 1941, Lavinia reluctantly had to allow Penny to start school.

Penny set off delightedly, with Rosamund in charge of her for the long walk to school. They had to make the trip four times a day, as they came home for dinner. Part of the journey entailed cutting across a park. The path cut through a field section, and due to the war, there was no labour available to keep the grass cut. It was now so high that it reached up to Penny's face. When they reached the other side, there was an A.R.P station. Most days the warden greeted them, and told them to be careful crossing the big road ahead.

Penny enjoyed school, and did well in class. She was reading and writing before, so found that no problem, and particularly enjoyed the arithmetic lessons, and learned her tables well. The school was an old building. The infants' classes were on the ground floor, and the juniors were on the two upper floors. Teachers were strict. Not starting school until she was six meant Penny had only to spend one year in the Infants. The teacher, Miss Harris, who seemed very ancient, had an awful temper. She would beat you across the hand with a wooden ruler. Fortunately for Penny, she only received it once, but some children, especially the boys, seemed to be forever holding out their hands.

“I don’t think Miss Harris likes children very much,” Penny told her Mother.

And it wasn’t much better in the first junior years. Another spinster, Miss Burrows, who was a very plump lady, seemed to be forever slapping children. She would call a child out to the front, roll up his or her sleeve, and then proceed to slap over and over across the arm, leaving very red marks and a pain which lingered on. She also shouted and perspired a lot.

Rosamund had now passed the scholarship to join her brother and sister at the Grammar School. This meant Penny had to walk alone to school. Lavinia made sandwiches for her lunch, and therefore she had only to make one return journey. But she did get very tired. She often became extra breathless. She couldn’t stand anything across her face. When her mother washed her, she pushed the flannel away when it passed over her nose and mouth. Having her hair washed was an ordeal. She couldn’t stand hanging her head over the sink, and would be fighting for breath.

About this time she began to have occasional turns of fainting. Lavinia was afraid that she was not providing enough good food, what with the rationing and little money. Milk was provided at school, and each day she would ask Penny if she had drunk her milk. Penny hated the school milk. It was delivered in quart bottles, and early in the morning it was decanted in to thick beakers. They were all chipped and cracked, and were laid out on a counter, which was positioned in front of the huge radiator. They were not to be drunk until break, by which time each mug of milk had developed a thick skin on top was covered in chalk and dust, and decidedly warm. It stunk, and Penny heaved each time she had to drink it. It was a smell that stayed with her all her life, whenever she poured milk, even when the days of fridges became a part of everyday kitchens. So, at school, if she got a chance, she would avoid drinking her milk, usually passing it to one of the boys. They seemed to like it!

Once again, the family moved house. Penny was very upset. She had enjoyed a lot of freedom in the old house. They didn't have a lot of toys, but shared what they did have. As a family, they played cards, paper and pencil games, and board games. Some, like Monopoly, could go on for days. Penny, Rosamund, Annie and Robert usually made up the foursome. Robert felt very much in charge, being older than the three girls. He was always the banker, and inevitably won. The sisters were pretty sure he cheated on them.

Penny's other main interest was the dolls and soft toys, which belonged to them all, although she had her favourites. She and Rosamund played their own game which they called 'Bundles'. They would go up to the large bedroom where the older girls slept, and proceed to share the dolls, teddies, and animals between them, then any clothes, covers, etc. They then each chose an area of the room to set up a home, named their characters, and let the game begin. It was a game of everyday life, and at some point, usually involved dances, and boy meeting girl, weddings and babies. Penny would be totally absorbed in the game, and it would go on for a whole day, until, usually, Rosamund would have enough and want to pack up. They named the game 'Bundles' after their aunt had visited one day when they were playing. She looked in on them just as they had tipped all the toys into the centre of the room for the share out. She exclaimed, "What a bundle!"

They didn't have a doll's pram, but were allowed to play with their own baby pram. Penny would pile in her babies, and walk up and down the road for lengthy periods. People in the street would stop to talk to her and look at the babies. There were two pretty cottages at one end of the road. A little old lady lived in one, and she seemed to take in all the stray cats. The family never knew her name, but just called her the 'cat lady'. Penny had a black and white cat called Timmy, and she often dressed him up in some of the doll's clothes; dress, jacket, bonnet, and then lie it in the pram, tuck it in with the covers, and proceed up and down the road. The cat was her favourite baby, and normally it was quite amenable to being dressed and taken for a ride. But sometimes it had had enough, and would take a running leap from the pram and dash off. Eventually it would turn up back home, sometimes fully-clothed, or minus a few articles, or without any! Goodness knows how many people must have thought they were imagining things to see a dressed cat running through the gardens! Sadly, the cat did not return home one night, and next day, the 'cat lady' told Penny a black and white cat had been found run over by a car. It wasn't dressed! Penny missed the cat very much. It was her first death.

Soon after this incident, Penny lost her pram too. She was out walking her babies one-day, when she recognised a friend of Annie's coming up the road with an older lady. They went in her house, and shortly after, Lavinia called her indoors. The lady's older daughter was expecting a baby shortly, and as things were scarce because of the war, she asked to borrow the pram. Penny was devastated as she watched her mother taking out the dolls and covers, hurriedly giving the pram a wipe over and then seeing her pram pushed away down the road. She never saw it again.

CHAPTER THREE
1943

So it was they moved house. It was the end of an era for Penny. She never played 'Bundles' with her sister again. The new house, rented again, was sizeable, and situated the other side of the borough in a pleasant area. It had five bedrooms, two of which were very small, and these were both allocated to Granny Saunders. One made a small kitchen and the other was just big enough for her single bed and an easy chair and drawers.

The other single room over the hall was for Graham when he was home on leave. The other three boys shared the large back bedroom, although Lenny was away at sea most of the time, and the three older girls shared the large front bedroom. Lavinia and Harry's bedroom was downstairs in what would have been the back lounge, and Penny had a small bed in with them.

There was a large front lounge, and steps down to a spacious morning room with a fitted wooden dresser and two pantry cupboards, and ample room for their wooden kitchen table and chairs where they mainly ate their meals, and on which Lavinia made her cakes and pastries. The back-boiler fire was in there, and a small kitchenette led off, with a butler sink and the old gas cooker.

The entrance hall had a fireplace, as indeed all the rooms

had, but it was hard enough to find the money for coal for the kitchen boiler and the front room grate. Also in the hall was a pannelled love seat behind which the stairs curved upwards. Outside was a long garden with a nice lawn and an apple and plum tree.

But the most exciting facility to the house, was one that they really should not have used. The first half of the long street, and in which the house was situated, backed on to a large playing field. It belonged to a school several miles away, which meant it was not in use all the time. According to the season, it would be marked out for football, cricket, running lanes with a jumping pit, and hard tennis courts at one end. A high wall ran along the ends of all the gardens backing on to it, but with a little ingenuity and assistance, it was easy enough to get over. There were trees and rough grass on the immediate stretch between the gardens and the main field. The children spent a lot of time over the field. There was a groundsman, but he was not resident, nor on duty every day. He would regularly chase them away, but they soon learned when he was and when he was not on duty. They acquired some old tennis racquets and regularly used the courts. Sometimes, when the older boys were all home, they all went over the wall for a game of cricket. And the trees, grass and hillocks were marvellous for exciting games of hide-and-seek, cowboys and Indians and such things.

The war was still on. Dorothy had had to go to work in the munitions-factory, and Neville's tool-making was now based on war assignments. Around this time, houses were being equipped with either Anderson shelters, which were sited in the garden, or Morrison shelters, which were of an indoor construction. The Saunders opted for the Morrison, and it was erected in the parents' downstairs bedroom. It was made of metal with a solid table-top, and meshwork sides allowing entry at one end. This now became Penny and Rosamund's bed, being the size of a double bed with the mattress on the floor. When the air-raid siren sounded, the rest of the family would join the two girls, already in there, and all huddled together until the all-clear sounded. So for Penny, the excitement was still on. The rest of the time, the shelter was wonderful for a game of table-tennis on the large, solid top.

Every man, woman and child had their own gas-mask, and these had to be carried to school each day. Very often there would be a gas-mask practice, and Penny dreaded these. Not only did she hate the smell of the mask, but, just as when she had a flannel over her face, she would be fighting for breath. Fortunately, they never had to use them in a real event of gas.

The Morrison shelter proved its worth one night. A raid was on, and there was a lot of gun-fire and bombing activity. The latest onslaughts had been from the German doodle-bugs. These droned through the sky, and then as the droning stopped there would be a silent pause of a minute or two before the sudden explosion as they hit the ground. With the bombs, you heard the whistling down and you could tell for a moment if they were coming your way. But with the doodle-bugs, the eerie silence after the droning sound left everyone holding their breath, wondering where it would fall. The activity sounded nearer than usual. The family was all gathered in the shelter, except for Neville, who refused to come downstairs, and for Harry, who was still in bed! The whole house was rattling and shaking as they listened to the barrage outside. Lavinia was terrified, and kept shouting for Dad to come in to the shelter with them, but he refused. Suddenly, there was an almighty explosion, much nearer than anything before. At the same time, Neville dived in to the midst of the family huddle. Glass was shattering all around, and things were crashing about. Lavinia screamed out, "Dad, where are you?" and he replied, "I'm under the bed." He had leapt out very rapidly. When they finally crept out to view the damage, they found slivers of glass embedded in the old mattress, which they kept standing against the side of the shelter, facing the window. Other lumps lay on top of the bed, which Dad had just hurriedly left and there were lumps of ceiling plaster on the shelter tabletop.

Next morning they found much devastation all around. The bomb had landed on the council estate just opposite their road. Some houses were flattened with fatalities, and others were extensively damaged. The children had a family of friends living on the estate, and were relieved to find that they had all survived, but were going to have to be re-housed. For the moment, everyone was temporarily living in the local church hall. The children went to see them. With the shock of the previous night's raid, and after seeing their friend's house in such a mess, and then the picture of them in the church hall, Penny began to have a different view of the war. Maybe it wasn't so exciting after all!

Living at the new home meant that Penny now had a very long journey to school. She did not want to transfer to the nearer, local school. It was on a rather rough estate catchment area, and apart from the friends who had been bombed out, they had not really mixed with the children there. The only local friends Penny had were two girls living towards the top of their road. They were two cousins, with their families, sharing one house. The older girl, Pat, was the same age as Penny, and her cousin, Sally, was nearly two years younger. They were both at the local school. Penny spent a lot of time with the girls, after school and during weekends and holiday times. Sometimes they climbed in to the field at the back of the garden, or played on the street and in one another's houses. These were two good friends for Penny, as due to the distance to her own school, it was not possible to play with her peers there out of school time.

Going to school now meant taking two buses each way. At a cost of one-penny fare for each bus, it meant four pence per day, which was quite an outlay for Lavinia. Some days Penny would hang around with some of her friends after school. Those living near would run home for a few pence and then go to spend them in the local shop. Not to be outdone, Penny sometimes spent a penny of her return fare, and would then have to walk the first leg, arriving home very weary, and wishing she hadn't done so.

She was still having fainting fits, and always appeared 'delicate' to Lavinia. So on many days she did not send Penny to school, and it also meant she didn't have to find the fare. But although Penny lost a lot of schooling, she maintained good results in her tests. She was now in the top two years of the juniors. They had a male teacher in these two years, and Penny found them more affable and reasonable than the previous ladies. The men were still strict, but without the shouting and slapping.

One teacher, Mr. Roberts, was forever falling asleep in class. He would get comfortable in his high chair behind the tall desk, and then commence 'reading aloud' around the class. This involved one pupil reading a passage from the set books, with the rest of the class following it in their own books. You read until Mr. Roberts called, "Next," and the next pupil stood up and took over, and so on around the class. However, Mr. Roberts invariably fell asleep, only to suddenly snap awake for a moment to call, "Next." Then he promptly fell asleep again. Sometimes, one child could be reading for up to ten or fifteen minutes. Meanwhile, the rest of the class would be quietly sniggering, and pointing out Mr. Roberts, or disrupting other children. But they were not malicious and really respected Mr. Roberts. Rumour was that he drank rather a lot, and he came from Wales. Penny didn't know anything about Wales.

During the last school year, they were prepared for the scholarship exam, which would decide who would go to the Grammar school and who would go to the Secondary Modern school. Mr. Sands, the master, gave them tests weekly, and the marks were totted up to see who had the highest, at the end of each Friday. He would announce the 1st, 2nd and 3rd places to the class. One boy was very, very bright, and in a normal week, he, another boy and Penny would compete between them for the first three places. Even though she was regularly absent, she found it quite easy to keep up with the work. But inevitably when she handed in her note, excusing her absence, the teacher would make a remark that she had been 'Off again!' with a look that said they thought she had been skiving. She came to dread being kept off school by her mother.

One day, Mr. Sands went around the class, asking each child what they hoped to do or become, when they grew up and left school. When it came to Penny's turn, she replied, "I want to get married and I will have four babies. Four boys, no girls. Girls are silly." The whole class giggled. Mr. Sands replied, "Well, that's not much of an ambition, Penny, and you will have to find a rich husband if you want four children!"

Penny didn't know a lot about the intricacies of how to

have a baby. What she did know, however, she had gleaned from secretive, break-time chats with the other girls. They would speak of men and ladies having to mix blood. One discussion was to why a baby should be a boy or a girl. Penny's suggestion was that as you had to mix blood, it would depend on if there was more of the father's or the mother's blood. The other girls thought her very knowledgeable.

During this last year at the school, two sisters from Scotland arrived. For some reason, the family had moved south to North London. These girls told tales concerning boys and girls, men and ladies, and making babies, that were very enlightening, and to Penny, almost unbelievable! They also told naughty jokes, and used language that most of the girls neither understood, nor had ever heard before. It was a real education for Penny.

One day, the older sister informed the circle of avid listeners that, "Men have two balls hanging between their legs, behind their dick." Now Penny had never seen a boy or man's private parts. Her brothers being so much older than her had always kept themselves covered in her presence. So that night when she went to bed in her parents' bedroom downstairs, she planned how she could see her father's parts. Early next morning, she heard her father getting out of bed. He moved to the end of the bed, and proceeded to bend forward to reach for his slippers. The back of the nightshirt rose up, and Penny saw things hanging down, but was not quite sure what was what. But that day she went to school and announced, "Well my Dad has got three, so there!"

Lavinia knew she kept Penny off school far too much. But she worried. She dreaded any of the family being unwell. There wasn't enough money for the general running of the house on a daily basis. To see the doctor and get medicine cost money. Every so often, she would go along with Penny to their very old family doctor, and ask for a tonic. But normally when one of them was ill, she would concoct some old fashioned remedy that had been passed down from mother to daughter. At one time, when Penny was very young, she was taken ill with whooping cough. Lavinia could not afford the doctor. The other children were getting ready for school, but Robert came in to the bedroom and gloated at Penny, "You're going to have turnip juice!" Sure enough, Lavinia came up later with the most revolting stuff. The smell and taste of it lingered with Penny for ages.

The war was now over, but the brothers were still in the forces. Robert, too, had to do his term. He was terrified of being sent down the mines, so he signed up for the Royal Navy. He was not very happy in Service life, and fortunately, his time was soon up, and he never even had to go to sea for any length of time. In fact, he was dreadfully sick on the one voyage he made as far as the Isle of Man! On demob, he went to the Bank. Lenny took up cable-jointing on his demob, and said that later on he intended emigrating to New Zealand: "The most wonderful country I came across in my world-wide travels of the war," he said. Graham went back to his tool-making and designing, after coming out of the R.A.F, where he had seen service as a bomber pilot. And Annie was now old enough to go in to nursing training.

Penny heard that she had passed to go to the Grammar school. At this time, after a dental check-up at the clinic, she had an appointment to have an extraction under gas. Lavinia took her to the clinic, and waited nervously in the waiting room, while the nurse directed Penny to the surgery, where the dentist and anaesthetist were waiting. Penny reluctantly went in. Lavinia waited. Suddenly, the door re-opened, and the dentist called her inside. "I'm afraid we have not been able to do the extraction, Mrs. Saunders. The anaesthetist has checked Penny over, and he is not satisfied that her heart sounds normal. We think you should get an appointment for her to see a specialist at the hospital."

As they made their way home, Lavinia could not get the words out of her mind: 'not satisfied that her heart sounds normal!' What could it mean? Back home, she lifted Penny's clothes and put her ear to her chest. She could hear her heart quite well. Why was it wrong? Then she listened to Rosamund's, but she didn't think there was much difference.

They received the hospital appointment, and Penny was put through a series of tests and X-rays. Finally, the specialist called them in.

"Your daughter has a congenital heart murmur. So she has been born with the condition. There is a small hole between her two heart chambers, so that valve does not fully separate the oxygenated blood from the de-oxygenated blood. We will write to your doctor with a full report."

The next visit was to the old family doctor. He was well in to retirement now, and kept his old-fashioned ideas. He read the report and then listened attentively to Penny's heart. He could hear the beat and then the purr of the murmur. Penny never forgot his words to her mother.

"I'm afraid you will have trouble with this one, Mrs. Saunders. She will never be strong, and really should rest every day, but of course she has got to go to school, so that's not very possible. Now there will be lots of strenuous sports and activities at the Secondary school, so I will give you a certificate to excuse her from these sessions. She won't be able to marry and have children. You will have your hands full. I am sorry." And he got up to dispense the usual tonic.

They walked home, wearily, hand in hand. Lavinia was in total shock. Penny was stunned, and could still hear the old doctor's words ringing in her head, 'she won't be able to marry and have children.' She hated that doctor, and made up her mind that she would prove him wrong.

CHAPTER FOUR
1946

Penny was now eleven and a half, and once more she was able to set off for school with Rosamund, who still had one more year to do at the Grammar school. They would take one short bus ride and then walk up the long road in which the school was situated, not far from their old house, really. Or they could walk via the back roads, which took them about thirty minutes, or they could go by bike. Work was more intense in this school, with different teachers for different subjects and much higher ability. Classes were streamed, and Penny had been put in the A class on the strength of her entrance exam results. Now if she was absent for any length of time, it was very hard to catch up with the work again. She didn't want to be absent, and tried not to let her mother know if she wasn't feeling too well. Several times she had a fainting turn at school. She would be taken to the medical room and Rosamund called from class to keep her company. Having handed in the doctor's certificate at the start of the first term, she had to sit and watch the P.E and games lessons.

This was all very frustrating for Penny. She was a naturally, well co-ordinated girl. She had always had a good eye for ball games, could skip, roller-skate - which she did up and down the street with her friends Pat and Sally, and had recently learned to swim. She was very good at table-tennis, which she had learned from her father, who ran such a club at work. There was a house system in the school, and Penny was put in the Red House. She knew she would be, as, if you had siblings at the school, you were always allotted to the same House. This meant Robert had been the first, followed by Annie, Rosamund and now Penny. "Well I won't be of much use to the Reds," she thought. "I don't do anything."

In the second year, she was re-streamed in to the B form, and this seemed the appropriate level for Penny. She had become friendly with two girls while in the A class. They were Belinda and Joyce. They lived near one another but came from out of the immediate area. Belinda and Penny were re-streamed together in the B form, while Joyce remained in the A. This was the start of a very close friendship, which they maintained throughout their school years.

One day, early in the second school year, the girls were to have a netball session, Penny watching. They were one person short to make up two full sides. The P.E teacher, who was newly appointed that term, explained which position they would play without. Penny put up her hand. "I'll play," she said. "I thought you aren't allowed to," the teacher replied. "Oh I'm better now, it's o.k." Penny lied. "Well that's good. Play centre attack," the teacher replied. And so began a turning point in Penny's life.

She loved the P.E and games lessons, and began to excel in most. At first, when she had lied her way into participating, she was very nervous, wondering what effect it would have on her heart. "I suppose I will just drop dead during a game one day," she privately thought. She did get breathless, of course, and at the end of each session, her face would remain flushed for several hours, long after the other girls had paled down. She dare not tell her mother, at first, that she was doing the activities, but it came to a point where she had to, as she needed the P.E kit to be washed. Lavinia became hysterical when she heard what she had been doing.

"You mustn't, you mustn't," she gasped out. "How did you feel? Did it hurt?" She questioned. "It doesn't hurt, and I like it. I'm trying to get in to the teams. They want me in them. I'm good at it. It's the best thing I do," Penny informed her. So Lavinia relented, making her promise that if it ever got to hurt, she would stop.

Rosamund had now left school, and was working in a solicitor's office in the city. She had become very moody at home the past year or two, and seemed to argue a lot with their mother. Penny had always been very respectful of her mother, and loved her dearly. She would never intentionally upset her, and became very upset herself when she heard Rosamund answering back and being very rude and stubborn. In fact, to hear her, brought tears to Penny's eyes and she would have to leave the room.

Rosamund had a boy friend, and a lot of the arguments were over her stopping out late. In fact, she and the boy were half way down the road, kissing and cuddling under a lamppost, for lengthy periods, on their way home from the cinema or wherever they had been on a date. Penny used to watch them from the top front bedroom window, having gone up to bed in the large room she now shared with the other girls. No doubt Lavinia was also keeping an eye on the couple from the downstairs front lounge window! In fact, this was the cause of most of the arguments, with Lavinia saying, "What will the neighbours think of you, Rosamund, making a spectacle of yourself right under the lamplight." Penny also wondered why they didn't go somewhere more private.

There were several changes within the family around this period. Neville married a young war widow, Ellie. They lived with the family for a while, taking the big back bedroom. Ellie was a very lively young woman, and used a lot of make-up. The girls used to watch her applying it very expertly, and began to experiment themselves. She was highly entertaining and dramatic, always spoke her mind, and several times instigated an argument within the family. She loved to go to the cinema, and as Neville was often making nick-nacks such as cigarette lighters, which he sold for extra cash, and did not want to go too, she would persuade Lavinia or one of the girls to accompany her. She was great fun at Christmas time and parties, singing and dancing and telling jokes, often very ribald. The girls learnt a lot from Ellie, in more ways than one!

Neville and Ellie soon had a baby, a boy, and called him Charles. The whole family adored him, and there were plenty of ready-made baby sitters. It made Penny even more determined to fulfil her ambition. She announced to her mother one day, not realizing what her statement implied, "Well, even if I don't ever get married, I shall still have a baby." Lavinia was shocked to hear her talk so, and said, "You must not talk like that!"

Later, Neville, Ellie and the young tot moved to the country, where Neville had been offered a tool-making job in a new factory. Ellie found the life very slow there, and lost the freedom she had with a family of baby sitters.

Dorothy also got married, literally to the boy next door, well almost. His brother was married, living two doors from the Saunders and the brother's in-laws lived right next door to them. This neighbour was a real gossiper, which Lavinia was not. If the woman heard her out in the connecting side-way, either going to the dustbin or getting in the coal from the cellar entrance, she would immediately come out too, hoping to chat. Poor Lavinia would have to stand for lengthy periods listening to all the gossip, and then worrying at how she needed to get on with the continual round of washing and other household chores. She never returned gossip concerning her own family, if she could help it, always feeling conscious of the fact that theirs was a life of hardship. However, the neighbours had obviously been planning an introduction of their young man, Jonathon to Dorothy. He was well educated, and had a good job with the Patent Office. The introduction took place, and after much courting, they finally got engaged and then married.

A wedding meant another head-ache for Lavinia. At least Neville and Ellie had just quietly married at a register office with a quick drink afterwards! There was no money available for a grand reception, and although the war was now over, rationing was still in force. Lenny came to the rescue with the wedding dress, buying a silk parachute, which at that time became available for material on the Black Market. He had a dressmaker friend, and she made a simple but attractive bridal gown. Lenny also bought material for bridesmaids dresses to be made for Annie, Rosamund and Penny, although now that the two older girls were working, they contributed what they could. He and Graham searched for, and paid for, a few bottles of spirits, which were also in short supply.

There was a near disaster concerning the drink. It was to be collected from the grocery store near to their old house. It was kept under the counter, but the arrangement had been made for its collection a few days before the wedding. Penny was sent as the courier, and was given a small case in which to carry it home. She had to take two buses there and two back. When she got to the store, she handed over the case to the manager. It was secretly dealt with in the back of the shop and then handed back to her. She went to sit in the bus shelter to await the first bus back, and stood the case at her feet, as it was quite heavy. She saw the bus approaching, and, as she went to pick up the case, the top suddenly flew open, and out fell one wrapped bottle. Quickly she pushed it back in, did up the case, and joined the queue. Getting on the bus, the conductor said, "You're leaking, girl!" The case was dripping, so she leapt off again. She was panicking, and, not knowing what to do, took off her cardigan and shoved it around the leaking bottle, jumped on the next bus, finally changing to the second route to finish the journey home. Walking up the road to her house, she was crying and worried sick. Her heart was pounding and her brain was a whirl. What would her mother say! What would her brothers say! What would happen about the wedding reception!

When her mother opened the door, she virtually collapsed in to her arms. "I didn't do anything," she wailed. "It just flew open, I couldn't stop it running out! What will the boys say?" Lavinia was worried too. It was a whole bottle of whiskey gone. She had neither the funds nor the know-how to replace it. She blamed herself. She should never have sent the child on such a task. And she, too, wondered what the boys would say. Harry had been laid-off from his Civil Service job now that the younger men were returning from war service. He only managed to get an occasional temporary job, so it meant that there was no regular income from him.

She tried to console Penny, and made her go to rest in bed. Penny lay there, listening for when her brothers would return from work, and wondering what they would say or do. Eventually, she did doze off, waking up late in to the evening, with Lavinia telling her to come downstairs for something to eat. She crept down very sheepishly, and found Lenny and Graham seated at the table, eating their meal. Graham looked sympathetically towards her. "Don't worry, Penny," he said. Lenny, as usual grinning at her. "Well, you could have waited 'til the wedding before you drank the whiskey. Got a headache now, have you?" he joked. "Don't worry, we'll replace it, somehow." Penny was so relieved, and felt a rush of blood to her face, and promptly went in to one of her faints.

The wedding went well, with the two families and just a few friends coming back to the house from the church. Lavinia had made sandwiches, sausage rolls, cheese straws, scones, small cakes and a wedding cake, which they got the local baker to ice and decorate. Everyone seemed to get a drink. The boys had managed to replace the whiskey on the Black Market. Dorothy and Jonathon left for a short honeymoon at Brighton, and then went to live in half of his parents' house, making a self-contained flat, and not too far away from the family.

Shortly after, there was a second wedding. Robert was now working in the Bank, and had become engaged to a young colleague. Now they were to marry. Delphine lived in Hampstead, and she invited Penny to be her bridesmaid, along with a cousin on her side. It was a much grander affair than the last wedding, with many people in the church and at the large reception held in the church hall in Hampstead. Robert and Delphine were to live in a flat in that same area, in a property owned by her father. Penny enjoyed the wedding and there was music and dancing at the reception. She longed for when she, too, would become a bride. This now made the third time that she had been a bridesmaid, as when she was only nine, she had also been one for her cousin, the daughter of Aunt Mabel. When they all arrived home, late, from Robert and Delphine's wedding, Penny remarked that she had now been a bridesmaid three times. Rosamund teased her, "You know what they say, three times a bridesmaid, never a bride!" Penny worried over that statement as she lay in bed that night.

CHAPTER FIVE
1948

Penny was enjoying herself at school. She was now thirteen and beginning to feel very grown up. She was developing a trim figure, curving out in the right places with a tiny waist, and quite petite in stature. She was doing away with the plaited hair and experimenting with a variety of styles. Lavinia would curl all the girls' hair sometimes, using squares of tissue paper or pieces of rag to twist the curls all over their heads. Penny could now do it herself, and used squares of toilet paper to fix the curls. When she finished, they looked like a load of walnuts all over her head. To sleep in them was murder, but 'Pride feels no pain', and she would suffer the night out so that she could comb out the curls the next day. By the afternoon it would be only wavey, and if it were a damp day, it would be gone altogether by the time she returned home.

She was becoming very conscious of her appearance. With her trim figure, fair, sometimes curly, shoulder-length hair, green eyes and long eyelashes, she was indeed very attractive, and the boys were noticing too. Possibly because she was quite short, and because the boys tended to be still quite short at the same age, she appeared more attractive to them. While sitting in class, she was aware that several of the boys were eyeing her. Of course, they were giving the other girls the eye too.

Penny too was beginning to look around at the boys, although it was the older boys in the school who seemed the most attractive. The girls' chat was very much boy-orientated now. There was a lot of note-writing and passing of these around. About this time Penny got her first 'crush'. There were two older boys in her year and they were certainly taller and more mature looking than the other boys. Most of the girls fancied them too, and her best friend, Belinda, was absolutely besotted with one of them, whose name was Steven. Joyce was much quieter about her feelings, but Penny and Belinda were quite sure that she was interested in the second boy, Patrick. Penny also noticed a funny feeling whenever Steven was around. Not that the girls ever called the boys by their Christian names. In school, all boys were known by their surnames by both their peers and by the Staff. They were Steed and Salter.

After school, Penny and her friends took opposite bus rides home after the long walk to the bottom of the school road. But usually, Penny would walk her friends' way to the second bus stop, and then take a longer ride all the way back to her home. Very often, the two boys would walk with them, which was most exciting, but none of them ever paired off. But it caused lots of heart- fluttering, sleepless nights, fantasies and plenty of note-writing in class next day. At this time, the school laid on a Ballroom dancing class for their year, in the lunch period. So there was much anticipation, excitement and disappointment, as to which of the three friends the two boys would partner. Soon after, Penny had a second 'crush' on the film star, Richard Widmark, in 'The Halls of Montezuma.' She went to see it three times in the one week it was showing at the local cinema. Belinda and Joyce were not at all impressed.

Thirteen was an age when the girls were becoming very conscious of their appearance, experimenting with hairstyles, make-up, clothes and footwear. In school they had to wear uniform, although there were ways of getting away with little individual differences. But of an evening, weekends, and holidays, one could really 'go to town'. Penny was very much disadvantaged in this field. On the whole, she had had to put up with hand-me-downs. Money was short at home and she was bought the minimum. She was given a shilling or two pocket money a week, and first thing she did, was always to go and buy a small bunch of flowers, usually violets at 6 pence a bunch, for her mother. But she wanted to be able to buy clothes and grown-up shoes for herself. So one weekend, she went and fixed up a paper-round with a local shop. She told Lavinia, who was horrified. "The paper bag will be too heavy for you, and you will be tired getting up early," was her reply. But Penny did the job, and got 12 shillings a week, which she saved, and bought all her own out-of-school gear, plus flowers for her mother.

The owner of the newsagent and confectioner shop also owned a second stationary store, which included a private library. He had a young lady running this for him, and he asked Penny if she would like to help out on Saturdays, mainly sorting out the books. This she did, and with some occasional Sunday work serving at the sweet counter in the main shop, she sometimes accrued what was to her a tidy sum. She told Lavinia that she need not give her any pocket money any more, and so she felt she was contributing to the household expenses. At Christmas time, she received a Christmas box at most of the paper-round houses. One year, it amounted to 7 pounds, enough to buy presents for her family and friends.

Greta, who was the other young lady at the library shop, was very friendly towards Penny. She was in her late teens, and when they were not busy, they had, what seemed to Penny, very adult chats. Greta knew about all the books, and would recommend one or other for Penny to read, and allow her to borrow them without paying the few pence which they had to charge the customers. Penny particularly enjoyed the American war-time novels such as 'From Here To Eternity', and romances. Lavinia was rather worried, and discussed with Dorothy one day the nature of the books that Penny was bringing home.

"I hope she isn't reading things she shouldn't know about yet." One of the books, an American novel that she was particularly enjoying, had a young man as the central character, called Ross. Penny had never come across the name before. It stayed in her head intensely, and she told Lavinia, "I shall call the first of my babies, Ross." Lavinia was even more worried! But her favourite book was 'The Blue Lagoon.' Penny was so involved in it, and identified herself with the young girl, all alone with a young boy on a desert island, growing up together, falling in love and producing a baby. She read it over and over. She was that young girl, but she wasn't sure who would be the young boy. She had gone off Steven and Richard Widmark!

They now had a new form teacher at school. The younger men were returning from the forces, and they were a change from what had been mainly elderly staff. He was Mr. McKenzie-Vernon McKenzie he told them, and he came from Yorkshire, having a slightly different accent from them. He was possibly about twenty-six or twenty-seven, Penny guessed, comparing him to her older brothers. As well as being their form master, he taught History throughout the school. His attitude to the students was friendlier than that of the older, more experienced staff, and the children enjoyed the more approachable atmosphere. As the weeks and months progressed, it became very noticeable that Mr. McKenzie paid a lot more attention to Penny. He would choose her to run errands, would hover by her desk a lot, and chat informally to her. When Penny went to his desk to pay her dinner money on a Monday morning, he would keep her chatting, maybe ask what she had done over the weekend. Of course the rest of the class noticed these things, and called her 'Teacher's Pet'. Penny couldn't deny that she did rather enjoy the attention, and found she could get away with murder when in his class. She was full of fantasies, reading her novels, and imagining herself in similar situations, forever drawing hearts with arrows through them, all over her books. They used to have P.S. and S.S.- for she and Steven, then it was P.S. and R.W.- for she and the film star, but of late it was just P.S. and who? Maybe the boy in 'The Blue Lagoon'. She found lots of notes in her desk from boys in class, but never filled them in on the hearts.

One morning, as Penny paid her dinner money, Mr. McKenzie asked, as usual about her weekend. And then he said, "Do you like ballet, Penny? I have some tickets for a performance at The Empire this Friday evening. Ask your mother if you can come." Penny's brain went in to a whirl. What was he asking? Was this a date? Was this a school outing? She didn't know if she wanted to go. Why had he asked only her? She was flattered certainly, but did she want to go? You couldn't say no to your teacher. So she answered meekly, "Oh thank you, Sir."

Lavinia was flattered when Penny told her what Mr.

McKenzie had said. Fancy choosing her daughter out of the whole class to take to the ballet! And so, she sent a letter with Penny next day, thanking him for taking an interest in her daughter's further education, and she was willing for her to accompany him to the ballet. But, as she sealed the envelope, she did rather wonder if she had done the right thing.

Penny was to go by bus to The Empire, about a fifteen-minute ride, and Mr. McKenzie would meet her there. She had tried to dress as different from the school uniform as she could, not that she had much from which to choose. But she still had on her white socks and plain flat shoes. He led her inside to their seats, and introduced her to the lady in the next seat. "This is Penny, one of my pupils. And Penny, this is my landlady." Penny quite enjoyed the ballet, and Mr. McKenzie bought the three of them ice-creams during the interval. As they left the theatre, he told the lady that he would have to see the girl safely home. They caught the bus back to the bottom of her road. Penny said she would walk up the road by herself, and thanked him for taking her to the ballet. "I'll take you to the opera next time, Penny," he said, and went. That night, Penny had mixed up feelings. Why did he ask *her* out?

The following week, Mr. McKenzie told Penny that he had tickets for the Royal Opera House for the Friday and the following week also, and again told her to ask her mother if she may go. Lavinia was very impressed. In her early years of marriage, when they were financially sound, she and Harry had often gone to the Royal Opera House. She thought it a wonderful opportunity for Penny. Penny was certainly flattered that it was only she that Mr. McKenzie invited out, but she wasn't sure in herself that it should be so. She told only Belinda and Joyce about it, and made them promise not to tell anyone else. They were intrigued to know what she wore for these adult dates. When she said she still had on her white socks and flat shoes, they said she must look rather odd to be out with a man like Mr. McKenzie.

This time, Penny was to take the bus to the underground station, where Mr. McKenzie would meet her, and they would then take the underground in to the West End of London. There were only the two of them going this time, no landlady, and Penny was quite over-awed as they entered the Royal Opera House, and were shown to their seats, which must have been expensive ones, being in the front row of the stalls. During the interval, Mr. McKenzie went in to the bar, leaving Penny in her seat.

They caught the underground train for the return journey, and then caught the Trolley bus towards Penny's home. However, that particular route stopped about three stops from the one at the foot of her road, so Mr. McKenzie suggested they walk. It was getting late now, and Penny was a little worried, but she guessed her parents would realize that she would be late after going to a West End show.

As they walked, Mr. McKenzie probed in to Penny's life. Had she had a boyfriend yet? The boys liked her, he said. What did she want to do when she left school? They were just passing a huge poster advertising 'Join the Army'. Penny said she might go in the Forces. Then he suddenly took her hand and said, "Well, where shall we go to the pictures tomorrow?" Suddenly, Penny felt things weren't right. She didn't know how to say no to a teacher, and hedged the question by saying there were no good films on that week. They reached her road and Penny turned to say goodbye, but Mr. McKenzie said he would take her to her house, as it was rather late. She wished he wouldn't and as they reached her house, and she said this was it, he said, "Oh let's walk a little further." Penny was now, very uneasy, and said no, she must go in. As she thanked him for the outing, and he said he was looking forward to the same next week, he put his hands on her shoulders, pulled her towards him and kissed her full on the lips. Penny went rigid, not knowing what to do. She eased away, turned, and walked quickly up the path, as she heard him walk back down the road.

Waiting for someone to open the front door to her in reply to her knocking, she noted that the front lounge windows were in darkness. She knew then that her mother would have put out the light, so as to watch out for her. Lavinia opened the door, looking at Penny in a very strange way. "Well, you can get to bed. And you can tell that teacher that you won't be coming next week."

Penny went to bed, but she couldn't sleep. Her thoughts were in turmoil. He had kissed her. He had asked her to go to the pictures. He had told her to call him Vernon. Was he trying to make her his girlfriend? But she was only thirteen. What would the other girls say? She was flattered. Wait 'til she told them. Then she thought, why had he wanted to walk further up the road? Good job she hadn't, what with her mother looking at them. What would they have done up the road? And suddenly, she wasn't flattered, she was horrified. How dare he kiss her! He wasn't the boy in 'The Blue Lagoon'. How dare he! And then she thought, 'I could get him thrown out of the school for doing that.' And she finally fell asleep, dreaming she was in 'The Blue Lagoon', running towards the boy on the beach, but as she got near, it was Mr. McKenzie, and he was leaning over her, trying to kiss her, and she was trying to say, "No," but the word wouldn't come out. Where was the boy?

Lavinia was threatening to write a letter to Mr. McKenzie for Monday, but Penny pleaded with her not to. "I'll tell him," she said. So, Monday morning, as she handed in her dinner money, she coldly said, "I can't come out again, Sir." She could hardly look at him, but she forced herself to do so. "I'm sorry to hear that, Penny," he replied, and it was he who shifted his eyes first. The following Monday, another girl in the class, who was a year older, and a very attractive, well-developed girl informed the others that Mr. McKenzie had taken her out to the opera. She said she found it all very boring. The girls eagerly asked her what had happened. "Nothing, he put me on the tube home, and left me. Can't understand why he didn't take you there, Penny. We all know you're his favourite." Penny didn't let on, but it proved that Belinda and Joyce had not spread the gossip around and had respected her secrecy. Although, some years later, she heard from another source that everybody did eventually know!

The outing to the opera had a profound effect on Penny. She felt spoiled, that her first kiss had not been with the boy in 'The Blue Lagoon'. She rebelled against Mr. McKenzie, refusing to do her work, sitting reading her novels, and drawing her hearts, challenging him all the time. She refused to do any History homework, or wrote a load of rubbish instead. Mr. McKenzie didn't know what to do with her. He tried to talk with her, but she just stared at him with eyes that said, "I could get you thrown out."

Apart from this episode, life was very enjoyable. Penny was in all the junior school teams and House teams. She had received her gymnastic badge, and did reasonably well in athletics. Dinner times could be fun, with sometimes table tennis in the hall, or dancing to records. Other times, they could play tennis on the courts at the back of the field, or practice netball shooting, which Penny often did, as this was her position in the teams. Other times, on fine days, they would just lie on the grass in the field, gossiping with the girls, eyeing the boys, and being eyed by the boys. After school, and Saturdays, when she wasn't in the shop, she spent her time wandering around the shops, and sometimes spending her paper round and shop wages, mainly on clothes. Other times, she would meet her girl friends and walk in the park, go to the cinema, and, in the summer months go to the local outdoor swimming pool. In fact, this was the favourite venue during the long summer holidays, and when they broke up from that term, they were able to buy a book of tickets at the school office, which gave them admittance to the pool at a special rate of one penny. And Penny very rarely fainted now. She felt stronger in herself, and could tolerate having her hair washed without fighting for breath. She still got very puffed and extra red in the face after games sessions, but she didn't worry about dropping dead anymore. The one thing that guaranteed her going in to a faint was if she had to have an injection, or just to see one, or even talk about injections or veins! Life seemed good. Many girls were pairing off with boys, and several boys tried to pair off with Penny, but she knew she had to feel something special before accepting a date with any one in particular. She was friendly with them all, and enjoyed the starry-eyed looks that some of them gave her, but none would be suitable for 'The Blue Lagoon'.

During the spring half-term holiday week of '48, Penny, Belinda and Joyce went on a holiday week for school children, on the South Coast. It was available for any Secondary School boys and girls in the borough. The three of them had the application forms filled in at home, and they were all accepted. It transpired that Penny's parents did not have to pay anything due to their circumstances, but both Belinda's and Joyce's did. Penny felt rather embarrassed over that. The week before going, they had to go for a medical check at the clinic. Penny was worried about the heart murmur, but it seemed the nurse was more interested in there being no nits in their hair.

They met at a central point, and the coach was full with children from various schools in the borough. There was an older girl from their own school, and she joined with them to make a foursome. As they got on the coach, making their way towards the back, a rather big boy who was already seated in the back, and unknown to the girls as he was from another school, winked at Penny, saying, "Cor, I'm glad you're coming. I've been watching you at the swimming pool!" He was a thick-set boy, possibly fourteen or fifteen, quite mature looking, but not at all attractive, not to Penny anyway. The friend with him was smaller, and very skinny. "We call him Belsen, 'cause he's so thin," said the bigger lad, "And my name's Barry." He patted the seat next to him for Penny to sit down at the back, but she, Belinda and Joyce moved further front.

The three girls enjoyed the holiday week. There were a lot of young people there from boroughs within Middlesex. They slept in bunk beds in huts, like barracks, had to help with simple domestic chores. They also had to keep their huts tidy, and these were inspected each day and points allotted to be totalled at the end of the week. There were organised outings to places of interest, and plenty of games, both inside and out. There were tournaments between the various boroughs. One day it was to be a rounders knock-out tournament. Each group had to organize their own team. Belinda, Penny and Joyce were

Bowler, Back-stop and First post positions in their own school team. These are the key positions, and they proved their worth. Their team slaughtered the others to win first place in the final.

The girls enjoyed the freedom of being away from home, and experimented with what they thought were grown-up hairstyles, make-up and dress. The two boys were forever hanging around, and the boy, Barry, had a camera, and kept jumping out and snapping away at them. He seemed to particularly swoon over Penny, and although she rather enjoyed having such an effect on him, she only teased, and would not get exclusively involved. In fact, she found Belsen the more attractive of the two. They were all at a fairground one day, and Barry was trying to get Penny to go on the Ghost Train with him, but she cunningly connived the seating arrangements to share with Belsen. He did put his arm around the back of the double seat so as to enclose her shoulders, but with all the screaming, bumping and frights, Penny was quite glad that he did so, but only as protection. There were dances on some evenings, and the girls were in high demand with the boys. Penny wasn't very happy when Barry kept asking her out on the floor. He held her quite tight, which she did not like. Sometimes, when she saw him heading her way, she would turn to Belinda or Joyce, to dance two girls together. But then he and Belsen would come over together to split them up. She was happier dancing with Belsen who held her limply and they would joke and giggle as they moved. It was an enjoyable week, and the girls had plenty to talk over on their return to school.

CHAPTER SIX
1949

The year of '49 had quite a few developments within the Saunders family. Grandma Dale died, and soon after, Grandpa died. But Granny Saunders still lived in her two little rooms. Dorothy now had a baby girl and she and Jonathon were moving to a house of their own a little further away. Robert and Delphine had a baby boy, and Neville and Ellie had produced a second boy. Graham was planning marriage with the daughter of a local publican, and Lennie was getting serious with the sister of an old school friend. Lennie had a work-mate, Morris, who quite obviously had designs on Annie. Annie was well into her nursing course now, and had a room at the hospital, so was not always at home. Rosamund seemed to have an on-off relationship with an old boyfriend, but it was now waning.

Penny had joined the Girls Life Brigade, along with Belinda and Joyce. They met on a Monday evening in a church hall near to Belinda and Joyce's homes, which entailed a double bus journey for Penny. They did a lot of activities there, and wore a uniform, which Penny liked. Occasionally, there were organised outings or competitions which entailed travelling further afield.

She was in all the school teams, which involved practices after school, some evening matches, but normally on a Saturday.

This meant that on such occasions, she could not work in the shop until the afternoon, but if there was no game, she put in a full day. She still did the paper round, getting herself up and out each day. They received regular homework at school, and this took up the major part of each evening, plus some of the weekend. Lavinia also expected the girls to help with various housework. So times were quite busy. Penny enjoyed wandering around the shops, going to the park, playing tennis, swimming and sunbathing at the local baths, and the cinema, whenever she could. When she hadn't anything to do, she would relax, listening to popular music on the radio or playing her records.

Since her Grandparents' death, Lavinia's youngest brother, Uncle Alfred to Penny, had taken to staying at their house at certain times. He was married, and lived on the South Coast, but worked in London. He had stayed at their Grandparents' house previously, Mondays to Fridays, going home at the weekend, but he had asked Lavinia if he could have the same arrangement with them. Harry was not very happy over it, and in fact none of the family were very enamoured of Uncle Alfred. He was only a couple of years older than Graham, being a very late child of Lavinia's mother.

One evening, Penny had finished her homework, and was lying on the settee in the darkened front lounge, with only the flickering light from the coal fire. She was listening to a music programme on the radio. Normally her father would have been there listening to his favourite programmes, but he had gone out for a drink, so Penny had grabbed the opportunity to hear her kind of songs. Uncle Alfred had come in late from work, had the meal that Lavinia had saved for him, and now came into the lounge. He sat down in their father's chair at the side of the fire, slightly back from where Penny lay stretched out on the settee. Penny felt awkward, and annoyed, as she was enjoying listening alone. Suddenly, she was aware of Uncle Alfred moving behind her, then the shape of him looming over her, then leaning nearer, and then kissing her full on the lips while pinning her down across her chest. She could hardly breathe, but kicked out with her legs. As he loosed himself, she leapt up, pushed him away and ran out of the room. She was gasping for breath and thought she was going to be sick. She could still feel him on her mouth and could taste the sickly smell of beer. She sat on the loveseat in the hall, wondering what she should do. Lately, there had been a lot of rows between her parents over Uncle Alfred stopping there. She didn't want to make more trouble, so she decided to say nothing. But she made sure she was never alone with him again.

The summer of '49 was a good summer. Most days in the long holiday were hot and sunny, and it meant that Penny and her friends could spend long hours at the local swimming pool. Using their one-penny tickets previously bought as a book of thirty, on the last day of term, entitled them to a whole day at the pool, if so wished. Sometimes they would have to queue for a long while before being able to get in. They would grab an area where they could spread out their towels, and settle down for several hours, sunbathing and swimming. The pool had diving boards of varying heights at the deep end, plus a chute. As the pool was not far from Penny's home, she was able to walk there.

Many boys and girls from the school gathered there, and each age-group tended to gather together. There was plenty of serious swimming and diving, as well as lots of horseplay, in and out of the water, mainly between the girls and boys. Penny and her friends were popular, and developed friendships among the various groups.

Some of the boys, especially, were very good swimmers, and they liked to show off their prowess in front of the girls. They would display their dives and silly jumps off the boards, and leap in near the girls to splash them. And the simple fun and games, gossip and remarks would continue around the sunbathers. Penny did not dive very well, but particularly enjoyed watching those who did. One boy was outstanding, and she was fascinated by his performance on all the boards, including the highest one; rarely did he make a mistake. The school gala was held at the same pool, and he always won the diving event for his house team. His name was Matthew, always called Matt, Matthew James Oliver. Penny thought his full name had a nice ring to it. She had always wished that she had a second name. He was in the year below her at school, but was her age, in fact eight months older. He had obviously entered the school at the second try at the scholarship.

Matt was fun. He had a great sense of humour, as indeed Penny had. It often got her into trouble in lessons at school. A lot of his friends were in Penny's year, or older, and his biggest pal was a boy called Jack Stewart, who was in her year but in a different form. He seemed very street-wise, and had a reputation with the girls. Several of Penny's peers, and older, had obviously had dates with Stewart, and he seemed to flit from one to another. Penny wasn't in the slightest bit interested in him, not that she had had the offer, but he was good fun within the group, although she thought at times that he got up to no good.

They didn't only meet up at the pool. Other times they would congregate in the park, or be wandering around the shops, maybe stopping in the coffee and milk bar. Penny enjoyed this mixed company, and she enjoyed the attention she drew from several of the boys, some her own age, some older, and some younger. But the best satisfaction she had was when the boy Matt, talked to her, swam with her, joked with her, or bumped into her at the park, shops or milk bar. Like her, he excelled at most sports, and was in all the school teams. He didn't live too far from Penny, so their paths would often pass. He, too, did a paper round, although for another shop, but sometimes she would see him early in the morning. Yes, it was a good six-weeks holiday and at the end of it, Penny realised that she was in love!

Attending school became even more attractive. Penny rated her best days according to how many times she had seen or spoken to Matt. She watched all the football practices when she could, and he often watched the netball or hockey practices. After school, she, Belinda and Joyce strolled through the shops, often ending up in the coffee bar. Sometimes, Matt, Stewart and others would be in there, and they would make a drink last a long while, so as to enjoy the company and attention as long as possible. Belinda and Joyce would then head off in the opposite direction to Penny for their journey home. Penny knew Matt's journey was her way, and she tried to time it to leave when he did. Just sometimes he would walk with her some of the way. But generally he hung back with Jack Stewart. Penny now found she could think of nothing else other than her meetings with Matt. She couldn't concentrate on her lessons, and would daydream or doodle on her books. And one day she found that on one of her arrowed hearts, she had entered P.S. and M.J.O. Had she found the boy in the Blue Lagoon?

Penny began to believe that Matt was interested in her.

Sometimes she thought he went out of his way to cross her path, as indeed she did to cross his. Her most exciting association was during some lunch breaks, when, especially if it was wet, they were allowed to have a mixed dancing session to records in the hall. Officially, most sessions were restricted to a particular year, but as the pupils tended to run it themselves, with the member of staff on duty only putting in occasional appearances, it was possible to gate-crash. The first time Matt asked her to dance, she thought she was going to have one of her fainting turns. It was wonderful to have him holding her. He was not very tall, but with her petite frame, they bonded very well. She felt she couldn't dance with any other boy after that, and she always had plenty of offers. Two particular boys in her form had been her suitors right through school. Both had tried dating her, but she always declined. They would do anything for her, but the nearest they ever got to her favours was to dance with her in the lunch hours. But now she felt she could not let any boy hold her, other than Matt. It was like being unfaithful.

Sometimes she would look in on a dancing session for his own year, and she noticed he went with other girls. It made her feel sick with jealousy. Being in love was a wonderful feeling, but it could be very painful too!

By chance, her sightings of Matt on the early morning paper round now became an almost everyday occurrence. Her shop took over his shop, and all the marking-up and sending out of the papers now centred on the one building. This meant that very often they both met up on their way to the shop, and if the papers were not ready they may hang around for a while together. But usually, Matt would bury his face in a paper, reading the sports pages. But at least it meant another meeting and some recognition. Each night, Penny would go to bed in anticipation of next morning's meeting. Most of their peers at school had noted the interest between them, and obviously, Penny had confided in Belinda and Joyce. She was forever finding pieces of paper in her desk saying, 'Penny loves Matt,' and she assumed that Matt found likewise, but in reverse. But although Penny inwardly swooned each time they had some kind of liaison, whether it be a dance, a walk home, or a wave on the paper round, he had not yet actually asked her out on a date.

Then one Friday at school, it was announced in the morning assembly, that one of the senior boys, an excellent footballer, was having a trial the following morning for Tottenham Hotspur Juniors. The headmaster was suggesting that some of the pupils would like to support him. After school, having said 'cheers' to Belinda and Joyce, and turned on her way home, Penny was suddenly bowled over when Matt ran up behind her, and then walked alongside. "Fancy coming to watch Brown play at Spurs tomorrow, Penny? Some of the gang are going." She could hardly get her answer out. Her mouth went dry, her legs went weak, her face flushed, and for one dreadful moment she thought she was going to faint. But recovering herself, she laughed out, "Smashing, I'd love to. I've never been to Spurs." They walked together almost all the way to her road, and he left, saying he would see her at the bottom of the road at 9.30 next morning.

It was the longest night of Penny's life, or so it seemed. She couldn't sleep, and kept looking at the clock every few minutes. Then it was time to be up for the paper round. As it happened, she didn't see Matt on the way to the shop. She hoped he wasn't ill and would drop out from the football date.

She rushed through the round, and also through her breakfast when she got back home. She had had to excuse herself from the shop work that morning, and Lavinia knew where she was going, and who with, although Penny had added, "Everyone's going there!" Walking down the road, she could see Matt already waiting at the bottom and quickened her pace, afraid she might be late.

They needed to take a couple of buses to get to the stadium, and Penny was very conscious of the nearness of his body as they sat together on the bus seats. She enjoyed being at the match, but being with Matt was the attraction rather than the game! They seemed more relaxed with one another on the return journey, and were joking and giggling about people at school, both pupils and staff. They called in the milk bar on the way home, and some of the lads from school came in. Penny had to work at the shop in the afternoon, so she had to leave quickly, but Matt stayed on with his mates. She was a bit disappointed that he hadn't seen her home, but she was still elated over the whole morning. They had had a date!

It was several weeks before they had a second date, but there was plenty of association in between. There were times of meeting on the paper rounds, watching one another in team practices, lunch hour dancing or table tennis, milk bar sessions, gatherings in the park, strolling round the shops, and swimming. Sometimes, Matt would walk with her towards home, and other times, he would ignore her. But Penny was obsessed, obsessed with just seeing him, even at a distance.

Then one day, shortly before the Christmas break-up, Matt caught up with the three girls as they walked down the road from school. It was growing very foggy, and they were not going to hang around the shops. Belinda and Joyce said goodbye and went their way. Penny and Matt turned their way. She was in heaven! They were chatting, laughing and giggling, possibly nervously, and then fell silent for a while. And suddenly, out of the blue, he said, "Like to come to the pictures tomorrow?"

"Oh, yes please, Matt. I'd love to."

"Well there's a good film at the Capital," he continued. "See you there at half past six then," and he turned off towards his way home.

Penny often went to the cinema with Belinda or Joyce, but now she had to tell Lavinia that she was going with a boy, or in fact, ask her if she may go. First of all, she thought of saying that she was in fact going with Belinda. But as it was a school day, Lavinia would expect her friend home for tea first, as it would be a Friday, even stay overnight, as they had done previously. So Penny had to tell the truth. "Can I go to the pictures tomorrow, Mumma?"

"I expect so," her mother replied. "Whose coming, Belinda and Joyce?"

"No, I'm going with Matt. You know I went to football with him." Lavinia was surprised but relieved, at least it wasn't a teacher!

Penny didn't know how to get through the next school day. She confided to Belinda and Joyce about the date. She couldn't concentrate on her lessons. It seemed all the staff were telling her off. She was doodling her hearts with P.S. and M.J.O. all over the place. The inside of her desk was covered with them. She got told off for not doing her maths homework, and ended up getting a detention after school. She ran down the road to the bus stop when she was finally let out, and then ran up the road to her home the other end. She would have liked to bath after scrambling her tea, but her mother said there wouldn't be enough hot water left for her brothers bathing after coming home from work. So she had to make do with a good wash. She changed out of her school clothes, did her hair three or four times, and sneaked some of her sister's perfume and a little make-up. Suddenly she realised she only had five minutes to get to the cinema. She grabbed her coat, and called out goodbye to her mother, and dashed out the door before Lavinia could see the make-up.

Matt was already waiting outside the cinema when she arrived quite breathless and flushed. He paid for them both; and they were shown to their seats, just in front of the back row. Penny couldn't have cared less what the two films were, but as it turned out they were quite good. She was only conscious of the proximity of Matt for almost three hours. They had no real contact with one another, but Penny noted that Matt's body was slightly turned towards hers. Walking home afterwards, they chatted about school mainly, and, stopping at the end of her road, they lingered on a while. And then it was goodbye. Penny thought he seemed as if to move towards her, but then it was "Cheerio," and he was gone. Penny floated up the road home.

Lavinia greeted her. "Had a good time, Penny?"

"Oh yes. They were two good films."

"Is he a nice boy?" her mother continued.

"Yes. He's ever so good at sports. He's a gorgeous diver," Penny volunteered.

"You should have asked him in, Penny. Make sure you do next time." Next time thought Penny. Oh please let there be a next time.

It was coming to the end of term, and there was plenty of lunch-hour dancing. Matt didn't always come in, but when he did, he would dance with Penny. Oh it was wonderful. She was as weak as a kitten in his arms. And if he didn't come into the hall, she found it boring, even though she had plenty of offers to dance. She preferred to listen to the music.

They broke up for the holidays, and Christmas came and went. One evening there was an outing with the Girls Life Brigade, organised by the leaders, to a dance in Hampstead. It was in a church hall, and was held by a Young Men's Club. The story was, that most of these young men were orphans, or in some way deprived, and they lived in a hostel there run by the church. The groups of young ladies were escorted to the venue, having to travel there by bus and underground train. The girls felt shy as they entered the hall, they seemed to be the only females there. The young men looked very pleased, and as each record started, they descended on the girls en masse. Some of the fellows seemed quite old to them, and Penny didn't want them holding her. But their leaders had told them that they mostly had poor backgrounds, and it seemed unfair to say no. But others were younger, possibly sixteen, seventeen, eighteen, and some were quite nice-looking, but they seemed more shy.

Fortunately, the pack of girls could not stay very late, as they had a considerable journey home. Penny's feet ached from all the dancing, so she was pleased when they left. They all walked to the station, and as they waited to get on the lift, a girl whom they had seen at the dance, apparently connected with the young men in some organizational way, rushed up to Penny with a pencil and note-paper, saying would she write her name and address, as one of the boys would like to write to her. Penny was taken so much by surprise, that without any consideration, she did so. As the door closed on the lift, and they descended, she thought over what a silly thing she had done. "I bet it was one of those old men who were there, Penny," Joyce commented.

"Well I won't reply anyway, whoever it is," Penny started. But she was inwardly a little pleased that it was only she who had been asked for her address, and she did wonder who it was.

In fact, two or three weeks later, a letter did arrive. It was quite a nice letter. His name was Douglas; he was coming up to eighteen, and was going to do his National Service. He was an orphan, although he had relatives living in the Midlands. He said how he thought Penny seemed 'so nice' at the dance party. He said he had been too shy to ask her himself for her address, but when he saw her leaving, was desperate he would not see her again. He reminded her that he had danced with her twice, and that he had been the one who offered her the tray of soft drinks, and he included a photo of himself to remind her. She did then remember him. Yes, he had seemed a nice, quiet, gentle lad. He was hoping Penny would write to him while he was in the Forces, and that maybe they would meet again sometime, and would she send him a photo, please. Penny thought it a pleasant letter, and in fact she felt very sorry for him.

She thought there would be no harm in writing to him, but had no intention of ever meeting him. After all, she was already Matt's girl. This was only the start. They would be together forever, she knew. They would grow up together, get through school. Get some sort of work, always be madly in love and would finally marry, have a family and live happily ever after. That's what real love was all about. And she lay on the settee listening to her latest record, 'Too Young', by Nat

King Cole. Well she and Matt weren't too young. They would show everyone. Penny didn't realise that boys don't think that way.

CHAPTER SEVEN
1950

It was now 1950. Penny had received a small diary among her Christmas presents, and she religiously filled it in each night before settling down to sleep. Every entry began with either 'Saw Matt' or 'Did not see Matt' - a reference to the paper round. The last comment on every day was 'I love Matt' with expletives of how much. In between were comments on anything that had occurred between them. Other than that it seemed her life did not exist.

Then one day at school, early in February, an older boy, Adam, who normally hung around with Matt and Jack Stewart, handed her an invitation to his birthday party to be held at his home that coming Saturday evening. It transpired that there would be four couples there - herself and Matt, Stewart and whoever was flavour of the month, Adam, another older boy and two older girls whom Penny didn't know.

Matt was to call for Penny at 7.00 p.m., as she didn't know where Adam lived. She had been so excited all day at the shop and had found it hard to concentrate. Seven o'clock came and went, and Penny was getting anxious. Finally, she told her mother she would walk to Matt's house and maybe meet him on the way. When she knocked at his door, his father opened it looking rather surprised to see a young girl there, and said Matt was out. She explained that he was supposed to be taking her to a party, and Mr. Oliver asked her in. Mrs. Oliver said that Matthew had been out since early afternoon, and she didn't know he was going to a party. But they told her to wait when Penny said she didn't even know where the party was. After what seemed an age, Matt arrived. His mother told him off for 'keeping the young girl waiting' and he rushed to get ready for them to go. As they left, his mother told Penny, 'Come round any time,' which Penny thought was very nice of her. Walking to the party, she asked Matt where he had been. 'Just out with Jack,' he said, and did not elaborate. He's always out with Jack Stewart. What do they get up to, Penny thought. Anyway, now he was with her.

They arrived at Adam's house, and shortly afterwards Stewart arrived. All the others were there. There were no parents at home, but obviously they had expected the young people as there was food laid out for them. Stewart hadn't brought a girl after all, so there was just Penny and the two older girls.

After eating, they went into a small lounge containing two armchairs and a settee. Adam put on some records, and then it was decided that the three couples should sit together using the settee and armchairs for each pair. Stewart stretched himself out on the carpet and said he would be in charge of the records. They were all listening and generally chatting and laughing. Penny was enjoying sitting close to Matt on the settee, and couldn't help noticing the other girls were on the laps of Adam and his friend on the armchairs. Suddenly Adam called out, 'Put the lights off, Jack.' With only the light of the electric fire, they were all plunged into darkness.

Apart from the music, it was all very quiet. Suddenly, she felt Matt's arm come around her shoulders, and his face near hers. She turned awkwardly, and then his mouth was on her mouth. She gasped at first, but then melted. It was a short kiss, but after a while he repeated it, and they lingered on. Penny was swimming with sensations that took over her whole body. This was what she had been waiting for. She shifted her body to turn more towards him, and as they relaxed into a further long embrace, she had this fleeting image of herself and Matt coupled together under the palm trees on the Blue Lagoon beach.

The record stopped, Stewart put on the light and called out, 'Right, change partners!' Penny broke away from Matt, wondering what was happening. The two older girls got up from the laps of Adam and the other boy. One came over to Matt, and Adam's girl moved on. Adam patted his knee, and said, 'Come on Penny.' Penny was horrified, but it seemed this was what you had to do. She gingerly perched on the arm of Adam's armchair, and Stewart put on the next record, and switched off the light again, just as she saw the other girl curling up on the settee next to Matt. Adam was trying to pull her down onto his lap. Penny began fiddling with her clothes, pretending to get comfortable, but really playing for time. How could you just kiss and cuddle someone you didn't love! She couldn't do it! But Adam was pulling her nearer and kissing her. She kept breaking off and pretending to cough, and then allowing a short peck of a kiss. She wondered what Matt and the girl were doing. It was very quiet and she wished the damn record would finish.

At last it did, and horror of horrors, Stewart repeated the process - on with the light, 'change partners,' off with the record, on with the next, and off with the light again. Penny now found herself with the second boy. He was a strapping lad, and he pulled Penny down onto his lap right away. She struggled a lot, but it was no use. He was kissing her hard and not letting go. She couldn't break off the kiss and she was losing her breath and thought she would faint. With one big effort, she did manage to break the kiss, and began coughing and spluttering. 'I've got a cold,' she told him, but he just pulled her down again and carried on where he had left off. At last, the music stopped and on went the light. Penny looked across at Matt separating himself from the older girl, and she thought she was going to cry. Jack Stewart was dealing with the records. Would she be with Matt next? Then Adam jumped up and said he would get them all a drink. They chatted a while, listening to more music, and then they were off again.

Penny was back on the settee with Matt. Adam and the other boy were with their original girls. Stewart was still on the floor doing the music. Penny felt rather sorry for him that he didn't get a turn with the girls - well not with her, the other two. Well I guess that was his fault for not bringing a girl to the party! As the light was turned out this time, Adam called out, 'We'll stay where we are now. No more swapping!'

And so Penny and Matt began a snog that lasted through record after record. At first she felt spoiled after having been with the other two boys, and could not stop herself thinking of Matt with the two other girls. But gradually, she relaxed, and their kisses became longer and longer, and the sensations through her body were so intense and wonderful that Penny wished that the party would never end. But end it did, and as they walked back to her home, hand in hand, she thought this would be the way it would always be now. It was 11.20 pm when she got home - late for her - and she told Matt as he left her it had been a smashing party. Strangely, he didn't kiss her goodbye. Lavinia asked her if it had been a good party. She answered nonchalantly, 'Yes, very good. We had lots of food!' That night, Penny wrote in her diary: 'What a party. Just in Matt's arms. I really love him. I know I do.'

Valentine's Day was coming up, and Penny had bought a card for Matt. There was dancing in the hall during the lunch hour the day before. Penny went in, but she was disappointed that Matt was not there. So as it neared the end of the session, she asked one of the boys to find Matt and tell him to come in. He did come in and had the last waltz with her. Having him hold her brought back memories of the party. After school that afternoon, she hung behind, and then sneaked into his form room to leave her Valentine in his desk. She did not see him on the way home. There was no Valentine in the post the next morning, nor in her desk, so it was a disappointing day for Penny.

But the next day proved better. They danced together in the lunch hour. Penny had a netball match after school, and Matt stayed to watch. It made her very self-conscious, and unfortunately, they lost. But he waited for her and walked her home, asking her to the pictures the next day. Penny was on time this date. She was more relaxed, and they sat much closer together, with him holding her hand. They took their time walking home, and chatted a while at the gate. This time he did kiss her goodbye. Now she really felt they were an item

Early the following week, they had yet another date to the pictures. It was half- term holiday and Jack Stewart was taking a girl out, so they made it a foursome. They all sat upstairs, and were in the back row. Matt had his arm around her all the time, and they had several long kisses. Penny couldn't see what the other couple were up to, but they seemed very close.

Afterwards, they all went to the usual milk bar before Matt took her home, except that he didn't take her all the way, only as far as the turn towards his own home where he left to walk the rest of the way alone, and he did not kiss her goodnight.

During the next few days, she felt that Matt was avoiding her. Something seemed different. She was worried that it was all over. Then came a terrible shock. She accompanied Annie to the hospital on the Saturday to help her carry some things she wanted to keep there. Passing through the shops on the bus, she suddenly saw Matt with Stewart and two girls waiting to go in the cinema. She was devastated. How could he! What had she done? Back home, she moped around the house, thinking of what she had seen. That night she wrote in her diary, 'He must like me, he must, he must. I'll die if not.'

She had a troubled week at school. Matt seemed to ignore her. She asked him to come into the dancing, but he didn't. Everyone noticed that she was moping, and she couldn't concentrate in class. She got into trouble with Miss Cook in Biology, and was sent to stand under the clock where everyone could see her. But later, she was playing in a House netball match, and she noticed Matt watching. He waited for her to finish and walked part of the way home. Were they back together? Next day he came into the dancing and danced with her. They walked home together that day, too, and as he left her he invited her to the pictures that evening. Oh, the excitement again! But when she met him, he said he couldn't stay for the pictures because his mother was ill. So that was that! But Penny didn't mind. He did like her, she was sure.

It was an intense time at school now, as this was the External Examination year. However, for the first time, an age limit was introduced, and this meant that Penny, along with many others, being among the youngest of her year, would not be allowed to sit the exams, even though they would have to undergo the course. They would take it the following year in the sixth form, when they would also be pursuing their chosen course of education.

Penny was finding it hard to concentrate on her lessons. It seemed that thoughts of Matt had taken over her whole life. Her worst subjects were the sciences, History and Geography. She had been able to give up the sciences, apart from Biology, which they had to pursue. Penny couldn't stand Miss Cook, the woman who took the subject. In fact, the feeling was probably mutual. Miss Cook was possibly in her thirties, and was very plain with untidy, straight, dark hair, glasses, and a harsh, boring voice. They were a group of girls only for this year's Biology lessons, and they were studying the rabbit as part of the course. Miss Cook stated that all the body systems of the rabbit were the same as in humans, hence they were to take special note. The course finished with the reproductive system, and Miss Cook remarked, sarcastically Penny thought, "We are supposed to tell you these things nowadays!"

The various diagrams of the body systems were up on the board, and they were made to trace the passage of the male renal system, then the passage of the male reproductive system, compared to that of the female systems, and note they connected during mating, the same for humans as for the rabbit. Penny looked at Miss Cook, and she wondered what she knew about such things. She was Miss, and Penny couldn't imagine that she had ever had a boyfriend. Who would fancy her? "Well, come on, girls, any questions?" There was silence. "What about you, Penelope? Or do you know it all?" Penny detected the sarcasm again. She knew Miss Cook didn't like her. Penny very rarely put up her hand to ask questions. She was furiously thinking what she could ask. "Please Miss Cook, looking at the man's renal system, could he possibly do a 'wee' when he is inside you?" All of the girls smirked. "What a ridiculous question, Penny. Of course not!" Penny flushed, and wanted to shrink under the desk. Looking at the diagrams, she didn't think it was a silly question. Well she wouldn't ask anymore. Anyhow, what did Miss Cook know about it.

But to make up for her disaster in Biology, Penny was very good with Maths, French and English. She enjoyed writing essays, and very often had to read hers out aloud to the class. And she could be very amusing. In fact, the English teacher, when giving out the choice of title usually said, "And one for Penny to give us a laugh." He often wrote a comment under her mark, saying it had amused him. However, her humour was her downfall. The following year when she did sit the External Exam, she searched through the choice of essay titles, and could not find one that lent itself to humour. She finally chose 'communication,' trying to add a laugh or two but she knew it was not of her best. She failed her English.

Penny put her most effort into the games activities. There were plenty of matches for both the school and house, and they all required regular practices. Matt was similarly involved with the boys' teams. There came a period of erratic association between the two of them. Sometimes he would acknowledge her, and other times he appeared to ignore her. Now and again, he would walk with her homewards, but he did not arrange a date. The last time he had asked her to the pictures, he hadn't turned up, and when she rang his home, his mother said he could not come. Penny went into the cinema alone, not wanting to return home and say she had been stood up. She now endured weeks and weeks of miserable pining, with occasional lifts if Matt walked, spoke or looked her way. Her diary was one long lament.

During the May half-term holiday, Penny went on her own to stay with Neville and Ellie in Somerset. It was very enjoyable, and she took young Charles and the new baby out most days. She was convinced that on her return, Matt would have missed her, and would show renewed interest, but she was wrong. He was always with Stewart, and as Stewart was forever taking different girls out, Penny wondered if Matt was too. But she heard no rumours. Then at the shop one morning she learned that he was away on two week's holiday. Two weeks! Two weeks without even seeing him. She counted off the days to his return.

Several of the boys began trying to chat her up again. They obviously felt that all was over between the young couple. But she wasn't having any of it. The girls thought her silly not to take up any other offers. But why would she want a date with someone she did not love? There was one boy, David, a year younger than herself, who lived further down her own road. His house also backed onto the playing field, and they often met there. He attended the same school, and Penny would occasionally walk to or fro with him, not by design on her part, but possibly so on his.

One day, Steven Steed - the first boy Penny had ever felt stirrings for some years earlier - walked with her after school all the way home. As it happened, Belinda had recently said that she was fancying Steed again, so Penny didn't encourage him. She had no designs on him herself. Shortly afterwards, there was a Leavers' Dance held at school, and their year was included, but not Matt's. It was held on a Saturday, and was quite a sophisticated affair. The three girls went along. Penny and Joyce knew that Belinda was fancying Steed, but the evening proved an embarrassment, as he quite obviously danced most of the time with Penny. During the last waltz, while with him, Penny came over all hot and excused herself from him and went outside. But he followed her, and stood holding her to him. "You're so exciting, Penny," he told her. He did not kiss her, thank goodness. If only it were Matt holding her. She could hardly look at Belinda when they both made their way back inside. The two girls were to stay the night at Penny's house, but only Joyce did so.

The following evening, Penny was out walking the dog, when Steed appeared and walked with her, lingering for a long chat at her gate. That night she wrote in her diary, "Steed is making a big mistake. If only it was Matt. I love him so much. Please come back to me."

It was almost the end of the summer term. There were very few set lessons, but lots of activities and free time. There was sports day, the swimming gala - Matt won the diving-rounders, cricket and tennis matches and social occasions, and a second leavers' dance, for the top half of the school, to be held one evening. Belinda and Joyce came back with Penny after school for tea and they took their time, changing into their finery, doing their hair and applying the make-up. Penny knew that Matt would be there, and was hoping that he would dance with her. And he did, over and over. It was wonderful to be in his arms once more.

Afterwards he walked her home. Belinda and Joyce were to stay the night with her, but they very diplomatically turned off to walk a different route. Matt held Penny's hand as they strolled along, and he kissed her long and hard at the gate.

Penny just knew it was all going to be fine between them once more. As he left, she sank down to sit on the step to await her friends. She was absolutely weak at the knees ... and it felt lovely!

CHAPTER EIGHT

Then, it was the long summer holiday time again, hopefully much of it to be spent relaxing at the swimming pool. All the friends did. Sometimes Matt would be there, and sometimes he wouldn't. There were trips to the park or the shops, or they would hang around in the milk bar. Penny played a lot of tennis with various friends in the park or in the field at the back of her house. But whatever she did, her prime thought was hoping she would bump into Matt. When she did, he often almost ignored her, and other times he was all chatty and walking her home. He might make arrangements with her for later but very often it didn't materialize.

But the one boy who was always on the scene was David, who lived down the road. Wherever Penny went, she seemed to meet him, and living so close she had no option but to walk home with him. He, too, spent a lot of time at the pool, but unlike Matt would always sit near her. His main preoccupation seemed to be with Jack Stewart. He, of course, was forever associating with different girls, and Penny often wondered if he made fun of Matt sticking to her instead of 'playing the field.' Matt was always practising his diving, and in fact had an All England competition coming up later in the year. Penny watched him performing on the diving boards at the deep end. She was filled with admiration and love. She positively adored him. And in her fantasy, she saw herself languishing on the golden sands as Matt dived off the rocks into the warm sea of The Blue Lagoon, before joining her to take her in his arms and.... She was brought to her senses by David asking her to come into the pool. "No thanks. Not now. I'm thinking," she casually replied.

One day, Penny did a terrible thing, well, that's what she thought afterwards. She had been through the shops as far as the coffee bar, then on to the park, but did not see Matt. Walking home, as usual, David appeared on the scene. "Coming over the field later?" he asked her. "Might as well, there's nothing else to do," she answered. They often saw one another in the field behind the houses. They lay in the long grass just chatting. Penny was feeling glum. They were gossiping about which boy was going with which girl, and Penny asked if he had ever been out with a girl. "Not yet," he said.

She sat up, and suddenly she felt very sorry for him. She found him a strange boy. Without thinking what she was doing, she leaned over and kissed him full on the lips. "Is that your first kiss?" she asked. He nodded. "Well, now you owe me one," she continued. He sat up and obliged. "Now we're quits," she said. That night she was filled with horror and disgust by what she had done. She hoped he wouldn't think she was interested in him in that way. He was O.K as a friend. And she hoped that Matt wouldn't find out. She couldn't even explain why she had done it.

A few days later, Matt asked her to go with him, Jack and two girls to another boy's home for an afternoon. They all took their records round and had lots of fun. There were no parents at home, so they had the run of the house. The two girls were sisters, not at their school, but were known for being friendly with several boys in the area. Jack seemed besotted with one of them. It won't last, Penny thought. The six of them split up into couples, and she and Matt had the sitting room to themselves. It was wonderful to be alone with him. They chatted and giggled, but kissed and cuddled most of the time. He had his hand on her breasts, which she thought rather naughty, but she didn't stop him. It was a lovely afternoon, just the two of them alone for so long. She never saw where the other two couples disappeared to. Walking her home afterwards, Matt held her hand, then had his arm around her. She was sure he must love her as much as she did him. That night, her diary read, 'We necked. Quite bad really. I must watch out.'

Matt began calling at the house more often now. Usually Penny's father would be in the front lounge, so there wasn't much privacy. But they would sit on the second settee at the back of the room, maybe playing cards or just chatting, and could hold hands discreetly. Sometimes they would stay in the hall on the love seat. That was the best, and as it got dark, they could kiss and cuddle while the family were in the other rooms. Or they might go for a walk, taking the dog as an excuse. They usually held hands, and if it was dark could stop for the occasional kiss.

The holidays were soon over, and it was back to school. Penny thought things were going fine with her and Matt. They had several dates to the pictures, and he came round several times to her house. One such evening, he told her that David had told him what she had done over the field. She couldn't explain why to him, but was relieved that he didn't seem too bothered. Another evening they were to go to the pictures after school, but he did not call for her as promised. She did not know why.

Then, the following day, as she and Joyce were wandering through the shops, they saw Matt going into the cinema with a girl. Penny was shocked, and went to bed early. She tossed and turned with the pain of what she had seen, and wrote, "I want to kill myself." All next day she thought of him and *her.* Why had he done it? Then shock of shocks, early that evening, he called to invite her to the cinema. And he seemed the same as he always did. She dare not ask about the girl, but wondered how many times he had seen her. For a whole week then, he did not date her. He would say he'd be round but not turn up. She was convinced he must be seeing *her.* Then he did ask her to the cinema, but while in there, neither kissed nor touched her. What had happened to them? When they reached her gate, she did not allow him to kiss her goodnight.

The following weekend, Matt was away for the All England Junior Diving Competition at Exeter. Penny went to the telephone box to call him before he left to wish him good luck. But he had gone. She went to her sister Dorothy's house on the Sunday, and was late home. Her father told her that the boy had called, and that he had come third. She was so thrilled for him, and congratulated him next morning when they met up for the paper round.

Their relationship now seemed to settle down. Everyone at school spoke of them as a couple, and Stewart was now dating Belinda. This meant they would go as a foursome on a cinema date. It was rather nice, but Penny wished that Joyce could have a boyfriend. She was an attractive girl, but she would never own up to being interested in anyone, apart from one boy older than themselves but not at their school. They could not get out of her if, how, when or where she saw him. But he did once turn up at the school gates asking for her. A couple of lads in school had tried tagging onto them, possibly to make up a six-group, but Joyce would not get involved. Penny and Belinda felt they were ostracising her by going out together with the two boys. The cinema dates were now becoming very amorous much to Penny's desire and pleasure. She was indeed a very tactile person. One evening she noted that Matt rested his hand across her lap. Her diary read, "I did not see the film at all!"

During the Autumn half-term, she and Belinda and Matt and Jack Stewart were to go to a show at the Empire. Nelly Lutcher was appearing, and they had some of her records. The two girls were to meet at Jack's house in the afternoon, and Matt would be there. They were obviously expected, as Jack's mother had left a nice tea out for them. They played records and generally talked. At one point, Matt and Penny began cuddling, but Stewart seemed to get annoyed with them. She noticed that he and Belinda seemed to be cooling off. Later, the two boys decided to iron their trousers in readiness for going out to the theatre. They were parading about in their pants, and the girls were giggling. Suddenly, the window cleaner appeared doing the job on the house. They all wondered what he would think about the scene of the two young couples with the lads in a state of undress, and that set them off giggling again. After tea they went on the bus to the theatre. It was a good show, but it was the last date that Belinda and Stewart had. She had bitten the dust like those before her! Penny was glad that Matt wasn't like him, and she was sure that Stewart probably ridiculed Matt for sticking to one girl for so long. She blamed Jack Stewart for a lot of Matt's erratic behaviour. But then she didn't realise that boys don't think like girls, that it was quantity not quality with them.

They now entered possibly the most stable time of their relationship. They had plenty of dates to the cinema, just the two of them again. Penny rather liked it like that again. Matt was always very amorous there, and she wrote up her comments: 'Love seems to pour out of our bodies,' 'You should have seen us this time,' 'Wow. Just can't control myself.' But in truth it was all very innocent.

They went for walks to the park in the dark, taking the dog for company. They would push the dog through the bars, then climb over the top themselves. It was very eerie at night, and the ducks would start quacking, so they were afraid of being caught. They would kiss and cuddle on a seat while the dog sat and waited. Other nights they stayed in, maybe on the love seat in the hall. They danced at school, watched each other in matches, and cruised the shops afterwards. Everyone knew them as a couple. One day, Mr. McKenzie said to Penny, when she was in a more affable mood towards him, "You and Oliver are the ideal couple. He's a lucky lad." Penny didn't know how to reply. She was remembering him kissing her that night two years ago. All she could say was, "Thank you. Yes, he is nice." And she wanted to say she was sorry for being awful in his lessons, but she didn't know how. She didn't do History any more now. She had dropped it in her Exam options.

Each year the school produced a Music and Drama Festival. The four houses had to make up a programme of items, which they then performed in front of an invited adjudicator. Staff were allotted to houses to help out and produce the finished entries. Mr. McKenzie had helped write a song of 'school happenings' for his house to perform as the novelty item. He was not in Penny's Red House, but when the day came, and the whole school assembled to watch the show,

Penny was surprised to hear one line of the song as: 'Penny Saunders got her Oliver!' Penny was in an item for her house. They did a skit on the staff room. It was obvious that they were taking off certain teachers, and Penny was the P.E teacher, tripping on stage in a short kit, wielding a tennis racquet, and moaning about the girls. She enjoyed performing, and enjoyed a wolf whistle or two that emanated from the audience. She was beginning to think she might take up P.E teaching as her career. At the time, she was in the Commerce group doing shorthand and typing, but she couldn't see herself doing that for long.

One day in the Commerce Class, she was taken ill and was violently sick in the toilets. Going back to class she promptly fainted which she found very embarrassing. She had to lie down for the rest of the day, and then Joyce and Belinda saw her home. About 6 o'clock, Matt called round to ask her mother how she was, having heard about her fainting in school. Penny thought that was very sweet of him. She didn't go to school next day, but Matt called again that evening, and they spent a couple of hours together in the front room. Penny thought there was a lovely closeness between them. Matt had just had his sixteenth birthday. He was getting broad shoulders, still not that tall, but taller than herself, as she was still tiny. He had blue eyes, and brown wavy hair, not blonde like the boy in The Blue Lagoon, but just as attractive. In fact, everything she could want. And he was *hers,* as she made quite clear to other girls.

The last two months of 1950 were probably the most intense the young couple enjoyed. Penny was very happy and contented. And there was the added excitement of the Christmas season, with school parties, family gatherings at home, shopping and presents. Penny bought a photo album for Matt. She, Belinda and Joyce discussed the idea of holding a party. It was decided that Penny's home would be the most suitable, with the other two girls living out of the area where most of their mutual friends were. Also, Penny's house was larger. She approached her mother about the project, saying they would limit it to five girls and five boys in total. She promised they would not be rowdy, and that they would not go on very late, would not do anything silly ... and please would everyone in the family go out that evening! Lavinia condescended to agree, and it was arranged for the evening before New Year's Eve, the 30th.

The three girls got very excited with the plans. Belinda and Joyce would come over earlier in the day, and would bring some contributions to the buffet. Lavinia had said she would take care of the majority. They put their money together to buy a bottle of ginger wine as a grown-up drink to the New Year. This was Penny's suggestion, as she loved ginger wine, which they always had at Christmas in her house. As it turned out, this was a waste as the young party guests were not so enthusiastic about the taste. Belinda and Joyce would stay the night afterwards. All the others lived locally.

Then they planned the activities. They would ask everyone to bring records, would definitely play Postman's Knock, and Penny said they would need to buy five different coloured cotton reels, one for each girl, for a game she'd heard of, but didn't know its name, something like 'Follow the string.' They could play 'Hunt the Thimble,' and give sweets for prizes if things got boring. They invited two mutual girl friends and asked them to name two boys. Belinda and Joyce chose two boys from class, and, naturally, Matt was on the list. The party would start at 6.00pm, and Penny asked her mother if they could go on until midnight if they promised to clear up.

The big day arrived, and the three friends busied themselves setting out the food on the large dining table in the front room. The decorations were still up from Christmas, so it was attractive, and the girls added more balloons. Penny told her mother they would use only the front room and the hall. Her two brothers who still lived at home had gone out. Rosamund was also going to a dance and sleeping at her friend's, Annie was working at the hospital and was sleeping there after a dance and Granny Saunders had gone to stay with their Uncle for Christmas and had not returned yet. So that only left her parents, who were in the kitchen when everyone arrived. Lavinia said she and Harry would be going out to visit Aunt Mabel later. She had prepared a nice spread for them, and waited a while to see that they were enjoying it, before she and Harry left. The loud music was playing non-stop, and she wasn't sure that Penny heard her call out goodbye.

Once Penny heard the front door shut, she relaxed more. There were only the ten of them in the house now. She cleared some of the crockery and food debris away to the kitchen, and on return, found the boys were doing card tricks, which was fun. "Let's play Postman's Knock now," she interrupted. The suggestion was well received! As well as the love seat at the foot of the stairs, there was also a chaise-longue in the hall, right opposite the door of the front room. There were coat hooks, and, being in a corner at the top of the three stairs down to the kitchen, it made a dark, secluded corner, ideal for a kissing couch. It was an enjoyable session. Penny couldn't wait for when she and Matt met up, and they took their time. But when she had one of the other boys, it was just a quick peck. She thought Belinda took her time with Matt though! They savoured this game for a considerable time, and then took a break playing their records again, and having more snacks.

There was a lull in proceedings, and somebody said, "What shall we do now?"

"I have a special game," replied Penny, and she proceeded to bring out the cotton reels. "The girls will go out in the hall and each have a different colour cotton. Keep the door shut, then poke the end of the cotton under the door. The boys must choose one, then give the girls five minutes before you open the door. The girls can go anywhere in the house but unwind the cotton as you go until you find a final place to stay and hide. Boys, follow your cotton 'til you find the girl, then you can have a kiss and a cuddle." It all sounded very exciting. As Penny went out the door, she whispered to Matt, "Mine's the pink!" and in the hall she told the girls that she was going in the small front bedroom - her brother Graham's - so they were to keep cut!

Penny carefully unwound her reel, through the hall, up the stairs, left across the landing, and into her brother's bedroom. She closed the door, lay on the bed in the dark, and waited. There seemed to be an awful lot of noise going on outside. Voices were saying, "That's mine!" "It's tangled up!" "It's broken!" "Mind my cotton!" "I'm going there!" "Where are they?" and so on. Doors kept opening and closing. Several times Penny's door opened and the light from the landing would illuminate who was there. Each time one of the other four boys looked in, Penny said, "Go away! I'm not your colour." The truth was, that all the cottons had twisted and broken, and no-one knew which they were tracking. It was a complete shambles, and was now a game of 'Hide and seek!' Eventually, the door opened and Matt looked in. "I'm here," Penny called from the bed. "Where have you been?"

"I couldn't even find your pink cotton in all that mess," he whispered.

And then he was on the bed, the two of them sitting next to one another. He was kissing and cuddling her for some time, and she settled herself back on the bed, and he was lying beside her, and then on top of her. They kissed long and passionately. The commotion outside subsided as all the others made their way downstairs again. "Where's Penny?" "Where's Matt?" they heard. Matt went to get up, but Penny pulled him back. This truly was heaven. This was how they belonged to each other. This was how it should be forever. And Penny melted and languished in his kisses and caresses. She, in her innocence, had no idea of the effect it was having on him.

Their bliss was broken by Belinda's voice sailing up the stairs. "Penny, where are you? We're all waiting!" They broke their hold on each other and left the bed. Penny straightened her clothes - and the bed - and they went down to join the others, where they received some very strange looks. Time was nearly up, so they played more records, had the glass of ginger wine and more snacks, and hearing Penny's parents returning, broke up the party. The three girls cleared up and retired to bed. They agreed it had been a good party. "It was lovely," Penny said as she turned off the light in the bedroom and climbed into bed, still tingling. "Lovely!"

The girls stayed for most of the next day and then returned home. It was the last day of 1950. Penny's final entry in the diary said, 'Did not see Matt, today.' Then, she added a statement to close the book: 'I thank Matthew for a year to remember. He has made everything different and yet super for me. He is everything to me, and always will be, for I swear I love him! xx'

As she closed the little red book for the last time, little did she know she would be closing that chapter in her life also.

CHAPTER NINE
1951

The New Year did not start too well. Penny and Matt did not meet for almost a week. She rang his home one day, but he was out. Then he called one evening, and everything seemed O.K. Next visit he stayed for the afternoon and evening, the last part of which they spent in the hall on the loveseat. Penny was trying to tell him how she felt, and then fetched down the diary, asking him to read it when he got home. "Keep it," she said. "I want you to have it." She thought the diary would spell out all she wanted to say. He took it, and they kissed goodbye. She didn't realise that the mature sentiments of its pages would be enough to frighten off any normal sixteen-year old boy.

They were back to school again, and there was plenty of lunch-hour dancing. Matt came in most days, and always asked her to dance, but apart from occasional walks home, they did not seem to date very often. Penny felt there was a change between them, sometimes having minor arguments. Then all would seem the same again. She was in turmoil, and was still besotted with him. No other boy featured in her life.

The gang of friends had started going to a local church hall where dances were held for young people each Friday evening. The venue was becoming very popular. Penny and Matt had been a couple of times, usually meeting up there, but walking home together. One particular week, talk at school was of who was going to the dance that evening. Matt told Penny he might be a little late as he and Jack Stewart had to go somewhere first, but he would see her up there. Penny had wished he would call for her. He was always doing something with Stewart! A boy, Paul, in her class, an avid admirer, told Penny he was going to the dance for the first time, and asked her for directions. She explained and explained, but he made out he wasn't sure of that area, hinting that she might show him. "Oh, okay, then. If you knock at my house at seven o'clock, you can walk up with me." And she thought no more of it. The boy lived near to a younger girl in school, who had come to Penny's notice very much lately. And she thought she had also come to the notice of several of the boys, too. Her name was Susan, and she was in Matt's year, a year younger than Penny, quite pretty and becoming very attractive. Of late, she had seemed to hang around Penny, bringing up the subject of Matt on occasions. Penny wondered if she was interested in him, and sometimes felt she was a threat.

She was just finishing dressing and doing her hair, when Paul called at her house. He looked very pleased with himself when her mother brought him into the lounge. "He's just walking up to the dance hall with me. He hasn't been before," Penny explained. They walked up, and Penny left him as soon as they got in, joining her close friends. She looked around for Matt, but he had not yet arrived. Paul kept asking her to dance, and she obliged while waiting. Finally, Stewart and Matt turned up, but he didn't come her way for some time. The girl, Susan, was there, and he danced quite a lot with her. Paul kept asking Penny to dance, very often before Matt could or so she told herself. But as the evening wore on, she felt Susan had him more. It came to the Last Waltz, and Paul stepped in quick. She thought Matt was walking her way, but seeing Paul, he turned to Susan. Penny was near to tears now, and as soon as the dance ended, she made her way to Matt ready to be walked home. But an argument developed. Paul was saying, "I brought her up, I'm taking her home." Penny was almost hysterical now. "You didn't bring me up. I only showed you the way. You are not taking me home." She was making a scene, and Matt condescendingly said, "I'd better take her." As they left together, she saw the look that Susan gave her.

Walking home, Penny had the feeling that this was now the beginning of the end. She had made a fool of herself. She could feel the tension between them. She stopped walking at one point and tried clinging to him, but she knew it wasn't the same. She sought desperately for what she could do or say. She said silly things such as, "We've never done anything to be ashamed of, have we?" She didn't know why she said that, but what she probably meant was that she would if that was the way to keep him. As he left her at her gate and she kissed him, she knew the end of her world had come.

Days passed into weeks, and then months. There were lots of meetings, but no firm dates. They danced together at school, and sometimes walked home together, but Penny knew there was an atmosphere between them. They often met up at the shops or in the coffee bar, although Penny was beginning to avoid it. Stewart would always be with Matt if he was there. Inwardly, she began to blame Stewart for her demise. She believed that he teased Matt for sticking to one girl instead of spreading his wings further. Of course, that is what he should have been doing, but it was not Penny's way of thinking. The school began to buzz with the gossip that they had finally broken up. Boys made advances, which she declined, and girls told her she should be enjoying herself on numerous dates. But she could not. March came, and she spent a miserable sixteenth birthday, seeing nothing but unhappiness ahead.

A letter arrived from the pen-pal, Douglas, saying he was being posted abroad, but although she had written regularly to him before, she didn't bother to answer. Strangely enough, some time later, a letter arrived from Hong Kong. The writer claimed to be serving in the army there, and said he had seen a photo of her posted up inside a fellow comrade's locker. He thought her very pretty and hoped she would write to him. His mate had given him her address, saying that she had apparently given up corresponding with him. Penny now felt very guilty, and also very sorry, thinking of two young soldiers looking at her photo in Hong Kong and waiting for letters. But she did not reply.

Another month came and went. Penny still did the paper round, but she felt Matt avoided her and believed he took a different route to the shop, and timed it so that their paths did not cross. At night she would plan how she would see him next morning, what she would say and do to put everything right, but it never happened.

The three girls were chatting at school one day, about boys mainly, and Belinda and Joyce were teasing her about mooning around after Matt still. "For goodness sake, go out with some others, Penny," Belinda advised. Without thinking, Penny replied, "Ok, I'll go out with anyone!" No doubt, this statement got around and one day, a letter arrived at Penny's house, from an older boy at school, saying how he had always been an admirer, and would she meet him outside the cinema at 6.30 on the Friday evening. She showed Belinda and Joyce the letter.

"Are you going?" they asked.

"I don't think so. Who is he anyway?"

"Well you said you'd go with anyone," they continued.

Friday arrived and Penny toyed with her conscience all day. How could you go with someone, just like that! Finally she made up her mind she would. She took the bus to the cinema, and saw him already waiting. She nearly changed her mind, and would have stayed on the bus, but the conductor was holding it up for her to alight.

The young man, Philip, by name, beamed when he saw her. "Hi. I never really thought you'd turn up," he greeted her.

He made sure they were seated in the back row, and Penny was feeling very uncomfortable beside him. This was the first boy she had been to the pictures with, other than Matt, and she was not very happy. After a while, he put his arm around her shoulders, trying to pull her nearer, but she just sat staring intently at the film. Then he was turning her way and putting his face next to hers. This was awful! And then he was kissing her cheek trying to move to her mouth. Penny thought she was going to be sick. This was really awful! She pulled away, turned to him saying, "I can't I can't. I'm ever so sorry but I still like Matt." So the date was a disaster. They watched the rest of the programme in silence, and Penny took herself back home on the bus. As she said goodbye, she said, "Sorry."

The only other date she accepted was from David down the road, whom she considered an old friend. He, too, asked her to go with him to the cinema. She knew she was the first girl he had ever taken, and as she still felt sorry for him - she never knew why - and as they were not in the back row - she did not complain when he rested his arm across her shoulders. But he got no kiss goodbye. Later, at school, she heard that he had told his peers of the date, and it seemed he bragged of more than he got. She wondered if Matt had heard about it. Probably!

Easter was coming up, and the following term at school would be a very busy one. Penny would be taking the External Exam, along with the others of her year who were too young previously, and from the lower year - Matt's year - who were of age. Now in the sixth form, she had to pursue some course of preferred education with a view to leaving school. Penny had opted for the Commercial Course, but she was not very happy with Shorthand and Typing, and couldn't really see herself working in an office all day. Occasionally, on a Saturday and in the holidays, she had gone with Rosamund into the city to the solicitor's office where her sister worked. She helped out with general filing and odd jobs, but it did not appeal to her as a career.

She had discussed with the new PE teacher, Miss Kent, the possibility of her going into teaching PE. Miss Kent thought it an excellent idea. She already delegated several tasks to Penny, having her umpire junior matches and practices. Penny, herself, was busy with her own senior teams in which she was in all of them, and captain of several.

There was a lot of chopping and changing of time-tables at school, trying to accommodate students in the classes of their choice, and it resulted in Penny and about eight other girls finding they had one short session at the end of two afternoons, when they had no fixed subject. The Head called them together and asked them to think if there was something they had not been offered in their years at the school that they would like him to arrange for the two blank sessions. Between themselves, they decided they would like to learn some conversational German.

The German master, Mr. Rogers, was assigned to take them. Needless to say, he was not very pleased to lose two free periods, and with them being at the end of the day, he had very often left for home early if not required to substitute. And, as he told other staff, “These girls aren’t really interested in learning anything!” He was possibly in his early forties, having come to teaching since war service as an interpreter in Germany. Each session usually took on the same procedure. He would arrive very late for the lesson, taking his time from the staff room to the upper-floor classroom. The girls would sit waiting, chatting, not bothered whether he came or not. Suddenly, he would fling open the door, stand a while in the doorway, cup of tea in hand, then slowly make his way to the desk. And then he would set out to embarrass the group of sixteen-year-old young ladies.

His most frequent ruse, was to complain that the room was too hot, and that the windows needed opening. The windows were high in such an old building, and required a long pole to manoeuver them. But inevitably, the pole was missing, which meant someone climbing from chair to desk top, to window ledge, and then fixing the windows by hand. He would look around the girls. ‘Now, who shall we have to open the window?’ The girls would cringe, knowing what was coming and inevitably it would be Penny. He looked around the small class. “Ah, Penny. You’re nice and athletic. Will you open the windows for us please?” You couldn’t say no to your teacher, so up she would get onto the chair, onto the desk, and finally clamber onto the window sill. Of course, they were given this task because as you stood silhouetted against the window, the light shone straight through your skirt. First one window, then another, he would say, then another, until you had gone right across the stretch of windows. Then it was the undignified clamber down again. "Very well done, Penny. That was very nice. Thank you."

Another day, he was teaching them German names of fruits. He came to plum - *pflaume*. He said that a term of endearment between a boy to a girl was, 'Meine kleine Pflaume.'- my little plum. He then elaborated that it was thought if a girl could say *pflaume* very nicely, she could kiss nicely. He made each girl come up to the desk, and say to his face, '*pflaume*.' It was just to embarrass them, and Penny decided when it was her time, she would refuse. But she could not summon up the courage. He asked her to say it three times right up near his face. "Very nice, Penny. Very nicely done." Possibly he was punishing them for making him lose his free periods!

One week the girls thought they would get their own back. As usual, they sat waiting for Mr. Rogers to arrive. The time went on. Penny said, "Let's hide behind the lockers." This was a tall, heavy piece of furniture near to the windows, but with quite a space, hidden from the view of the door, in which eight girls could huddle together. One girl kept peeping out the door with a view along the corridor. They waited and waited. Finally, she darted back in, whispering, "He's coming," and joined the rest behind the lockers. They dare not speak, or hardly breathe. Suddenly, the door was flung open and there was a long silence. They pictured the huge frame of Mr. Rogers in the open doorway, cup of tea in hand. Still there was silence. Penny thought she was going to burst with holding her breath. Was he still there? Then his voice boomed out something in German, followed by what they presumed was the translation:

'The birds have flown!' Then the door closed. The girls didn't know if he was in the room or not. They waited, silently. Finally, one girl peeped around the lockers.

"He's gone." One by one, they emerged, going back to their seats. The stupid girls had left their school bags at their desks, so he must have known they were there. Now, of course, they wondered what he was doing about it. Would he go to the Head and report them? They sat and worried.

"It's all your fault, Penny. I bet we get a detention," one girl blurted out. Of course, this was the situation that Mr. Rogers knew would ensue. Let them suffer. What did he care? They weren't interested in learning German, anyway, just as he wasn't particularly interested in trying to teach them any. They were an attractive group of girls, but not worth having to give up a free period. And he sat reading the paper and enjoying a second cup of tea in the staff room, waiting for the end of school bell.

April lapsed into May, and the days became longer and warmer. Break times could be spent sitting on the school field. Sometimes, Matt would join Penny, and chat with her. They seemed just friends, she thought. He never asked her out on a date now. Although they still occasionally walked back through the shops from the coffee bar, and once or twice strolled around the park when their paths crossed. Penny tried to feel indifferent, as she believed he was, but then memories would come flooding back, and she would long for them to become reality again.

The girls still teased her about not dating any of the other boys, and she had offers. One day, they were lying on the field, gossiping. Belinda and Penny were tackling Joyce to see if she was interested in anyone. "I'm sure you have got someone," Belinda stated. Joyce was still doing Science, and she said there was a young man working in the laboratories as a technician, who she thought looked rather nice. "He's not a teacher," she directed at Penny. "His name is Mr. Jenkins. I think he comes from Wales." Belinda and Penny had never seen the fellow, so they began to look out for him. Sometimes he would stroll out on the field, and the two girls would tease her about him. But Joyce was very timid, and she did nothing outwardly to show her interest.

It became a game with Penny to spot Mr. Jenkins, and as the days and weeks went on, she found she really was looking for him! The laboratories were off the main hall, and she often diverted to cross it and go out the other side. One lunch hour, the girls were lying on the field, and she spotted Mr. Jenkins coming out, and then sitting on one of the seats. He was talking to Miss Kent, but she thought he kept looking their way. She nudged Joyce, but she showed no sign of emotion. Each time Penny looked at him, she felt he was looking at her. She lay on her front with her head propped up on her elbows, studying him. He had very dark hair, and she thought his eyes must be dark brown. He was not very tall and was very slim, skinny really, she thought. Wonder what he does when he's not at school, she mused to herself. Don't think he's particularly athletic. Can't imagine him in The Blue Lagoon, and she diverted her gaze. But then she came back to him. Miss Kent looked pretty interested! Wonder how old he is. "How old do you think Mr. Jenkins is?" She asked her friends. "I say twenty-five," replied Belinda. "Perhaps younger," stated Joyce. "Well I reckon he's younger than Mr. McKenzie," continued Penny, and she took another look and found Mr. Jenkins glancing her way again.

The following day, the same thing happened. They lay on the field, and then Mr. Jenkins came out to sit on the seat.

"Here comes your flame, Joyce," Penny teased her. "Oh, him, I'm not interested any more," her friend replied. Penny was relieved at her answer, because she felt that maybe she was! Miss Kent was taking a Junior team rounders practice. She came over to Penny and asked if she would like to take over the umpiring for a while. "Good practice for you, Penny." Miss Kent had become extra friendly to Penny of late, and sometimes spoke to her more as a friend. She was quite young, the girls guessed, having come straight from college. She was very encouraging to Penny about taking up teaching, and had recommended her own college on the South Coast.

Penny got up to join the girls playing rounders, and Miss Kent handed her the whistle. Why, Penny didn't know, as you didn't really need it to umpire a rounders game. Miss Kent went to join Mr. Jenkins on the seat. As Penny glanced her way, she caught Mr. Jenkins looking at her, and she got a funny feeling inside. It rather disturbed her because she knew that feeling! She finished the practice game, and was organising the girls to clear up the apparatus. Miss Kent made her way back to them and Penny handed over the whistle. "Thank you Penny," Miss Kent said, "I'm trying to get Mr. Jenkins to have a look at my iron that's not working. He wants me to bring it into school, but I can't be bothered. I'm trying to persuade him to come round to my flat to do it." What a strange thing to tell her, Penny thought. I think she's got designs on Mr. Jenkins. The whistle blew for the end of lunch break. She and her teacher walked together, and as they passed Mr. Jenkins, he raised his hand to them, or was it to her, thought Penny. No, to Miss Kent, I expect. Then he got up to follow them back into school.

May ran into June. It was the exam time, but when you didn't have an exam, there was a lot of free time. The three friends played a lot of tennis on the school courts at the far end of the field. Boys would be playing cricket, and others practised their athletics. Penny and Belinda often fetched out the hurdles for a practice, as this was their special event. Belinda, especially, was very good, and represented the school along with Penny, and the two of them had gone from the area sports to represent the borough at the Middlesex competition at the White City Stadium, although Penny was only reserve there. But Belinda did very well.

One day in the German session with Mr. Rogers, he seemed less enthusiastic at taking the girls than normal. Then, he asked them, "Today is the first Wednesday in June. Do you know what takes place today?" They looked blank. "It is Derby day," he volunteered, "and any moment now, the horses will be off." He kept looking at his watch, and then looking around the girls, his eyes resting on Penny. Oh no. Not the windows again, she thought.

"Penny. I would like you to go across to Mr. Allan, the caretaker, at his house, and ask him who has won the Derby. He will have been listening to the race on the radio." Penny got up. Well, that was a relief. She left the room, hurried along the corridor, tripped quickly down the two flights of stairs, flung open the door of the main hall, which was empty, and then ran straight across to the far door which would lead to the nearest exit to the caretaker's house. As she sprinted through the hall, the far door opened, and in walked Mr. Jenkins, or at least he would have if Penny hadn't run straight into him. She gasped as he put out an arm to stop her. "Don't run in school!" Mr. Jenkins uttered. Penny had stopped, and so had he. Her heart was pounding and she felt her face flush.

"Sorry, Mr. Jenkins," she puffed out. "You needn't call

me Mr. Jenkins. My friends call me Gareth. You're Penny aren't you?" he continued. "Were you going to ask Mr. Allan the result of the Derby?"

"Yes, Mr. Rogers sent me. I'd better go and find out," Penny almost whispered, as she was beginning to feel almost faint, for some reason.

"I can tell you who won. Tell Mr. Rogers his horse came third." He then reeled off the names of the first, second and third horses, and Penny turned to go, saying thank you. But he called her back. "Penny, perhaps you would like to come out one evening. Maybe to a show. I'll see what's on." Penny's brain began to whirl, she couldn't think and she seemed to hear herself answering, "Oh, thank you," but she was somehow up above herself, looking down on this scenario, as if it wasn't her at all.

Mr. Jenkins disappeared into the science laboratories, and she started her way back through the hall, up the two flights of stairs and along the corridor back to the classroom. But her legs wouldn't seem to move, her heart was still pounding, her head was throbbing, and she was afraid she would faint. She pushed open the door, and stood there panting. Mr. Rogers and the other girls gazed at her. "Well come in, girl. Did you get the result? Who won?" Penny's legs would not move, nor could she get a word out of her mouth. "What's the matter with you, girl? Who won?" Still she couldn't answer. "Did you go to Mr. Allan's house?" Mr. Rogers continued. She struggled with the words. "No," was all that came out. "No! Well where have you been? Whatever's happened to you, Penny?"

"I met Mr. Jenkins. He heard the race, so I didn't go," she answered almost incoherently. "Well, who won then?" Penny thought. She had forgotten. "I don't know. I've forgotten, Sir."

"You've forgotten," he roared at her. "Well, think, girl. What did Mr. Jenkins tell you? Now just sit down, pull yourself together and think. I don't know what you have been up to. You look dreadful." Penny felt dreadful! She sat at the desk. All she could hear Mr. Jenkins saying was, 'My friends call me Gareth,' and, 'Would you like to come out one evening.' Suddenly, she remembered: "I don't know who won, but he said your horse came third."

"Well that's something then. I won't send you on an errand again!" The bell sounded for the end of school, but Penny still sat long after Mr. Rogers and the other girls had left. Had Mr. Jenkins really meant what he said? He obviously knew her name. She didn't say anything to Belinda and Joyce as they walked down the road. They weren't in the German group, so they had no idea of the event. She would wait and see first if he did ask her out. What would her mother say! Well, he wasn't really a teacher!

As they walked down the road, Matt passed on his bike. Penny looked his way ... funny, her tummy didn't give a jump! Mr. Rogers and Mr. Jenkins were also walking home together, but their journey took a different route, through the park. In fact, Mr. Jenkins was lodging with Mr. Rogers and family. "I don't know what happened to that girl I sent out who you gave the result to. I've never seen a girl in such a state. I was worried one of the boys had got hold of her and raped her! Unless it was you, Taffy," he laughed.

As it happened, Gareth Jenkins was waiting for payday, so that he could indeed get tickets for a show at the Empire and ask the young girl out. He had certainly noticed her before the encounter in the school hall. He had watched her out on the school field, and had heard her name called. While working in the science labs, he often heard the students' idle chat, and he recalled hearing a boy saying that Penny Saunders and some boy or other had now broken up. The lad was daring another to ask her out.

This was his second term at the school, and he did not intend continuing any longer once they broke up for the long summer holiday. He would go back to Wales again. He didn't really know what he wanted to do. There wasn't much opportunity back home. He was twenty-five, and knew it was time to sort himself out. He was well educated, having done three years at University, studying science. He had then done his two years National Service as a Bevin Boy in the local mines. This was the main occupation in the South Wales village of his home. But he didn't want to pursue it. He had one or two other jobs in various industrial laboratories, but nothing with prospects. So he had suddenly taken himself to London to seek his fortune, having got fed up with his nagging, dominating mother at home. He had an Aunt, Uncle and family living in North London, and they had accommodated him initially, even though they really had no spare room. He had to sleep on a settee in the kitchen-cum-lounge. They only had a two-bedroom flat of a large converted old house, in a rather run-down area, but they did their best to look after him.

His Uncle was a prolific drinker, and as this seemed to be the norm amongst the men of the Welsh valleys, Gareth was happy to partner him. He spent a lot of time in the West End of London, frequenting a nucleus of pubs, which other Welsh people seemed to patronise. He was popular with the ladies. At one time he was seeing a Welsh girl, a Scottish girl and an Irish girl - sounded like the start of a joke! But he needed money to frequent these pubs, and most of the time he had to rely on his mother sending him money, which she did believing it was payment to his Aunt for his board. He really had looked for a job, and accepted the laboratory technician's post at the school as a stepping-stone to higher things. The hours were short, long holidays enabling regular trips home to Wales, but the wages were not enough for high-living in London. So, he was now going to give it up, go home, and think again. His family were getting fed up with him not settling down to some kind of career. He was wasting his brain, they preached.

He was a popular member of the male staff room at the school. They knew he was wasted in the lab assistant's job, and had suggested to him that he undertook a teaching course. Mr. Rogers was particularly friendly with him, and when hearing of the circumstances of his stay with his Aunt and Uncle, offered him lodgings in his household. He lived in a large house with his wife and child, his sister and his mother, it being his mother's house. Gareth had been very grateful to the family for taking him in, and they appeared happy to have him. However, they now knew that he intended to return to Wales at the end of the summer term.

Payday was due, and Mr. Jenkins looked for Penny out on the school field. As it happened, she was sitting with Matt, who had made a point of joining her, and they were joking and chatting, very non-commitally. At one point, Penny felt he was going to ask her something - maybe to come out - but other friends joined them, and the moment was broken. It was a hot day, and she got up to go to the drinking fountain. As she did so, Mr. Jenkins quickly crossed her path. Her heart skipped as he walked beside her. "I think there is a good show on this week, Penny. Would you like to come one evening? What about tomorrow?"

"I'll have to ask if I can, first," she replied. "I'll let you know tomorrow."

Penny went home that day very excited, but also very worried about asking her mother if she could go out with Mr. Jenkins ... Gareth. She knew the family had noticed that she did not go on dates with Matt now, and that he didn't call round as he used to, although he had sometimes walked home with her if they bumped into one another, and they had chatted at the gate.

Her mother seemed extra busy that evening with household chores. Lavinia had been worried lately, as Graham was marrying the publican's daughter in a couple of months, and it was going to be quite a posh affair. She wanted a new outfit, but money was short, and they would also need to buy a present. Penny was not to be a bridesmaid this time. Her sister, Annie was the one chosen. Penny helped with the washing up after all the family had their evening meal.

She kept opening her mouth to ask her mother, and then she could not. It was almost time for bed, so she had to do the deed now or never. With one big effort, she blurted out, "I've been asked out to a show at the Empire tomorrow evening. Can I go?"

"Oh Penny, is it with Matthew? I knew he would be back," her mother asked.

"No, it's someone else - another boy - well, not really a boy - his name is Mr..... Er...Gareth," she replied, trying to sound very matter of fact. "I haven't heard you speak of him, Penny. How old is he?"

"Well I don't really know, maybe twenty....ish," was the vague reply.

"Twentyish! Oh, Penny, it's not another teacher, is it? Well, you're not going."

"He's not a teacher, Mumma. He just works in the school. He does things in the science labs. I don't know what he does but he's not a teacher. He comes from Wales, and he's ever so nice - really Mumma. Oh please let me go. I'm sixteen now and he's only a few years older than me." She was beginning to get hysterical and raise her voice. For one dreadful moment, she thought she was going to start arguing with her mother, like her sister Rosamund. She never did that. So she pulled herself together, fought back the tears, and asked once more, meekly, "Please, Mumma. We're going to the early show. I promise I won't be late."

Lavinia looked at her. She had always worried so much over Penny, and yet out of all the girls, she seemed so capable, and had a lovely temperament. And she was getting very attractive. Twentyish could mean anything!

"Well go on then,' she answered. "But be sensible."

Penny ran and hugged her mother. "Oh thank you. I will." As she went up to bed, she thought over to herself what being sensible meant!

Next day at school during the morning break, she made her way to the science labs, looking for Mr. Jenkins. Luckily, the classes and teachers were not there, and she found him preparing some apparatus for the next session. She knocked on the open door, and he turned around. "Ah, Penny. How nice to see you in here. Are you coming out tonight?"

"Yes. My Mum said it's okay. But I mustn't be too late," she told him, shyly. He arranged where and when he would meet her, and she turned to go out for break.

"Don't go," he said. "Stay here a while." Penny was in a quandary as to what to do, but then decided. "No, I'd better go out with the others. See you later then," and she turned and made her way outside. Just as she got to the playground, the whistle went for the end of break.

There was no time to tell Belinda and Joyce her news. Their next lesson was a double commercial session. Penny typed out, "I am going out with Mr. Jenkins tonight. We are going to see a show. His name is Gareth." She passed the note to Belinda and she passed it on to Joyce. Penny was doodling on her books, drawing her hearts. She drew in the arrow and filled in her initials, P.S. She toyed with filling in the other end, and finally entered, G.J. She went to scribble it out, but changed her mind, and closed the book. Then she looked inside the back cover where she still had an old heart saying, P.S. and M.J.O. She went to scribble over that one too, but left it as it was.

That lunch-time break, Matt came and joined the girls on the school field again. They were all chatting like old times, and Penny didn't know what to think. Why hadn't he behaved like this some while ago? She really felt that she had fallen for Mr. Jenkins ... Gareth, but she felt unsure again now. Of course, she had fallen on the rebound from a failed love relationship, always a danger. Still, she thought, no harm in trying. Could be interesting. No doubt, news of it all would get out sooner or later, even though she had sworn Belinda and Joyce to secrecy. Wonder what Matt would make of it all. Why was she worrying herself what Matt would think, she didn't expect he cared? But he was being rather sweet today. If he were to ask her out tonight too, she would really be torn between the two dates. Which would she accept? But it was her fantasy running away with her again. Matt suddenly got up, and left to join his friends.

Penny hurried home from school that day, rushed her tea

and then took her time getting ready. She took the bus to where she was to meet Mr. Jenkins. He was already there, waiting for her. They took the last part of the journey to the theatre, and he bought the tickets for seats up in the circle section. They were quite early for the programme, so he suggested they sit in the bar. It was quite posh in there, thought Penny. He asked her what she would like to drink. She had no idea what to say. "I don't know," she answered. He obviously knew she was only sixteen and shouldn't be having alcohol in a bar, but he didn't want to make it obvious, so he said, "Perhaps a port and lemon will do." She agreed. He had a beer, and they sat drinking, but not saying much. Then he asked her how her day had been at school, how the exams had gone, and what she intended doing when she left school. Penny was taking particular notice of his accent; it was rather nice. She was studying him now. He had gorgeous eyes and she always thought she didn't like dark eyes. Then he was telling her that he lodged with Mr. Rogers, and how he had told him about the state she was in the day of the Derby. She blushed when she remembered it. "Does he know that you've asked me out?" she asked rather worriedly. But he said he didn't, which made her feel more relieved.

Then the bell sounded to say the show was about to begin. So they finished their drinks, and hurried to their seats. They were good seats for seeing the stage. Some rows back from the front, but not near the back row. The show was good. During the second half, when the main act was on - he happened to be a hypnotist - Gareth slipped an arm around her shoulders. Penny jumped a little at first, and then, as she was getting interested in what was taking place on the stage, she began to relax. She leaned nearer to him, and was wishing he would hold her hand as she didn't know where to put them. He whispered in her ear to rest her head on his shoulder. She could feel the warmth of him, and she was beginning to tingle inside. His face was next to hers, and suddenly, without thinking where she was, with an almost uncontrollable urge, she turned to him, just as he turned to her and she kissed him full on the lips. She felt him startle from her action, and then indulge in it. As she released herself, she was quite shocked to realise what she had done. "Oh Penny, you're so warm," he said. The show ended, and they got up to leave. Penny looked around, wondering who, and how many had seen her. There were people behind and around them, but fortunately not that near. But she felt embarrassed, as they had obviously seen.

Leaving the theatre, he told her to take his arm. She found this strange, and wished he would hold her hand instead. There was a cinema opposite, near the bus stop where Penny assumed they would catch the bus home. "Let's go to the pictures," he said.

"No I can't. I should be home by ten," was her worried reply.

"Come on, just half an hour. I want you somewhere where we can spoon a while. You're so cuddly and loveable," was his next retort. Penny thought what a funny expression 'to spoon' was, but he was already leading her to the kiosk, buying the tickets, and then asking the usherette for two nice seats in the back row.

As soon as they sat down, he had his arm around her, pulling her to him, and kissing her long and hard and Penny was beginning to melt, and all the old feelings were coming back. It seemed so long since she had been kissing and cuddling in the back row. And it was very nice! And then his hand was across her breast, and when she didn't object, he was fumbling at the buttons of her top. Penny had put on a short-sleeved top, which had buttons right down the centre front. It gave the appearance of a cardigan, but the front fastening was an illusion, as in fact the row of buttons were just affixed to the outside of the plain front, and therefore did not undo. He was fumbling and fumbling, trying each one, and Penny almost got a fit of the giggles knowing her top could not open, and wondering what to say, as all the time he was still kissing her. Eventually, he broke off, and whispered, "These buttons are too tight."

"They don't open", she assured him, and he moved his hand to edge himself up from the bottom of her blouse. But by now, Penny was worrying about the time, even though her body was telling her to stay. She whispered in his ear, "I really must go home now, Gareth". It was the first time she had used his name to him. It sounded strange, but she liked him.

So they broke away from each other, and got up to leave, Penny thinking to herself that it had been an expensive kiss and cuddle. He made her take his arm again as they waited for the bus, and sitting up on top deck, he pulled her close to him. They had some general chat, and then alighted at the foot of her road, turning up towards her house. She told him she lived half-way up, but said she didn't want him to walk all the way with her. Well, she was sure her mother would be 'spying' and she didn't want a reoccurrence of the Mr. McKenzie affair! He honoured her wish, and they had a long kiss by the wall at the foot of road. He said he wished he could see her over the weekend, but he had other arrangements. "I'll see you at school on Monday. Would you like a game of tennis lunch-time? We can go down the park courts," he offered.

"Oh that would be lovely," she answered him. "The hard courts in the park are better than the school grass ones." Also, she thought, they are out of view of prying eyes. That's probably what he had thought too. So they parted, and she took herself up the road.

"Had a nice time, Penny?" Her mother enquired. "Yes, very nice. It was a good show - a hypnotist. I'm glad he didn't ask me to go up. It went on a bit late though," she lied.

"What about Mr. Jenkins. Is he nice?" The inquisition continued. "Are you seeing him again?"

"Yes he's very nice. He's got a funny accent. He comes from Wales. We're going to have a game of tennis at school on Monday. His name is Gareth - it's a Welsh name". She turned to go up to bed, then called back to her mother, "He's got gorgeous eyes!" As she lay in bed, thinking over the evening's events, she came over all gooey again. Guess I'm in love again, she thought. Then she giggled to herself over the expression 'to spoon.' Well, they went quite a long way, if that was spooning! And then she thought, 'I wonder what the film was!'

Penny was on a high all weekend. She met Belinda and Joyce at the shops on the Saturday, and told them all about the date. They all went into the coffee bar, and Matt and Stewart were in there. Penny felt uncomfortable and had a guilty feeling. The girls left before the boys did, and that evening went to the cinema together. It brought back feelings of Penny's half-hour in the back row with Gareth, and then her mind wandered to back-row memories with Matt. She wondered if, and who, he was taking out now. Probably that young girl, Susan, although she hadn't heard any talk at school.

She also wondered what Gareth was doing over the weekend. He had told her he had made arrangements. Maybe he had another girl, well; she would be a woman probably. Why would he want to date herself, only sixteen, when he could go with older women who must be much more exciting? They might do really naughty things. She tried not to think of Gareth and an older woman. He had told her that she was cuddly and loveable. What would she do if he tried to get her to do naughty things? The films finished, and her friends went their way home, and she hers. She spent a restless night, but was up to do her paper round and she even saw Matt. It was a lovely day, she thought of going swimming. It was likely that Matt would be there, and she decided against it. Tomorrow she was to play tennis in the lunch-hour with Gareth. She hoped it wouldn't rain.

Monday was a lovely day. Penny took herself along to the science labs during the morning break to check that the game was on. Gareth said he was borrowing a racquet from Mr. Rogers, and would meet her outside the school gate lunchtime. Then he said, "Come here a minute, Penny." There was a small storeroom between the two laboratories. The door was open and he called her inside. He shut the door behind them and it was now completely dark. He put his arms around her, and began kissing her. "I've been thinking of you all weekend, Penny." She was enjoying the kissing when she suddenly realised where they were. The bell sounded for end of break and she panicked, pulled away, and crashed into some apparatus in the dark. He opened the door and she dashed out. Her heart was pounding. Supposing they had been caught!

They met, having missed lunch, and made their way down the road to the park. Gareth booked the court. They were the only ones there. Penny was a good tennis player, and was in the school team. She wondered what Gareth's play would be like. It turned out that he didn't have much style, but obviously had more power than Penny, so they had a reasonable knock-around of a game. They had been playing for about half-an-hour when she suddenly saw Mr. Rogers and a second language teacher, Mr. Weston, strolling through, along the path towards the tennis court. She was facing them, Gareth had his back to the path and had not seen them. When they reached their court, they stopped and stood watching awhile. Penny felt awful and didn't know if she should acknowledge them or not. At that moment, Gareth turned to retrieve a ball, and saw them, too. The three men had a few words of conversation. Penny couldn't hear what and busied herself by undoing and doing up her plimsoles. She looked up, and the two teachers had turned and walked back.

Time was getting on, and Penny said she would have to hurry back for afternoon lessons. As they walked back, she said to Gareth that she wished Mr. Rogers and Mr. Weston hadn't seen them. "I'm sure they were spying on us," she told him. "I expect they were. They knew I was going to play with someone, because I had to borrow the racquet and the shoes."

"Don't worry, they won't make anything of it. Anyhow, there's no harm in a game of tennis," he reassured her. The next day, he told her that after school, when walking home with Mr. Rogers, he had told Gareth, 'I admire your choice!' The bell was ringing for the end of break as they got back to school. Penny rushed in, but not before Gareth had arranged to take her to the cinema the following evening.

And so began some weeks of regular dates. Penny was now getting heavily involved. Several times she visited Gareth in the little storeroom of the labs during break times. One day, Belinda told her that Miss James, the senior mistress, had called her aside, saying she wished to speak to her. She told Belinda that if she ever could not find her friend, Penny, she wanted her to let her know. As it happened, at that very moment, Penny and Gareth were 'spooning' in the little room. When her friend told her what Miss James had said, Penny was shocked. It meant that the school staff must know of her association with Gareth. It also meant that her peers in school must know about it also. She wondered what Matt thought. He often sat on the field with them, but never mentioned the matter.

Then one day, Belinda told her that Matt had asked her out to the cinema. Penny was a bit shocked, but then why should she be bothered? "Do you like him then?" she asked Belinda. Belinda answered that she had been tempted way back at their New Year party when they played Postman's knock. Penny was surprised, and then remembered how long Matt and her friend had spent on their turn in the hall. This stirred memories of herself and Matt in the bedroom that day. Why, oh why had he finished with her? They say you never forget your first love, and she knew she never would. She brought herself back to what Belinda had just told her. "Have a nice time," she remarked. "I'm going to the cinema, too, with Gareth. Think we're going to the Ritz. We always sit upstairs there. It's great in the back row."

It turned out that Belinda and Matt went to the same cinema, but they sat downstairs. It was a Friday night, and at school on the following Monday, Penny asked Belinda how she got on with Matt. "Yes, it was okay. But when I told him I believed you and Mr. Jenkins may have been upstairs, he kept bringing up the point, and saying he couldn't imagine you up there. Quite honestly, I think he was more interested in thinking what you were up to than in me! But he's nice, and I like him," was her friend's reply.

Penny's mother was getting anxious about the dates her

daughter was having with the young man at school. She saw a change in Penny and wondered what she got up to on these dates. "I hope you're not silly in the cinema, Penny," she told her one evening just as she left for another date.

"No, of course not," Penny called back. But in truth, their spooning, petting, cuddling, whatever you liked to call it, was very intense. Penny could not stop thinking that it was obvious that Gareth was very experienced, and it bugged her so that she could not stop herself thinking about how many girl or women friends he must have had by the age of twenty-five. Why did he bother with her, when she always held back from going too far? Did he still see the ex-girlfriends when he still obviously visited the pubs in the West End? They wouldn't say NO, she imagined. What did he want with a girl of sixteen? She could not believe that he loved her. But he was always telling her that he did.

They didn't only go to the cinema. One weekend, they went to the Battersea Fair, which was fun. They went walking across Hampstead Heath, rode out to Epping Forest, where they lay in the grass together. When they walked together, they stopped often to kiss, or hovered in dark shop doorways and alleys for more intense sessions. Penny was such a tactile person, Gareth could not resist her presence, and under it all was her innocence still. He told her that he had given in his notice for the school job, and would be going home to Wales as soon as the term ended. Then he wasn't sure what he would do. Penny assumed that was going to be the end of it all. She told her friends, "This is just an affair. He is going back to Wales in a few weeks." She didn't really know what was meant by an affair, but she could not imagine that he would want to return to her. I guess he's just amusing himself with me, she thought to herself, but she didn't want to believe it.

Up to now, Penny had not invited Gareth home. She still made him leave her at the end of the road. But Lavinia was pestering her to bring him in. Well, she wanted to assess this fellow. So she told Penny to invite him round for tea one weekend, which she did. Her parents were there, of course, and Annie and Rosamund. Rosamund had teased Penny all morning about his coming round, and Penny hoped she wouldn't tease her in his presence, and she was on edge waiting for him to arrive.

What she didn't know was that Gareth was also on edge about coming to meet the family. He was very self-conscious about his accent, and told Penny later that he had been practising speaking correctly in the mirror! The meeting went off okay and as everyone relaxed, Gareth and the three sisters played cards while Lavinia prepared the tea. Later, he talked about his home in Wales, and told Lavinia he would like Penny to visit there. It was the first Penny had heard of it! Then the two of them took the dog for a walk to the local park, where they could both relax and have some kisses. There was a small, wooden, open shed in the park. It had a bench seat all around, and they sat in there, cuddling together, while the dog waited patiently. They went back home, and Gareth left, saying he was meeting his uncle for a drink.

It was almost the end of term now. Penny had to sort out her course of education for the following years. She really did hope to get to a College of Physical Education in two year's time. This meant she would have to study one or two subjects for a higher certificate. Miss Kent had also told her that a science was normally required. So Penny was going to have to take up chemistry once again. The headmaster suggested she go and have a chat with the chemistry master. Penny went along at the end of one morning session. She explained her position to him, and he said perhaps she would like to take a book home to study in the long summer holiday break. He also said he looked forward to having her back in the class. As she left the laboratory, she noticed Gareth in the storeroom. When they next met, he told her that as she walked out, the teacher remarked to him, "Well that will add a bit of glamour!"

The end of term did arrive. Gareth was returning to Wales the very next day. They had their final date, going to the cinema, where they never looked at the film, only indulging in one another in the back row, completely oblivious to those around them. They walked homewards afterwards, and stopped in several shop doorways. Their final farewell was in the alleyway near to Penny's house. Gareth promised to write to her, and insisted that he wanted her to visit him in Wales.

"I will send for you," he promised. "As soon as I can arrange it with my parents." He took her to her house, and they kissed goodbye for the last time. As she went indoors, she thought to herself, well that's that! I know he won't write. The affair was over. And she cried and cried in bed that night. She had felt this despair before.

CHAPTER TEN

Once again, it was the start of the long summer holiday. At first, Penny was at a loss as to what to do. She was missing Gareth terribly, and at the same time, telling herself she had known from the start that this is how it would inevitably end. She wasn't sure if she really belonged with her friends. The past few weeks she had been plunged into the world of adults. She watched for the postman every day. He had promised to write but nothing came. It suddenly dawned on her that she didn't even have an address for Gareth. Oh well, it had been an experience!

She wandered the shops with Belinda or Joyce if they came over, and she confided in them what a fool she had been. Several times she saw Matt and some of the gang, and they still sat together in the coffee bar, and he even walked home with her. Neither of them mentioned Gareth. One such day, Matt asked her if she wanted to go to the usual dance at the Church Hall. She was getting fed up with mooning around, so she said she would. She did love dancing. It was an enjoyable evening, and she danced more with Matt than anyone else. But she walked home with some of the girlfriends.

One week slipped in to two, and then during the third week, she received a post card from Scotland. It was from Gareth, and he said he was touring, driving the car for his parents. He said he would write as soon as they got back to Wales to arrange for her trip there. Penny was stunned! So he had remembered her! That day she went to the swimming pool with some of the girls. Matt was there too. He was with Jack Stewart and some other boys. The two groups of girls and boys gradually mingled, and there was a lot of fun between them all, in and out of the water. Several times, she felt Matt seemed on the point of asking her something, but nothing materialized. She thought it over as she walked home. Was she willing him to ask her something?

A few days later, a letter did arrive from Gareth. It was quite short, saying he was back from Scotland, and was looking forward to her coming to Wales. She could come any time now to suit herself, just let him know if she was coming by train or coach, telling her to book her ticket to Neath, and he would meet her with the car. He finished by saying he was missing her very much, and looking forward to holding her again.

Penny told her mother about the letter, and asked if she could go. Lavinia did not know what to answer. She had met the young man and he seemed very nice and she thought he was genuinely fond of Penny. But to let her go on her own for a week, was rather worrying. How did she know if there were indeed any parents at his home? He might be enticing her down to take her off on his own. And she was still only sixteen. What should she do for the best, and what would people think of her for letting a young girl go off with a twenty-five year old man! She decided to write to his mother, thanking her for inviting her daughter for a holiday, that it was a wonderful opportunity for Penny to see South Wales, but as she had never been away on her own before, and still young, she was naturally concerned. She would like to know that everything was in order for her to visit. She asked Penny for the address, which she now had, and posted off the letter to Mrs. Jenkins.

A couple of days later, a reply came, saying that they were looking forward to Penny visiting them, and that everything was in order. Penny would have her own bedroom, and Gareth would be sleeping next door, in his cousin's house. So Lavinia felt more relieved, and she told Penny it would be all right for her to go. She and Harry decided she should go by coach, which would be cheaper, and Penny and her father went to book the ticket. The day coaches were all fully booked, so they had to take a night coach out, but were able to get a day ticket for the return, one week later. Penny then wrote a letter to Gareth, telling him of her arrival the following week.

That same week, the results of the External Exams were available. She was quite shocked to find that she had failed both her English Language and Literature subjects. She had always considered them her best, and she needed them for entry to College. She had passed Maths, which she expected and also passed French and Geography, although she had considered herself hopeless at Geography. Oh well, she would have to re-sit the two English exams next year and aim for a higher level the second year. She would have to concentrate more on her school because she definitely wanted to get into the PE College. And she suddenly remembered the old doctor, five years ago, writing out the medical certificate to say that she was not permitted to take part in physical activities at school. Well, she had got away with it up to now, and she was determined to prove him wrong! At that moment, she thought it meant more to her than anything else, even more than going on holiday to Wales with Gareth. Then she thought, would she have felt the same a year ago, would it have meant more than her relationship with Matt! She didn't think so!

There was more than a week to prepare for the holiday. Suddenly, Penny was having second thoughts. It seemed as if she was forgetting what it had been like when she and Gareth were together. Each day she went to the shop, she seemed to bump into Matt, and he would walk home with her. They had long chats, and she would remember their past dates when she looked at him. She was feeling troubled. One day she would be excited at the coming reunion with Gareth, and another day she felt a sense of panic and she felt that she could not go.

The last weekend before she was due to leave, she met Matt and their peers in the coffee bar at mid-day. He walked home with her to the bottom of her road, and suddenly said, "Fancy coming to the pictures tonight?" She could not believe what he had said, after all this time he was asking her out again, and she was only one week away from going to see Gareth. But without hesitating, she answered, "Yes."

After tea, she began to get ready, and told her mother she was going to the pictures that evening. "Oh, are the girls coming over?" Lavinia asked. Penny told her that she had met Matt, and that he had asked her. Her mother looked shocked. "Well, you better make up your mind, my girl, who it is you want." Penny didn't know what to answer, and eventually said, "Matt is my friend." But underneath, she was pondering on her mother's words. She was indeed feeling a sense of doubt as to what or whom she did want.

She finished getting ready and left to meet Matt. He was already outside the cinema. As it happened, it was very full, and they were lucky to get in, having two seats in the very centre of the rows. No back row now, not that they had asked for it, and it was occupied anyway. Although the two films were reasonable, not that Penny was concentrating, she found the whole three hours a strain. There was an atmosphere between them. They almost sat apart, each in his or her own seat. There was no contact whatsoever. Penny knew she was longing for him to take her hand, but they finally left the cinema as they had entered. He walked her home, still with no contact, and they stopped at the end of her road. For a while they chatted idly. Why doesn't he take hold of me, Penny wrestled with herself. And then it was goodbye. Please, please kiss me, she thought. But he was gone. "See you," he called! She turned the corner, and then leant against the wall, thinking and crying. So that was it! Obviously, he had no further designs on her. She would go to Wales next week. But she still had a sense of panic when she thought of it. It had been some weeks now since she had seen Gareth.

That night, she lay in bed, turning her life over in her mind. She was having difficulty remembering what it felt like 'spooning' with Gareth, the word still making her giggle to herself! But she could remember what it had felt like 'playing around' or 'necking' with Matt as they both called it! But this evening had shown her that Matt was in no way interested in her, well, that is what she believed! She finally fell asleep, but then woke suddenly from a dream. She was on the sands of the Blue Lagoon, crying desperately and the boy - was it Matt-was diving off the rocks and swimming further and further out to sea. She was trying to call, "Come back," but the words wouldn't come out, and he disappeared way out to sea, without hearing her or looking back! She lay awake now, feeling very disturbed, and she felt she had seen and thought of the Blue Lagoon for the last time.

Penny now had less than a week to get herself organised for the trip to Wales. Her mother permed her hair for her, and she bought a few new clothes with the money saved from the paper round. Belinda and Joyce came shopping with her. They could not believe that she was going away with Mr. Jenkins for a week! Penny knew that everyone was talking about it. Matt hadn't mentioned it on the cinema date, but obviously, he too knew. Well, it would be of no consequence to him, she assumed. And still there was this little doubt at the back of her mind. Did she really want to go? She was too involved now. She had her coach ticket already booked, Gareth was expecting her, his mother was preparing for her, and Penny's own mother had written a letter. Too much was involved for her to 'chicken out.' The one person who could make her change her mind, obviously did not care! So, she would go.

Friday arrived. Her coach was not leaving until very late at night. It was going to be a long journey, involving a change of coach at Cheltenham, although she had no idea where that was. Her parents were taking her to the coach station in London, going there by bus. She packed and repacked two or three times, and her mother kept saying had she remembered this or that.

Lavinia suddenly asked her what she had packed to wear in bed. "I haven't got anything," she answered. Penny never wore anything in bed, hadn't done so since she was in her teens. She could not tolerate clothes around her in bed. She was a restless sleeper, and found she would get tangled up in nightwear, start getting overheated and then feel she would faint. Hence, she did not possess pyjamas or a nightgown. She hadn't thought about it. And they both panicked.

"Penny, you must take something to wear in bed. You'll have to borrow something from Rosamund or Annie."

"But I can't stand anything on me in bed. No one will see me in bed, anyway," she moaned.

"Well you're taking something, even if you only leave it folded on the bed, so it looks as if you wear it," was her mother's reply, and she found some pyjamas from Annie's drawer, and supervised Penny packing them in the case.

After tea, she was finally ready and packed. Then, later in the evening it was time to go. She had said goodbye to her two brothers and sisters still at home and Granny Saunders and then her mother and father were ready, and they were telling her it was time. Her father carried her case. They had one short bus ride before changing to the second bus for the hour-long ride to the coach station. She sat next to her mother, and gazed out of the window.

The first places on the journey she recognised. The bottom of the road to school - no one about now. The cinema where she had gone with Matt a week ago - wonder if he was in there with some girl! The milk bar where the gang always met - maybe Matt and Stewart were in there. The big shopping centre where she shopped with the girls - the shops were shut now. And then the Empire theatre - Mr. McKenzie had first taken her there, and Matt and Stewart and Belinda and she had gone as a foursome, and she had kissed Gareth there on the first date. Gareth! She was on her way to spend a whole week with Gareth! Did she want to go? Yes! No! Then her mother was asking her again, "And have you packed…and remember to help…and speak nicely and thank them for having you…"

She was automatically nodding and saying "Yes," but not really taking it all in. Then they were passing places she didn't really recognise. Oh, Trafalgar Square - she recognised that, a glimpse of Buckingham Palace - her father behind was telling her to look, and suddenly they were stopping and they were getting off, and making the last walk to the coach station.

There were so many coaches, but her father seemed to know which one they were looking for. There was a long queue of people already there, and then everyone was getting on board. The driver said the coach would be full, and please get seated quickly. Her case was in the hold, and she was seated next to the window towards the front. An elderly man was seated next to her. Her mother and father were trying to say goodbye to her, and the driver was saying it was time to leave. Penny felt as if she was going to cry, and she was sure that her mother was actually crying.

Lavinia said to the elderly man next to Penny, "Look after her, please," and then her last words to her daughter in her ear, as she kissed her for the last time, "Have a nice time - and do be good, Penny."

"I will, Mumma," she whispered. And then they had left the coach, the door closed, and it was reversing out of the parking bay. Her parents were waving, Penny raised her hand gulping back the tears, and then they were off. Off and away to what, she wondered. She had a feeling that she was leaving behind a lot more than her Mum and Dad!

It certainly was a long journey, and night time all the way. As they left London, Penny read the sign posts, although most meant nothing to her - just names. The elderly gentleman next to her had initially tried to chat to her. He said he was going home to Treherbert in the Rhondda valley. He had been visiting his daughter and family in London. "I don't like London. It's too big," he said.

Penny said she had always lived in London. "But it's very nice where I live. Not like the West End," she volunteered. He then asked her where she was going in Wales and why. “I’m going to stay with…a friend,” she faltered. “I have to go to Neath, and then we go to the village somewhere. I can’t pronounce the name. I shall only be away a week,” she continued.

“In that case, we will both have to change to different coaches when we get to Cheltenham. We’re not going the same way,” he continued.

Penny looked around the coach. Everyone seemed to be sleeping, leaning on the windows, on one another, slumped forward or heads back, some with mouths open. Eventually, she heard quiet snoring coming from her companion. He had his arms folded and his head propped back on the far corner of his seat. She was glad he wasn’t leaning on her, but he was a nice man. Penny wondered how people could sleep on a coach like that. She couldn’t. In her own bed, she liked to lie on her tummy, flat out, with her arms bent up to her pillow with just her finger tucked under it, and her head turned to one side- and no clothes on, of course. But she did tuck down more in the very cold of winter, curling up on her side and pulling the covers around her neck. But she still wore no bedclothes. Her sisters laughed at her. Her mother called her a piece of warm toast! Wonder what the bed will be like in Gareth’s house, she mused. Poor Gareth had got to sleep next door - how odd!

She began to think about Gareth. It had been quite exciting really, sneaking into the lab store at break times. That was fun, quite naughty she supposed. Fancy Miss James telling Belinda to sneak on her. Lying in the grass in Epping Forest when she had taken her blouse off and Gareth removed his shirt, and kissing and cuddling and getting so hot and sweaty that they were slipping about on each other. Made her imagine lying in the heat of the Pacific Islands' sun on the white sands of the Blue Lagoon. No, Gareth didn't fit in the Blue Lagoon. But Matt did! And then back came the feeling of doubt. She really hadn't expected this to go further than an affair. She could not believe that Gareth really loved her. Why would he want her, sixteen, when he could have grown women, and he must have had lots at his age? And yet he had been forever telling her how he loved her. Matt had never said that to her. She couldn't imagine any of the boys at school actually saying that. Steven Steed had told her she was 'exciting' when he followed her outside at the school dance. Gareth had said she was 'lovely' and 'cuddly.' No, Matt had never said such things to her, although one of the boys at school had once told her that Matt told him she was smashing. But when she remembered their innocent love-making, surely that had said it all. She reminisced to herself, and pondered on the New Year party when she and Matt were together on her brother's bed. Now how she wished they had gone further with their session. If only we had, I think I would feel on a level with Gareth then, she thought to herself. I would have a little past too, as I'm sure he has a very extensive one.

She looked out of the window at a signpost for Oxford. Well, she had heard of that! Then it was back to wrestling with her thoughts. She had found Gareth pushing her to go further with their 'spooning,' and at times she found it hard not to give in. Would she cope this week? And what had he been doing these weeks when they had been apart? He must have girlfriends in Wales. Well, he had been to Scotland for most of the time. Maybe he had played around up there. No, he had been with his parents. And as thoughts went round and round in her head, she did finally begin to doze.

She was brought round with a jolt. The coach had stopped. “Cheltenham,” the driver called out. Everyone began to stir, and gather up their belongings to make their way out into the bus station. It was still dark. The old gentleman said goodbye, and wished Penny an enjoyable holiday, and he also enquired on her behalf, which was her second coach. There was a thirty- minute wait, and as there was a small stall selling snacks, Penny bought a hot tea. Her mother had made her a sandwich and put in some biscuits and sweets. She had already eaten the sweets on the coach, offering the old gentleman some. Wonder what his name was; he never said. It was quite cold at the bus station in the middle of the night. She sat in the small waiting room with her jacket pulled tight around her.

Suddenly, she saw the driver of her coach getting in and calling them on. He called out a list of town names, and Penny heard Neath, so joined the short line of people. Not so many on this leg of the journey, and she had a seat to herself, half-way down the coach. And once more, they were off. She did not doze this time. The first part of the trip was still in darkness, but dawn began to break, and it revealed some very beautiful countryside. Eventually, they passed a sign saying ‘Welcome to Wales.’ Her heart jumped and her stomach turned. They must be getting near! They began to stop at one or two towns and some people got off. She knew she was due in soon after seven in the morning, and it was well past six now. They must be near, she thought. And the driver called out, “Neath, next stop.” Penny almost panicked. She felt odd. Was it excitement at seeing Gareth again? She didn’t know. The coach pulled in, and looking out of the window she saw one or two cars parked at the opposite kerb. And then Gareth was getting out and waving to her and walking towards the coach. She stood up, and was making her way off the coach, and suddenly thought, 'I must look an awful sight!' As she got off, the driver was asking which was her case in the hold, so she only said, "Hi," to Gareth before pointing it out. Then he was taking the case to the car, opening the side door for her, jumping in the driver's seat, and they were away.

There seemed an awful silence at first. "How did it go then," he asked her. She looked blank. "The journey," he continued.

"Must have been tiring."

"Oh, it was okay. I had a nice old man next to me for most of it. Then everyone went to sleep. I didn't though." Again they were quiet.

"What was it like in Scotland?" she asked.

"I was just the driver," he answered. "I had my parents and my Aunt, so it was pretty boring. We've been touring that way several times. They always want to go to Scotland. I don't really like it, and we usually have awful weather, although it was quite good this time. The only bit of peace I had was to get out for a drink on my own after dinner at night. And the pubs shut early in Scotland." Wonder if he chatted anyone up, Penny thought.

Gareth was pointing out a few things on the way, some mountain, a coal mine, an Aunt lived down there, and so on. Suddenly, he turned into a secluded lay-by and stopped the car. He turned to her, "Come on then, let's have a cuddle. I've missed you, Penny." He turned to her and put his arm around her, pulling her towards him and started to kiss her. But Penny pulled back. Why did she do that? I can't, she thought. I don't feel the same way. "What's wrong?" he asked.

"I don't know," was all she could answer. He tried again,

and she tried to respond, but she was very impassive. He drew back, and looked so disappointed. She felt sorry for him. What is the matter with me? Her thoughts ran on. I've got to get through a week of this!

"I expect you're tired, Penny. We'll soon be home and you can go straight to bed for a while. It's a strain travelling all night. We'll have some fun later."

There was a period of silence again, then he asked, "Have you had the exam results yet?" She was a bit embarrassed to have to tell him that she had failed the English, the most important one.

"Never mind, it's not the end of the world," he answered.

"Yes, but I need it to get into PE College. I'll have to re-sit it, plus the higher exams."

"You are going back to school then?" he continued.

"Of course. I have to do two more years and go to College when I'm eighteen. You know that," she almost snapped back.

"You don't have to go back, Penny."

"But I want to. I love school. I've always enjoyed school. But now I shall have to work hard."

"I won't be there," he stated, and then she contemplated that.

A little later, he said, "I haven't told my parents you are still at school, or that I met you there. If they ask, say you are working somewhere, in an office or something."

Penny felt worried. Well, she had been to Rosamund's work place sometimes, she would say she worked there. "Do they know how old I am?" she asked him.

"They haven't asked," was his reply.

"Well here's the village, all one road of it. Five pubs and five chapels, and that's it." Then, they turned up a very steep lane with some small houses to one side. "My house is at the top," he continued, and they slowed to a stop. "This is it, Penny." As she got out of the car, she thought, "Yes, this probably is it, in more ways than one!"

There was a short, elderly man with an old trilby hat on his head doing something in the garage. He turned when he heard the car pull up. He reminded her of the dear old man on the coach. "Here's my Dad. This is Penny, Dad." Gareth introduced them, and he was leading her through the open door, of the low, stone-built house. The door opened straight into a room. There was no hall-way, which Penny thought strange. It appeared to be a small sitting room, but there was also a dining table and chairs pushed against the small windowsill. A woman who she took to be Gareth's mother was polishing the table.

She turned as they entered. "Oh, you soon got here. I didn't expect you for a while."

"The coach was early," Gareth interrupted. "Here she is. This is Penny, Mam." They acknowledged one another and Penny thought the woman looked rather surprised when she turned and saw her for the first time. She was indeed surprised, to see such a young girl. Pretty, yes, but so young. There had been much discussion between the family of Aunts and Uncles, etc, about Gareth bringing an English girl, and from London, too. They had been expecting someone very sophisticated and street-wise as all the London women-folk were! But this young girl could have been plucked from the village itself. No wonder her mother had sent such a letter of concern. She would have to have a word with Gareth to behave himself with her. But she certainly was pretty.

"Well, I'll put the kettle on for a cup of tea first, then we can have some breakfast. Gareth can bring in your things, and perhaps you would like a wash after all that travelling. You must be tired," his mother rambled on.

"I've told her to have a sleep to get over it," Gareth interrupted. Then he took her up to see the bedroom.

"Where's the bathroom?" Penny asked him, and he told her it was downstairs. It led off the large stone-floored kitchen, and she spruced up and then joined them for tea and something to eat. Penny was trying to pluck up courage to ask where the toilet was. There wasn't one in the bathroom, and she hadn't seen one upstairs. As his mother took out the dirty dishes, she turned to Gareth and whispered, "Where's the toilet, I'm bursting!" He apologised and took her outside, right around the house to the back, and it was there. She was rather embarrassed, and thought it a long way to go to the toilet. 'Well I won't be getting up in the night,' she thought.

When she came back in, Mrs. Jenkins told her to go up for a sleep now, and she escorted her up to the bedroom, showing her where she could put her things. Gareth called up that he would call her by midday so that they could go out somewhere.

As his mother left the room, she turned and said, "There's a pot under the bed for the night time!" Well I won't be using that either, Penny thought. She looked around the room. It was quite small and square, with a low ceiling. There was a double bed and a dressing table and wardrobe in very dark, old-fashioned wood, and a washstand, on which were a jug and a bowl. The room was above the one they had been in downstairs, so the small window looked out over the front and the garage. She could see Mr. Jenkins going in and out of it, doing some job. Somehow, she didn't feel that this was Gareth's room. No, it must be his parents' room. So they had moved out for her, into the room next to it. She had glimpsed in there, and that, too, had a double bed. Wonder why they hadn't put her in there. Maybe this was the best room. She climbed into bed, after laying the pyjamas out on the top of it. There was a huge feather quilt on the bed, and layers of blankets. She pushed half of them back, and turned on her tummy. She could hear them talking downstairs. They all spoke very loud but she couldn't make out a word. They were obviously speaking in Welsh to one another- and it was probably all about her! And in no time at all, she was fast asleep.

CHAPTER ELEVEN

Penny woke with a start. Where was she? She was still flat on her tummy with her head turned to the wall, looking at the jug and bowl on the wash stand. Then she remembered. She wondered what the time was, rolled onto her back and was turning towards the door, when she jumped. There was a small, blonde-haired boy standing beside the bed. He looked about five or six.

"Hello Penny. Are you getting up?" He seemed to be saying the words as if he had learnt what to say from someone. Penny sat up, remembered she was naked, and pulled the sheet in front of her.

"Hello. Who are you?" she asked the shy boy.

Very quietly, he answered, "Martin," and then dashed from the room, leaving the door wide open. She heard him downstairs jabbering excitedly and then Gareth was talking too. But then Penny realised they were speaking Welsh. Of course, that was why he had spoken to her strangely. Gareth must have coached him what to say to her. She remembered he had once told her that as a child, he and his brother only spoke and understood Welsh for many years, and that if their parents didn't want them to know what they were talking about, they would speak in English to one another. So that little boy wouldn't know much English.

She jumped up and changed into fresh clothes, did her hair, tidied the bed, and went downstairs. Gareth and the little boy were in the downstairs room. "You're up then. Had a good sleep? You've met Martin. He's my cousin's boy from next door. He's been in and out all morning, asking when you were going to get up." Penny told him how the little boy had made her jump, but she was glad to be up, and felt much better after the sleep. The little boy was looking at her all the time, and then said something to Gareth in Welsh, and they both laughed.

"What did he say?" Penny asked.

"He said you're very pretty and am I going to marry you?" Penny had no answer to that.

The boy was tugging Gareth's hand, and then came to get Penny's. He was still jabbering in Welsh. "He wants you to go next door with him. Come on. You've got to meet my cousins. They are all waiting for me to take you in. My mother's already in there." They walked out the front and what Penny thought was next door turned out to be two doors away, another neighbour lived between them. The three houses were all joined together, Gareth's one end, his cousins' the other end and a very tiny terraced house between, where the neighbour lived.

They all seemed to be expecting them, as Martin had dashed ahead. They entered through a tiny side door, through which they had to stoop. "It's really the coal store but it's the quickest way in," Gareth informed her. The cousins were two sisters, older than Gareth, one of whom was married - Martin's mother. Her husband was there, and the sisters' mother, who was virtually blind, being Mrs. Jenkins' oldest sister. It turned out there were three other sister aunts that Penny would have to meet.

Everyone was very nice and welcoming and saying how

they had looked forward to meeting her. The older sister said they hadn't believed Gareth when he said he was bringing home a young lady from London. The blind aunt didn't seem to speak English very well, and they seemed to translate to her all that was being said. Penny was sure they were commenting on how young she looked.

Then the younger sister asked, "Do you work, Penny?" Penny looked at Gareth, hoping for help in answering.

"She's in an office," he quickly volunteered.

"Do you have to travel far?" the cousin continued.

"Well the office is in London - in Holborn - my sister works there too. It's a firm of solicitors."

"And what do you have to do?" Penny was beginning to panic. And she didn't want them to think she was just a filing clerk.

"Not a lot. I can type a bit, but I'm really working to go to College. I'm going to teach PE." They all seemed to agree that sounded good, but Penny noticed the younger sister half-smiling, and she commented, "I teach too, Penny. History." Penny was sure she knew that she wasn't old enough to go to College.

The interrogation was broken by the little boy bringing some toys for Penny to see, and she was relieved to have his attention. Then they all had tea and sandwiches and cake, and Gareth said he wanted to take Penny out around the village. His mother was telling him to make sure that they called to see Aunty this, Aunty that, it seemed a long list. Gareth groaned and said there was plenty of time. As he and Penny made their way back to his house, the door of the little middle house was open. Gareth called out something in Welsh and out came the neighbour. "Mrs. Price, this is Penny." And in they had to go, and start all over again. Her husband was also there, but he seemed a very sick man. Miner's Disease, Gareth told her later. Penny immediately liked Mrs. Price. She didn't talk so loud, as everyone else, and had a very gentle manner, and such a pleasant face. She reminded Penny of her own mother, and she even had auburn hair like her. She was very welcoming to Penny, and told her that Gareth was her favourite. They had no children of their own, and she went on to say that he had been a very naughty, young boy, but that everyone liked him. She said she was pleased to see him with such a pretty young girl, and hoped she enjoyed her stay there.

"Come on. Let's go for a walk around the village," Gareth told her. She ran upstairs for a cardigan, and as she came down again, he was waiting at the foot of the stairs. She knew what was coming, and just as he was putting his arms around her, they heard his mother returning from next door, and she was calling out something in Welsh. He turned quickly, and with Penny behind him, they returned to the main room. His mother looked searchingly at them, and again, spoke in Welsh. Had she thought they were in the bedroom, Penny thought. She wouldn't know they had been in next door with Mrs. Price. Penny felt guilty, for nothing!

Gareth told her they were going for a walk, and when did she want them back for tea. And they left. They walked behind the house and went up a path that he said led to a farm. As they climbed higher, they turned for a view of the village and the valley. He pointed out the places. The coal mine - his uncles used to own it, now it was Nationalised, the single track railway connecting the villages and used for the coal trucks, the small station, the coal tips, the pubs, the chapels, the mountains and the river meandering its way from the Black Mountain, through the villages on its way to the sea at Swansea. He pointed out various little houses, and it seemed an aunt, uncle or cousin lived in every one. Penny wondered how many aunts, uncles and cousins there were. 'Must be the whole village,' she thought.

Eventually they reached the farm. The dogs barked their arrival, and out came a man from the barn. He was Gerwyn, and obviously knew that Gareth was bringing a girl home, as he greeted them with, "So this is the young lady, then." He was about eight years older then Gareth and they seemed to be friends.

Then his wife joined them, and they were invited into the old farmhouse. Penny loved the house. There was a wood fire with oven, and she could smell bread baking. There were heavy, black beams in the ceiling, and lots of brass things hanging on the walls. She liked the couple and they were very friendly, and the two men were talking Welsh and laughing in such a way that Penny thought they must be making some ribald remarks. She felt it was about her, and then Gareth said, "I've got to sleep next door, haven't I, Penny?" So it was about her! The couple wanted them to stay for tea but they said they were expected back for a meal, and so left after Gerwyn had shown Penny some of the animals.

They cut down a path, which took them to the railway line, and followed it back to the far end of the main village street. As they walked through, Gareth pointed out the shops. "But they're just houses," Penny said. "I know. The men go to work in the mine, and the women set up a shop in a room of the house. They just serve, if and when someone comes in, otherwise they are just getting on with the normal housewife chores." It fascinated Penny. There was an ironmongers, a shoe shop, clothes shop, two fish and chip shops open of an evening, several sweet and tobacco shops, wool shop and a hairdresser. There was a cobblers shed, and there were two real shops - a small post office, and a Co-op. Then there was the village hall, where they could play snooker, hold meetings and present local drama groups and concerts. And of course, the five pubs and five chapels of various denominations.

As they walked the village, they passed or met several people. Gareth appeared to know them all, and they had to have words with each one. Lots of them seemed to be cousins, but as Penny later found out, many were cousins of cousins, etc. But that's how close they all considered themselves. Finally they made their way up the steep lane back home. They were supposed to call on several aunts, etc. on the way up, but Penny was grateful when Gareth said they would do it tomorrow, as tea would be ready.

After tea, Penny offered to wash up, but she wasn't allowed to. But she noticed that Gareth's mother told his father - even though it was all in Welsh - that he was to help her. It was very obvious to Penny that Mrs. Jenkins was in charge in this household. Gareth seemed to get very heated when he spoke to her, and she appeared to dictate to him. No wonder he said he left home to go to London. Gareth apparently asked to take the car - he asked his mother, not his father, which Penny thought strange, and then he told her they would go for a drive.

It certainly was a lovely drive. They went to the top of the Black Mountain, and saw the wonderful view of the other side. "We'll go over that way on another day. My brother's wife comes from over there, so we'll all go for a day trip in the car." They returned towards the village, but then took another mountain road where he said there was a wonderful sight when it was dark. And it was now almost dark. They finally stopped very high on the road, and were on the opposite side of the valley to his home. He said if they got out of the car, and walked a short way across a rough grass field, they would see for miles down the valley, all the way to Swansea, with the night time lights shining.

They walked across the field, and were now on the top of a very steep drop. Penny did not know that Gareth could not stand heights, and he stayed a little way back from her, not wanting to look down. Penny was looking at the view of the twinkling lights exclaiming how lovely it was, and turned to Gareth, who she thought was just behind her. Looking from the lights back to the pitch dark, for a moment she couldn't see. And in a few fleeting seconds, she panicked. Suddenly, a string of terrible thoughts flew through her mind. Why had he brought her to Wales? What did he want with a sixteen-year-old girl?

She recalled one of her girlfriends telling her she was silly to go away with Mr. Jenkins. "You know nothing about him," she had said. "He might attack you, or be a murderer!" Penny panicked. Why had be brought her up here, and she was standing on the edge, and she couldn't see him. But she followed his voice, and her eyes adjusted to the darkness, and she made out his silhouette. "Come back, Penny," but she couldn't move, and then he was coming towards her, and she thought, 'Is he going to push me over?' She felt she was going to faint, when she felt him, not pushing her over but drawing her to him, and holding her tightly. "Penny, you frightened me, going near the edge like that. I can't stand heights. You're shaking all over. What's the matter?" And then she was crying and saying, "I was frightened, I thought you…" but she broke off. "You thought what, Penny?" "Oh, nothing," she answered. "I just came over faint. Probably the height." He drew her further back across the field, stopping by the gate, and held her tight, and began to kiss and caress her fiercely. This was their first close association since she had arrived, and Penny now felt tremendous relief, and all the old, lovely, exciting feelings welled up.

He was leaning and pushing against her on the wall beside the gate, and wrestling with her clothes, and telling her how he had missed her, and how he loved her, and how he just had to have her. Penny was in turmoil. She was now overflowing with feelings of love again, and she felt she was on the point of giving in, but it all felt wrong, up against a stone wall with her feet slowly dampening in the night grass!

She pulled away, saying the wall was hurting her back. "Let's get back to the car," she said. So they did, and drove a little further on, and turned into a very secluded opening. The 'spooning' started again. There wasn't much room in the car, but their love-making became more and more intense. Gareth was telling her to take off her top, and then more. Strange, Penny never had inhibitions about removing clothes, and she loved the feeling of skin on skin, but now she knew she was holding out for the loss of her innocence. "Come on, Penny," he was saying, but still she would not. So after plenty of petting, she put her clothes back on, and after more kissing and cuddling, they set off back to the house.

It was quite late when they entered the house. Gareth's parents were up and waiting for them. There was an inquisition as to where they had been, which he answered. They all had supper and Mrs. Jenkins said he better get in next door to sleep before it got very late, and then they could lock their door after him. His parents went into the kitchen to wash up, leaving them to say goodnight. He kissed her and whispered in her ear, "You're a killer, Penny. I'll never sleep tonight," and left for next door. Penny said goodnight to his parents and went up to the big double bed. She thought over the day. Well, they had certainly carried on from where they had left off in London! She was glad she was feeling full of love again. But would she manage to hold out for the rest of the week?

Sunday turned out to be a day of visiting relatives. They wandered down the lane after breakfast to first visit the aunt, uncle and cousin in the 'Big House.' They were the ones who used to own the mine. Then there were more relatives in the next row of houses, and even more at the bottom of the hill, plus close friends of the family. They all seemed very pleased Gareth had a young lady from London stopping, and all were very pleasant to Penny, although she felt they remarked - in Welsh - on how young she looked. Several asked if she worked, and she knew the story about working in the solicitor's office by heart. But she liked to add that she was waiting to go to College. One or two added that it was good to see Gareth settling down. There were many implications that he had been a 'wild lad,' and Penny wondered if they thought that she was the bride-to-be!

By the time they returned to the house for dinner, she was completely bewildered as to whom they had seen. All their names sounded similar, they all had the same accent, and almost everyone said the same thing to her. Gareth's mother asked, "Well, who did you see then?" Penny really had no idea, but Gareth came to the rescue. There was a half-hour before lunch was ready, and he said they would sit in the parlour. Penny had only glimpsed inside this room. She had never heard a room called a 'parlour' before. It was a small room off the passageway, and had a large, leather three-piece suite, plus a huge bookcase that almost touched the low ceiling. Penny thought it must be very old, and it was full of old books, and, Gareth said, his College books, and his father's schoolbooks. Mr. Jenkins taught in the local Primary School. The small room was absolutely full up with such large furniture. Penny guessed that the 'parlour' was the 'best' room for special visitors.

They sat on the settee, and Gareth drew her to him. Penny was so worried his parents would come in, so was a little withdrawn, but they had some nice moments, and his mother even knocked on the door to say that dinner was ready. After dinner, he was taking her to see his brother and wife, who were recently married, and now lived in another village, about two miles away.

Penny insisted on helping with the washing up, and then they set off in the car. "See you're back in time for me to go to Chapel," his mother called. "And I shall want the car."

"That's good. We'll have the house to ourselves while they're at the Chapel. Then we'll go out afterwards," Gareth whispered to Penny.

"That's nice," she said, but then thought, 'Oh dear!'

She enjoyed visiting his brother and wife, and was intrigued by their cottage. It was so tiny and basic, and they were overrun with ants on the stone slab floors. Penny thought she could never live in a house like that. But it was a pretty village. Gareth's father came from there, and so there was the inevitable round of visiting even more relatives in several houses. Before leaving, they arranged to have a day trip in the car, later that week, with the brother and wife, and go over the mountain to where she had lived when single.

They hurried back, and as they had eaten with his brother and wife, there was no need for tea. Mrs. Jenkins was getting ready for Chapel, and was putting on all her finery. Penny noticed that Mr. Jenkins was not. It was almost time for them to go, and Gareth told his father he better hurry up. "He's not coming today," his mother said. "He'll drive me there and be back. Then he or you can collect me after Chapel ends."

"Dad always goes," Gareth stated.

"Well he's not coming today," was the reply. Gareth looked across at Penny, and, she, too, thought, as he did, that it had been a crafty move so as not to leave them in the house on their own. Penny didn't know if she was sorry or pleased. As they left, his mother called out, "Dad will only be five minutes taking me!"

The young couple went around the back garden, and sat on a low wall, in the early evening sun. "We'll go for a nice drive later, Penny." Out came the little boy from next door, and Gareth kicked a ball around with him, and then Penny joined in. The little boy chatted away in Welsh, and Penny had no idea what he was saying. His father came out to chat - the two sisters were at the Chapel - and so Penny and Gareth went in to see the blind aunt. Penny liked her, but they had to translate all she said. As they left, to sit outside again, Gareth said, "You'll have to learn Welsh. Penny - Cariad."

"What do you mean, Cariad?" she said.

"It means Darling, or Dearest, or Lover. You say it to the one you love," he answered. He made her repeat it properly.

"Teach me some more," she asked. "Well 'ydw' means yes," he continued. "Say it, Penny, o-do". Penny repeated it several times, then said, "Well, what's no, then?"

"Oh, I'm not teaching you that, because I only want you

to say ‘odo’,” he laughed. Penny thought awhile, and then got the joke, and had a lovely feeling through her body, and this time, leaned against him at the wall, and put her face up to kiss him. “Odo, Cariad,” she said.

They had heard his father return very promptly from delivering his mother to the Chapel, and now they heard him setting off to bring her back. “We’ll drive down to Swansea when they get back, and go along to one of the bays and look at the sea and the lights at night,” Gareth planned. And this they did. Penny was feeling very warm and tactile, and she nestled in close to him as he drove. She liked watching him drive. “If you don’t watch out Penny, I’ll have to pull in somewhere before we get to the sea,” but when he started to drive with one hand on the wheel and the other on her knee, she thought she’d better stop teasing him.

It was lovely sitting on a bench above the sand and sea. It was gradually growing dark. They had previously walked a short way along the coastal path, but kept stopping to cuddle, so had retired to the seat. It was now quite dark. “Let’s get back in the car. It’s cold,” he told her. The car park was almost empty, and it, too, was in darkness. Penny had soon divested herself of some clothes - but not all! She really was teasing him, and kept calling him ‘Cariad,’ which made them laugh. He said something to her in Welsh, which she had no idea of its meaning, and he was saying, “Just say ‘ydw’ Penny,” teasing her back

But she never said ‘ydw’ or ‘yes,’ and after a very lovely and frantic session, she re-dressed and they set off home. “You’ll be the death of me, Penny,” he remarked as they drove back, and his hand was on her leg for much of the journey.

His parents were up when they returned. Once again, they

had supper, and then he was packed off next door. “It was lovely at the seaside,” Penny said.

“We’ll go down in the day and get the sun next time,” he answered her.

“I thought it was lovely in the dark,” she said, as she closed the door after him, and then re-opened it, calling him back and adding, “Cariad. I’ll practice the other word in bed tonight,” she teased him.

CHAPTER TWELVE

The next day, they were all to visit his mother's three sisters in turn - the remaining aunts and uncles. They were to have an evening meal with the one furthest away, and so called at the other two houses on the way. Penny could see that they were Mrs. Jenkins' sisters, and it was the usual round of questions, but they were all very friendly and welcomed her. Two lived within two miles of Gareth's home, but the third lived further, almost at Neath.

It was a very nice house, and was furnished with beautiful furniture and fittings, and lots of lovely ornaments of china and cut glass. They had no children, so there were no cousins there. The table was set out immaculately, and the aunt had prepared a very lavish meal for them all. They waited for his uncle to get home from work. He was a lovely man and Penny took to him right away, and he seemed to take to her. He joked a lot with Gareth, and at one point she and Gareth had been left alone in the lounge - or was it the parlour - and he called out for fun, "Stop that kissing in there." Penny was a bit embarrassed - they were only looking at photographs - but she realised he was joking with them.

They were there a few hours in all, although while the others were clearing up after the meal, Gareth took her for a short walk to see a local waterfall. Then, they had to chat some more on their return, which made it quite late when they left. Gareth was driving, and his father sat in the front and she and his mother in the back. As they drove back home, now in the dark, Penny felt an overbearing urge to be in close contact with Gareth, and could hardly stop herself from reaching forward. In fact, at one point, she did rest her hand on the back of the driving seat, leaning forward, and rubbing the back of his neck with her fingers. She had looked across at his mother, and she had her eyes closed.

Reaching the house, his mother said they wouldn't need supper, having eaten so late, and she was tired and she and Dad would go straight up to bed. "Make a cup of tea, if you want," she told them. "And don't you be late going next door, Gareth. And make sure you lock the door behind him, Penny." She nodded, and could not believe they had been left alone downstairs. Maybe his mother realised that they had had a long day under scrutiny, and had hardly been alone.

They didn't make any tea, but sat on the fireside chair, next to the fire, now made up for the night, she on Gareth's lap. He had already turned off the light, but there was a small glow from the fire, and, added to the warmth, Penny felt real cosy. They spooned and spooned on the chair, then he said "let's get on the settee". They tried lying together, but it was very small. So Gareth put two of the small cushions down on the mat in front of the fire, and pulled Penny down there.

"Take your things off, Penny," he whispered, but although it was feeling lovely on the mat in front of the fire, she felt that any minute one or other of his parents might come back down. "I can't," she said. "Your mother may come down." He tried to persuade her otherwise, but she only loosened everything instead. She really was feeling lovely inside, and certainly felt she would have liked to take off her clothes. Then he was pulling her pants down, calling her Cariad, and saying, "Come on, you've got to this time, Penny." And she was saying no, but not really stopping him. Her pants were off and he was kissing her furiously, and then fiddling with his trousers, and he was coming down on top of her, and she was thinking, "Yes, this is it then," and just as she felt something pressing against her, there was a Bang, Bang on the ceiling, and his mother's voice calling out something!

Penny gasped, pushed him away and off her, rolled over, grabbed her pants, and leapt up, furiously trying to put them back on. Gareth was exclaiming something to himself in Welsh - she imagined he was swearing - and then calling something back to his mother.

In the glow of the fire, Penny glimpsed him on his knees, with his trousers half down, and she began to giggle. "For goodness sake, Penny, don't laugh. Come back here. We can't stop now. It won't take a minute."

But she refused, saying, "Saved by the bell!" He tried to coax her back, but she wouldn't. It was as if his mother had been watching them. Of course, she hadn't but had obviously given them long enough, before they could get up to mischief. To Penny, it was the Hand of Fate. She had been wrong to give in, and certainly would not be saying 'ydw!' She told Gareth he better get in next door, said 'sorry,' as she closed the door after him, and felt very guilty going into the bedroom, when Mrs. Jenkins called out to ask if she had locked the door and put out the light.

Penny felt rather uncomfortable when she came down the next morning. She was sure Mrs. Jenkins must have known what they were up to. She wished Gareth would come in from next door and relieve the tension. But he didn't. The plans were that they were all going to Swansea today, to go around the big shops and the covered market, and then, if time allowed, go on to one of the bays. Mr. Jenkins was eating his boiled egg. He had one for breakfast every day, and said he had done so the whole of his life, except for when he had served in the First World War. He was a very gentle man, and very hen-pecked. Penny liked him. He was dispatched next door to call Gareth from bed.

Penny had something to eat, and was just clearing the table, when the little boy, Martin came in. He said very sweetly in English, "Penny, come here, look." He ran out the door, and she followed him. He led her around the back of the lane where a series of stone steps led down to one end of the village. Then he pointed to the ground. Penny looked and jumped. There was the most enormous slug she had ever seen, in fact she thought it couldn't possible be a slug, more like a small snake. Then he pointed to another, and another. He poked one with a stick, and it shrank up. Just then, Gareth appeared, coming to look for them.

"What are you looking at?" he said, rather surly, Penny thought.

"Well I don't know if it's a slug or a snake," she answered.

He looked. "They're slugs. They've come out, because it was wet in the night- and I know that because I was awake for most of it," and he gave Penny a searching look. "Well I've never seen slugs that big," she continued. They went back to the house, and Gareth said he didn't want anything to eat, so they all got ready to go to Swansea.

Penny bought postcards, and wrote them right away to post home and to her friends. Thinking of her friends made her wonder what they were all doing. If it was fine, all the gang would probably be at the swimming baths. I bet they are all gossiping about me being on holiday with Gareth, she thought. And she pondered over last night's happening. Would she have behaved like that with Matt? Probably yes, if he had only tried. But that was 'old hat' now.

Penny and Gareth split up from his parents, and he took her into the covered market. They went to the cockle stall, but the lady said it was the wrong month for them to be in season. Gareth was disappointed, and he told Penny how you bought them alive in their shells, and then took them home to boil up while still alive. Penny thought it sounded disgusting - she had only ever seen them ready prepared in pots. Then he showed her the black laver bread.

"Whatever is it? It looks like cow poo," she exclaimed. He explained it was made from seaweed, and that you fried it up with bacon. But he didn't like it. "Well I don't want to try it, thank you," she said.

Then they met up with his parents, and they drove on to one of the bays, where they sat on the beach and had a picnic. Gareth said he and Penny would walk a little of the coastal footpath for half an hour. It climbed gently along the side of the golf-course, with some rough bracken, grass and shrubbery between the path and greens.

"Let's sit down here a while," Gareth said. They stepped through the bracken, and found a small grass patch, where he spread out his jacket, sat down, and patted it beside him for Penny to sit. It certainly was a lovely spot. The view was fantastic. Penny loved the coast. Gareth turned to her, and gently pushed her down on her back. He was kissing and fondling her, and then said, "Take your clothes off, Penny."

"No way," she answered. "Not here. Someone will see us." He tried to assure her there was no one around, and he stood up to check. He could see his parents sitting on the beach way back and far below. There was no one on the path at the moment. He went to her on the ground. He was groping with her clothes and pushing against her.

"Come on, Cariad. You were going to last night." But she just couldn't, and certainly not there in broad daylight. So they got up, and made their way to the path. "I don't understand you, Penny. You don't mind taking your clothes off and teasing, and yet you won't go further. You should have been an island girl, in the South Seas, running around with hardly any clothes on."

His statement struck home. 'Yes, she should have been just that, on the white sands of the Blue Lagoon with…' They reached the beach, and they all packed up the chairs they had brought with them for the parents, and made their way back to the car and home.

Gareth seemed very moody that evening, and finally said, "Let's go down the Cwm for a walk." They said the 'Cwm' when they meant the village. So they walked down the steps and stood on the bridge by the river for a while. Suddenly, he said, "I'm coming back to London again. I'm not stopping here. I'll go back to my aunt and uncle there, and look for a job again. Why don't you look for a job, Penny? You don't have to go back to school."

"I have to go back to school. I've got two more years before I can go to College," she answered. "I don't like to think of you back at school," he said. Penny wondered why. Was it because he thought there would be scandal about her having gone away with him? Or was he afraid she would take up with her old flame? But she really did want to go to College. Or was she just trying to prove to that old Doctor that she could do it.

"Well I'm coming back on Sunday, when you go home," he stated. "I'll go by train." He still seemed very moody. "Come on Penny, I want a drink. Let's go in the pub." They made their way towards the old character building the other side of the bridge. "Now the only thing is that women don't go in pubs here - well only a certain type. You'll have to sit in the kitchen at the back." So in they went, around the back. Gareth knew the elderly publican and his wife very well, and introduced Penny. The wife entertained her in the kitchen, Gareth bringing her in a port and lemon. They left the door into the bar open, to try to include her. There were several men in the bar, and Penny could hear that everyone only spoke in Welsh. There was lots of laughter, and then Gareth came for Penny and took her in the bar for them all to see her. Then she went back in the kitchen with the wife, and they chatted about where she had been so far on the holiday.

Eventually, they left the pub, and went on to the next one, where they repeated the scenario. Penny sat in the kitchen with the lady of the house, although she had to keep serving in the bar, and Gareth joined the men there. Finally they left. It was dark, but the two fish and chip houses were open and they went to have some chips. Several people were having fish and chips, and everyone knew everyone, so there was much chat and laughter. Gareth was introducing Penny to everyone, young and old. There were several groups of men chatting on the road, and eventually they joined a group of fellows, mainly around Gareth's age, Penny thought, who were gathered by the second bridge at the foot of their lane. They all wanted to be introduced to Penny, and were very complementary to her. "Hey, Gareth, are there any more in London like Penny to bring back for us?" They all stood chatting for ages, and then finally broke up, and Penny and Gareth started the steep climb up the lane.

Penny had hold of Gareth's arm - as he always liked her to do, when he broke away and said he was having a 'wee' by a tree. Penny was waiting, when, without warning, all the streetlights suddenly went out. It was completely black everywhere. She panicked. She had never known complete blackness since the Blackout of the war, and she was very rarely out then, being young. There were always lights on in the streets back home. She was calling Gareth and saying she couldn't see him. She imagined things rearing up in front of her, and was terrified. He was saying he was nearly finished, and that it was okay. Eventually, he re-joined her, which made her jump, and she clung tightly to him.

"What happened?" she asked him.

"Oh, all the street lights go off at midnight." She hung on to his arm, and they continued up to the house, Gareth seeming to know exactly where to walk. His parents had already gone to bed, and Penny said she was going up too. She didn't want a repeat of last night's performance!

The following day, they went with the brother and his wife - Jim and Lena - for the day, in the car. They collected them from the small cottage about eleven in the morning, and drove up the valley to the Black Mountain, and down over the other side, through lots of farming country, towards Lena's small country home town. It was a picturesque drive, and Penny enjoyed the company. Lena was about twenty-two, and Jim was nearly two years older than Gareth. "Well, we've done this trip enough over the years haven't we?" one brother said to the other, and they laughed, and continued in Welsh and then laughed a lot more. Penny got a strange feeling, and wondered what the significance was of that statement.

"We call it going over the country," Gareth told her.

"Well why did you want to go there?" she asked.

"For the girls of course!" Jim answered.

"Yes. The girls in the country were always willing," Gareth added.

"Well I wasn't," Lena stated.

"No, but we didn't marry *them*," Jim continued.

Later, she asked Lena how she and Jim had met. "Well, it's like they said. Weekends, crowds of the lads from their side of the mountain would come to our town, go in the pubs, and then go out courting the girls."

Penny turned to Gareth. "Well how did you get there, Gareth? It seems a long way."

"We had a motor-bike. Jim's still got it. Or sometimes we took the car."

"We never cared how or when, or if we got back though," Jim added. Suddenly, Penny didn't want to go over the country. This was the 'past,' with which she felt she could not compete.

They got to the little town. It was a rural market town, plenty of pubs, and quite attractive. Gareth seemed a different person here. All the time, he was saying remember this and that, and then there were names, and then he would lapse into Welsh. They parked the car, and strolled through the town. Lena pointed out the store where she had worked before marriage. She went in to see the lady owner, and then the four of them went to buy fish and chips. The men were laughing, and chatting to the young woman behind the counter while the girls waited outside. Then they went to sit on a low wall to eat them.

Jim said, "Let's get a pint before they close." They were pondering which of the many pubs to choose and Jim and Lena seemed to be wanting to go to one in particular. Gareth was asking them something, and seemed to be holding back. The only word Penny could make out from the whole conversation was the name Rita.

The four of them went into the bar. It seemed more like a small hotel, thought Penny, not like the old pub they had visited in the Cwm the previous night. They were the only customers, and the young lady behind the bar jumped with recognition when she saw them. Lena was immediately conversing with her and they were obviously friends. Then she welcomed Jim and Gareth. Penny had no idea what they said to one another, but she noticed a certain look between the woman and Gareth. They seemed to have almost forgotten that Penny was there, and she held back. Suddenly, Gareth turned to her, and said she was Penny from London.

Penny sat with her drink at a table, but the others were all at the bar, laughing and talking with the girl. Penny just knew that this woman was an old girlfriend of Gareth's. She could feel it. Then Lena joined her at the table, and said that Rita was her best friend, and had been her bridesmaid at their wedding last year. Penny recalled having looked at a wedding photo on the wall in their cottage. Yes, this girl was the bridesmaid, and Gareth was the best man. Penny was not happy here, and was relieved when they finished the one drink and left. Gareth had paid for the round, and she noticed that the girl had a drink, too.

After, they drove a short way out of the town, to visit

Lena's parents' home. Her father was not there. He was at the pub, her mother said. So, after a short while, the men said they would go for another drink with the father, if they found him, and would be back in half-an-hour for Lena and Penny. Lena's mother made them a cup of tea, but Penny was worrying. She wasn't happy over here in the country. This represented the past that she knew would haunt her. It was obvious that the girl in the pub was an old flame of Gareth's. She was a grown woman. Who knows, maybe the woman in the fish and chip shop was another, and what about all the people they had stopped to chat to in the town? She hadn't got a past! Well, there was only Matt, and he was a very special past. Gareth would have had at least ten years of a past if he started when she had. How ever many would there have been in ten years, and what would they all have done? He had said the girls in the country were always willing. Why oh why hadn't she and Matt gone further with their relationship, so that she, too, had a past? Their innocent love of holding hands, walks in the park, kisses at the gate, and cuddles in the back row, were much more special than crowds of fellows converging over the mountain to the willing girls of the country.

She was brought back from her thoughts by Lena saying it was time the men were back. Penny panicked. Maybe they had gone back to the old girlfriend in the pub! But then, the car drew up, and the two brothers got out, plus Lena's Dad, whom they had found in another village pub. After giving Lena time with her father, the four of them got in the car ready for the drive back. Jim drove this time, and Lena sat in the front with him, and Gareth and Penny got in the back. "No looking in the mirror," he said to his brother as he cuddled Penny up to him.

But Penny was not happy, and in fact was near to tears.

The day had revealed the age gap between herself and Gareth and all its implications. She could not believe that he would be happy with a sixteen-year-old girl who did not say 'ydw' when there was a whole lot of grown women over the country who were 'willing,' as he had said. Then what about all those women he acknowledged back in his village - they couldn't all be cousins? And what about his time in London? Why did it all torment her so? Gareth was pulling her close, kissing her neck, and wandering his hands, but she could not respond. Why oh why had they all gone over to the country? She wanted to go back, back home, back home to London, back home to… No, she hadn't got anyone to go back to. She was Gareth's girl now, and she tried to enjoy his kissing and caressing, but she was quietly crying. Eventually, with his arm around her and his head leaning on her shoulder, Gareth fell asleep, and she could let the tears out.

When they got back to Jim and Lena's cottage, they went inside and had tea together. The four of them did their round of visiting the relatives in their village, and then she and Gareth drove to his home, where they found two of his mother's sisters and their husbands visiting. The blind aunt from next door was also in, so there was quite a houseful. Then the two cousins came in, and it was such a babble of Welsh, Penny was quite bewildered, but they tried to include her. By the time everyone had eaten supper and left, it was quite late. Penny started to help clear up and started the washing up, but Mrs. Jenkins insisted that Mr. Jenkins do it, and he was enjoying talking to Gareth about the day out. There wasn't much left to do, but he did as he was told and took over from Penny in the scullery.

Gareth said he was tired and would go in next door earlier than usual. "Let's have a word with Mrs. Price next door for a few minutes, first."

So in both called. Poor Mr. Price was already up in bed. "He's had a bad day with his chest," she explained. As they left, Gareth said they would have a look at the back, and they stopped by the wall, looking down on the village lights.

"Do you like Wales, Penny?" Gareth asked her. Penny thought over her answer carefully. "Yes I do. Some places are lovely. But I could never live here."

They were leaning together, and he turned to face her, and began kissing. She felt a little more amenable, but still there was the nagging thought of the past. "I better not start again tonight," he said.

"Because you're not going to say 'ydw' are you?"

"Na," she answered him, giggling. "You said 'Na' - that's no in Welsh.

Who told you that?" he asked.

"Well I've heard so much Welsh today, it was easy enough to work out what 'Na' meant." And they both laughed and then kissed goodnight.

CHAPTER THIRTEEN

It was a glorious sunny day when they got up, and it was decided to go to the coast again. They were all going at first, but then his mother said she and Dad would not. They packed a picnic and put in the canvas chairs and set off. Penny was pleased they were going to the seaside. It was the opposite way to the mountain and 'over the country'!

They went to several little bays on The Gower, and sat in the sun, lay on the beach, and spooned in the sand dunes. It was hot and Penny soon had her clothes off, just leaving on enough to be decent. Once more, Gareth was pleading with her to give in to him. She was enjoying the feel of the sun on her naked skin, and his bare chest on hers as they lay in the dunes, but it was not the deserted Blue Lagoon and she teased him with 'Na'. It was a lovely day, and they were quite sun-tanned when they got back. They had a pleasant evening playing cards with his Dad, who, as Gareth had warned her, was a terrible cheat if you didn't watch him. But it was good fun.

Next day, Gareth told his parents that he was going back to London. There was such a heated discussion going on, that Penny left the house and wandered round the back. The young boy came out, and Penny asked if she could take him for a walk. His mother said she was waiting for the fish van. Presumably, once a week, the van came through the valley selling fresh fish. It seemed that almost everyone was waiting. It tickled Penny to think of the whole village having fish for dinner today. And sure enough, that is what they had. The cousin told the boy in Welsh that Penny would take him for a walk, and his Mum translated for him that he would like to go to the farm.

"Oh lovely. I like it there," Penny responded, and she went to tell Gareth where they were going. He was still talking over things with his parents, and said he would follow after them.

As she and Martin started up to the farm, he raced ahead, then waited for her by the cattle grid. Further on, there was a lot of buzzing, and Penny was sure there was either a bee or wasp nest. She was nervous, but tried to appear calm for the boy's sake. He however, was not bothered and took her hand. For one moment, as she and the boy walked hand in hand, she thought of Matt. But no, this was different. This is what it would be like when she had a little boy of her own. And she would love one, or two, or the four that she once told her teacher she would have. But first she must go to College to prove that doctor wrong, and later she would have a baby to prove him wrong again. Of course, she would marry first.

They were greeted at the farm, and they too had a young boy. Penny wondered why they had not seen him before. They explained he had been out with grandparents. The two boys immediately went to play, climbing on the tractor, throwing hay, and larking with the dogs. Then they all went to collect eggs and as she took them into the house, Gerwyn, the farmer, took the boys for a ride on the tractor. Then he called Penny and gave her a demonstration of his dogs getting in the sheep. He was evidently well known in farming circles for the breeding and training of his sheep dogs. Penny was very impressed. She was leaning on the field gate watching when Gareth crept up behind her. "Well that's all settled," he said. "I shall go back to London on Sunday when you go. I can't stay here, and you there." After chatting with the couple at the farm, they called Martin and then strolled back to the house. Walking back, Gareth kept patting and squeezing her bottom. "You've got a lovely little bottom," he told her.

They spent the rest of the day lazily in the garden, and later in the evening, after the fish dinner, they strolled through the village, called in one of the pubs and stood chatting to the group of men. Walking up the hill home, Gareth once again brought up the question of Penny going back to school. He told her the work for the higher level would be quite hard, followed by three years at College, which she said was at the South Coast, and he wanted to be near her. Then he pulled her under a tree and started spooning with her, pushing her against the bark. He was telling her he loved her and couldn't stand to think of anyone else having her. And he was lifting her skirt, and forcing himself upon her. It was dark, but the few streetlights were still on, although not one was near. Penny felt she was weakening, but she was hurting pushed up against the tree and managed to weedle her way to the side, pulling her skirt down as she did so. "Penny how can you say yes one day and then no another? You know you were going to do it the other night. Come on." But she would not, and they broke apart and carried on up to the house.

There was only one full day left of the holiday. A letter arrived for Penny from her mother. She said they had received the post card, and hoped she had enjoyed herself. She also reminded her to thank Gareth's parents for having her, and to give her the box of chocolates they had put in her case. Her father would be meeting her at the coach station in London. And they had all missed her.

The last day was spent running a few errands for Gareth's mother and calling on various relatives to say goodbye. They drove around some of the local places, and then Gareth gathered his things together, ready for packing the next day. Penny left him and his mother to it and went for a walk with the little boy. That evening, the cousins and neighbours were calling for a last chat with them. Everyone said they hoped to meet Penny again, and she had lots of invitations to visit them next time. She also noticed how everyone said that Gareth had been much better behaved than usual. It made her wonder what he normally got up to!

His father and mother escorted them to Neath, although Gareth drove. Penny was pleased she was on a day coach this time. Gareth's train would leave soon after her, but it would get to London some hours before her. She said goodbye to his parents, and thanked them, as they turned into the coach stop. Gareth took her case and then saw her to the door. "I'll meet you the other end to make sure you've arrived OK even though your Dad's coming," he told her, then gave her a quick kiss, and dashed back to the car. They moved off to go to the station before her coach did

As she sat on the coach, she thought over all that had happened that week. She actually felt very grown up. It dawned on her that she had been in the company of adults all the time, apart from Martin next door. Everyone had treated her as an adult and spoken to her as an equal. She wondered what all her friends would think of her, and she was looking forward to reporting the week's events to Belinda and Joyce. She wouldn't tell them everything, of course, and certainly wouldn't say she had nearly done it. Bet everyone at school will be wondering if I did, she thought. Suppose the staff got to know about her going away with Gareth. They would be wondering what she had got up to, too. Suddenly, thinking of school, she realised she was going to be a pupil again, a child really, and there were going to be all the silly girls and boys around with silly childish talk. She wouldn't be treated as an adult there. Well, maybe Miss Kent would. And suddenly, going back to school didn't seem such a good idea now. If she left and got a job, she would be treated as an adult there. And then she thought about going to College. Well she would be a long way from home, and her friends, and…Gareth, too. And she did suppose he loved her, and he did make her feel so much in love with him. But what about his past… and there she was again with this obsession, that he had a past and she didn't! Well, in a week's time, she would be back at school. And tomorrow she would have to do her paper round. It had been rather nice not having to get up and out so early every morning. Maybe she would give up the paper round. But then she wouldn't have any money, unless, of course, she had left school and was going to work. Maybe she would leave school then. But what of her ambition to teach PE and prove the doctor wrong? Well, she had achieved a lot at school in that field, and the fact that Miss Kent thought she was capable of it was proof in itself. She would talk to her parents about it. And the other part of the Doctor's statement she could prove otherwise, later!

She now cleared her head of her rambling thoughts, and settled back to study the countryside, most of which she had been unable to digest in the dark of the previous week's journey. There was the change of coach at Cheltenham again, but this time she felt quite capable of seeking out the second bus herself.

She found herself seated next to a young woman, probably, Penny thought, in her twenties. They both chatted freely to one another, about holidays, jobs, friends and family, music, films, etc. and Penny felt very much an equal. In fact, the young woman said she thought her much older than sixteen. Penny had grown up!

Her father and Gareth were waiting to greet her when the coach drew into the bus station. Gareth said he had rushed from the station over to his aunt and uncle's house and dumped his things, and then come back to meet her to make sure she had arrived okay. But now he would leave her to her Dad, and was going to his old pub haunts at Marble Arch. I'll call for you in a couple of days, give you time to sort yourself out again. His bus was coming, and he whispered to her as he left, "Ask your Dad about leaving school." And he ran for the bus and was gone.

Penny and her father waited for their bus, and she chatted about the holiday and Wales on the journey home. He reminded her that Graham's wedding was in just over a week's time, and that Lenny had now finalised his papers for emigration to New Zealand. He would be leaving soon. That will be all the boys gone, Penny thought to herself. That only left Annie and Rosamund contributing to the house income. So, she had better go ahead and leave school then, to help out.

Only her mother and sisters were in at home when they finally arrived and, of course, they wanted to hear all about her week. So she was once more relating this and that. "They all talk Welsh, you know. I did learn a little." Lavinia was looking at Penny. She was different. She seemed to have grown up. And she wondered was it only some Welsh that she had learned!

CHAPTER FOURTEEN

There was only one week of the school holidays left. Penny couldn't wait to see Belinda and Joyce, to report on her week away with Gareth. She didn't go into too much detail, but she did tell them that she was thinking of leaving school. As yet, she hadn't approached her parents about the matter, but the more she thought about it, the more she believed that her parents would be pleased. They wouldn't be able to put her through College anyway, and any money she could contribute at home would be very welcome.

Gareth called for her later, and they went to the cinema. He said he would have to look for a job now, and he also asked her if she had asked her parents about leaving school. "There's only a few days of the holidays left. You'll have to decide soon," he told her.

"I will," she answered. "But they're all tied up with my brother's wedding next week, and got a lot to think about." Coming back to her house, they went up another back road, and across to an alley, which ran between the back gardens, and there they ardently spooned. Before it got out of hand, Penny said she better get home. "Why don't you come up to my aunt's place one afternoon? All the family are at work in the day," he asked. She knew what the implication was, said no at first, but then thought it could be rather cosy. "Well how do I get there?" she asked as they strolled back to her house. He told her which two buses to take, and the name of the pub where she should finally get off, and where he would meet her, and then said, "Come tomorrow afternoon. Get there at two." She wasn't sure, but then agreed.

She daren't tell her mother she was going to the aunt's flat in case she asked for more details. So she told her she was going to meet Belinda and Joyce at the big shopping centre. Then she panicked, what if the girls called for her after she had left. So she went to the phone box at the top of the road and telephoned Belinda to tell her that she was going out with Gareth that afternoon. She did some shopping for her mother, took it home, and then got ready to go.

Getting off the bus at the pub stop, which the conductor called out for her, she saw Gareth already waiting for her. She was a little late, as she had to wait a while for the second bus. As he took hold of her, he said, "I thought perhaps you had changed your mind. Come on then, it's a little walk." It took them about ten minutes, and finally reached the large semi-detached, double-fronted house. Penny didn't think it a very nice area.

Gareth opened the front door with his key and led her inside. It was a large, downstairs flat, and a second front door was for the upper flat. There was a long dark passage with two doors on one side and two on the other. He said the large front room was a bedsitter for his older cousin, who was divorced from her husband. Another room was the younger cousin's bedroom, the third door led to the aunt and uncle's bedroom, there was a bathroom-toilet, and then two steps down there was a kitchen-cum-sitting room and a scullery. There was also a large settee, and Gareth said that was where he had to sleep.

Penny felt rather sorry for him, but he said as soon as he got a reasonable job, he would look for some digs. He assured her that everyone was at work, and no one would be in before half-past five.

He sat on the settee, and patted the space beside him, "Come on Cariad." Penny sat beside him, then curled up, leaning on his chest, and they started their spooning. After ten or fifteen minutes, he said, "Come on, let's go in the other room." Penny couldn't think where, as this seemed the only place they could go. But he got up and called her into his cousin's bed-sitter, she saying she didn't think they should, but he said it was OK.

It was a well-furnished room, with a three-piece suite, a dining set, a wardrobe, and a single bed in the corner, up against a wall. He drew her to the bed, saying, "Come on, Penny. No one will come in." She took off her shoes, and joined him. He had already removed his shoes. They started petting on the bed, and Penny suddenly had a fleeting vision of herself and Matt on her brother's bed, when they had played the cotton-reel game at her party. But they got disturbed ... if only they hadn't! She was brought back to reality by Gareth asking her to take off some clothes. Between them, they had soon removed most of hers, and again were furiously petting. Penny was feeling lovely and enjoying the love-making. But then he was tugging at her pants.

"No, I'm not doing it," she told him, but he was getting more forceful.

"Penny, you must this time. No one's going to disturb us now." But still she refused. She loved making love, but she wasn't going that far.

"I'll be careful," he tried to reassure her. But she kept her pants on. “You know, Penny, in a court of law, if we had been found like this, it would be assumed that we had done it.”

“Well, we haven’t, and we’re not going to!” she retorted. After more cuddling and caressing and coaxing, Gareth said it was just too frustrating, and they better leave off.

“I don’t understand you, Penny. You take off your clothes quite happily, and yet you still hold back. Don’t you know what it’s like for a chap?” Penny got dressed, and put the bed tidy and they left the room, and the house. He walked her back to the bus-stop, and said he would meet her at the park in two days time.

As she sat on the bus, she thought over the afternoon. Now she was almost wishing that they had made love. Why did she still say no? Was it fear of doing it, or fear of getting pregnant, or wasn’t she sure of Gareth. But she wasn’t his first, that was pretty obvious. It wouldn’t be like the boy and the girl from The Blue Lagoon. If only she had had that experience first, then she was sure she would be giving in to Gareth. She did love him, she did, and she did want to do it with him, but it wasn’t the image she had always had of a first time. Then her thoughts wandered to what he would be doing tonight. Maybe he would be in the West End at his old haunts. Maybe the old girlfriends would be there. One of them might do it with him. Oh, no! Please don’t do it with them, Gareth. I do want to. I will! She was jolted out of her thoughts, by the bus stopping suddenly. She continued the rest of the journey home, and then determined that tomorrow she would tell her parents she wanted to leave school.

Next morning, she saw Matt when she was going to do her paper round. This was the first time she had seen him since going to Wales. He gave her a wave, and that was all. She thought maybe she would go swimming that afternoon, but then she wondered how all the gang would react to her, knowing she had been on holiday with Mr. Jenkins. It wasn't a very fine day, anyway, so she decided against it.

After breakfast, she hovered around her mother, trying to find the best time to ask about leaving school. She helped with some jobs in the house, and by now they were having a snack lunch, just her parents and herself. Her brothers and sisters were all at work. Just as she was plucking up to say her piece, her mother said, "I hope your school clothes are good enough for the first few weeks. I won't be able to buy any new ones until we get over the wedding." Now for it then, she thought.

"Well, I've been thinking. I don't think I want to go to PE College. I don't want to have to go away from home. So there's no point in my going back to school. If I look for a job, I can give you some money, because both the boys are going away."

Her mother looked surprised. "What are the other girls doing?"

"Oh, some are leaving, and some staying on. There's nothing I want to do at school now, so I might as well leave," Penny went on, "And I'll still be able to see my friends."

Her father joined in the conversation. "Well I better take you up the school this week then, and tell them you won't be back. Then we'll go to the Labour Exchange, and see what jobs they can recommend." So that was it. She'd done it!

Next morning, her father was ready early, and said he would go with her to the school right away after breakfast. They walked there, and Penny said maybe there wouldn't be anyone in the school, as the term hadn't started yet. "I expect the secretary will be in, and maybe the Headmaster," her father stated. Penny hoped the Head would not be there. He was new and had started the previous term, and no one really liked him. He had told the school 'there would be changes.' The previous Head had been such a lovely man. In a way, she was pleased she wouldn't be going back, now that she recalled the new man.

They reached the school, and found the office. The secretary told them the Headmaster was busy with interviews that morning, and would not be available, much to Penny's delight. Her father explained that circumstances had changed, and that his daughter, being sixteen years of age, intended leaving school. She asked her father to put it in writing for them, and then turned to Penny.

"We'll be sorry to lose you, Penny. Good luck with whatever you do, and come and see us sometimes. I will send you an invitation for Prize Giving towards the end of term."

Penny thanked her, and believed the woman was studying her sympathetically. As they left the office, she thought, 'Expect she heard about me and Gareth. Her father had said circumstances had changed. I bet she thinks I'm pregnant!'

Leaving the school building, Penny felt a lump in her throat. She had enjoyed her school years, and was sure she would miss it. The office was upstairs, not far from the classroom where Mr. Rogers had tried to teach them some German. He wasn't bad really! Then they went down the two flights of stairs, the stairs she had hardly been able to climb, after the shock of first speaking to Mr. Jenkins. What a fool she had made of herself! As they reached the bottom, she told her father she had to leave a book in the Chemistry Lab, the book she was supposed to read in the holiday in readiness for her intensive study to get to College. She hadn't opened it! She pushed open the door of the hall, that was where she had collided with Mr. Jenkins, and he had told her, 'My friends call me Gareth.' She knocked at the door of the Laboratory. No one spoke, so she entered, and was just laying the book on the teacher's bench, when a voice said, "Can I help you?" Swinging round, she came face to face with a young man coming out of the storeroom. "Oh, I'm just leaving a book here for Mr. Marshall. He lent it to me for the holidays. I go to this school ... well I did .. but I've left now."

"I'll see he gets it. I'm the new Lab Assistant," he said. "I'm just sorting things out before term starts next week. Finding my way about. Expect you know the place well enough."

Penny looked into the storeroom, and thought of the illicit breaks she had spent there with Gareth. "Yes, I know it very well. It's a lovely school. I've enjoyed myself. Hope you do, too," and she waved him goodbye. Well, he might be all right for Joyce, she mused.

Her father had come to look for her, and she said they may as well go out the back. Her last walk across the hall where she had played table tennis and danced and danced with Matt. She would miss that. Wonder who he would dance with this year. Probably that pretty little girl, Susan, the one she had made a fool of herself over. Yes, she really would miss her dancing as Gareth did not dance. They didn't go anywhere to do it anyway. She certainly wouldn't be going up the weekly Church Hall dance, with all the gang there!

And then they were out the back door leading on to the netball courts. She really would miss that. She looked across at the field and the far tennis courts. The groundsman was setting up the pitches ready for hockey, which she had found rather strenuous, and for football. She used to enjoy watching the soccer teams. Matt was in the first XI. He would be busy there from next week. It was still warm weather, so all the boys and girls would be lounging on the field in the breaks. Matt had often joined her there, and sometimes made a date for later. Wonder who he would be chatting up. Maybe the new Head wouldn't let boys and girls mix. He said there would be changes. Her father called her, having gone ahead. "Come on, Penny. We've got to get to the Labour Exchange, now."

They walked down the long road from the school, and through the shops. They had to pass the coffee bar. Penny dare not look, in case some of the gang, especially Matt, were in there. She didn't think they would be, it was a bit early. A little further brought them to the Labour Exchange, and they went to the Young People's Dept., where they had to wait awhile. Eventually, a man called them in, and her father explained that Penny had now decided to leave school, and would be looking for a job. She had to fill in a questionnaire, and said she was good at figure work, and would like something with prospects, and the man said he knew one of the Big Five Banks were recruiting staff. Would she like to work locally or in the City? Penny said she thought local would be best. So he said he would make enqiuries, and she should wait to hear in the post. So that was that, and she and her father caught the bus home.

She was quite excited relating the events to her mother on their return, and couldn't wait to tell her brothers and sisters. Wonder what Belinda and Joyce would think about it all. She would see them tomorrow. Today she was meeting Gareth. She bet he would be pleased with the news. She told her mother she was meeting him, and she said to bring him back to tea. So, after lunch, Penny got ready, and left to meet him in the park.

She sat on the seat by the small yacht pond where she knew she had a good view of his arrival. Seeing him in the far distance, she hurried to meet him, and said, "Come and sit on the field. I've got something to tell you." She was quite excited, and was hanging on to his arm, and turning her face up for quick kisses as they went on to the field. Then they sat down under one of the big trees, Penny pulling her knees up under her chin, and announcing, "I've done it!"

"Well, not with me, you haven't," he laughed.

"No! I've left school. And I've probably got a job. I'm going in the Bank."

He looked surprised at first, and then said, "Well that's good. I didn't want you back at school. I won't feel so bad about loving you so much now." And he pulled her legs down from under her, rolled her towards him and started kissing her, and during a pause, said, "And now I can tell you I've applied for a job too. Got an interview tomorrow. It's in the Laboratory of a local factory." Penny knew it. Not far from where Belinda and Joyce lived. Her brother, Lenny, had worked there a short while when he first came out of the Navy. "So now we can both plan," he continued. "But first of all I want to catch up on not seeing you yesterday!"

After some time in the park, they made their way to Penny's home as she told him that her Mum expected him for tea. "Well, after tea, I'd like you to meet my aunt and uncle. They keep on asking when they are going to see you," he said.

It was getting on in the evening by the time they arrived at the flat, which Penny felt she knew quite well. His aunt and younger cousin were there, and were very friendly to her. Gareth seemed to speak to his aunt as a friend, not as Penny would speak to her aunts, and it was a very relaxed atmosphere. She liked his cousin, and it turned out that she was working in the office of the factory where Gareth was having the interview the next day. The older cousin served in a bar, and so was not there. Penny felt relieved, as she thought she would feel guilty about having been on her bed with Gareth. But there was something between him and his Aunt when they lapsed in to Welsh that made Penny feel she *knew* and that she was quite willing.

His uncle was evidently in the pub, and Gareth said they would call in there to see him when he walked her back to the bus. He was a lively character, and seemed very popular in the bar. All the customers seemed to know Gareth, and were interested in the 'young lady' with him. His uncle bought her a drink. He asked for the best drink in the house and they brought her a Pimms, which had lots of fruit in it. Penny liked it, and he was after giving her another, but she declined. It was getting late, and as she had to make her own way home, Gareth said he would take her to the bus, and she assumed he told his uncle he would call back to the bar. The bus was a while arriving, and they had a lovely cuddle in a dark shop doorway. Penny was feeling very amorous, and Gareth felt this. "I think you should have had that second Pimms after all," he told her. But the bus came along at that moment. "There's always something spoils it, Cariad!"

Getting on the bus, she called out, "Good luck with the interview tomorrow."

Gareth got the job and was to start the following week. Penny spent the day with Belinda and Joyce. They played tennis, and then went swimming at a large pool out of the area, joining other girl friends who were having a day out. Penny told everyone her news that she had left school, and they all seemed to envy her, although two others were also leaving. She also made it known that she was still with Mr. Jenkins, and that he had followed her back from Wales. “Seems it was more than just an affair after all,” she informed them. That evening, Gareth called for her, and they went to watch Speedway, which was fun. Afterwards, they called in the pub where his cousin worked, which was near to the Stadium, so now she had met them all. He took her home, and they spent a long goodbye in the alleyway. He said he wouldn’t see her the rest of the weekend, and would call after he had started the job.

CHAPTER FIFTEEN

The school term started the following week. Penny found it strange that she would not be going. She still did the paper round, but didn't see Matt at all. She supposed he had gone extra early because of school. She shopped for her mother in the morning, and then later in the afternoon said she would walk to the school to see her friends. Waiting at the gates, she saw Matt. He stopped to talk to her, and had noticed that she hadn't been at school.

"I've left," she told him. "I'm probably going to work in the Bank. Expect I'll hear this week." Then they chatted generally, and rather awkwardly.

"See you around," he said. "Good luck in the Bank." Penny didn't know what she felt as she watched him walk away. She thought for one moment, he was going to say something more, but then her group of old classmates came out. They knew by now that she had left, and after some words with them all, she walked down the road with Belinda and Joyce.

Saying goodbye, they arranged a date at the cinema mid-week. "We must stay in touch," she called, as she turned her way home.

Next day, she received a letter from the Bank, inviting her for an interview. She saw Gareth the evening before, and he said his job was okay so far, and he gave her some tips for an interview. She had to travel to the Head Office in the City. Her father accompanied her, and it all went well. They agreed to take her on, and said she would hear shortly where she could take up the appointment. Penny felt excited at the prospect of starting work. She told them at the newsagents, but said she would continue with the paper round until she started the job. She did see Matt a couple of mornings, and when she told him her news, he said he would like to take over her round, as it was more convenient than his own. So they arranged it with the boss.

That Saturday was Graham's wedding, so there was a lot of excitement at home. All the family were gathered together, and Neville and Ellie, and their two young boys, came up from Somerset to stay. So there was quite a houseful. Annie was bridesmaid. It was a very lavish wedding, and the reception was in the large banqueting room at the bride's, Bab's, pub. Graham had a car, and when everyone left the reception to see the couple off on the start of their honeymoon, they found that Lenny had organised the decorating of the car with tin cans, old boots, streamers and graffiti. As they drove away, Bab's mother turned to Lavinia and said, "Expect one of your girls will be the next one." It had been a good day, and when they all got back home, one of the girls remarked that Lenny was the only one of the boys left at home. But not for long, as he was due to leave for New Zealand in less than two weeks. Penny noticed that Lavinia was quietly crying.

Early the following week, Penny received a letter telling her to report to a local branch of the Bank the following Monday. Penny knew where the bank was, being in the block of shops where she had been sent to fetch the drink for Dorothy's wedding all those years ago. It would be quite convenient for her, and she could even cycle there. She told them at the newsagents, but promised to continue with the round while they found another boy or girl. This they did, and it was agreed that Matt should change to her round. On her last day, she and Matt did the round together. It took them about half-an-hour, and was the longest they had been together for a very considerable time. As they finished, and said goodbye, it really did seem it was for the last time.

Penny enjoyed working at the bank. It was a small, local branch, and there were only seven working there, including the manager. He lived above the bank in a large flat, and had six children. He acted in a very fatherly way towards Penny, and said one of his daughters was her age. During the lunch hour, Penny sometimes went home if she had gone on the bike in the morning. At other times, she might go on the bus to a café near to the coffee bar where the gang used to hang out, and treat herself to a cooked lunch. Sometimes she just took a snack with her to work, and sat in the basement where there was a kettle and cups for making tea and coffee. One of her jobs was to make the tea and coffee for everyone at break time, morning and afternoon, and collect in the few shillings at the end of each week to cover the cost. Out of that, she was responsible for buying the necessary groceries. Sometimes she had a balance of a few shillings, and then she bought biscuits, and served them extra. Once in a while, Lavinia would make a few cakes and send them with her to work. The staff were very appreciative when she served them with the break time cuppa. "You certainly look after us all," the chief cashier told her one day.

It was almost time for Lenny to depart for New Zealand. Lavinia was getting very emotional over the impending parting.

Some of his friends held a party in his honour, and invited Lavinia and Harry. The girls were at home, and eventually, quite late, their parents were brought home by car from the party. There had obviously been plenty of drink, and Harry staggered to the door, telling the girls to come and help their mother. Lenny was assisting her out of the car. She was in a terrible state, not only intoxicated but very ill. The girls helped Lenny get her inside and into the bedroom. She was crying and moaning, and obviously had no idea where she was. Lenny left the girls to see to her, and went back to the party. He told them that their mother had had some drinks at the party, but had not eaten anything, so it had affected her badly. The girls got her into her nightclothes and into bed. She was calling out about the boat leaving, and calling for Lenny, and crying. The girls had never seen their mother in such a state, and were very concerned. Annie said she would sleep with her, and their father went into Graham's bed.

Next day, all was well, except that Lavinia had a sore head, and was very off-colour. She said she was most ashamed of herself.

Lenny left a few days later, and the brothers and sisters all went to the station to see him off on the train to Southampton, where he was to board the ship. Many of his friends were also there, and his best friend, Morris, accompanied him to the port. Lavinia and Harry said their goodbyes at home. "I'll be back to see you all," Lenny told them. "And once I've got a home out there, make sure some of you come to visit. Start saving now." As he left, he called out. "It's not the end of the world, you know." But really it is. You can't go much further!

With all the boys now left home, and Dorothy married with children, and in her new house, there were only Annie,

Rosamund and Penny still living with their parents. Granny Saunders still managed in her too small rooms, but she was becoming very feeble. Sometimes, Uncle Alfred would stop a night or two, but, much to everyone's joy, he did not come so often as in the past. The three girls still shared the large front bedroom, and if Annie was on night duty shift at the hospital, it left only the two girls sharing of a night. If their uncle was not stopping, it left two vacant bedrooms.

One day, Penny heard her parents discussing the question of some unpaid bills. She knew they now missed her two brothers' contribution to the running of the house. She hoped they weren't going to have to move on again. These years were the longest they had ever lived in one place. She approached her mother. "Gareth is looking for somewhere to stay. He has to sleep on the settee at his aunt's place. He's sticking at the new job. He could have Graham's room, now that he has gone. That would help you out with extra money. Would you like me to ask him?" Lavinia thought it over. She did like Gareth, and he seemed genuinely fond of Penny. It would certainly help out, as they were definitely missing the two boys' income. She discussed it with Harry, and then answered Penny. "Well if you think he would like to come here, you can ask him."

Penny was meeting Gareth to go to the cinema, and she told him of the offer. He agreed to take it up, and, instead of stopping in the alley for a long goodbye session, they came straight back to the house, had some supper with her parents and sisters, and discussed Gareth's moving in with them. Penny got the feeling that her sisters were rather doubtful about the arrangement, but it wasn't up to them. So it was agreed that he would move in that weekend, and would have the smaller front bedroom which had last been Graham's. As they kissed goodbye at the front door, Gareth remarked, "Seems I'll be kissing you goodnight at the bedroom door next!"

He moved in, as arranged, that weekend, and so began the situation of the young couple living under the same roof, with all the pros and cons relevant to the circumstances. Previously, they had not met every day. Penny never really knew what he did those times when she did not see him. She rather thought that he went drinking with his uncle quite often. She also assumed that he still went to the West End to meet up with other people from Wales. She tried not to think that it was possible he still saw ex-ladies there. Now, living under the same roof, he always asked her out with him, not that they went to the West End haunts.

They often visited the aunt and cousins, and usually joined the uncle for a drink. They still went to the cinema and the Speedway, and had taken to going to the Greyhound Racing now and again. It happened that Mr. Rogers, Penny's old German teacher, and with whom Gareth had once lodged, was a regular patron of 'The Dogs,' as it was called. Several times they met him, and sometimes his wife, too, at the Stadium. It seemed a strange situation to Penny to be on social terms with an ex-teacher. He was very friendly to her, and his wife was happy to include her with Gareth, saying how much they had enjoyed having him living with them. At other times, the four of them met in a pub for a social drink.

Although living together, they were not very often actually alone. Penny's father was almost always in the front sitting room, and then her mother and sisters could be around. So most evenings, they went out somewhere. If nowhere in particular, they would usually take the dog for a walk, stopping somewhere for a cuddle session. Often, they would climb into the park, just as Penny and Matt used to, and make their way to the hut or gazebo. The dog was very patient. Other times, they went for a drink in one or other of the local pubs, or went further afield to meet the uncle. And if they got back home and the rest of the household had already gone to bed, then they could spoon in the warmth of the front lounge or kitchen. But separating to go to their own bedrooms was becoming more painful.

Lavinia and Harry were to go away for a week's holiday. Lenny had insisted on booking it for them before he left for New Zealand, as a going away present. Lavinia asked Dorothy and Jonathon to come and stay with the sisters while they were away. They had two little girls now, and they were all to sleep in the parents' bedroom downstairs. Harry was a member of the Holiday Fellowship, and they were spending the week in a centre in South Devon.

One night, Penny was unable to sleep. She never did really sleep well, a condition she put down to having had to get up early for the paper round for several years. Rather stupidly, she had never invested in an alarm clock, believing that she would disturb her sisters. Consequently, she kept a watch beside her bed, and a box of matches, which she would strike to see the time. This exercise could take place over and over all night, as she waited to get up in time. Now that she no longer did the round, she found that she was still waking several times all night. Unlike her, Rosamund had always been a very heavy sleeper, and could lie in for hours of a morning if she were left alone. The sisters used to call her Lazybones.

Penny tossed and turned in bed. She had only had a short doze, and now could not get back to sleep. She could hear Rosamund's heavy breathing. Lucky her! She was in a good, sound sleep. Annie was on night duty at the hospital, so her bed was empty. The house was silent. Then she heard coughing. It was Gareth in the adjoining bedroom. Penny lay there listening. Again she heard the coughing. She thought of going downstairs to fetch him some water, then decided against it in case she disturbed the two little ones in with Dorothy and Jonathon in her parents' bedroom. She began to think that Gareth must be lying awake in his bed, and she was lying awake in her bed. She would love a cuddle. Maybe she would be able to sleep after a good cuddle.

Slowly, she sat up. Rosamund was sound. She slipped out of bed, naked except for panties, as usual, and felt for her dressing gown somewhere at the foot of the bed. Rosamund really was sound. Then, creeping past her sister's bed, pausing to make sure that she was still sound, she slipped out of the room. She stopped awhile outside Gareth's bedroom door. He didn't seem to be coughing now, and she intended asking him if he wanted a drink. Slowly and quietly turning the handle, she eased open the door, slipped inside, gently shutting it again behind her. There was a little light from the street lamp outside, and she could just make out that Gareth was turned towards the wall, against which was the bed.

Gliding to the side of the bed, she bent over and whispered, "Gareth." He turned quickly. "What's the matter? What's happened?" he gasped. "I heard you coughing. Are you OK? Do you want a drink?" she continued. He said he didn't and she better get back to bed before her sister came looking for her. "She won't. She's sound asleep. But I can't. I want a cuddle." And she dropped the dressing gown and slipped into the bed beside him. He was taken completely by surprise, saying at first she should go, but here was Penny, almost naked in bed with him, warm and loving, pressing against him and kissing. He was kissing and fondling her and rolling her over and lying on top of her, and still she was whispering that she only wanted a cuddle. The situation was becoming unbearable. Penny was getting so hot and breathless under him. "Oh, I'm so hot," she told him, trying to push him over. "I'm sweating," she said as she felt her tummy soaking. Sweet, innocent Penny did not realise that it had been impossible for a young man to control himself in such a situation.

As they both lay there, recovering, they suddenly heard Penny's bedroom door open. Penny's heart jumped. "Rosamund's looking for me," she whispered, "What shall I do?" They heard her sister go to the toilet, then the bathroom, the empty back bedroom, and finally downstairs. Penny leapt up, grabbed her dressing gown, and made a quick, quiet dash back to her own bed. Maybe she hadn't seen that her bed was empty. Maybe she had got up for herself. But she knew she was looking for her, and the only place she hadn't looked was Gareth's room. So it was obvious that was where she was!

Penny lay in bed, waiting for her sister to return, and pretending to be asleep. She heard her coming up the stairs, back into the bedroom, and then stop. She had obviously seen her back in the bed. Penny's heart was pounding, but all she heard was Rosamund exclaim, "Huh," and get back into bed. She lay there, worrying and worrying. She was sure that her sister had reported her missing from bed to her older sister, or maybe she hadn't wanted to wake the babies. They would never believe her that she hadn't 'done anything.' To Penny, she hadn't 'done anything,' only had a cuddle. Would they tell her parents? They would make Gareth leave. They would never believe that it had been none of his doing. And she lay there dreading having to face her sisters in the morning.

She eventually dozed off long after it was light and suddenly awoke to hear Rosamund up and dressing, ready for work. She lay still until she heard her leave the room, and then dashed to the bathroom to wash and get herself ready. Gareth's door was open and his room empty. He had already left for work. She hurried downstairs. Only her two sisters and the children were in the kitchen. Her brother-in-law had also left for work.

Her sisters looked awkward as she entered. "And what do you think you were up to last night?" Dorothy threw at her firmly, but quietly. She always spoke calmly and never seemed to argue, very much like Penny. "I wasn't up to anything," was Penny's reply."Well you weren't in your bed, and you know it." Rosamund had now joined in, much more heated. "I heard Gareth coughing and went to see if he wanted a drink," was Penny's weak excuse. "You planned it. Annie was on night duty, and you thought I wouldn't hear you." Dorothy now joined in again, but still quietly and calmly. "How could you have done such a thing with Mumma away? She trusted you both." "I haven't done any bloody thing. It's your dirty minds," Penny screamed at them, and grabbed her jacket and ran from the house.

She worried all day at the Bank, and couldn't concentrate at all. She was sorry, too, for shouting at her sisters, especially Dorothy, as she was always so sweet and kind to them. She felt she couldn't face going home, and what would they say to Gareth? She didn't think he had seen them before leaving for work. And would they tell her mother? None of them would believe it was all her idea. She felt sorry for Gareth. He would get the blame.

Around midday, there was a phone call for her at the Bank. It was Gareth. He wanted to know what had been said at home. He was worried, too. "I'll meet you at the shops after work," he told her. Penny was early, for once, finishing work. You never knew what time you finished in the Bank, as no one could leave until the day's business was balanced. Even if there was only a one-penny discrepancy, everything had to be checked and re-checked until it did balance. Sometimes it could take hours. But today, all was well, and as it was early closing day, the shops had paid in early, and the balance was correct, and they could all go home.

She had gone to work by bus that day so caught the first bus to the shops where she would wait for Gareth to meet her. She wasn't far from the coffee bar and wondered if some of the old school gang were in there. Maybe Matt and Jack Stewart were there. Wonder what they would think of what she had done, or not done, last night. As she sat on the pavement seat, she thought over the escapade. As far as she was concerned, she hadn't really done anything wrong, nothing more than she did in the park shelter or in the alley, except it was more comfortable. And remembering, her thoughts went back further, to when she and Matt had cuddled on that same bed. But they were on top of the bed, and she had her clothes on. For a moment, she imagined what it would have been like then, under the covers, and her naked!

She was brought to her senses by Gareth sitting next to her. They decided to walk home and not take the second bus. He had had a worried day, also. He asked her what her sisters had said. "I'm sorry, Gareth. It was all my fault. I don't think they will tell Mumma, because they won't want to worry her. I'll talk to them, but I know they won't believe that we didn't do anything." Gareth looked at her. "You really believe that, don't you Penny?"

They both felt very sheepish entering the house. Gareth stayed in the front lounge, reading the paper, and Penny joined Dorothy and the children in the kitchen, trying to help prepare the meal. Then Rosamund came in from work. Annie was asleep upstairs after her night work, and would be up shortly. Penny wondered if Dorothy had told her about the night's happening.

The three sisters were having a cup of tea, Penny having taken one in to Gareth in the front room. Finally, Dorothy spoke up. "We're not going to tell Mumma about last night. We don't want her worrying. But I'm upset because you did what you did behind Mumma's back. And you swore at me this morning. You've never done that before, so you can just say you're sorry."

"I am sorry, but I didn't do anything. I never have. I heard Rosamund sneaking about, and I knew what you'd all think," Penny replied.

"I wasn't sneaking on you," Rosamund retorted. "I woke up and thought you'd gone to the toilet. When you didn't come back, I was afraid you were ill or gone into one of your faints. When I couldn't find you, it was obvious where you were. What you and Gareth do is your business, but don't do it here!"

Penny got up to leave the room. "We don't *do* anything," was her last retort.

Their parents were due home in two days' time, and the night's episode had left an atmosphere between the present household. But when Lavinia and Harry did arrive back, it was obvious to Penny, as time went by, that her sisters had not reported the escapade. Everything was soon back to normal, Dorothy and family having returned to their home.

CHAPTER SIXTEEN

Returning from the Bank one day, Lavinia told Penny that a letter had been delivered to her, by hand. Penny opened it, and found it was an invitation from her school for the Prize Giving Evening. The examination certificates and prizes would be given out. It was in two days time. She could not make up her mind if she wanted to go, or not. She would only have her certificate with its three measly results, to collect. All the school would be there. There were several she would like to see again - and some she wouldn't. There must have been a lot of gossip about herself and Gareth, and of her going to Wales, and then of her leaving school. She bet a lot of the women staff would look down their noses at her. What would she wear to go there? And thinking of that, she remembered that she had only that day left her most grown up and fashionable shoes at the menders, and they wouldn't be ready for another three days. That settled it then. She wasn't going! Gareth said he thought she should. He probably wanted everyone, staff and pupils, to see that she was still the same Penny, and not pregnant, as might be assumed. But she made up her mind finally, and said she did not want to go. They could send her certificate, for what it was worth, to her.

The following week, the certificate duly arrived. But in with it, was a second certificate ... a prize! She had been awarded the school prize for Girl's Physical Education. There was only one awarded each year for the whole of the school, with a parallel one for the boys. Penny was stunned, and tears came into her eyes. Oh how she wished she had gone to the ceremony. She would have been so proud to have received it. She felt she wanted to find that old Doctor and wave it in his face and say, 'See, you were wrong! Look what I did!' And the next thing she would hold out for him to see, would be her babies! Proud as she felt, she was very upset that evening. She would have loved to have heard them calling, 'And the school prize for Girls Physical Education goes to: Penelope Saunders!' She wouldn't have cared if she hadn't had her best shoes on! How awful to have had her name called, and to have not been there! She bet everyone was nudging one another, and winking, as if to say, 'Yeah, wonder why she's not here. That's the girl who went off with the Lab Assistant. Expect she's pregnant!' Yes, the staff and the pupils would have thought that. But Belinda and Joyce knew it wasn't true. Her only hope was that they would quell any rumours.

Penny was upset for some while after receiving the certificates. Gareth tried to pacify her, telling her that she really should have gone, but that made things worse. Thinking it over, she felt better by telling herself, that even though she was no longer thinking of going to College, maybe the school award made up for that. It showed that she could have done it. Out of the whole school, she had been found worthy of it. With the prize certificate came a voucher for a book of her choice, and that weekend, Gareth accompanied her to the shops to select one. She eventually decided upon a good, hard-bound dictionary, in which she could stick the Prize certificate on the inside cover. "A dictionary is always useful," she said, "and people who use it will see my name on the prize. I expect my children will use it and I can tell them what I did at school to win it, and maybe they will be proud of me."

The next weekend, Penny was at the shops again, alone. Gareth had started playing Rugby for the factory team, on a Saturday. She was strolling past a small café, when there was a tapping on the window from inside. It was Miss Kent, her old PE teacher. Penny waved, and was going to walk on, but Miss Kent beckoned her inside. She seemed very pleased to see her, and insisted she join her for a cuppa. Penny felt a little shy at first, but then relaxed, and enjoyed chatting. One of the first things the teacher asked was why she had not been at the Prize giving.

"I know you were sent an invitation because I checked with the secretary." Penny made all sorts of excuses, even telling her the truth about the shoes. "I gave you the best I could, Penny," she continued. "I'm so sorry you left school. We miss you in the teams. I know you would have had a good career in teaching. It's not too late, you know. You can still come back."

It sounded so tempting. She wondered if they had a netball or hockey match that morning. Yes, they had, Miss Kent informed her.

"Well I changed my mind," Penny was looking for excuses again. "I wanted to get out to work. Two years more at school was a long while, and then another three at College. My parents are elderly. It would be very hard for them to support me all that while. Anyhow, I enjoy working in the Bank."

"And you're still friends with Taffy Jenkins, so Belinda and Joyce inform me," Miss Kent went on.

"Yes, we're very good friends. He's playing Rugby today."

"Why don't you both pay us a visit some time at school,

Penny? Taffy was very popular in the men's staff room, I know."

But Penny replied that she didn't think it a very good idea.

"Mind you, Penny, school is not quite the same under the new Head. I'm looking around myself." They had exhausted the topics of conversation, and both got up to leave, going in opposite directions. Miss Kent's last words were, "Come and see us any time, Penny ... or come back."

Penny's last words were, "Thanks," and "Thank you for the prize."

Autumn was turning into winter and life went on as usual. Most evenings, Penny and Gareth would make some excuse to go out. The dog was happy, because if they were not going anywhere in particular, they would walk the dog. Climbing into the park was a regular ritual, and spooning sessions in the alley were another. And it was here that Penny gave in to Gareth's lovemaking, and went 'all the way.' It just seemed to come naturally. They had been on the brink of it long enough, and this particular night, she knew that she wanted to as much as he did. Afterwards, she thought to herself, 'Well that was it then.' She had finally done it and yes it had been lovely. Hardly the white sand of the Blue Lagoon, swaying palm trees, and the sea lapping under a moonlit sky. No, her image of the innocent lovemaking of the boy and girl of the Blue Lagoon was gone forever. In its place had been the innocent young girl with an experienced man in the messy back alley where the dogs went to the toilet, enveloped in a cold, damp autumn fog. And the dog had waited so patiently!

Walking the short way home, she realized she would never be the same again. She was well and truly in the world of adults now. This would be the pattern of their lovemaking from now on, she guessed. Entering the house, she felt all her family would know what she had just done. Did she look any different? She went out of her way to speak to everyone, trying to sound very matter-of-fact. She thought her mother looked at her strangely, but no, it was just her imagination. Only three of them knew what had taken place, herself, Gareth ... and the dog! Thank goodness the dog couldn't talk!

Penny now felt a deeper love. Whenever and wherever they could make love, they did. The hut and the gazebo in the park became their love nests, although it was very cold now of a late evening and the benches were hard. It wasn't much better in the alley. Just once or twice, they had been alone in the front room or the kitchen at home when everyone had already gone to bed. But Penny could not relax there, expecting someone to interrupt them, and it felt very wrong at home. There were one or two more comfortable sessions.

They had been to visit Gareth's aunt, and there was a very open relationship between them. As they were leaving one evening, Gareth said something to his aunt in Welsh, and she replied pleasantly and smiled. They said goodbye and left the aunt in the kitchen. No one else was in that evening. Passing through the long, dark passage, Gareth pushed open his cousin's bed-sitting room. "Come in here, Penny."

"No we can't. Your aunt is in," she whispered. "It's alright. I just told my aunt we would have a little while in here. She doesn't mind. She knows what we're up to."

Penny couldn't believe it. How could he ask his aunt such a thing? How awful, that she knew what they were doing. But he was already taking off his shoes, and calling her to the bed. It was certainly tempting, and she succumbed. Yes, it was lovely to have comfort and warmth, but she did feel guilty about performing on his cousin's bed. Then, having put the bed tidy again, they quietly left the house. And on a subsequent visit, they repeated the session.

It was coming up to Christmas, and Gareth was to go home to Wales for a break. He would have taken Penny, but she had very little time off from the Bank. Gareth had longer, as he had in fact recently applied for, and got a new job. It was in the Analytical Laboratory of a Pharmaceutical firm. It was a slightly further journey, but offered more money. He was to start after the New Year, and would finish the old job just before Christmas.

Most of the family would be home for Christmas at Penny's house. Neville, Ellie and the boys would be staying a few days up from the country, and Dorothy and family, and Robert and family would be visiting day times. So there would be a lot of fun at home, although Penny thought she would never get through more than a week without seeing Gareth. They had not been apart for that long since the break up of school way back in the summer.

The last few days together were very intense. They went to the cinema, the Speedway, the Dog Racing where they met Mr. Rogers and his wife, visited his aunt and uncle, spending a couple of hours with him in the pub. They went in one or two pubs local to Penny's home, and of course, walked to the park, where they climbed in to visit the love-nest. One evening, it was quite thick with snow, but it didn't deter their love-making. And then there was always the alley.

Their last evening together arrived too soon. Gareth had finished with the job, and was going by train to Wales early next morning. They planned a last stroll to the pub, and the inevitable love-session somewhere afterwards. After dinner that night, Gareth went to pack ready, and Penny started to wash up. She felt there was something different about her mother. There was a strange atmosphere between them. Perhaps she was extra tired, Penny thought. She knew she was already cooking and preparing for the influx of family over Christmas.

Gareth came down and said, "Shall we go for a last drink then?" Just as Penny was nodding yes, her father joined them in the kitchen, shutting the door behind him. Lavinia moved in from the scullery. "Sit down, Penny. We want to talk to you both," said her mother. "Yes we do," echoed her father. Penny looked across at Gareth, who was leaning against the dresser beside the fire.

"What's the matter?" he asked, looking around them all.

"We know what you two have been up to," her father spoke. "You know what we mean."

Penny was struck dumb. She couldn't believe what her father was trying to say. Then her mother joined in, "You can't behave like this. She's still so young. What if she had a baby!"

Then her father took it up again. "You're going back home tomorrow Gareth, and we think it better that you don't come back here. We don't want you seeing Penny anymore."

"But I love her. I've got to see her," Gareth blurted out.

"No, it's best you don't," Harry went on. Penny's head had been spinning, and her mouth went dry.

She was trying to think straight. She couldn't believe what she was hearing. She just threw herself at Gareth, screaming, "No. Don't go Gareth. Please Mumma, I love him," and she was sobbing into his chest as he held her.

"It's for the best, Penny," Harry mumbled. Still she sobbed out, "No, no. I'll go too, then. I'm sorry, sorry, but I love him. Mumma, please!" It was a terrible scene, and then Gareth was sobbing too and saying, "I love her. I want to look after her.

She means everything to me."

Then Lavinia was weeping, and Harry was looking uncomfortable. The young couple clung to one another, Penny still sobbing uncontrollably.

Lavinia composed herself. "We're sure you do love her, Gareth. But we can't have this going on. We are only thinking of Penny."

Then Penny turned to her mother. "Please Mumma, don't make him go. I do love him."

"I know you do, Penny. Well, this behaviour has got to stop. Come back then if you want to, Gareth. I'm sure you do love her and we don't want to spoil the happiness for you, but we are concerned for Penny."

The tension eased. "Well I think we need a drink after all that," said Harry, and turned to get one of the Christmas bottles out

"Yes, that's right," Lavinia emphasised. "Is it all right if Gareth and I go out for a walk now, Mumma?"

"Yes, go on, dear. I expect you're feeling bad too. I'm sorry for you but it had to be said."

As Penny and Gareth strolled up the road, holding on to one another tightly, and stopping on every dark corner for a long kiss, they discussed the past experience at home. "You will come back, won't you Gareth?" Penny begged.

He assured her he would, but she was worried that he may not want to after her parents' warning. She also thought over her mother's words "What if she had a baby?" Not only would she have been worried about the embarrassment and stigma to the family if her young daughter became pregnant, but also at the back of Lavinia's mind, would be the worry of that old Doctor's words when he told them: 'She won't be able to marry and have children!' Gareth didn't know about that.

They strolled to one of the local pubs, and sat close together with their drinks. As Gareth drank his pint, he said, "I needed this after that dreadful scene. You'd better drink that brandy, Penny. It will make you feel better." They had a second drink, and then started walking back home. Gareth was leaving very early the next morning. They did not stop in the alley this time.

Penny kept saying, "You will come back, won't you?" and he was trying to reassure her that he would and was telling her that he loved her too much to leave her. They had their last cuddle up the road this time. Both were thinking the same. How could they be together and not make love anymore? It was easier said than done.

"Well love," he said, "what are we going to do?" Penny was silent a long time as they stood cuddling. Then she said, "We could get married."

"Me, with my meagre job. I've got nothing behind me," he answered. "I'd love to marry you, Penny. Where on earth would we live?" After another long silence, Penny continued. "We could live at home. There's only Annie and Rosamund at home now. We could have one of the big rooms upstairs, like Neville and Ellie did when they first got married. There were loads of us living at home then. We could make a lovely bed-sitter upstairs like your cousin has. I could cook down in the kitchen. We would look after ourselves, and just pay my parents some rent. We could save with both of us working."

Gareth listened to her, and held her. "I'd love to marry you, Penny, but I've got nothing to offer you yet." They went in the house, and kissed a last goodbye. He left early next morning.

Christmas came and went, and then New Year's Eve.

Penny suffered her way through it all, wondering and worrying whether or not he would be back? 1951 had certainly been a year of changes and excitement for her. But would 1952 be one of happiness or sadness?

CHAPTER SEVENTEEN
1952

Gareth was due to start the new job on the first Monday in January, which was the 6th. He had told Penny he would be back the previous Saturday. All over Christmas and the New Year, she thought of him, wondering what he would be up to while in Wales and why she was never able to trust her boyfriends? She still could not believe that he saw in her, a sixteen-year-old girl, something more desirable than the mature women with whom he had been involved. More worrying, was whether or not he really did intend coming back, after all that her parents had said to him.

Thinking back over that dreadful, embarrassing evening, her parents had been quite fair over the whole business. They could have sent him packing there and then. But it took 'Two to Tango,' and she was as much to blame as he was! So often it had been she who orchestrated the scenarios, and he was only human, after all. She felt sorry too, for having put her parents in that awkward position. Out of all their large family, she guessed she was the only one who had caused such a problem, and she knew her mother was concerned about her health. But she was over the age of consent, so they hadn't broken any law! She remembered Gareth once telling her that, if she had been under sixteen when he was first attracted to her, in school, he would have resisted the temptation of asking her out. Would he or wouldn't he come back? It would be quite easy for him to stay in Wales. He had given up the previous job, and not yet started the new. She could only wait and hope.

They were very busy at the Bank. She had spent New Year's Eve there until almost midnight. It was the end of the year balance day, and the staff had warned her not to make any plans for New Year's Eve. She had seen Belinda and Joyce a day or two before, and they had all gone to the cinema. It was good seeing them again. They had not met up for a while, so she heard all the latest school gossip. It didn't seem that Belinda and Matt had dated that long.

"I don't think he was very keen on me," Belinda informed her. Penny did not follow up the conversation to ask if they knew who he was dating. That water had now flowed under the bridge. But as she thought of him, she knew she would never forget him. They had had a very special relationship that she would always cherish. In fact, she felt, was it possible to love two people at the same time? She could only ever think of Matt with love. In years to come if someone asked him, "Do you remember Penny Saunders?" Would he answer, "Who?" But she would always remember Matthew Oliver. She had thought she would be Mrs. Oliver one day, stupid girl that she was. Now, perhaps, she was going to be Mrs. Jenkins. Well she was now, really, in all bar name.

She was brought out of her reminiscences by Joyce telling her that they were going to the Church Hall New Year's Dance, and why didn't she come too, as Gareth was away. She had not told them about the dreadful scene at home, nor of the circumstances that had caused it. They did not know that she and Gareth were now full-blown lovers! She declined the offer, telling them how she had to work late in the Bank on that particular day. She was glad of the excuse, thinking of who would be at the dance, and with whom she might dance. She did miss going to dances. But it wouldn't be the same now, with Gareth or without him. This was one pleasure she had given up. Still, they had found other pleasures!

Saturday arrived, and Penny was edgy. Her mother had asked her the previous evening when Gareth was expected back. Lavinia thought he would have returned by now, and was feeling guilty, that maybe he had decided against it after their words. She felt sorry for Penny, and knew she must be in doubt, also.

The afternoon dragged on, and it was soon dark. Penny was beginning to despair. She was sitting in the front room, and her father was listening to the football results on the radio. Rosamund was in there too, and the two girls had been talking. But now, once the results came on, they knew to be quiet as their father checked his Pools coupon. Penny thought she heard footsteps outside on the path, then a key turning in the front door. Her heart jumped. Annie was in the kitchen with their mother ... it could only be Gareth! With one dash, she was up and out of the room, startling both her sister and father, who cursed her for giving him a shock as he was adding up his points on the Treble Chance.

Gareth was just putting his bag down and shutting the front door. He was nearly knocked over as Penny threw herself at him. He felt frozen, but she was clinging on, with her face in his cold chest. They hugged and kissed, and she was holding back tears. "I thought you weren't coming," she told him. He told her about the snow in Wales, the train being delayed, and a busy tube and bus journey through London, and then whispered, "Missed you Cariad." Her mother emerged from the kitchen to see what the commotion had been when Penny bolted from the front room. She was confronted by the couple kissing in the hall.

"Oh, it's you, Gareth. We wondered what all the fuss was about. Had a good journey? Nice to see you back. Perhaps Penny will brighten up a bit now."

They stayed in that evening, and her sisters did, too. So there wasn't much privacy. When Gareth went upstairs to unpack his things, Penny slipped up after him. They snatched a few moments together, and both were longing to get on the bed, but Penny knew she mustn't push her luck too far with her family, and so returned downstairs, tingling all over. After a late tea, they had a very pleasant family evening, with everyone in the front lounge together, relating tales of Christmas and New Year, and Harry pouring drinks for them all, and then discussing Gareth's coming new job. Morris called to see them, Lenny's best friend. He had called a lot lately, and had taken Annie out a few times. It was obvious that he was very interested in her, but none of then knew if she really felt the same. Penny thought not. They were not really suited to one another. But he was good company, and he and Gareth always got on well together.

Eventually, the party broke up. Morris had left, Penny's sisters went up to bed, and her parents discreetly retired, leaving the two of them alone. Penny thought her mother gave her a special look as she said goodnight. "Don't be up late, Penny," was all she added.

Now, at last they could indulge in one another, but no way would they allow themselves to go too far, not yet, and certainly not there! Breaking away from a long kiss, Gareth said, "I've got something to tell you, well to ask you, I suppose." Penny couldn't think of what it could be, but he continued. "Next weekend, I'm taking you shopping."

"But you gave me my Christmas present, and it's not my birthday for another three months," she stated.

"It's not for your birthday. I'm taking you to choose an engagement ring."

Penny was shocked and elated, then she thought, "You're not just doing this because we got caught?"

"No, I want to marry you, and if you think it will be okay for us to move in here together, then we may as well do it soon. But you have to have your father's permission at your age. Perhaps he won't be willing."

Penny's brain was racing around in her head. "He'll have to,' she said. 'I expect they'll be pleased to know you're going to make an honest woman of me. They must know that we're not going to be able to lay off one another."

Then she thought on, "But you won't have the money for a ring. I don't mind not having one. We can still say we are engaged. "

"No. I've got the money now, as long as you don't choose the very best!" Penny was bubbling over with excitement. Wait until she told ... asked ... her parents. Surely they would be relieved. Bet her sisters would be jealous. What would Belinda and Joyce think? And everyone at school and in the Bank!

What she did not know was that Gareth's mother had given him money to spend on rigging himself out with new clothes for the winter. But he was going to spend it on a ring for Penny. "You'll be seventeen in March, Penny. So perhaps we can get married anytime after that. I would marry you now, but somehow, seventeen sounds better than sixteen. I don't want people calling me a cradle-snatcher!" Penny was thrilled, and was already planning inside her head. Just three months and she could be called Mrs. Jenkins. She would ask her mother if they could have the larger front bedroom where she and her two sisters now slept. Her sisters would fit nicely in the large back bedroom, and there would still be Gareth's small bedroom as a spare room if Uncle Alfred or anyone else came to stay. Yes, the front bedroom would make a lovely bed-sitting room. They kissed goodnight. "We'll tell my parents tomorrow," she said.

"No Penny, we've got to ask them."

Penny was so excited going to bed that night. She didn't doubt that he loved her. Her sisters were both asleep, but she couldn't get to sleep herself. She was looking around the room, planning what furniture they could have. Oh, it would be so cosy, and she and Gareth would have a lovely double bed, and they could kiss and cuddle and make love whenever they wanted, and no one could tell them off for doing so. It would be very comfortable, much softer than the hard bench in the park hut. But, until that time, she supposed it would still have to do. It was only three months until she was seventeen. Three months to plan for the most wonderful day of her life. Mrs. Penelope Jenkins sounded good. She would start practising signing that. In three months time, Penny Saunders would not exist anymore.

Next day was Sunday. Lavinia had invited Morris round for the usual roast dinner. Annie was on a weekend off from the hospital. Penny was up early, and wondered what would be the best time to approach her mother about the engagement. Just as she was plucking up courage to do so, her sisters came down. Gareth never got up early on Sundays. The girls helped out with preparing the dinner vegetables, while Lavinia was making her renowned apple tart. Their father was up, and the family had all had some breakfast. Only Gareth wasn't down, but he never ate breakfast. Eventually, he did appear, had a cup of tea, and then retired to the front room to read the paper, their father already having done so. He looked enquiringly at Penny as he finished his tea, as if to ask if she had said anything to her mother, but she shook her head.

About midday, Morris arrived, and shortly after, he, Gareth and Harry said they would go for a walk and a drink before dinner. The girls had done all they could do to help in the kitchen, and Lavinia asked if one of them could do some dusting and tidying upstairs in the bedrooms and the front room. They argued a little as to who would do what, eventually deciding Annie would do the bedrooms, Rosamund the front room, and Penny said she would lay the dinner table in the kitchen while their mother sat awhile.

Now was her chance, she thought. Several times she opened her mouth to speak and then couldn't. Penny thought her sisters would be back soon, so it was now or never. She just blurted out, "Gareth wants us to get engaged. He's going to buy me a ring at the weekend."

Her mother seemed struck dumb. She stared at Penny. "Don't you think it's a bit soon?"

"No," Penny went on. "What's the point of waiting? I'll be seventeen soon. We thought we'd get married then. Anyway, you were married at eighteen, so there's not much difference." It was quite true, Lavinia had been only eighteen, so she hadn't much to argue about. And, like Gareth, Harry was quite a lot older than herself, twelve years, in fact. She knew how Penny felt, but unlike Penny, she had behaved herself until marriage.

She knew it would be impossible for them to stop what they were doing. It would probably be a relief if they were married. Would it work out though? They seemed happy enough together, but Penny hadn't had much experience of life yet.

"Well that's lovely that Gareth wants to get married. But you don't seem to be wanting to wait long before getting married. You are all right, I hope!"

Penny was shocked. Her mother thought her pregnant! "Of course I am. But what's the point in waiting?"

"And where are you thinking of living?" her mother went on. "You're not going to Wales, are you?"

"No I'm not going to Wales," Penny emphasised. "Well, you'll miss us all living here. I thought we could make a lovely bed-sitter up in the big front room. Annie and Rosamund can go in the back room. I can cook down here, and we'll look after ourselves. So you won't have so many to cook for. And we'll pay whatever rent you want." Penny blurted it all quickly, wanting to get it off her chest before her sisters came back in the room.

"Well, you certainly seem to have it all planned out. Did this all come about last night?" Lavinia went on. "Well, yes. I suppose it did. Gareth said he wanted us to get engaged right away. But Dad would have to give permission for me to marry. He will, won't he, Mumma?"

"If I say so, he will, I suppose," Lavinia said quietly, just as the older girls came into the room.

Her mother asked if she was going to tell the girls her news.

"What news, Penny? You're not giving up the Bank are you?" Annie remarked. Rosamund seemed to look her all over.

"Well come on, What's up?" Penny didn't know how to

tell her sisters, but her mother chimed in.

"Penny and Gareth are getting engaged this week."

"You're a bit young, aren't you?" Rosamund retorted.

"So when's the wedding then?" Annie asked. "Have we got time to make our dresses? We are bridesmaids, I hope."

And so the conversation developed on plans for a wedding. None of them had money to make expensive plans. Penny said she would borrow Dorothy's wedding dress. Annie and Rosamund said they would buy material for bridesmaids' dresses, and would ask Lenny's old friend who did dressmaking to make them. The girls were quite excited now, planning the wedding. But Lavinia was already worrying, thinking of a reception. Well, maybe they wouldn't get married for a while.

Penny went upstairs, and while she was out of the room, Lavinia explained how Penny would like to have the large front bedroom to start married life. The sisters were not too happy at first, but then, thinking there would only be the two of them left, they agreed the back room could be quite comfortable, and they went upstairs to plan the arrangement.

Meanwhile, Gareth was enjoying a pint or two with Morris and Harry. He wondered if Penny would have told her mother by the time they got back. Should he mention it to her father now? Morris was always very easy-going. Maybe if he said something now, and her Dad wasn't very agreeable, Morris could help to keep the peace. Harry seemed to be loosening up with the effects of the beer, so Gareth timed his announcement. Morris asked him about the new job he was to start the following day. It was just the lead he needed.

"Yes, well it has got more prospects, and of course a little more money than the last job, and there's regular rises. So I can plan ahead now. And my first plan is to get engaged to

Penny. In fact, I want to take her to choose a ring this week." He'd said it!

"Well you're a fast worker, Gareth. Good luck to you. They're all fine girls." Morris quipped.

It seemed to take a while for it to sink in for Harry. "Did you say you want to get engaged? She's only sixteen, you know."

Well he didn't sound too cross, so Gareth continued. "We wouldn't marry until she was at least seventeen. But I'm twenty-five, so it's time I settled down and I want to look after Penny."

"And where are you thinking of going to live?" Harry enquired now, sensing that the fellow was serious. "Well Penny hoped we could live upstairs with you in the big front room. We could help out with the rest of the house then," Gareth went on.

"I expect that's possible," Harry answered.

"We also have to ask for your written permission to marry while she is under twenty-one. You will give it, I hope," was Gareth's next question.

"Of course he will. He'll be glad to get rid of one," Morris laughed.

Harry was thinking about it. He liked the feeling of power this gave. "I'll think it over," he said. "Come on, dinner will be ready by now. I said we'd be back." They finished their pints, and set off on the short walk home. Gareth breathed a sigh of relief. It was all in the open now. He wondered if Penny had told her mother and sisters!

Needless to say, the dinner and the day's conversation revolved around the imminent engagement. It had always been the custom in their home to have a glass of cider with Sunday lunch. The boys of the family had regularly provided it. Now they were gone, but Morris had taken over today. However, after lunch, Harry said they better get out something stronger to toast the 'young couple' and between them all, they drained the remains of the Christmas tipple. This resulted in the three men falling asleep later on, having previously indulged at the pub.

Leaving the snoring trio in the front room, Lavinia and the girls returned to the kitchen to clear up, and then sat there discussing wedding arrangements. Dorothy and the children would be visiting tomorrow, so Penny would ask about the wedding dress. Annie and Rosamund discussed the colour and style of what they would like for their dresses. They chose lilac, and Annie said she would look at patterns that week. Lavinia said she would, once again, make the cake and get the nearby bakers to decorate it. She asked Penny how many guests she thought would travel up from Wales. "No idea," Penny answered. "There's quite a lot of aunts and uncles, and thousands of cousins, but they won't come, and then there are his relatives in London."

"And we are quite a lot on our own," continued her mother.

"I must have Belinda and Joyce there," interrupted Penny. So it would be another headache for Lavinia to think of.

That evening, Graham and Babs called. They usually did this late of a Sunday evening, and took Lavinia and Harry in the car for a drink, locally. They were surprised to hear the news, but joined in the discussion on the plans. Babs offered Penny the loan of her wedding veil, which they all remembered as being very long and lovely. So this was gladly accepted. The plans were progressing at a fast rate. Penny couldn't wait to gather all the finery together and dress up.

Next day at the Bank, she was longing to tell someone,

but decided she would wait until she had the ring, and then flash it around. But that evening after work, she telephoned Belinda to tell her. She had hoped to have finished work early, for once, and would have dashed to the school, hoping to meet her friends coming out, but there had been no chance of that. She wondered what she would have said if she had met Matt. Well, the news would soon get around, now that she had informed Belinda. She would like to have invited them to be bridesmaids. but she couldn't very well ask them to pay for their own dresses, and it would be too much for her family to do so, so it was best just to keep it to her sisters.

When she arrived home, Dorothy and the girls were still there. She had been surprised at the news, and seeing her sister reminded Penny of the painful scene between them, after she and Gareth had been together in the bedroom when her parents were away. She felt very mean, now. Dorothy was always so placid, and Penny had sworn at her. She didn't think her sister had told her mother. Actually, Dorothy, being ten years older than herself, seemed to be a confidante of their mother. Wonder if Lavinia had told Dorothy of the confrontation they had when they knew she and Gareth were misbehaving. Anyway, what did it all matter now? They would soon be married and legal.

Penny couldn't wait to borrow the wedding dress, so after they had all had their evening meal, she and Gareth said they would accompany Dorothy and the children back home on the bus journey, and collect the dress. This they did. The dress was brought out from the wardrobe, and Penny and Gareth returned home with it. On the bus, she kept peeping in the carrier.

"It's made from a parachute you know," she informed Gareth. When they got home, she couldn't wait to try on the dress. She paraded for him to see her.

"I'm not supposed to see you like that until the wedding," he told her.

"Oh, it doesn't matter," she answered him. "I haven't got the veil and the bits and pieces yet. Anyway, I'm going to have the neck changed a bit on this to make it a little different. And I'll have to have it taken in a bit, because Dorothy was plumper than me. Anyhow, how do I look?"

"Beautiful. I can't wait. And if we take the dog for a quick walk, we needn't," he quipped at her.

She got the message and laughed. "No it's a bit late. Let's take him out earlier tomorrow evening and have longer." So it was just a quick kiss and off to bed. Penny felt so excited as she climbed into bed. Just over three month's time, they would be together in this room, every night!

She couldn't wait for the weekend to come, when they would be going to buy the ring. They caught the bus to the big shopping centre, where there would be plenty of choice. After window shopping them all, they settled on which one to enter. She wasn't long in choosing. First, they selected the price range, and second, there were not many that fitted her, with her finger being so slim. The salesman said that any ring could be made smaller, but she wanted it there and then. This narrowed down the selection, and she finally chose a neat cluster of small diamonds. Even that one was a little loose, but they were advised to leave it as it was, and have a small clip inside.

"When you start doing all the housework, your hands will soon get fatter, then you can remove the clip," the man told her. Penny loved the ring, and wore it to go home. Everyone at home thought it beautiful, and she knew her sisters were envious.

That evening, she and Gareth went to visit his aunt, uncle and cousins. They were all congratulating them, and asking when the wedding would be. They had decided on the first Saturday after Penny's seventeenth birthday in March. This was a very popular time for weddings, as it meant that the groom could claim back a year's tax allowance from the Inland Revenue, with the financial year always commencing in April. As usual, Gareth's uncle was going to the pub, so they joined him for a celebratory drink on the way home. Then they rounded off the night with a long session in the alley. It was extra cold, but they didn't seem to notice. At least it wasn't raining!

Next morning, Lavinia suggested that the couple visit Aunt Mabel to tell her the news. This they did, and then Robert, Delphine and the baby were coming for Sunday dinner, so they were all able to receive the news, and view the ring. Lavinia said she would write to Neville and Ellie, and also to Lenny.

That evening, Gareth suggested to Penny that they go to the pub, which he knew Mr. Rogers and his wife always visited of a Sunday evening. Penny was reluctant at first. She thought she would feel awkward telling her old teacher she was engaged. But they did go. Mr. Rogers' wife got very excited at the news, and hugged and kissed both of them, but continentals are like that! Coming home, she said to Gareth, "Well it will be all over the school staff room tomorrow."

The next place to flash the ring around was in the Bank the next day. She popped out to the bakery in the morning, and bought a box of cakes to serve with the morning tea. They were all very surprised at her news, and when she took the tea into the manager, he asked her to sit down for a chat. He told her he, too, was surprised, and said he assumed it was a long engagement. When she told him they planned a March wedding, he looked most concerned, and told her he certainly wouldn't let his sixteen-year-old daughter get married. She corrected him that she would be seventeen, but he said he would still feel the same. "Please consider it very carefully, Penny." She was disappointed at his reaction, but as she left his office, he called her back. "Congratulations, anyway, and the ring is great."

There now began a very busy three months of preparations. They had chosen the local Congregational Church where Dorothy and Jonathan had married. They met the minister and confirmed the date, and then attended the evening service each Sunday. Penny had arranged with a neighbour to alter the dress for her, and her sisters had settled on the material and pattern for their dresses, and they were being made.

However, the reception remained a problem. Penny had told Gareth they had previously had a good reception in the house at her sister's wedding, but he said they should book a restaurant reception with a large number of his relatives travelling from Wales. She explained that no way could her parents pay for such a thing, and she herself wasn't bothered about having anything lavish. She just wanted to get married! But Gareth insisted on having an outside reception and said his parents would foot the bill. This was very embarrassing for Penny and her family, but they had to settle on the arrangement. So they booked a very pleasant restaurant which was situated above one of the local cinemas, called the Palm Court. It would be the nearest Penny would get to the palm trees of the Blue Lagoon.

The weeks passed into months. Gareth's parents gave them a tidy sum of money for their wedding present, and they used this as a deposit on furniture for the bed-sitter they were to have. They spent an exciting Saturday shopping, finally ordering a three-piece suite, a dining table and chairs, a kitchen cabinet and a bed. Penny's parents had said they could have a wardrobe and drawers from the house. She knew exactly how she would set out the room. Her sisters moved into the back room, leaving the large front room empty for the delivery a week before the wedding.

They had to go to the registrar to apply for the licence, and for the bans to be called, three weeks previous to the wedding. The ceremony had to be planned. Gareth thought they should have one Welsh hymn and one traditional English one, and he spent several hours coaching Penny and her two sisters on the words of the Welsh hymn, and of course the tune. This was difficult, because unlike the tradition of all Welshmen being good singers, Gareth appeared to be tone deaf, and the girls really had no idea what the tune sounded like. But Penny, particularly, persevered with the words and their pronunciation. It transpired that Gareth's uncle was an exceptional singer, and once he had sung the hymn to Penny in the pub a couple of times, she kept the tune going over and over in her head, and then relayed it to her sisters. Lavinia had made the cake and it was being decorated.

This only left the question of a honeymoon. There was no spare money to book anything elaborate. Penny would have been quite happy to just go home to their cosy room. Gareth wanted them to go to his home in Wales. He had two weeks holiday he could take off work, but when Penny approached the bank manager, he told her she was entitled to only one week. She would have been happy with this, but gave in to Gareth's wish for the two weeks. This resulted in her having to resign from the Bank. "There's plenty of other jobs about,"

Gareth told her. "Give it up if they won't let you have two weeks for a honeymoon. You can find something else when we get back." All the arrangements were now complete.

A few weeks before the wedding, Penny went from the Bank in her dinner hour, to the shops near the school. Hurrying along, she suddenly heard someone say, "Hello Penny." She turned and was surprised to see Mr. McKenzie, the History teacher, so she stopped to chat. She felt shy at first, as he asked how she was getting on, and then continued to say that he had heard she was getting married. "Congratulations, Penny. Taffy is a lucky chap. I wish I were in his place." Penny blushed, and had no idea how to answer him. She was remembering the date to the ballet and the second one to the opera, after which he had kissed her goodnight. She was searching herself for words, when he continued. "Do you know Penny, I was really fond of you, and seeing you now, I still am. If Taffy hadn't come along, perhaps it could have been me and you." Penny was dumbfounded. What was he trying to say? And as she forced herself to look right at him, she noticed his eyes were watering. He leaned forward and brushed her cheek with a peck of a kiss. "I hope you'll both be very happy." She thanked him, and suddenly remembered how terrible she had behaved towards him after the opera date episode. She had been a bitch to him in class. Now, how ashamed she felt of herself. She wanted to say she was sorry for her behaviour, but could not find the right words. If only she could say it, but no, nothing came out and Mr. McKenzie was saying he had to get back for afternoon lessons. She came back to her senses, and said she, too had to get back to the Bank. They said goodbye, and he called after her, "Give my congratulations to Taffy."

CHAPTER EIGHTEEN

Two weeks before the wedding, they arranged to make a quick visit to Wales, mainly to collect some of the many presents that had arrived there. They booked to travel on the Friday night coach, and return on the Sunday night. This meant they had to go straight to work on the Monday morning. They both hurried home from work on the Friday, had a quick meal, and then set off on the bus journey to the coach station. It was cold of a night time, so they took a small rug with them. As Penny was sitting on the coach in the dark, it brought back the memory of her first trip to Wales just over six months ago. How undecided she was then. A lot had happened since. Here she was two weeks away from getting married!

As the journey progressed into the dark night, all around them passengers were nodding off. Penny nestled against Gareth. Then she turned herself towards the window, and curled up. He wrapped himself around her, and they pulled the rug up over themselves. It was quite cosy, and they were able to fondle under the rug, assuming that no-one would know what they were up to. Penny did sit up and look around them at one time, and she thought a lady in the seat opposite was giving them a nasty look. Eventually they tried to sleep, Gareth achieving more than Penny.

It was a busy weekend, with the usual round of visiting,

and visitors to the house. Gareth was not sent next door to sleep this time, but the arrangement was that Penny and his mother would share one room, and Gareth and his father the other. The couple had hoped that if they managed to be alone in the house for some time, they would be able to snatch a cuddle in comfort in one of the bedrooms. But it had to be a very quick session while his parents were visiting the aunt and uncle in the big house down the lane. There were many presents for them; they selected those items they thought they should take back with them, mainly sheet sets and blankets for the bed. They packaged up what they could carry, and then made the return night trip. Once more they cuddled up together under the rug. Penny made her way straight to the Bank, and Gareth took all the parcels home and said he wouldn't go to work that day.

The final arrangements were now being made. The church minister called them for a last chat. They had brought the music for the Welsh hymn with them from Wales for the organist. They went over the order of the ceremony. "I shall have to ask if there is anyone present who knows why you should not be joined in matrimony," the minister told them. "You haven't got any skeletons in the cupboard have you?" he joked.

Penny was thinking to herself how awful it would be if someone did call out. Then she smiled to herself, thinking, maybe Matt would be there, and he would jump up and say, "Yes. I object. She is my girl. I am supposed to be her first lover. We are the couple in the Blue Lagoon." Sorry, Matt, too late now!

The big day was fast approaching. The dresses were ready, the flowers ordered, the wedding car booked, and for Penny's seventeenth birthday, Gareth took her to buy the wedding ring – a plain gold band. "Only six more days now, Penny," he told her as they cuddled in the kitchen, she straddling him on a chair. Everyone else had gone to bed. Guess they thought there was nothing to lose in leaving them alone at this late stage of the proceedings!

The furniture was arriving on the Monday. Annie and Rosamund had now moved into the back bedroom, and said it was very comfortable in there, and they liked looking out on to the back garden. Penny had given the front bedroom a good clean out, and it was now empty, awaiting their new possessions. They had asked Lavinia to tell the delivery men to just plonk it all in the room, and they would set it out when they got home from work. Penny couldn't wait to get home that evening. After their meal, she and Gareth set about the arrangement. Finally, they had it as they thought looked best. The bed was in one alcove to the side of the small fireplace, the kitchen cabinet the other side, the settee in front of the fire, the armchairs either side of the bay window, and the table and chairs against the back wall, with her mother's chest of drawers in a corner, and the wardrobe out on the landing. Penny made up the bed with the new covers.

Everything looked lovely. They had ordered extra coal with her parent's delivery, and when they were married; they would be having a coal fire in the room. It would be so cosy to sit in front of it on the beautiful settee, and then turn into bed, still in the glow and warmth of the fire. Penny could hardly wait. But for now, she would be sleeping in here alone for the last few days leading up to the wedding, as there was no room for a third bed in her sister's back room.

The next evening, Belinda and Joyce called to see her,

having let her know beforehand that they were bringing their wedding present with them. Gareth had gone to visit his aunt and uncle. Penny took the girls up to see the bed-sitting room, and they all stayed there, having a good chin-wag. They were very enthusiastic over the room and its contents, and Penny got out the wedding ring to show them, also her dress, although she did not put it on.

It was now just two days before the wedding. Penny spent her last day at work. She brought cakes again to serve with the tea. Then the Manager gave a little presentation talk wishing her well, and handing her a box of cut glass tumblers from all the staff. She was allowed to leave early, and after a round of farewells, she left the Bank for the last time. Gareth finished the next day. Penny had spent some time writing out the place names for the reception, and they took them to the restaurant to leave with the seating plan.

Gareth's relatives arrived that day. His parents and brother were to stay with another relative near Epping Forest, and others were in hotels in town. A cousin, who was to be best man, and Gareth's old college friend stayed in Penny's home. For that last night, Penny went into Gareth's bedroom, and he and his cousin and friend, shared their bed-sitter.

At last it was the big day. Everyone was up early. The ceremony was at mid-day. All the arrangements went smoothly. Penny and her sisters dressed in the back bedroom; Gareth and his fellow men were in the front. The bridal car arrived and took the men first, then Lavinia and the bridesmaids, and finally Penny and her father. She was bubbling over with excitement. There seemed so many people in the Church as she walked down the aisle on her father's arm. And when they sang the Welsh hymn, Penny had the words right and sung her heart out. And no one answered when the minister asked if there were any objectors! Then the ring was on her finger, and they were going into the vestry for the signing of the certificate. It was all over. But when they studied the wedding certificate, under the column for bride's age, it stated sixteen!

"But I'm seventeen," Penny said.

"Well when the details were filled in by the registrar three weeks ago, they would have seen you were sixteen," the minister explained.

"So we waited for nothing!" said Gareth. They thanked him, and he wished them well.

"Do you know," he continued "I have never had a bride so obviously enjoy her wedding as much as you have today, Penny. Or should I say, Mrs Jenkins!"

The reception went smoothly. Not too many speeches, but Mr. Rogers was called upon to make one. It was a bit unfair, Penny thought, as he hadn't been forewarned. But he was very good, and mentioned one or two happenings in school, saying that his lively lodger and popular colleague had met an equally lively and popular pupil of his and that they both shared a tremendous sense of humour. "They are very well suited, and should have a lot of fun together", he concluded.

When all was over, Penny changed into the new grey suit that she had bought for going away. They were booked on an early evening train from Paddington to Swansea. Gareth's father was to drive them to the station in the family car, and as he did not know the London roads, Penny's father accompanied him as guide. Harry knew London extremely well. They did the rounds of the guests to say goodbye. Gareth's mother kept telling them the key to the house would be next door, which bedroom they were to have, and over and over she told Penny where to find the eggs for breakfast. Quite honestly, she wasn't even interested in the eggs! And then they were off.

Finding their reserved seats on the train, Penny was leaving a trail of confetti everywhere. There were two other gentlemen in the compartment, and it was so obvious that the young couple were newly-weds that very shortly they both excused themselves, and left, going further along the corridor. Diplomatically, neither returned, which was very sweet of them, Penny thought, but rather embarrassing.

The journey was long, and after alighting at Swansea, they still had to get two buses up the valley, before they would reach the village. "I should have asked someone to meet us," Gareth said. It was dark on the final stage, and getting off the last bus, they had to climb the steep hill to reach the little house at the top, and carry the luggage, although they hadn't brought too much with them, as his parents were bringing the rest when they returned next day in the car.

Reaching the top, they now had to call next door for the house key. One cousin was not at the wedding, staying at home to look after the blind mother. The cousin's husband said she had walked her mother down the lane to the aunt at the big house, and that he didn't have the key. So down to the big house they went, and sure enough, everyone was there, and they had the key with them. But then they all wanted to hear how the wedding had gone off. Penny thought they would never get to bed that night. Eventually, they got away, and back at the house, just as they were putting the key in the door, Mrs Price, next door, came out asking them inside, and she too, wanted to hear all about the wedding. Finally they got into the house, and eventually climbed the stairs to the front bedroom. It was almost midnight. The two of them were absolutely whacked. But they made up for it in the morning!

After two week's honeymoon in Wales, they returned to their little love-nest in Penny's home. It was heaven! Gareth was back at work, and Penny now had to find a job. She signed on with an agency, saying she was good at figure work. She filled in the form, and was just about to hand it to the lady, when re-reading it through, she saw that under 'name', she had written Penelope Saunders. She snatched it back, saying, "No that's not my name." The woman looked at her strangely, but Penny was explaining that she was very recently married and wasn't used to her new name. She then filled in another form, and entered Penelope Jenkins with Mrs. in brackets.

She was sent almost immediately to a small engineering firm about three miles away, and was assigned to the wages office. There were only two other women working there, and they warned Penny that she would get plenty of wolf whistles and banter from the men. It was all in good fun and they were quite harmless. True to form, this did happen. The two women were very friendly, and Penny spent an enjoyable few weeks there. However, by now, she knew she was probably pregnant. She confided in one of her colleagues who told her, "Well, you might not be, it sometimes happens like that, with all the excitement of the wedding". She knew someone who had been mistaken in similar circumstances, so Penny tried to ignore the possibility.

Gareth came home one day and said that there was a job going in the pharmaceutical factory, for a laboratory assistant. It's in the Bacteriological Section where the products and the water are tested for bugs. "It's next to the lab I am in, where we do the chemical analysis and testing. Why don't you apply, Penny? We can travel to and from work together, go on the bikes when it's fine, and there's a good friendly atmosphere there, and it's slightly more money."

It sounded a good idea, but she was worrying about her condition. "Yes, but what if I'm pregnant?"

"Well, you're not sure yet, and who knows what may happen. Anyway you can do a good few months. I'll speak to them tomorrow. The chap you will work with is very nice. You met him at that work's dinner dance I took you to just after the New Year. His name is Alec." Penny certainly did remember him.

"Oh, no. I'll never be able to face him again. Remember what I did!" What she had done was that while they were all sitting at the long dinner table provided for their party, above the dance floor, Penny had started playing 'Footsie' under the table, presumably with Gareth. She kept her eyes on him, and he remained quite unmoved. Only later did she learn that it wasn't his leg, but the man next to him, this Alec. He was there with his wife, but he told Penny he didn't like to correct her, as it was most enjoyable! The men had a good laugh over it, but Penny wanted to hide away.

Gareth brought the application form home, and told her that he had spoken to Alec first to see if he was interested in her applying, and that he had said, "Not half. I'll have her anytime!" Penny got the job, and it was both pleasant and interesting working in the laboratory. They were secured off from the main lab, completely enclosed, and with a special ray at the door to de-bug anyone entering. In fact, she and Alec were known as the 'buggers'! Once a week she had to do a round of the whole factory plant, taking samples of all water outlets, and then making cultures back in the lab to count the contamination. This was also done with the products. Through the windows of their little room, she could see Gareth at work in the main lab. They met up for the breaks and dinner times, and sometimes strolled in a park opposite or even had a half hour on the rowing boats there. It was a very satisfactory time for them both. But all that time, Penny certainly was expecting.

One evening, after their meal, they had cuddled together on the settee, listening to the radio, and then succumbed to going to bed very early. It was so lovely to just step from the settee to the cosy bed in the corner. They had made love, and then slept. Penny suddenly awoke. It wasn't eleven o'clock, yet. She sat up, felt terribly sick and rushed to the toilet just in time.

"Well that's it," she told Gareth. "I'll go to the doctor tomorrow." Next day she told her mother she hadn't felt well, and had been sick, and that she would go to the surgery. Lavinia looked at Penny sadly. "Yes, that's best", she told her.

The doctor confirmed the pregnancy. "You'll have a baby by Christmas," he said, and then asked where she thought of having the baby.

"I shall have it at home," she informed him. "It's no problem. My mother is there." So far, she had got away with him not sounding out her heart. He had only taken her blood pressure. He wasn't the same old doctor, and she didn't think he had read any of her notes.

"In that case, you will attend the local midwives' clinic," and he gave her a letter to take on her first visit, and wished her well, telling her to come back to him if she needed anything. "Well you're young, and you look fit," he added.

"Oh yes, I'm very fit", she said as she left his surgery.

Returning home, she found her sister, Dorothy, and the children there. Penny didn't quite know how to tell her mother, so she just blurted it out as she joined them in the kitchen. "Well, I'm having a baby". It was obvious that her mother and sister had been talking about her visit to the doctor, and had guessed what the outcome would be. "The end of the year," she continued, thinking that put her within the nine months from the wedding, "and if it's all right with you, Mumma, I shall have it at home."

Lavinia looked shocked and worried. "Do you think that wise, dear?"

"Of course. There's nothing wrong with me," Penny emphasised.

Gareth seemed rather disappointed at first, when he came home from work. But they had both known in their hearts that she was pregnant. They had really buried their heads in the sand, trying not to face the inevitable. As they nestled together that night, and Gareth stroked her still flat tummy, Penny felt a wonderful glow about herself. So this would be the first of her four boys. Baby Ross was on his way. And as she sank into sleep, curled up against Gareth, she heard those words again: "She won't be able to marry and have children, Mrs Saunders!" She came to with a start. Well, she was married, and she was having the first of her children!

Penny kept well throughout the pregnancy, and worked up to six weeks before the expected birth. They were sorry at work that she was leaving, and she, too, was disappointed, as it had been an enjoyable few months. On her last day, their colleagues from the laboratory presented her with a beautiful cradle, full with baby items. She and Gareth had already ordered a lovely grey pram, which was awaiting collection as soon as the baby arrived. Penny couldn't wait to be pushing it around the neighbourhood. And there was just room at the foot of their bed for the cradle.

She had attended the midwives' clinic regularly, and the house arrangements had been sanctioned for a home birth. No one had queried her heart condition. There were no complications in the birth, and in the early afternoon of the third of December, Penny was nursing her baby boy. It had been a wonderful experience, and she was now completely satisfied. Never again would she be haunted by that doctor's words. Kissing her baby – who was the image of Gareth – she thought, "And I'll prove him wrong again and again."

That Christmas, the family of three travelled to Wales by train for the festive season, and to show off the new baby to the many relatives and friends. They stayed over the New Year, and as Penny and Gareth kissed for the last time in 1952, she whispered in his ear, "I've had a marvellous year, thanks to you, Gareth ... and baby Ross".

"You've made it for me, too, Penny, both of you," he said, as they made love for the first time in 1953.

PART TWO

MATURITY

CHAPTER NINETEEN
1953

Penny, Gareth and baby Ross now settled into their small family life routine. They both adored the baby, and they were fortunate to have Lavinia, Harry and the two sisters still living at home, to advise and help out. In fact Ross got quite spoilt with so many adults around him wanting to hold and play with him.

Gareth would come home from work and want to pick him up right away, and sometimes Penny had just got him to sleep. She would tell him not to disturb him, but inevitably he would. He liked to wrap him in the large Welsh woollen blanket off the bed, twisting it around himself, so holding the baby snug to his chests, and then walk around the house, the garden and sometimes the street. This was the Welsh tradition of nursing a baby in the 'Carthen'. But Penny never got the hang of how the blanket had to be draped and fixed, and so nursed him her way.

The baby was not a good sleeper at night, possibly because he got so much attention from such an extended family all day and also because Penny and Gareth were in the one room for most of the time. But with so many baby sitters on hand, they were able to go out for an occasional evening. Penny enjoyed going out with the pram, much more exciting than the dressed up cat of her early years. Some times she met friends from school. The girls seemed envious of her and the baby, and Belinda and Joyce still came to see her. Strange, though, she never crossed paths with Matt. Not that she thought of him any more, but who knows, perhaps he had seen her from afar. She attended the clinic regularly, and tried to undertake all they advised, and noticed that she seemed to be the youngest mother there.

Life was good, and although bringing up a baby was hard work, and what with sleepless nights, she did feel tired at times, the profound love that she felt for Gareth and little Ross filled her whole being. Sometimes, as she sat feeding her baby, her thoughts would drift to what would be going on at school. Well, she was glad she wasn't there. Mind you, she missed all the activities sometimes, and she and Gareth occasionally slipped over to the tennis courts at the back of the house for a game, while one or other of the family baby-sat. They even went to the park on occasions to play on the better courts. But, strangely, she never went to the swimming pool!

It was summer time, and it dawned on Penny, now that she was eighteen, she should have been sitting her higher exams, and applying for college. No, she wasn't disappointed. She was sure she was more fulfilled in the position she now found herself. But at the back of her mind she thought it would have been nice to know that she could have gained entrance.

Gareth, too, had been thinking over his position. He needed something with prospects now that he was a family man. They wouldn't always want to be living in one room of her parents' house, even though they had the run of the rest of it, and Ross would not have to be confined to just one room as he got more active. He applied, and was accepted for Teacher Training College. It was situated just a bus journey away, so he didn't have to leave home, and with his age and qualifications, he only had to undertake a one year mature student course. In fact, with the year starting later and finishing earlier than school terms, it only took nine months. Now, with a reasonable salary and a steady job, they could plan for the future. However, during this period of study, Penny found that she was pregnant again. Their second little boy was on the way, and she began to decide on his name.

On the night of 1st March, Penny awoke suddenly and realised that the baby was on the point of being born. Gareth rushed out to call the midwife, and it was all happening so quickly, they didn't have time to get Ross, asleep in his cot, out of the room. It was St. David's day, the Welsh National day, and Penny gasped that the baby would have to have David as a second name. But it passed midnight, when the baby arrived very quickly, crying loudly. Ross awoke and stood up in his cot to view the performance going on at the bed a few feet away. As the midwife held up the baby, he pointed, and said "Baba".

"Well that was a quick job," the midwife exclaimed, as she handed the baby to Penny, "and a lovely little girl for you." For one moment, Penny was stunned. She had never imagined herself with a girl; she had once told her teacher that, "I will have four boys, girls are silly." But as she drew the baby to her she saw it was indeed a girl. Well, what a surprise, and she was lovely!

Gareth was thrilled to have a little girl. They named her Lynette, although she was eventually always called Lynn, and chose Megan for her second name, after Gareth's Mother, as was the Welsh tradition. If she had been a boy, she would have had a name after Penny's father, being as Ross had his second name after Gareth's father. Well, there was still time for that, Penny thought!

So now they were four in their little love-nest. Fortunately they could overspill into the rest of the house. Babies certainly kept you busy, as Penny found out. Luckily, she had plenty of help on hand from the rest of her family. And there were quite a few developments within the family.

Lenny was now married over in New Zealand, having sent for his girlfriend from England, and Neville, Ellie and the two boys were waiting to get their passage out there. Graham and Babs had a baby on the way, Robert and Delphine also had two boys, and Dorothy now had three girls.

Morris was no longer courting Annie, but had been going with Rosamund lately. In fact Morris had to go away with his work to Canada for a while and Rosamund was to join him there. But he suddenly returned, and they got married very quickly and quietly soon after. Annie had a steady boyfriend, having met him in the country when she had gone to stay with Neville and Ellie for a week. The young man then followed her back to London, found work there, and they seemed very much involved. Granny Saunders had become very feeble, now well into her nineties, was taken into hospital, and died there soon after.

And to add to all these developments, Penny realised, to her dismay this time, that she was pregnant again. As her Doctor told her, "You must be the most fertile thing on God's earth Penny. I reckon your husband only has to wink at you, and you're pregnant!"

Penny did wonder how they would manage with another little one. In fact when the new baby arrived, there would be three of them under two and a half. They had to have more room, and they probably could have had an extra room at home now, but Gareth said they would have to get a house of their own. Very kindly, his mother gave them the deposit on a house, and they had soon chosen what they wanted.

It was a very large four-bedroomed Edwardian property, with two lounges, a large morning room and kitchen, and a pretty square hallway with a fire grate, but no loveseat, and a large garden, where young children would be able to play safely. And it was in the road which led from Penny's old school, the very one that Gareth and Mr. Rogers used to walk on their way to and from school. It led to the park where they had first played tennis, and where Penny had had many assignations, both with Gareth and Matt!

Early in the winter months, the little family moved in to their new, grand love-nest. They wandered through the rooms. There seemed so many, and they had so little furniture, as yet, coming from just one room of their own.

"Never mind, Penny. We'll gradually get more things," Gareth told her, "but at least it's ours, I'll do some extra evening work to earn a bit more," he continued.

"I wish I could help out, but with all the children, I can't," Penny answered him. "Not yet, anyway. Maybe when they are older," she added. "But then I haven't got my four boys yet," she teased him.

CHAPTER TWENTY
1955

It was a cold, hard winter, and lovely as it was to have such a large property to themselves, it was a major operation, and a costly one, to keep the place warm. All the rooms had open fire grates, but there was no way they could keep them all going. They had to maintain the one in the kitchen, the morning room, as it also provided hot water, and light the one in the only sitting room they were using, later in the day. But going to bed was a cold experience for them all. At least Penny and Gareth had each other to keep cuddled up and cosy, but Penny was continually checking on the little ones to see that the covers were not kicked off.

Their third baby arrived on the third of January. Penny awoke while it was still dark in the early morning hours, and knew that things were happening. Gareth lit the fire in their bedroom for the first time, and then went out in the snow to telephone for the midwife and also sent a message to Lavinia's neighbour, asking that Penny's mother come as soon as possible to help out. They had previously arranged that she would stay for about two weeks when this latest baby arrived.

It was an easy birth, and the little boy was soon delivered. He was a small baby, and was possibly a week or two premature. They called him Gerald, Gerry for short, of course, and

Raymond for his second name after Penny's father's middle name.

It was a lot for Lavinia to do looking after Penny, a new baby, and two other young ones, so Penny soon got on her feet and insisted that her mother return home earlier than was planned. Lavinia seemed so tired, but was always so willing to help out. But Penny's sisters said that she shouldn't keep having these babies and expect their mother to take on all the extra work. Penny quickly made sure that she was back running her own household.

Gareth started to do some extra private coaching work, which brought in a little extra cash, and even took another part-time job working in a local pub of an evening and some week-ends, often helping out at functions. And, of course, during the daytime he was teaching locally. Penny hardly saw him, apart from meal times. Her days were so busy with the hard work of looking after three young children and all that it entailed, that the only time she and Gareth had to themselves was when they finally got to bed at night. And even then, they were often disturbed by one or other of their brood.

However, Gareth didn't always stop at school for every dinner break. Sometimes he would cycle home just to see Penny and the children for half and hour or so. Once or twice it would happen that all the little ones would be having a nap, and then it would be like old times, and Gareth would take Penny and they would 'spoon', and very often make love.

"You're just as exciting as ever," he would tell her, and then dash back to school. But for all the hardship, Penny was very satisfied. Loving Gareth and her babies was everything to her, and she wouldn't have it any other way, although it would have been nice to afford more things. But she was sure it would come easier one day.

Gareth had made a friend while he was at college. His name was Rhodri, and he came from North Wales. He, too, was teaching and was in lodgings, but he spent a lot of time with them in their home. They discussed whether he would like to move in with them. They certainly had the room, and when he said he would, they furnished a bedroom for him, and he became one of the family.

Penny now had two men and three children to look after. But it was a good friendship, and in fact he stayed with them for ten years. He never interfered, but helped with the decorating of the large house, so was a huge asset. The children loved him. Gareth's standard joke was to say that, if he ever caught him in bed with the wife, he would put up his rent! Yes, it was a good relationship between the three of them, and he never put a foot wrong.

During the next couple of years, two other young men joined the household. They were teaching with Gareth, and both from Wales. They were looking to share accommodation together, and Gareth discussed with Penny the possibility of them having the second largest bedroom, and the second lounge which led on to the old conservatory which could serve as their own kitchen area. He told Penny that she would not have to do anything for them, but the little extra money would be a help towards the house expenses. So, after suitably furnishing the rooms for them, they moved in.

There was quite a houseful for some time, but after several months, one of them returned to Wales, but the second young man stayed on for a couple of years. They made the lounge a bed-sitter for him then, and once more had their own use of the large bedroom.

Gareth now undertook evening class work several nights a week. He always called at the pub on the way home, and also went out on the other evenings. Weekends were one long drinking session, and if it was the rugby season, he would be at some game or other, and then drinking with the lads after. Penny felt she never saw him. Very often he brought one or other of his friends back to the house. She enjoyed meeting them, and they had some entertaining times. But she longed to spend an evening alone with her husband after a busy day, once the children were in bed. This was her image of marriage, but Gareth seemed to think he should carry on as he did in his bachelor days. Quarrels developed, always instigated by Penny's comments on his drinking and time away from home.

She could not understand why he should not want to be at home with her. She longed to spend an evening curled up on the settee with Gareth, relaxing after a day's hard work, cuddling like they used to, and then making love. Oh yes, they did make love at night, and it was their only time together really, but she came to resent the time he spent away from her. She could not understand that he did not want to be with her quietly at home instead of drinking in the pub. She saw more of Rhodri than Gareth!

Sometimes Lavinia would baby-sit for them, and they could go out together. But they only ever went to a pub, except for a very occasional invite to a party or an evening with friends. That was always pleasant, and they often held such evenings themselves with the many friends associated with Gareth, and their respective wives or girlfriends.

With Gareth teaching, there were plenty of holiday breaks. They could not afford a proper holiday, but most times they went as a family to Gareth's home in Wales. But sometimes his parents visited them. To get to Wales, Gareth would go by train and drive back in his father's car so as to transport the family back. Then they would return in the car and he would take it back and take the train home again.

The children loved going to Wales, where they enjoyed the freedom of country life, and visits to the seaside, although so often the weather was bad. But Penny always found it a strain. Gareth spent every night in the village pubs. There seemed to be no drinking hours and men were still indulging hours after normal closing. They would stay and chat in the village, so that it would be well into the night when he returned. Then there would be such rows in the house. His mother was still as dominant, and the arguments continued for days. This caused Penny to quarrel with Gareth, and she found most holidays a strain.

She yearned for when they would be able to afford a holiday for just themselves and the children somewhere entirely independent. She was sure that one day it would materialise. Maybe when the children were all at school, she would be able to get a job and save for a holiday. But her plans were short lived. By the spring of '57, Penny realised she was pregnant again. Their second daughter was born the day before New Year's Eve. They called her Jacqueline Lavinia, after Penny's mother. Ross was now five and was starting school, but with four children, they would be a very busy family.

CHAPTER TWENTY-ONE
1958

Penny was twenty-three in March, and as she sat feeding her baby, she mused on what she had and had not done with her life. Well, she was married, had four children, and lived in a big house. That was it really. Other than that, she had done nothing.

She loved her children, and she loved Gareth, even though she wished he would find more time for her. She was such a romantic that loving and being loved meant so much to her. She could cope with stress and trouble as long as she felt loved. But of late, she felt she came second to Gareth's time spent drinking and enjoying himself with his friends. And when she waited for him to come home at night, she turned over and over in her mind the situation, even dwelling on his past life before he met her. Still it came to haunt her, and still she regretted that she had no past. If only. If only she and Matt ... but then one or other of the children would rouse her from her thoughts, and it would be back to reality.

Gareth loved the children too, and made sure he provided for them as well as he could. Times were hard, and he needed to do the extra evening class work to manage. He had promotion with his teaching posts and was gradually making his way up the ladder. And Penny knew in her heart that he loved her. She was very subservient, and held her tongue as much as she could. No way was Gareth going to have her dominate him as his mother had tried and had succeeded with his father. But at times Penny would snap, and they would quarrel. Quarrelling made her feel very ill, and she would have palpitations and feel faint. Paradoxically, she seemed able to cope with hard and strenuous work, but emotion really affected her. But their lovemaking was still as intense.

There were changes within Penny's own family. After Rosamund and Morris had suddenly married they moved from London to wherever his job of cable jointing took him. For some time they lived in Scotland, but eventually they went to South Wales, living in a caravan on a farm, then moving into the farm, and later on buying their own bungalow in the village.

Annie finally married the boy from the country. Initially they made their home with Lavinia and Harry, taking the top of the house as a flat. But then Derek, Annie's husband, went into the RAF and they were stationed at a variety of places in Britain and abroad. Lavinia and Harry could not afford to keep the large house, and went to live with Dorothy and family who had now moved to the coast.

Penny missed having her parents near to visit. In fact, out of their large family, there were now only two of her brothers and herself within that London area. Graham lived with Babs in her family's pub, and Robert and Delphine and two boys had bought a house actually in the road of the old family home.

Apart from Rhodri, who still lived with them, there were no longer any other lodgers. Well, the family needed all the rooms. Penny's parents came to stay sometimes, and Gareth's parents made regular visits, and his many aunts and uncles often stayed.

The house was now more comfortable. Rhodri had helped with much of the decorating, and the rooms were all reasonably furnished. And Penny now had a washing machine. Up to then she had always had red, raw hands from the continual hand washing, much of which was a succession of nappies. Penny could not remember a day without nappies since Ross was born. But the children were always clean and well fed.

Gareth's uncle had called one evening with a new lady-friend. The aunt had died and the family moved away. He had moved in with the elderly widow. She felt sorry for Penny, so young, and with such a large family and so much work. But she admired her. Gareth and his uncle had gone out to the pub. Penny was getting all the children to bed. Each one was bathed or washed top to bottom, cleanly dressed, and then settled in bed. The new lady watched the whole operation, and when Penny came down from taking up the last one, she complimented her on how she coped. "Those children are shining like new pins," she told Penny.

One summer, the family had their first real holiday other than going to Gareth's home in Wales. Gareth came home from school one day and said that the Headmaster, with whom he was very friendly, had offered them the use of a cottage he owned in a country village near the south coast. Facilities were basic, but they could have it for one week at no cost, other than putting money in the meter. Gareth arranged to borrow his parents' car and fetched it from Wales. They were all so excited. Jacqueline was now a year and a half, Gerry was four, Lynne was five and Ross nearly seven. It was a wonderful break for them all. The cottage certainly was basic, but it led out on to a field where the children could play freely. They spent days on the beach, visited a castle, and generally explored. And Penny and Gareth were together with their family, with no distractions of old haunts as they had when they went to Wales. And although Gareth would go for a drink in the small village pub of an evening, he had none of his mates there to encourage him to over-indulge. Penny loved the week's stay, and she determined that in some way they would have a proper holiday each year. Somehow they would try to afford it. Maybe soon she would be able to get a job to help out.

However, shortly afterwards, they heard from Gareth's brother Jim, that he and Lena and two young boys were going to pack up in Wales, and come to London. He had been offered a clerical job, and was leaving the mines. It was arranged that they come to stay with Penny and Gareth while they looked for a house.

The house was certainly full up now. They gave them the front lounge for their own use, and the large back bedroom, and they shared the kitchen and bathroom facilities. The two boys were good company for Ross and Gerry, being of similar ages, but now with six lively children, days were very busy. And Rhodri was still living with them. Penny often wondered why he continued to stay, with so many of them in the house, and the noise of six children. But he was so placid and never complained. Everyone loved Rhodri.

Penny enjoyed having Lena to talk to. But it now became a very Welsh household. Gareth, Rhodri, Jim and Lena always spoke in Welsh to each other, and their two boys had Welsh as their first language. Penny and her children were the only English. Very often she felt the foreigner in her own house. And when her in-laws came to stay it was even worse! But the more she heard, the more she found that she was beginning to follow what was said, although she often got it wrong. But she never attempted to speak it herself, other than the odd words which Gareth had taught her.

CHAPTER TWENTY-TWO
1960

The house was certainly crowded, and as weeks went into months, Penny began to feel the strain. There was no sign of her brother and sister-in-law looking for a house. Gareth, too seemed to be finding it too much, and Penny asked him several times to prompt them into finding a home. His parents, who were going to put up the deposit as they had for themselves, seemed to think it a fine arrangement for them all to live together for a while. "Well I don't know what we would do if there were any more of us," Penny announced one day. They were the famous last words!

They were coming to Christmas of 1960, and Gareth's parents were to stay. Fortunately Rhodri had gone home to North Wales. Penny was worried. She was pregnant! Gareth knew and she had told him to tell his family. "We can't possibly have another baby here in this situation," she told him. "They must find a house now!" But he wouldn't say anything. In fact each time they had had a baby, his mother had lectured them about having so many, as if it was a crime. The baby was due the end of June, and that only meant six months for them to get organised.

Christmas came and went, then New Year, and Gareth's parents returned home, and nothing had been said. Jim and

Lena did not know of Penny's condition. Penny always remained small when pregnant, so they hadn't seemed to notice. But Penny was not as well as usual. The pressure of the baby was giving her trouble with the veins in her legs and groin. And all the time she was worrying as to where they would put another baby.

Gareth's parents made another visit in early February. Penny approached her mother-in-law. "When do you think Jim and Lena should buy a house?"

"Well there's no hurry is there. They can save while they're here." Now for it, thought Penny.

"Well not really, we're having a baby early summer." So it was said.

The mother was shocked. "In the summer, well you haven't said. Does it make any difference then?" Penny was almost in tears.

"Yes it does, we need the room." Jim and Lena couldn't believe the news, and wondered how they hadn't noticed.

However, by Easter, Gareth had seen a house he thought would suit them, and they soon moved in,

They got their own house back to normal. But Penny was in a lot of discomfort with the vein trouble. The only relief was to lie with her legs higher than her head. But how could she rest with so much to do. It was a great disappointment for her, as she had always enjoyed pregnancy. She once said, "I love making babies, having them, and looking after them!" But now she was suffering. The doctor could offer no help other than rest, which was impossible. He referred her to the hospital. Penny was loathe to go. She had a horror of needles, injections etc., and had always managed to bluff her way out of blood tests and such things at the local midwives' clinic.

She was also afraid of anyone investigating her heart condition. But she did go to the hospital, hoping they might ease her discomfort.

She was given the whole works, so it meant a blood test, which nearly made her go into a faint, and they sounded her heart out, and asked what she knew of her condition. They really could not help the baby pressure on the veins, echoing her doctor's advice to rest, which she knew she couldn't. And they also recommended she come in for the birth rather than a home delivery. But Penny was adamant that she would not. So, all in all, she gained nothing. How could she rest with all the work of the family and home? So she weathered the remaining time.

The baby was born on the hottest day of the year, and arrived shortly before midnight. It was not such an easy birth as the previous ones, and the baby girl was heavier than the others. They called her Georgina Mair. Mair after Gareth's spinster cousin.

"I think she will be the last one," Penny told Gareth as she sat nursing her. "I guess three girls and two boys is a good score." Lavinia had come to stay once more to help out, but Penny was soon taking over.

Daily life went on as usual. The three eldest children attended school, and Penny found it very pleasant to have Jacqueline and the new baby on their own for a few hours. But there was still so much work to do each day. Apart from the time when Gareth returned from school until he left again for evening classes, Penny had to manage alone. At least he could entertain the children or hold the baby awhile for her to get an evening meal. But weekends she hardly saw him. She thought it a waste of time when they could have been together as a family. But she knew he worked hard with two jobs. How she wished she could help out.

Sitting once again feeding her baby, she thought over her life as she had done so often before. She had done nothing except have babies. That was her whole achievement, and she was now twenty-six. She had no intention of having any more. Her veins were still playing up after the last one. Another year or so and Jacqueline would be going to school. Maybe Penny would be able to undertake some job a bit later when Georgina was a little older. It would have to be something that gave school holidays, so as to be home with the family. Well, what could she do? Lena was working in a school canteen. A possibility.

But Penny knew that what she was yearning for was to be teaching as had always been her intention. And she did want to teach P.E. Her thoughts went back to those days at school. She had loved school. Yes, she should have stayed on and pursued her ambition. But then she might not have married Gareth. Gareth! Oh, how she loved him, despite all his faults. She wouldn't have had the children. The children who were her whole life. No she wouldn't have changed all that. But it would have probably been better to have got a qualification. She had nothing to her name. What could she offer?

She lifted the baby from her breast, and burped her before placing her the other side. Her thoughts were now racing. Why not do it now. Did it matter that she was married with a family? She still had years to offer to a profession. If there was a college near enough to attend daily, she would not have to go away. She thought there must be. But first she would have to gain entrance. As a mature student, she needed a basic five passes on her certificate, and two had to be English Language and Maths. Well she had the Maths. She could easily sit the English again. She never did know how she came to fail it. That and Literature were her best subjects. She would sit the two again.

That night in bed she told Gareth of her plans for sitting the two exams. She did not elaborate on why she needed them. "I just want to achieve something," she told him. "Bring some old papers from school for me to look at, and get the list of set literature for this year, then I can read up on it"

"And when will you have time to read?" he asked her.

"Well, the only time I sit awhile is when I'm feeding Georgina. I'll do it then," she told him.

And so began a time of intense reading and feeding sessions. When she could make extra time, usually when all were in bed, she would set about written answers, as a practice, from the old paper. Gareth took some of her work to the English teacher at his evening class centre, and usually she received a good mark or a helpful criticism back.

The following summer, Penny attended an outside examination centre in the city to sit two English papers. Delphine looked after the two youngest girls while she went there. The other children were at school. Penny felt a great sense of satisfaction coming home from the last exam. Now she had to wait a couple of months for the results.

It was the summer holiday of 1962. As usual the family had gone to Gareth's home in Wales. Penny was anxious to get back as the exam results would be due. Arriving home to a pile of letters, she scrambled through them, and found what she was looking for. It was there, and her fingers trembled as she ripped open the envelope and pulled out the sheet. She hardly dare look, and when she did, there it was, a pass in both subjects. Penny now had the five required for College entrance. She was on her way! She screamed with delight, and rushed to

Gareth, throwing her arms around him. “I’ve passed,” she gasped, and was kissing him long and hard.

“Well done Penny. You deserve to pass.” That night in bed she told him of her plans to try and get into College.

“And how do you think you’ll manage that with all that you have to do?”

“I’ll manage it all right,” she answered him, “and then when I start teaching, we will have money for lovely holidays, a car, new furniture, alterations to the house, more things for the children, and you won’t have to do evening classes, and we’ll have lots more time together,” she rambled on.

Gareth was cuddling her and fondling her and finally silenced her by kissing her. “Penny you’re wonderful, and I love you so much. I don’t know why I spend so much time without you. I’m so lucky to have you Penny, and I know you gave up a lot for me. All these years I’ve had you when you should have been out free and easy and enjoying yourself. And I’ve been such a heel at times. No one else would have put up with me.”

“But I love you Gareth. I only want to be with you,” and she melted into his love-making. Teasingly, she added, “I’d better not get pregnant again, or I’ll never get to college.”

But she lovingly succumbed to the moment.

CHAPTER TWENTY-THREE
1965

Early in the year, Penny's doctor referred her to the Gynaecologist because of the discomfort she was still experiencing with the veins in her legs and her severe backache. The only relief was rest, and that was not possible.

It was ascertained that she had a severe prolapse of the womb, causing pressure on the main arteries to the legs and also the pain in the back. The specialist discussed with her the best course of action. "You are twenty-eight and I should give you a repair job, but looking at your record, you are just as likely to go and get pregnant again, and then you will be back to square one. And even if I give you a repair now, you will almost certainly be back for a hysterectomy at forty. The alternative is to have the hysterectomy now. Of course there will be no more babies, but although you are still young, you have a sizeable family. The decision is yours."

Penny was taken aback. No more babies. Well she didn't really want any more, but to know she couldn't seemed another matter. But he said she would have to have it done by forty anyway. She just could not decide. "I'll think it over and discuss it with my husband," she answered.

"Yes, don't rush into it. But I guarantee you will be back later on if you don't have it now. I know you are young, but you will probably recover quicker now than later. Let me know when you and your husband have made up your minds. There is a waiting list, so the sooner you decide the better."

Penny felt rather numb returning home on the bus. Delphine had looked after Georgina for her. The other children were all at school now. Discussing it with her sister-in-law, Penny virtually decided that she couldn't possibly have such a drastic operation. And when Gareth came home from school, she was still leaning that way. But standing cooking the evening meal, and as usual experiencing the sickening pain in her legs and back, she began to have second thoughts. She knew that they should not have any more children. But Penny always got longings in her body for a baby, and sure enough, when she was so inclined, whatever they did she would find herself pregnant. And she was making plans for maybe getting to college, or doing some kind of job to help out with expense. So, maybe she would go for the big op.

That night in bed, snuggling up to Gareth, she gave her views. He, too, thought maybe it would be the right decision. But he wondered how she would get through the operation and cope with the recovery. "There will be no lifting or strenuous work for at least six weeks after," Penny told him. But what she was already worrying about, were the injections, needles, blood tests and everything involved with an operation. And what about her heart. Would that be a problem? But, between them they decided to go for it. "Just think," she told Gareth, "we will be able to make love any time, any day or all day, and I won't get pregnant. That's settled it, I'll ring the hospital tomorrow."

Weeks went into months, and there was no word from the hospital. Penny had hoped that it would all be over by Easter, so that Gareth would be at home during the school holidays to help out with the children. Lavinia had promised to stay. But Easter came and went, and summer was looming. Penny began to worry. She had a feeling she might be pregnant. How, she did not know, as they had been extra careful, knowing that this was the last short time before the op. But the weeks went on, and it became more definite, and already the discomfort in Penny's legs was becoming more acute. Why, oh why, had they not sent for her by now.

She went to the doctor, and he was furious with her. "You should have been more careful, girl. They won't do the operation now."

"We were careful" she told him, "but when my body wants a baby, I always get one. If they had sent for me sooner, it wouldn't have happened. Anyhow, I'm not going through with it. I'm in agony already. I'll never make nine months this time."

Her doctor took her words as a threat that she was contemplating taking things into her own hands, and said he would consult with the specialist. The outcome was that two doctors had to assess her state of mental health, and recommend that the operation take place. Penny was advised to see a psychiatrist privately, to save time, and proceed from there.

As Penny made her way to the 'Millionaires Row' of houses where she had an appointment with the chosen doctor, she thought over what she would say. Was she supposed to act mental? She felt she couldn't do that. The door opened, and she was shown into a very sumptuous lounge and then into the consulting room. A tall, distinguished, middle-aged man sat at the desk, and he motioned her to sit down. Well, thank goodness she wasn't made to stretch out on the bed like they always did in the films.

He smiled at her, and took the letter she had brought

from her own doctor. After reading it, he smiled again. "Well, Mrs Jenkins ... Penelope ... you've got yourself in a bit of a fix. Five children and possibly number six on the way, and waiting for a hysterectomy. Just tell me how you feel about it all please."

And Penny talked. Out poured her story, from when she first married at seventeen and six days, of Gareth, of her babies, of how she loved her babies and having them, but of the disappointment at the discomfort of the last pregnancy, of how she felt this was going to be even worse, and how she and Gareth had decided on the operation for her health, and now this had happened. It all came out, and the man just listened to her tale.

When she finished he just said "And?"

She stared at him and continued. "I suppose now I am supposed to get hysterical and threaten that I intend to do something dreadful to myself or the baby. But I can't say that. In fact, in spite of all the discomfort, I will love the baby if it comes. But I don't think it would be fair to all of us."

He studied her, and then came round to her side of the desk, sitting back against it in front of her. "No ... Penny ... I think that's what you're known as. No, you don't have to say that. Enough is enough, and you have come to know that your body has now had enough. You seem to have a happy marriage and family. Enjoy them and don't ever blame yourself for what you are about to do." He put out his hand to help her from the chair, and led her to the door. "I shall recommend the termination and hysterectomy right away. My secretary will see you out. You may like to settle the account first. Good day Mrs Jenkins, and good luck."

Penny was called to the hospital within a week. She got the impression it was all very hush, hush, as to what was to be done to her. She was the youngest in the ward. There was a lot of consultation about her heart condition and for one dreadful moment she thought they were going to refuse to do the operation. Penny kept emphasising how she had led a normal life, been very active and had five home confinements without any trouble. She suffered all the needles, injections and blood tests. She noticed the other patients seemed to have various tubes in or out of their bodies, with an assortment of drips and bags, and was dreading what she would find about herself when she came round from the anaesthetic, but she could not back out now.

Having had the pre-med injection, she was the first one to be taken to the operating theatre. Waiting in the anteroom, she felt quite calm. Then the anaesthetist came to her and read her notes.

"You've come to us a bit early, haven't you!" the woman stated. Penny glanced up at the clock. It was ten to nine.

"Have I?" she answered. "What time was I supposed to be here." The woman laughed. "I didn't mean the time. You're only twenty-eight. Most of them are at least forty with your operation." Then Penny felt something in the back of her hand, and there was no more.

Coming back to her senses again, she found she was back in bed in the ward. A nurse was talking to her, and offering her a drink. She was immediately sick, and relieved when they said they would let her sleep. She hurt inside a lot, and she began to move her hand slowly about her body. She felt no tubes, thank goodness, and then lapsed into sleep. Next time she opened her eyes, Gareth was sitting beside her.

He kissed her, and showed her the flowers he had brought, and there were sweets from the children, and they had all written on a card for her, all except Georgina, of course.

"Your Mum's got them all in order," he told her.

"Well I'm getting out of here as soon as I can," she told him. "Thank goodness I haven't got any tubes or bags. I just hope they leave me alone to get better my way."

Then her eyes clouded over. "I wonder what the baby was Gareth."

"Don't think about it, Cariad. Well it won't happen again." Penny cried a little, and then drifted off to sleep. When she next woke, it was dark, Gareth was gone, and a nurse was giving her an injection.

Penny managed to get herself discharged in under two weeks instead of the obligatory two and a half, promising to lay up at home and take things easy. But of course she couldn't, but managed to get through the following six weeks and be given a clean bill of health at her check-up. Fortunately it was the long summer school break, so Gareth was home to help, and he did help with the children. Lavinia also stayed on for a while, and then Gareth's parents arrived. By the time everyone was back at school, Penny felt she was fit and well. Now to pursue her plans.

CHAPTER TWENTY-FOUR

Everyone was settled back in school after the summer break. Penny had recovered from her operation, and now felt her legs and back were no undue problem. She only had Georgina at home now, with the others at school, and she found it very pleasant to have just one to concentrate on for a few hours. And it also gave her time to think over what she could do about making a career for herself.

She was beginning to feel unfulfilled. They had plenty of friends calling, and often held parties. It was easier for them to host them as they were the ones with all the children, which made going to others for an evening or a party rather difficult. But Penny felt inadequate amongst such gatherings. What could she offer to the conversation? All she had to discuss were the children, and lots of these friends didn't even have a family yet. She began to dwell on it, and felt that even Gareth only saw her as a sex object and someone to run the home. He still spent all his spare time away from her, and she was quarrelling with him far too much.

She enquired about any Teacher Training Colleges within daily travelling distance, and in fact discovered that there was a Ladies college within four miles. It would entail a two-bus journey. They had just acquired their first car. Gareth's uncle had died, and his mother kindly bought his old car for them. It was a wonderful step up, but of course Penny didn't drive. Maybe one day she thought! To Penny's delight she discovered that the college ran a specialist P.E. course. It couldn't be better. She wrote to the Principal asking if she might call and have a chat to discuss whether it was worth her applying, although she knew it to be too late for that year's entrance. She was given an appointment, stressing that the present year's places were full.

Penny hadn't told Gareth about it, and she asked Delphine to look after Georgina for her, while she went to the college. She was so excited as she passed through the gates, and felt a whole new life was opening up for her. But her discussion proved rather disappointing. She related all her background, and emphasised that her plans had always been to teach, and stressed how well she had done at school in the field of P.E, but that marriage and motherhood had made her defer her plans.

The Principal asked how many children she had, and Penny lied, saying four. But then she was deflated, when the woman told her, "I've taken on young mothers before. You think you can manage, but then one or other of the family fall ill and you can't continue, or another baby comes along. And Mrs Jenkins, you have four! I'm afraid you are too much of a risk. And there is a lot of studying and written work and exams."

Penny tried to put her case by telling her how she had taken and passed the two English exams in her own time and that she could not have any more children, but the Principal told her to wait a few years and then try. She was sorry. Penny turned to leave feeling thoroughly dejected, but then she rounded and said as a last gesture. "If I can show that I can hold a job down for a whole year without too much disruption, would you please consider me then?"

"If you can prove that, Mrs Jenkins, then, yes, I will," and the door was closed behind her.

Penny felt very depressed as she sat on the return bus, but then pulled herself together, and determined that she would find a job for the coming year. Doing what, she did not know. It would have to be something with hours to fit in with the family schooling, and the holiday breaks too. That night she told Gareth where she had been, and of the outcome. He was not pleased.

"You are crazy Penny. Three years at college. You'll never do it. And you needn't think I'm holding the fort for you to go out to work. The only school job you could get would be in the kitchen, and I'm not having you do that. So you can just forget it." But she didn't.

She began to study the job vacancies in the local paper. There were nearly always ones for school canteens, but she disregarded these. Then an advert took her notice, appearing several weeks running, implying that no one either applied or got appointed. It was for a Grammar School just a short bus ride away. In fact en-route to where Gareth now taught. This would be the same Lab Assistant job that he used to do when they first met at Penny's school. She began to ask him what he used to have to do.

"Mainly setting up apparatus and keeping everything clean, maybe mixing chemicals," he explained.

"Do you think I could do it" she asked him. "Probably," he told her, "once you had been shown what to do the first time."

Penny thought it over. Well, she had worked in the laboratory at the Pharmaceutical factory when they first got married, and she had had to deal with the apparatus and chemicals there. So she made up her mind to apply. "Maybe it will be in the Biology Lab, and I'll have to look after rabbits and things, that would be nice!"

The application form arrived by return of post, and after filling it in and posting it back immediately, Penny was given an interview. The vacancy was in the Physics Lab. Penny had given up Physics at school as soon as she could because she could never get the hang of it. So she was disappointed, but they were obviously very desperate to appoint someone, and she stressed that she had previously worked in a laboratory and knew how to maintain apparatus, and was offered the job to start as soon as possible.

She travelled home on Cloud Nine, and couldn't wait to tell Gareth. But first she stopped off at a day nursery where she was hoping to enrol Georgina for the hours she would be in work. She knew someone who had sent her child there, and had given the place a good report. It was agreed that she could start Georgina the following Monday, and then she informed the school that she would be available to start work that day also

Gareth congratulated her on getting the job. "Well, I don't think they had much choice," she retorted. "I guess it was me or no one. The man I will be working for seems very nice," she said. "The nursery seems good. I think Georgina will like it there. You can drop her off first, then me, and you should be at your school in good time. Then by the time you leave and pick me up, I should have cleared up after the last lessons, and then we can get Georgina. And the other children will have just got home. So it should work out okay. I've worked it all out."

"Well if it doesn't work out, you will just have to give it up. We're not that desperate," Gareth answered her.

Penny was both excited and nervous all the weekend. She had taken Georgina to see the nursery on the last two days of the previous weekend, and spent an hour with her and then both came home. But she had not left her before.

Monday arrived, and it certainly was a mad rush getting everyone ready, the children off to school, and finally herself, Gareth and Georgina sorted out to set off in the car. She hurried into the nursery, and settled Georgina with the others and left. Gareth was hurrying her up, and she was feeling a lump in her throat as she waved the little mite goodbye.

Penny enjoyed her day at the school. She spent most of it clearing out and tidying up the many cupboards of apparatus. There were two laboratories situated on the top floor of the modern building, and she had a little room situated between the two of them, where she spent her time if a lesson was in progress, unless she was called in to help. A storeroom led off this centre room, and contained chemicals and other apparatus. It was similar to the one at her own school, where she and Gareth had snatched illicit cuddles. She tingled just remembering.

These laboratories looked out onto the school playing fields, and she could see the boys playing football and the girls playing netball. Her thoughts now drifted back to Matt on the football pitch and herself on the netball court. Yes, they had been happy times. She wondered what Matt was up to now. If he was married, and who had been the lucky girl. She hoped it wasn't that girl Susan. She was sure she had been the undoing of herself and Matt. Anyhow, what did she care now.

There was a kettle in the little room, and Penny decided to bring cups and supplies to make her own tea. It was quite a way to the staff room, and then it was a bit of a 'free for all'.

She asked the Physics master if he would like her to make tea for him, too, and he said that would be very welcome. As she finished her first day, he told her that the apparatus and cupboards were already showing a woman's touch, and looking very clean and tidy. Tomorrow they had an experiment to set up for the senior class, and he would show her how to do it.

All the children and staff had left, and Penny locked up the storeroom, took a last look around, and went to look out of the window above the stairway. She could see Gareth waiting in the car, so she hurried down, and across the corridor to the main door, and out into the car park. She jumped in the car and gave him a kiss. Running down the stairs and across the school had reminded her of her first real encounter with Gareth, when she had collided with him in the school hall. Why did she keep thinking back to those school days? It must be the situation she found herself in here.

"How did it go?" he asked her.

"Oh, good. I have a white coat, a lovely room to myself, and a storeroom with possibilities! Fancy coming up?" she teased him.

They hurried to collect Georgina, who rushed into Penny's arms when she entered the room. The staff said she had been good, but had not slept during nap-time. The children had just got home when they reached the house, and Penny set about getting a meal. She was telling Gareth about the apparatus, and what the experiment was they had to set up tomorrow. Gareth recognised it and explained what would be entailed.

"So you're going to be a physicist, are you Penny?"

"I don't think so," she answered. "I hated Physics at school. But I must say I was quite interested today. I even looked at some of the books."

Next morning she was up and ready early, and seemed more organised getting everyone else ready. Hurrying into the nursery with Georgina, she felt her hand tighten. She led her to where a group of little ones were playing with sand toys, and after getting her interested, left her to join Gareth in the car. As she left the building she heard crying. Was it Georgina? She hoped not.

Again Penny enjoyed her day, and Mr. Howell, the Physics master, complimented her on her assistance and said her tea was much nicer than that in the staff room. What Penny enjoyed was having a dinner prepared for her.

"I don't know why you complain about school dinners," she told Gareth later, "I thought it was lovely," and then she gabbled on about how the experiment had gone. "I thought it was interesting, but those sixth form boys looked pretty bored, and kept whispering and laughing."

"Perhaps you were the distraction Penny. I know what I would have been looking at!" Gareth remarked. Penny hadn't thought of that. But she had reminisced while she had sat in her little room during the break time, that the boys reminded her of Matt. He would have been their age when they were last together. It was an exciting age. Strange, here she was in a reversal of roles, she the mature lab assistant and young innocent boys in the class. Those years before, she had been the young innocent in class, and Gareth had been the mature lab assistant. Well, she certainly wasn't getting involved with young boys.

It was her third day. Georgina was crying when she dressed her, and she didn't want to get in the car, and she pulled back when they walked towards the nursery. As they entered, she clung to Penny and wouldn't go with the lady. Penny didn't know what to do. "Don't worry, we always get this on the third day," the assistant told her. "You go, she'll be okay in no time."

But Penny was upset and felt she shouldn't leave her. Gareth was tooting outside, Georgina was crying as she was led away and Penny felt she was going to cry. She hurried outside to the car, but she felt she shouldn't. Gareth revved off. "Don't hang around Penny, I only just make it in time you know, after coming here and then dropping you off."

"But she's crying," Penny almost sobbed out. "She'll be okay now you've gone," he tried to reassure her. But Penny was not happy at work that day, and when they collected Georgina, she looked very forlorn and was very clinging when they got home.

Next morning was worse. Georgina cried and screamed through the whole getting ready process. Gareth was telling Penny to hurry up, and the little girl was hiding herself in Penny's skirt and sobbing bitterly. Penny knelt down and cuddled her child and was sobbing herself.

"I can't leave her there, I can't. She wants me."

"Well what are you going to do, Penny. I've got to get off," Gareth retorted.

"I can't go, Gareth. I should never have left her. It won't work." And mother and child clung to each other, crying profusely.

"I'll ring them up and say you're not well, Penny," and he hurried off.

Penny was upset all day, even though Georgina soon became her usual happy self when she realised she would not be taken to the nursery and parted from her mother. Penny was searching her conscience. How could she have done such a thing to her own child? Well, that was the end of her going out to work. It was too soon. But she had enjoyed the little she had done, and she had felt appreciated. Oh well, she would have to send a letter of resignation. That was a short-lived career! But first she would go out to telephone the school and explain, and also to the nursery.

The nursery told her not to be hasty. She needed to give the child a little longer to settle in. Try short periods first, and gradually build up to leaving her longer. They always settle in eventually. And the school was very sorry to hear of her reason, and said they had been very satisfied with her work, and would be happy to wait while she got her daughter settled, and that she could return to the job when she felt ready. How sweet of them, Penny thought. So perhaps she would try again.

Penny did try again, and took her time, gradually settling Georgina in to the Day Nursery, and when she was quite satisfied that it was not detrimental to her development, she informed the school that she was ready to resume work in the laboratory.

Mr. Howell welcomed her back with open arms. "Well, you weren't here long, but we've certainly missed you. Afraid some of the cupboards are untidy again, apparatus needs cleaning ... and I've missed your tea! The pupils have been asking where you were, and the sixth form boys said where was the pretty lady with the nice legs! So they'll be keen to turn up again."

Penny thought it very sweet of him, and she really was pleased to be back. Now to prove that she could hold down a job for almost a year. She would apply for college next year.

CHAPTER TWENTY-FIVE

The following months were very satisfying for Penny. She became more confident and felt appreciated for what she did and for who she was, other than being just a housewife, mother and wife. And the wage packet, small as it was, was a tremendous bonus, making the difference between their scrimping and just existing, to managing reasonably well. The added satisfaction was knowing that she was contributing. Gareth was paid monthly and by the time the mortgage and bills were paid, there was little left. But she was paid weekly, and each Friday the Council pay van brought her pay packet to the school, along with those of the canteen and domiciliary staff. So, with a few extra pounds for the week, they had something to manage on.

She loved the whole school atmosphere and realised just how much she missed her school days. They had been a very enjoyable episode of her life. She always felt sorry for young people who said they disliked school. When she had prepared all that was required for a lesson, and if she was not needed to assist, she would often take herself outside and feel almost drawn to the activities going on. She longed to join in the netball, and in fact she often did so during lunch break when the girls were practising. The P.E. teacher liked her company, and if she was called away, Penny would take over.

Other times she wandered over to watch the boys playing

football, and her thoughts would drift back ... back to….. She knew full well what or who this took her back to. Yes, she and Matt had been so well suited to one another. She wondered what he was doing now. She supposed he was married, well he would be about twenty-nine. She and he would never be the young couple in the Blue Lagoon. But they could have been. And oh how she wished they had been. She knew she loved Gareth, but Matt had been so very special to her, and always would be.

The headmaster told Penny to feel free to use the Staff Room at the school, and not to think she had to stay in her small room between the laboratories. She did wander in there at times, and some of the staff would chat to her. They were a large staff and most of them didn't seem to know what she did in the school when she wasn't in her white coat. She did feel with some, mainly the older women, that they thought she should not be in there, but the men chatted to her and appeared much friendlier. Penny reflected that, hopefully, in just over three year's time she would be of equal status to them all.

The one member of the staff who very rarely entered the staff room was the boys P.E. master. Penny had seen him from afar out on the sports field, but had never spoken to him. One day, she was late going to the dinner hall. Most of the staff had been and gone, and she was alone at a table.

"Mind if I join you?" a voice asked.

She looked up, and a tall track suited figure was placing his meal opposite her.

"No, that's fine," she answered.

There followed a period of silence. Penny felt awkward. "You're the new lab assistant, aren't you?" he said. "I've seen you about, and thought you were a P.E. student at first. Seen you on the field and courts," he continued.

"Yes, I'm in the Physics lab, but I'm hoping to get to college next year. And I do want to teach P.E." Penny answered him.

"Well, I'm Nick, Nick Masters. What's your name?"

"Penny," she replied, "Penny Jenkins."

"Pleased to meet you Penny, and I see you're Mrs by the ring on your finger."

They continued with their meal, but Penny was looking at him. He seemed to remind her of someone. The soft curly brown hair, the shape of his eyes. He didn't seem so tall sitting there at the table. She was sure he reminded her of someone. But then when he spoke, he didn't. He had a northern accent .

"From Darlington," he told her, "and you're a Londoner, obviously. With a name like Jenkins you should be Welsh."

"Well, my husband is. But you're quite right. I haven't moved from North London, although we do go to Wales often."

He pushed his empty plate away. "Well I'm going to have half hour to myself on the trampoline. Have you seen the gymnasium, Penny? It's quite a showpiece."

Penny hadn't. She knew where it was situated and had been wanting to look in for a long while. She told him she hadn't. "Come along then. I'll show you around." He got up to leave, turned, and continued, "Go through the girls entrance and I'll meet you inside."

She finished her dessert - he hadn't had one – and she pondered what to do. She should go back to the lab, but Mr. Howell had said he did not require apparatus for the next two periods. She had intended tidying out the store cupboard, but it could wait. She would like to see the gym, but she was feeling uneasy inside. Who did he remind her of?

Penny went to the gym. She pushed open the girl's changing room door. There was no one in there. There was another door inside which she assumed led to the teacher's room. She knocked but there was no answer. She tried the handle; it was locked. She must be in the staff room she thought. Further on was a second door, which Penny assumed opened into the gymnasium, and she could hear a slight repetitive sound coming from within. She quietly pushed open the door. The gym looked huge. Wall bars along both sides, ropes tied up across the centre, a badminton net made ready across one section, and several pieces of gymnastic equipment standing by a store section. And set up at the end nearest to her was a trampoline, on which Mr. Masters ... Nick ... was bouncing. Hence the repetitive noise.

He had heard the door open, and seen Penny looking inside. He stopped re-bounding and called "Hi! Come in and have a look around." She felt awkward, almost shy. She had expected some of the pupils to be in there.

"Sorry, I'm interrupting you," she answered, and turned to go.

"Don't go," he called, and sat on the edge of the tramp. "Have you ever trampolined, Penny?"

"No, never. We didn't have such a thing at school. But it looks lovely. Is it difficult?" she asked.

"I'll show you," was his answer, "Take a seat on a bench. See if you want to try one day."

Penny sat and watched enthusiastically. She studied him closely. He wore tight gymnastic trousers with shoulder straps. He re-bounded, reminding her of the spring board action at the swimming pool diving boards, his arms extended above his head, hands and fingers pointing. As he elevated, his toes stretched together. She studied the line of his body, and then he was curling and somersaulting and … suddenly pangs of memories shot through her body. She was back at the poolside, gazing at a boy performing his beautiful dives, admiring him, loving him. Matt! Matt! Of course! Now she knew of whom Mr. Masters reminded her. If he wasn't so tall, he could well have been Matt. She pulled herself back from her thoughts. Nick was now performing front and back drops, but Penny was feeling very disturbed. Why should she feel like that!

The young man had now stopped and was alighting from the trampoline. "Gives you a strange sensation in your feet if you get off too quick," he told her. She could see the beads of perspiration on his rippling body.

"Would you like to try one day?" he asked her.

"Oh, I couldn't. But it did look exciting," she timidly answered.

"Have a go. Bring something suitable to wear some lunch time when I don't have a training session, or if I have a free period and the girls aren't in, you could come along then if you're not needed in the lab."

Penny thanked him. "I'll think about it," she told him.

"Well you're bound to have to do it at college. I'll give you a 'How to trampoline booklet," he continued. "I've got one in my little room. Follow me."

He led the way through the second door, into the boy's changing room, and unlocked his own teachers' room. "Come on in. It's a bit untidy," and he motioned her inside. She felt she shouldn't be there, but he seemed unconcerned. There was a table and chair, some drawers, several wall hooks on which were clothing articles. Penny noticed a whistle and coloured team bans. She saw a tennis racquet in a corner, there were various trainers and football boots lying around. There was a small sink and mirror, a locker, and then a curtain, which she assumed housed a shower cubicle.

He was rummaging in a drawer, and then pulled out the small booklet for which he was searching. "Here it is. Keep it as long as you want. Now I must shower before the boys arrive for lesson."

Penny turned to leave. "Yes, I must hurry back too. Thanks for the demonstration."

"You'd better go out of the girls way," he called, turning to switch on the shower, and lowering his shoulder straps and then closing his door after her. "See you." Did you say you're in the Physics lab?" he called.

She hurried away, calling 'yes' over her shoulder.

"I must come up there sometime and see what you get up to," were his last words as the door finally closed.

Penny hurried back up the two flights of stairs to the laboratory on the top floor. The bell was sounding for the afternoon session. She entered the lab. Mr Howell was already in there. "Oh, there you are Penny. What happened to the tea lunch time?"

She had forgotten that she always had a cup of tea ready for him before the session started. "Oh, I'm sorry, Mr Howell, I got talking to one of the staff. I didn't realise it was so late."

"Never mind, I'll enjoy the next one even more," and he smiled, paternally, Penny thought.

Then, he added. "You know, my wife says she's fed up with me saying that she doesn't make the tea as nice as Mrs Jenkins."

Penny looked alarmed. "It's okay, she won't divorce me over it. And I'll forgive you this time." As Penny entered her little room, the class was filing in for the lesson.

Penny was disturbed. She felt strange and unsettled. And why was she seeing all these pictures of herself and Matt. She was remembering the swimming pool, the cinema back row, the lunch hour dancing, hand in hand in the park, and the party with the two of them on her brother's bed. And she was thinking, if only! Why did it still come to haunt her so? She thought she had got over all that. And then she was thinking of Mr. Masters ... Nick ... on the trampoline. He certainly was a taller version of Matt. She wondered how old he was, possibly older, thirty, thirty-one maybe.

Next thing she knew the bell was sounding for break. She had done nothing! And she hadn't made the tea! She rushed to put the kettle on. Luckily she heard Mr. Howell chatting to some boys after the lesson, and when he came in his tea was ready. She caught up on the work during the last session.

Everyone had left. Penny knew Gareth would be collecting her soon. She finished clearing up and then stood at the top of the stairs where she had a clear view of the car park. As she did so, she saw a track suited figure leading some boys to the gate, where they all set off, presumably on a road run. She felt her tummy jump, and then she saw Gareth turning the car in. She bounded down, and out of the building. As she opened the car door she felt an awful guilty feeling. And then a surge of love. She lent over and kissed him.

"What's that for?" he asked, looking very surprised.

"Because I love you," she answered. That night she made advances to Gareth, and pushed other images from her mind.

Afterwards, he told her, "I don't know why I spend so much time away from you. You're the best thing that could ever happen to anyone, and I do love you Penny."

CHAPTER EIGHT

The arrangements for Penny working, and Georgina attending the nursery, and the older children at school, were working well. They all had to be very organised. Penny, obviously, had to be extra-organised to still get done all the work involved with a home. But by giving every minute of her time, she seemed to achieve it. Yes, it was hard work, but she believed it was worthwhile, and not just for the extra money it was giving them. She had gained confidence, she enjoyed conversing with people, was more competent and she could see her ambition of getting to college drawing nearer to fruition.

The week after the trampoline episode, Penny sorted out a pair of shorts and a simple top, which she thought would be suitable to wear on the trampoline. She was still doubtful as to whether she wanted to, or if she should take up Nick's offer. Well, she would keep the gear at school, just in case. She already kept her plimsolls and socks there for the occasional game of netball.

That lunchtime, Penny was in the dining room early. Hardly had she sat down before she saw Nick coming her way to sit beside her. They acknowledged one another and Penny felt her face flush. "There's no one in the gym this lunch hour. Do you want to come on the tramp?" he asked her. She deliberated a while, feeling she was wrestling more with her conscience than her wishes. "Well, I just have to put out some apparatus, but it will only take a few minutes. I could come down after," was her answer.

So they arranged to meet, and she left her dessert and hurried back up to the lab. She had soon done the job, put everything ready for the tea, and grabbing her shorts and top, was crossing the hallway to the gymnasium.

Nick was already performing on the tramp when she entered after having changed in the girls' room. He stopped and alighted, looking at her.

"You look nice," he told her.

"Is this OK?" she asked him.

"Yes fine. Come on, I'll help you up." Before Penny could heave herself up, he came behind her, put his hands on her waist, and easily lifted her up. Then joining her, he held out his hands, to take hers, positioning themselves near the centre, and proceeded to rebound. At one point Penny seemed to lose the rhythm, and felt she was falling forward. He quickly moved his hand to her shoulder to steady her. The rhythm was broken, and they stopped, but he still had his hand on her shoulder, and his other hand on hers. Penny felt a shiver go through her body. He dropped his hold, and jumped to the floor.

"Well done. Now try alone," he told her. Penny wasn't sure that she could continue, but continue she did, and under his vcry cxpert coaching she knew she was progressing. By the time half an hour had passed, she was doing seat and knee drops. They weren't perfect, but she had a tremendous sense of achievement, finally collapsing onto the trampoline after a bad landing. She lay there panting, and then had a fit of giggling.

"Oh, that was super," she gasped out. He held out his hand to her as she scrambled to the side. She sat up, and this time he lifted her down. It seemed that he held her a moment.

"I need a shower after that, but I didn't think to bring a towel," she told him.

"I can let you have one," he offered, "come and get one from my room." She followed him inside. As he was sorting out a towel, they heard the outer door of the boys changing room open, and then footsteps. He pushed her into his shower cubicle, pulling the curtain after her. "Keep quiet," he whispered. It had happened so suddenly and quickly, that Penny had hardly grasped how she had ended up being hidden away in the shower cubicle. He seemed to have pushed the door to. There was a knock on the door and she heard him opening it. A boy's voice asked if they might have a football to play outside. He answered the boy in the affirmative, there was some scuffling sound as a ball was taken out of something, then the boy was saying "thank you, Sir," followed by running steps and the door closing.

He pulled back the curtain. "Sorry about that," he said, "but you know what these boys are like. Don't know what they might think to see us both alone in here."

Penny had hardly recovered from having been bundled into the shower. "Well I'm going now," and she grabbed the towel and pushed past him. But she turned. "Thanks for the lesson," she called back.

"It was a pleasure. Any time," she heard him answer. She showered quickly, dressed, and hurried back upstairs to her little room, quickly putting on the kettle and making the tea ready for when Mr. Howell came in. She would take the towel home to wash before she returned it. Mr. Howell came in. "You look flushed, Penny. Been playing netball with the girls, have you?" She paused before replying.

"Oh, yes."

He always called her Penny now, but in front of a class she was Mrs Jenkins. But Penny always called him Mr. Howell, out of respect. In fact, she didn't know what his Christian name was.

Penny felt elated the rest of the afternoon. She really had enjoyed the session on the trampoline, and she thought of how Nick had held and guided her through the movements. Then she remembered hiding in the shower, which was rather funny, and she giggled to herself. She still felt a sense of excitement when Gareth arrived to take her home. She just had to tell someone what she had done. "I went on the trampoline today," she blurted out as they drove to the nursery to collect Georgina.

"What on earth did you do that for?" was all he said.

"It was great. The P.E. master coached me," she continued, and then regretted she had said that. Gareth looked across at her.

"What, just you?" She noticed a searching look upon his face.

"No, there were a few of us," she lied.

"Well you watch out you don't break your neck. You're not sixteen now, you know!"

No, she wasn't sixteen, and she thought back to when she was. She had had some wonderful moments, innocent yes, but so wonderful. She was jolted out of her thoughts by Gareth stopping the car.

"Go on, then, Georgina will be looking for you. You look as if you're in a dream, Penny." She jumped out of the car and hurried into the nursery.

A couple of days later Penny was at lunch and Nick came in to join her. He asked when she was going to try trampolining again. Between them they worked out one or two mutually convenient times. She told him she had washed his towel and would return it to him. "I have it upstairs," she told him. "No hurry for it," he replied "I'll call up for it some time."

Gareth had told her he would be a little later collecting her that afternoon, something to do with exams. So Penny took her time clearing up, and began to sort out some things in the storeroom. All the children had left, and Mr. Howell had called out 'good-bye' and also left along with the majority of the staff. Penny thought she heard the cleaner coming into the lab, but in walked Nick.

"So this is where you hide out," he said, coming into her little room. She was surprised to see him, and said she was working on a bit later, as her husband would be delayed a while.

He looked around the room. "Quite cosy in here," he told her.

"Yes it is. I can make tea and coffee when I want, and a lot of time is my own."

"Well, let's have a cuppa then, Penny, if you've got the time."

She put on the kettle, made the tea, and they chatted generally. He told her he was married, not long, just a couple of years. He couldn't believe that Penny had been married for eleven years. He got from her that she was twenty-eight. He was thirty-one, as she had rightly guessed. He had no family yet, and was stunned when she told him she had five children.

"You must have started young," was his comment.

"Yes, I sure did. But I don't regret it," she answered.

They finished the tea, and Penny said she had to get the equipment and chemicals back in the storeroom and lock up. He helped her carry some in, and then stayed in the storeroom a while looking at the various things on the shelves. They were both well inside, when Penny heard the cleaner coming from the laboratory. She suddenly thought of the image of her and Nick alone in the cupboard, and its implications, and remembering the two of them in Nick's room when he pushed her in the shower, she suddenly said, "Keep quiet," and quietly shut the door. Shutting the door automatically turned off the light. They were now plunged into darkness. Penny held her breath as she heard the cleaning lady sweeping out her little room. It seemed to take ages. Nick was completely silent.

The cleaner wasn't long, and they finally heard her cross into the second lab. "Thank goodness," Penny whispered, "sorry about that." She was now trying to find the light, when she felt Nick's hand also searching. But he was searching for her. His arm came around her waist, and he moved nearer. He was pulling her back to him. She dare not call out in case the cleaner heard, and she dare not pull away suddenly in case she crashed into the apparatus. She felt his breath upon her, and then his face was brushing hers, and then he was kissing her. Still she was afraid of all the equipment around her, but then she was relaxing and enjoying the kisses. For one moment, it was she and Gareth in the storeroom back in school, and she really was enjoying it. Coming to her senses, she did pull away, and was once more feeling for the light switch. She found it, and turned to look at Nick.

"Sorry, Penny, but I just had to." He moved towards her again, and this time she wanted him to kiss her. Breaking away, she told him it was just madness, and to be quiet while she opened the door to check the cleaner had gone.

She had gone, and Penny called him out, checked all was well in the store, and locked up. She was scrambling to clear up the tea things and trying to avoid looking at him. She was disturbed. Something had stirred inside her, and when she looked at him now, it was Matt she was thinking of. But he was Nick. And in the cupboard she was remembering her and Gareth. She was confused. What were these feelings? Suddenly she heard distant tooting. She ran to the top of the stairs and out of the window she saw Gareth getting out of the car and walking towards the building. He was coming in to look for her. She rushed back to her little room, and gathered up her things. As she grabbed her jacket and bag, she shouted out to Nick, "Get out, Gareth's coming up," and pushed him through the door into the second lab. She exited her room as Gareth entered the Physics Lab.

"Come on, Penny. What on earth are you doing? Georgina will think we're not coming."

"Well you said you would be late," Penny replied, trying hard to control her voice, although she almost felt she had a faint coming on, "so I've been doing some tidying up."

"Well now I'm up here, let's have a look around," he said. He wandered around the lab, and then into her little room. "Very nice and cosy, and clean and tidy, too, Penny. Congratulations." He looked at the door to the storeroom. "I bet that's the store cupboard. Remember us, Penny, years ago. Want to go in the cupboard, Penny?"

He pulled her towards him. "Not now, Gareth. I thought we were in a hurry."

"Yes we are, Cariad, but let's have a kiss anyway." Penny was flushed and still trying to fight off a faint. But she kissed him, and she felt so guilty. So very guilty. It must never happen again.

CHAPTER TWENTY-SEVEN
1964

The many months that Penny spent at the school, working as the lab assistant, was a time of great satisfaction. Beforehand, she had been going through a bad patch with Gareth, feeling unappreciated, unfulfilled, and often unloved, believing she was taken for granted. But the children had been her drive.

At the school, she was made to feel capable, appreciated, and as she found out, still attractive and desired. She knew she was treading on dangerous ground with Nick. Both determined their relationship would not go further. But their paths crossed so often, whether by accident or design Penny would not consider. But he had made her feel good again.

She now felt very much part of the school, and joined in many of the activities. She was popular with the pupils and the staff and was included in their lunch-hour chats, and she felt welcome in the staff room. She had pursued the trampolining for a short while, and had succumbed to an occasional kiss or embrace with Nick, but no way would she allow adultery to become part of her life. Yes, he had made her feel good, and she was grateful for that.

The first term finished with her very much on a high. She had played in the staff v school netball match, and proved her worth in her old team position of shooter. There had been plays and shows and parties and dances, and she had invites to them all, and put in an appearance when and where she could. Watching the young teenagers dancing together brought back so many memories. She felt she fitted into school regime so well, both as a schoolgirl and now as a member of staff.

They spent a good Christmas that year. Penny's wages had helped out with the present buying, and with the children getting older, although still making much work, things were less stressful. Gareth's parents came to stay for the festive season, and Jim, Lena and the boys joined them. And as they all saw in the New Year, Penny thought that this would be the one that would see her in College.

Back in work the second term, she thought it time to get her application form. The college where she had the chat with the principal that time, was not very far from the school in which she was working. Talking one lunch time with Nick, he offered to drive her there to collect an application form. He had encouraged her all along, and she was grateful to him for that.

"You'll make an excellent P.E. teacher, Penny, I know. Maybe you'll come back to us here."

She thought how she would like that. But first she had to get into college, and then survive three years. As they set off in his car, little did she suspect the disappointment that lay ahead.

They drove the short journey and passed through the large gates. "Just drive to the Admin block," she said, "and I'll run in for the form. I won't be long."

This she did, and knocking on the door, waited to be called inside. She explained to the secretary that she wanted an application form for next year, and this was sorted out.

Thanking the lady, and turning to leave, she was called back.

"You do know that the college is being re-located next year don't you, Mrs Jenkins?"

Penny did not know. "Where is it going? Will it be far?" she asked.

"We have a lovely new site in Hampshire," was the answer.

"Hampshire!" Penny echoed, "but that's miles away."

"You'll read all about it in the prospectus," the woman continued.

Penny's heart sank. Hampshire! How on earth would she travel there each day? It was impossible, and no way could she go resident. So that was it, then. No point in putting in an application. She felt tears welling up in her eyes. Nick opened the door for her, and she flung the literature inside.

"What's up, Penny? Are they over subscribed already?"

But now she was crying, and could not speak. He put his arm around her, and pulled her close, but still she sobbed. She was so absorbed in her sorrow that she hardly noticed how he was fondling her, and then kissing her so forcefully that she couldn't breathe. Coming to her senses, she forced herself away.

"Well, I can't go there now. They're moving miles away, and I know that there isn't another one near enough for me to get to. It's all been for nothing, Nick, and you can just stop that!"

They drove off in silence. As they turned into the school, Nick said, "You can apply elsewhere. There are plenty of colleges."

"Not for me, there aren't. They're all too far away," and she jumped out of the car to make her way back into the building, but turned and called back, "thanks for the lift," then pushed through the door, dashed up the stairs to the sanctuary of her little room, putting on the kettle ready for Mr. Howell's cuppa. 'Guess I won't get further than a lab assistant,' she thought to herself. 'Oh well, could be worse'.

She was still feeling upset when Gareth called for her. She told him what had happened and then sat quiet.

"Well you don't have to go there Penny, apply somewhere else. Go where I went, that was quite easy to travel to."

"It's not a P.E. college," she shouted back.

"Penny, it doesn't really matter what it is. You get the same Teacher's Certificate at the end, and then you can offer what you want. I had to do drama there, but I've only taught Science at first and now only Maths, so go there. You'll probably enjoy the Drama course. Then when you get to a school they always want help with Sports."

"I'm not doing Drama," she emphasised. "I'll just always be Penny the lab assistant. So that's the end of that!"

The weeks went on with the usual routine. Penny had resigned herself to her present situation. One day at school lunch, she sat opposite an older, senior teacher. She had spoken often to him, finding him very friendly and he had discussed her future plans previously. It transpired that each Easter holiday break, he led a party of senior pupils for a hiking holiday to the Lake District. They stayed in Youth Hostels. Moving on to the next one every two nights. This meant that one day they hiked light, and then one day with the full pack. He took a large mixed party each year with about six staff.

There were a few weeks left of term before they were due to leave. Mr. Bennett, the man in charge, was saying one of the girls had to drop out, so there was a place to fill. He suddenly looked across at Penny. "Fancy coming to the Lake District, Penny. I've got one vacancy, and you'd be useful as extra staff. Have you ever been there?"

"No, never," she answered. "Well now's your chance. Ask your hubby if you can come. They are a good bunch coming. Nick Masters is my mainstay." Penny stated immediately that she couldn't possibly leave her family, but thanked him for asking her, and said it sounded lovely. "Well let me know by next week if you change your mind. I'll' keep it open for you," and he left the table.

His place was taken by Nick. "John just told me he's asked you to come on the school trip."

"John? Oh, Mr. Bennett. Yes, he did. Sounds lovely, but I couldn't possibly," was her reply. Nick went on to say he had gone last year and found it great. "Some of it's tough, but it's fun, too. We climb Helvellyn, you know. And we trek miles. You'd love it, Penny. You have to do a little job in the Youth Hostels, but in the evenings we play games or go to the pub for a drink. John has lots of walking boots and rucksacks and stuff for those who haven't got any. Ask your husband if you can come."

"You must be joking!" was her only comment.

But she did ask. She waited until they were in bed, cuddling, that night. "I got asked to go on the school trip this Easter. One of the older teachers asked me." She tried to sound blasé about it, but her heart was pounding as she came out with the words.

"Where are they going?" he asked.

"Oh, the Lake District. They go every year," she answered.

"The Lake District! On a day trip!" Gareth exclaimed.

"No, not a day trip. They stay in Youth Hostels. About ten days, I think," Penny continued.

"Ten days. How on earth do you think you can go for ten

days? What are the children supposed to do ... and me. You needn't think I'm looking after them while you're gallivanting in the Lake District. So you can forget that!" and he pulled away from their cuddle and turned his back to her.

Penny lay quiet a while, but then felt cross and continued talking. "I only said I was asked. I knew I couldn't possibly go, but it was nice to be asked all the same." She paused. Gareth didn't speak, so she carried on. "It sounds such a lot of fun, and quite strenuous, too. He said he needed another woman member of staff, and he gives you all the gear. I've never been to the Lake District. Have you Gareth?"

"Yes, and it always rains," he answered sourly. "It's even worse than Wales."

She paused again. "Well I've never been anywhere except Wales, and I don't get much holiday there. You're in the pub all day, and I'm left looking after the children. Next time you can go on your own!" She was now looking for a row, and she was cross with herself for starting it. She hated quarrelling ... it made her heart go haywire and she felt ill.

Gareth was silent, but he was thinking over her words. He knew she had never really been anywhere, and at times he felt guilty that he had taken her so young in her life, when she should have been doing exciting things and going places. He knew he had been selfish with her. She worked so hard, and really had no time to herself. But he thought she had been more satisfied since working at the school. He would be lost without her but she did deserve a break.

He turned around to face her. "I suppose I could take the children to Wales. Mam and Dad would be pleased to have them, and I can take them around. Wait until I ask them before you answer. Mind you, it's not my type of holiday. You'll be worn out."

Penny couldn't believe what he was saying. "You'd really let me go?" she asked.

"Why not. I trust you, Cariad," and he cuddled her once more, and felt her respond to his lovemaking.

It was all arranged for Gareth and the children to go to Wales for Easter, and Penny informed Mr. Bennett that she would go on the trip. He fitted her up with walking boots, a rucksack and waterproof anorak, and gave her a list of other requirements. "Practice walking in the boots as much as you can," he told her. She was getting very excited about it all, but each time she put the children to bed, she had second thoughts. How could she be away from them for ten days! But the time was drawing near, and all the arrangements were made now, and she felt it was too late to change her mind. And when Nick said to her one day after a trampoline session, "I'm glad you're coming on the trip, Penny. Should be fun," she suddenly felt worried. What had she gone and done!

CHAPTER TWENTY-EIGHT

Gareth took her to the main-line station in London where the party were to meet. She cried after saying goodbye to the children, and she felt an awful longing for Gareth, too, after they had all left her. He was driving straight on to Wales. Ross was on a Scout camp holiday and would then stay with Jim and Lena, so that was one less for Gareth to have to contend with.

The party assembled, and then boarded the train. They were a capable group of older pupils, so were given freedom on the train as to where they sat. But the staff were all together, and Penny was staff. Nick sat opposite her and they all chatted together. The journey was long, but interesting, both for the scenery and the conversation. Penny kept thinking of the children, but as the journey progressed, she began to think of what lay ahead.

She enjoyed the whole experience. Yes, a lot of it was hard work. They hiked many miles each day, and the alternate days with their full packs could be exhausting. But they had plenty of stops. Mr. Bennett knew every nook and cranny, and if there wasn't a café, he would knock at a house ... often remote ... and they would be offered drinks and snacks. The occupants knew him well and welcomed him and his party each year. They paid, of course.

The hostels were basic, but served their purpose. Usually they slept in large dormitories, but some had smaller rooms for smaller groups.

Penny enjoyed talking and listening to the gossip of the teenage girls. It reminded her so very much of her school days, and her friends. She hadn't seen Belinda and Joyce for a couple of years now. In fact she didn't know what had happened to Joyce. She had kept in touch with Belinda more, and she was married with two children at the last count. But she, too, had not heard from Joyce.

After a hard day's hike, it was good to relax following the evening meal. Sometimes they played cards or table tennis, or listened to music. Most hostels had a good supply of board games, and it all seemed innocent fun. And if there was a pub nearby, the staff might walk there for an evening drink. Generally it entailed a walk back to the hostel in total darkness, as the pubs were often in remote places.

One such evening, six of them were on the return walk. They had had a strenuous day and Penny's calves were really aching with all the climbing they had done. She, Nick and a second young master were walking together behind the other three. The fellow moved forward to catch the others up, wanting to ask something.

Penny and Nick walked together, but she felt she was lagging behind. It was all uphill, and she couldn't see the others ahead now in the dark. Nick asked if she was okay, and she said her calves ached, but there was nothing wrong. "Come on, I'll help you along," he said, and took her hand firmly. The gesture made Penny start. Walking on, she had the image of herself and Matt. They had always walked hand-in-hand, and how she had loved that. Gareth always made her hold his arm, and it wasn't the same. She was going to withdraw her hand, but she didn't. A little further, and Nick released her, but then put his arm around her waist which, although he was pushing her forward up the hill, was also pulling her nearer to himself.

Halfway up, they paused for a rest. "Let's take a breather. I don't know where the others are," he said. Penny now felt awkward, and wanted to go on, but he pulled her even closer, turned her around, and she felt her back against a tree. Then he was kissing her, and forcing himself against her. The image of her and Matt had gone, and she remembered when Gareth had her against a tree on her first trip to Wales, and he had tried to lift her skirt and force himself upon her. Nick was also struggling with her clothes, which brought her to her senses.

He was strong, but she managed to push him off. "Stop it. We agreed we weren't getting involved," she almost hissed at him.

"I know, Penny, I'm sorry, but I couldn't control myself. You don't know what it's been like being with you all day and evening, and trying not to touch you."

"Nick," she said, "you've been good for me these past months, and I've really valued your friendship. But that's it. It's not going any further. I should never have come on this trip and put us in such a situation. You're just missing your wife. Come on, let's catch the others up."

But the others were already in the Youth Hostel and when she and Nick entered, she thought they got funny looks. "My legs are aching like mad," she stated. "I'm going straight to bed." And she left them all without having the usual late-night cocoa and discussion on the following day's walk. As she lay in bed, she thought of Gareth and the children. She missed and loved them all. She needed Gareth.

The end of the holiday was in sight. Nick seemed to avoid walking with her. He joined the fast boys on the hikes, and she joined the fast girls. And in the evenings they kept within a group. The final day arrived and as they all clambered into the train for the return journey, Penny felt extra excited with the anticipation of the imminent reunion with her family. Once more she was seated opposite Nick. Everyone seemed to be dozing, but suddenly he leaned across to her and whispered,

"I'd like to buy you lunch on the train, Penny, and talk to you."

"No thanks, Nick. You can talk to me here." He looked around at the two who were left in their compartment. They appeared asleep. "I'm sorry I didn't walk with you Penny, but the temptation was too much. Sorry if I offended you."

"That's okay. We won't be in such a situation again," was her reply.

The train finally pulled into the London station, and as Penny alighted, she saw her girls running the length of the platform to greet her. Gareth and the boys waited at the barrier. It was a lovely welcome, and after kissing and cuddling the children, she turned to Gareth. How she loved him! She was sure of that. "We've all missed you, Cariad," he told her, "I don't think I can ever let you go off again."

"I don't intend to. I've had a good time, but it's far nicer to be back home," she said. As they all sat squashed in the car on the journey back home, she said, "Well, did you have a nice time in Wales with Dadda?"

Lynette answered first, "Yes, but it wasn't the same without you."

Then Jacqueline said quietly, "You won't go away again, will you, Mumma?"

"No, I won't. I missed you all too much. You're quite right, it's not the same without you and Dadda," and she squeezed Georgina closer as the tears ran down her face onto the little girl's hair. "I've got all I want at home."

CHAPTER TWENTY-NINE

There were only a few days left of the Easter break, and Penny set about enjoying them with her family. The children had come back from Wales very rich! As Penny knew from previous visits, it was tradition to give children a few pennies, or shillings, and sometimes pounds, when you visited friends and relatives in Wales. They had obviously done plenty of visiting with Gareth, as was shown by the amount of money each one brought back. They were very happy that Penny was going to take them out to see what they each wanted to buy.

She was pleased to know that they had behaved themselves without her. Well she was always told her children were well behaved, which was a credit to her. She put it down to the fact that with so many of them, it was not possible to spoil any one in particular. Consequently, they were all very capable and helpful to each other and herself. Of course, they had their little squabbles, but nothing terrible. And they seemed to appreciate the little they had, looking after their toys and possessions, and saving for any extras. Penny witnessed other children who had much more, but who didn't look after things or seem so satisfied.

The children were ready, and they set off for the shops. The boys would go off on their own to spend, and had soon left Penny and the girls. But this day was to prove a turning point in Penny's life. As they walked down the road, they met a young woman who was living further up the road. Penny had known her for some years. She used to live with her parents, then married a chap from Wales and moved away. But the marriage didn't last long, and she was now divorced and back with her parents. She was younger than Penny, about twenty-five.

They had not met since the divorce, and stopping to chat, Penny commiserated with her. Rosa said how she now had to re-build her life. "I'm going in for teaching," she said. "I've just been accepted at the local college for the next intake in September."

Penny told her that Gareth had gone there and how he had suggested she apply. "But they specialise in Drama, Art or Music, and I don't want to do any of those."

"Oh no. They also do one called Art of Movement ... it's like expressive dance, called Modern Dance by some. Anyhow, I applied for Art, but they are full, so they offered the Movement class, and I'm doing that. It's not really for me, but we all end up with the same Teacher's Certificate. Why don't you apply Penny? They are still interviewing."

Penny was indeed thinking. Dance, she loved dancing and it must be a physical course, something like gymnastics, she imagined. "Thanks Rosa, perhaps I will. I so want to teach P.E. Sounds similar."

But Rosa warned her, "Don't mention P.E., Gymnastics or such things. The old girl who runs the course is quite mad and dramatic. She insists it is an ART, hence Art of Movement, and won't have it linked to P.E. So you have to appear all dramatic and expressive. Have a go Penny. It will be fun if we are both together."

Penny thanked her for the information and said she would think about it. And off she went on the shopping trip.

That evening she told Gareth of her meeting with Rosa, and all she had told her. "Well send for an application form. It's worth a try. You can't get more convenient than that, and it sounds like your kind of thing."

"Yes, I think I will," and she wrote a letter right away, ready to post next day. That night she was even more restless than usual. She felt this was it!

Penny soon received confirmation of an interview, and making her way to the college, she felt sick in her stomach. So much depended on this interview. She felt the two educational lecturers appeared satisfied with her. She was asked how many children she had, and lied by saying four. She made the point that she could not have any more children and could therefore give a good number of years to the profession, whereas the younger unmarried girls would be likely to interrupt a career by marrying and having a family. They agreed that there was now a tendency to appoint more mature settled students.

Penny felt the interview was going well, and when they asked about what she had done at school, she related her achievements in the sports and physical side, and of her wish to always teach P.E. And she suddenly realised she had put her foot in it. The elderly Art of Movement lecturer, of whom Rosa had warned her, then interrupted.

"If you think this is P.E. then you are entirely wrong." And she went on to expound on the artform of her subject. After what Penny felt was very much a dressing down, the woman became more passive and then spoke as if she was already including her in the group, which would be of about twelve students. As Penny left, she was told that she would hear shortly, by post, if she had been accepted.

She was so excited going home, and couldn't wait for Gareth to come home. And when he did, she couldn't stop talking. She told him about the dance studio they would be using, and of all they had told her was entailed. She would have to buy leotard and tights, and they had to have a tambourine, and then there were books on dance, plus all those for the rest of the course: psychology, health, education, etc. etc. "But," she said, "if I do get in, I will probably receive a grant. So that will help us." Then she flung herself at Gareth, put her arms around his neck. "Oh I hope I get in, Gareth. I must. Then just think, after three years I will be bringing home a good wage. Think of what we will be able to do."

"It won't be the end of the world if you don't get in, Cariad," and as they enjoyed a lingering kiss, two of the children started quarrelling, and, as usual, they were interrupted.

The following week a letter arrived offering her a place on the three year Teacher Training course, specialising in Art of Movement, commencing the end of September. She couldn't wait to tell them at the school that she had been successful.

However, the letter also said that she was to have a medical with the college doctor, and an appointment was enclosed. Well, that would just be a formality. Mr. Howell said he was very pleased for her, but would certainly miss her assistance .. and her tea.

She searched out Nick during the lunch break. He was playing cricket with some boys. Penny often joined in with the boys playing cricket. She would take a turn behind the wicket, likening it to her position of backstop in the rounders team at school. The boys were very impressed.

However this time she called Nick over to hear her news.

He congratulated her, and said he knew the P.E. lecturer at the college. "You will get some general work in that field, but there should be some coaching courses you can take. I'll tell him to look out for you, and point you in the right direction. I hope this won't be the end of us. We must keep in touch. I admire you Penny. I think if we both hadn't been married, we would have made a good couple."

"Yes, well, we are married. But we can still be friends. Anyhow, I shall bring the girls to your swimming club soon. So we're bound to see each other," she offered.

There were only a few weeks of the school term left. Penny almost felt she would be sorry to leave. The months spent there had been good for her, but of course what lay ahead was much more important. She really was on a 'high', and she didn't quarrel with Gareth about his always being out. Things were looking good these days.

But her elation was short lived. A week after her medical, a letter arrived from the doctor informing her that due to a heart disorder, and because her proposed course was a physical one, he was unable to recommend her as medically suitable.

Penny read it and re-read it. She could not believe that all her aspirations could be dashed by such a thing. She cried and felt desperate. Gareth could not console her, and he said he would telephone the school to say she was unwell. But she stopped him, and said she was going. Once at school she looked for Nick. He was in his little room. She showed him the Doctor's letter. She was not crying now, but felt angry ... angry at the system.

"Well, you've got more energy and drive than that P.E. woman here. You were up with the best walkers and climbers on that trip, Penny."

The bell went, and she dashed off. But that break she went into the office and telephoned the doctor, saying it was urgent to his secretary, and that she needed to speak to him. He did come to the phone, and she tried to control her voice, sounding competent and choosing her words carefully.

"I'm surprised that you thought me unfit to undertake the course. I am already working in a large secondary school, and there was no query at the medical I had for this appointment," she informed him.

This was quite true, as she did have to have a medical for the lab assistant post. But of course he did not know what job she had at the school, and she hoped he assumed it was some sort of unqualified sports work. She could not believe his reply.

"Oh, I did not know that you were already in school, Mrs Jenkins. Well if you were considered fit, perhaps I will alter my findings." She thanked him profusely. She couldn't believe that once again she had bluffed her way out of an awkward situation over her heart condition. College, here I come! she thought.

CHAPTER THIRTY
1964

Going to college was a wonderful experience for Penny. During the first week all the new entrants were made to sit a Maths and English test, and depending on the results, the students were allocated to their respective groups.

To her dismay, she was put in the top group of each. Penny was appalled how many of the young people who were coming straight from school, and who should have been used to tests and the form of things, had to go into a remedial for basic arithmetic and spelling the first term.

Alongside these general subjects there were lectures on History of Education, Psychology, Sociology, Art, Music, Health, General P.E., Religion, Speech, and of course her specialist subject of Art of Movement. She had the expense of buying books and equipment, but received a sizeable grant, which was paid at the start of each term. This was very useful, as they used it to pay off the large household bills.

It was certainly hard work, and there was a lot of home study and written work. She enjoyed the company of the various groups, even though the majority were obviously younger than herself, coming straight from school. But they included her, although she did not enter into the out-of-college social activities.

The Dance lectures were strenuous at times, but stimulating. Once Penny got out of thinking of it as P.E., as the lecturer stressed, she became very dedicated to it, and spent her time at home with the radio on, always searching for inspirational music suitable for Dance themes and choreography. And she enjoyed the performance work. She knew she had to obtain extra qualifications if she was going to be able to teach in a Secondary P.E. department, undertaking activities other than Dance. So she enrolled for any extra coaching course that was provided, often lunch times or late afternoons. She had made herself known to the P.E. lecturer there, as Nick had advised her, and in fact he had already put in a word. In this way she qualified to coach several games and activities, and in her final year went on an external residential gymnastics course.

The arrangements at home worked quite well. On the whole, the college hours were short, and Penny missed very little time through her domestic responsibilities. In fact, she thought some of the young, unattached girls skipped more lectures than she did. The grant she received certainly helped out with the financial pressure at home, and, all in all, she was feeling very self-satisfied.

During the first year, Rhodri informed them that he was going to move to a place of his own. He had been with them for ten years, as part of the family, and had never put a foot wrong. The children loved him, and they, and Penny and Gareth would certainly miss him. He was taking a flat nearer to the centre of London, where he spent most of his leisure time, visiting the Art Galleries, Museums and Theatres, which were his interests. He had formed a relationship with a young woman at his school, and obviously they desired a convenient place in which to spend time together. Sorry as the family were to see him go, it did mean one less for Penny to look after, and also an extra available bedroom. And with the family growing up, it was very useful.

Penny still saw Nick occasionally. Sometimes if she did not have lectures of an afternoon, she would visit the school for a chat with old friends. Nick was very interested in how her career was getting on, and always enquired after her activities. Penny knew she was 'treading on dangerous ground' with him, but managed to keep him at arm's length. She enjoyed the attention, but felt she could manage it without getting too involved.

Later, when the girls were a little older, she enrolled them in his swimming club, and a gymnastics club with which he was involved. They did very well there, and it obviously entailed more liaison between them. Very often he would call at the house. Penny felt that Gareth was a little hostile towards him, and, in fact, she recognised the faults in Nick. He was a terrible boaster, very full of himself, and could be quite aggravating at times. But he did seem genuinely interested in their family, although possibly he would not have been if Penny hadn't been there. But she could deal with that, and tried not to encourage him emotionally.

During the second year at college, she learned to drive, and passed her test at the first sitting. Not that she had a car of her own yet, but maybe when she had taught a while, and earned a good wage, she might be able to afford one. They had bought a newer car than the first one acquired after Gareth's uncle died, and Penny did drive it sometimes, but did not have the use of it for college.

However, during her final year, Nick called to see her one

college lunch hour. He told her he was buying a new car, and did she want to buy the old one as it was still in running order. It was a large car, and of not much value, but he wanted her to have it. Penny didn't think they could afford it, or that Gareth would be willing, but she said she would ask. She knew how useful it would be for her to have her own car, and that she would gain a lot of time each day, which she now spent travelling to and from college, and fetching and carrying the family. Gareth said no right away. A week or two later, Nick called at the house and told them that no one had been interested in buying the car, and rather than let it go for scrap, he would like Penny to have it.

"Tell you what," he said, "if it goes for a year, you can give me fifty pounds for it then."

Gareth still said they could not afford the running costs, and he certainly didn't want an old banger about the place. But Penny pestered and pestered over the next few days, and pointed out what she could gain, so he relented, and they became a two-car family.

The last Easter of the three year course, Penny enrolled for a week's residential gymnastics coaching course, to be held in Blackpool. She also had a final thesis to complete, and knew she would never get it done at home with all the children around. So, as the course took place in the daytime, she planned to do the written thesis work in the evenings. Gareth's parents were to stay and look after the family while she was away.

Unexpectedly, she was also invited to accompany the Lake District trip from the old school. A member of staff was unable to go at the last moment, and they hoped she could step in. At first Penny thought it out of the question, but then realised she could travel on from the Blackpool course, the short trip to the

Lake District, and meet up with the group. It was tempting. She had been under a lot of pressure that last year, and after this break she had the final exams and Dance performance. Gareth was not keen, but once more relented when she put her case. She was to meet up with the school group for only the last week of the trip. Nick would be going, as usual, and Penny hoped she would not be compromised, and determined that she would not be tempted – even if he had given her a car!

She enjoyed the gymnastics course, and each evening, when everyone else went out on the town, she was Cinderella left in the small hotel, working on her thesis. But she did get it completed. And the week with the school party in the Lake District was an enjoyable change, even though it was strenuous. And she also managed to keep Nick at bay, taking extra measures to ensure she was always with a group.

On her return, she had a wonderful reunion with the family, and promised them that next year when she had begun to teach, they would have a special holiday together.

Penny got through the final weeks, passing the written exams with average marks, but achieving good comments from the examiners for her Dance work. She was overjoyed to have survived the course, and it was now only left to have a college medical dismissal. She wasn't even bothered about that now. But she made one slip. Once more she was asked how many children she had, and answered five. "Oh, did you have a baby while you were here?" the Doctor asked.

"No, certainly not," she replied. He looked at his notes. "But it says here, on your admittance, you have four children," he told her. Penny had forgotten that she had lied. "Well it must have been a mistake," was her only comment.

Cuddling in bed that night, Gareth congratulated her on

staying the course. “I knew you would make it Penny. But I don’t know how you did it.”

“And now I have to get appointed to a school,” she stated, “and then we can start to get all the things we couldn’t afford before. We’ll start on the house. Thanks for helping me Gareth, and putting up with it all. I’m now an Art of Movement specialist. Like me to show you some,” she teased, cuddling closer.

CHAPTER THIRTY-ONE
1967

Penny served her probationary year in a large comprehensive school in a tough area of North London, teaching games and dance. And she stayed on there for a further year. There were three staff in the department, and she taught throughout the school, and contributed Dance performance work for the annual music festival. It was a new venture for the school, and was well received.

She was managing to run the home quite smoothely, as well as going to work, not that she ever had any time to relax. Gareth still undertook the evening class work for three or four evenings a week, and was still out most of the rest. Penny's salary certainly made a big difference to their financial position, and Gareth received promotion, which increased his income. They set about home improvements, and having lost Rhodri to do the decorating, Penny undertook the paper hanging. Gareth had told her that the women in Wales did it! She worked it out for herself, and improved throughout the years.

The children were older now, and Penny thought, easier to manage. There were always friends of one or other of them calling, and with the many friends that Gareth had, there was usually a houseful. It certainly was open house, and they held many parties. Life was definitely improving, but Penny still regretted that Gareth did not spend more time with her. And then tragedy struck.

Penny received a message at school one day, to say that Lynette had been taken ill at her school. She left right away, and hurried to fetch her. She found her extremely sick with a high temperature and severe aches and pains, mainly in her neck. She took her home and immediately called the doctor, who diagnosed 'flu', but said to call him if she did not improve in a day or two.

But that night, Lynette seemed to worsen, and a rash appeared on her body. The doctor this time admitted her to hospital. She was no better next day, and after tests, the diagnosis was a severe form of Meningitis. Penny knew nothing about the sickness, but she felt desperate as she watched Lynette deteriorate. She and Gareth stayed at her bedside throughout, having got the other children off to school. Gareth returned home to them at the end of the day, then left Ross, now sixteen, in charge, while he returned to the hospital. But, early that evening, Lynette died. She was just fifteen years old.

Everyone was devastated. Penny thought life could never be the same again. Things had been going so well, and then this! She searched her thoughts for why it should have happened, and felt she must blame herself. She remembered Lynette being born, and how she had only wanted boys at that time, and her initial disappointment and shock when the midwife told her the baby was a girl. Was this her punishment? But it had only been momentary. She loved Lynette. She loved all her girls and boys. Then she wondered if she had been selfish in pursuing her career. Had she neglected the family? She didn't really think so. And Gareth tried to reassure her that there was nothing she could have done to prevent it.

Penny reflected on her hysterectomy. She had now lost one of her beloved children, and she couldn't have any more. She would never have agreed to the 'op' if she had thought of this happening. What if she lost any more? Gareth, too, found it very hard to come to terms with their loss. They were both absent from their teaching for some time, but inevitably had to return.

At first, Penny thought she couldn't go on with it, but knew inwardly that she owed it to the rest of her children, and to Gareth, to pull herself together and carry on with life. She applied for a post in another school and on being offered the job to start the following term, gave in her notice. It would be a fresh start in a much smaller school, just as her family was now smaller.

Penny enjoyed the atmosphere in the smaller school. It was situated on an estate in a neighbouring borough. Everyone knew everyone, staff and pupils, and if it was thought anyone was 'playing hooky', the Head would stride down the drive, out the gates, visit the house and yank out the offender. Penny was in charge of the whole of the girls P.E. Department and enjoyed the responsibility. In fact there was not enough for a full timetable and the rest of the time was taken up with taking remedial classes in the basic subjects.

Family life had settled down once more after the trauma of losing Lynette, but there was something lacking between herself and Gareth. Penny knew she was nagging a lot about the time he spent drinking with his friends, and also the fact that he did nothing to help her in the house. The more she nagged, the worse things became. She tried to bite her tongue, and she did so for long periods, but he still carried on the same, and then she would have to give vent to her feelings. Then they would be quarrelling again. It came to a point that it was only at school that she felt appreciated.

At this time, there were some developments within Penny's own family. Her parents had been living with Dorothy and Jonathon and family on the south coast. However, Jonathon had suffered a nervous breakdown and had to give up his good job. So they were moving to a smaller house elsewhere and hoped that one of the other sisters or brothers could give a home to their parents. Penny was very concerned about it and discussed with Gareth whether her parents could come to live with them. They could have the back lounge and the bedroom that Rhodri had vacated, and share the kitchen and bathroom. As the rooms were already furnished, it meant they would only be able to bring a few items with them.

Penny was very close to her parents, especially her mother, and she thought it would be nice to have their company. Also, her mother had always been very helpful with things about the house whenever she stayed and would baby-sit for her and Gareth to go out together. If they came to live permanently, Penny and Gareth knew they would make themselves very useful, and of course, if any of the family were unwell, they would be on hand, which would allow them to fulfil their teaching jobs. So he agreed that they should come to live with them if they wished. Penny wrote to invite her parents and they eagerly accepted. They would move back to London in a few weeks and Penny promised to collect them in the car.

It proved to be a very satisfactory arrangement. Lavinia and Harry never interfered with anything within the family, and only set out to make themselves useful. The children were very fond of their grandparents and Penny and Gareth did not quarrel so much. In fact, they could now go out of an evening or weekend, and so had a much more sociable life. Sometimes they went away, just the two of them, for a weekend break, and Penny found such times exciting and romantic. Gareth had none of his distractions, and she adored the attention she received once more. They were now able to afford more things for the house, making some major alterations. Gareth had a new car, and Penny also had a small almost new one, the old banger from Nick having long seen its last day.

The children were growing up fast, and of course, different ages brought different problems. Gareth loved babies and young children, but he did not cope very well with the teenage years. Whereas Penny identified very much with that time. She could remember so well how she had felt, and said to Gareth, "Don't you remember what it was like? You always said how you resented your Mother's nagging during those years, and how you rebelled. And yet you are doing exactly the same thing yourself."

Quite a lot of hostility built up between the boys, especially, and their father. And Penny often made excuses and covered up for them. She thought that age such an exciting time of life, and often wished herself back to her teenage years in school. But then, marrying at seventeen, meant she had missed out on such a lot: parties, dances, partners, etc. But then she would reassure herself that she would not want to change things.

The family were now able to take a holiday each year, other than just visiting in Wales. They settled on holiday camps, as this seemed to work well with the range of the children's ages. They all seemed to make friends there and join in activities, and it left Penny and Gareth time together. The girls always took part in the wide range of competitions, etc. that were on offer. Jacqueline invariably won the swimming, and

Georgina the talent. She was very much of an extrovert, and had a delightful singing voice. Penny, too, competed in some of the activities, and always did well in the table tennis. The boys enjoyed the evening discos and there was entertainment for Penny and Gareth.

A year or two later, Penny moved school once again. This time she went to teach at a special school for the Educationally Subnormal, having got interested in such work through the remedial teaching at the previous school. She stayed for fifteen years, and during that time obtained a second diploma for teaching the handicapped.

Time came for each of the children to leave school. Ross became an Environmental Health Officer and Gerry started work on the papers in Fleet Street, first as a photographic darkroom assistant, progressing to photographer. Jacqueline became a Legal Secretary and Georgina took up hairdressing.

About this time, Penny and Gareth both lost their fathers. Lavinia stayed on living with them in the house, but she now had a little bed-sitter upstairs. This meant they had the use of the second lounge again. With boy friends and girl friends, it was very convenient. The next development would be weddings!

CHAPTER THIRTY-TWO
1973

All the children married young. Penny wondered if they wanted to escape from home! Gareth certainly did not cope very well with the traumas of their growing up. So he was quite happy to see each one of them settle down, even though it was a costly business, what with each wedding plus helping them set up a home.

He set about having an extension built on the back of the house, knocking down the conservatory and old coal store, making a bed-sitter arrangement using the back lounge, and adding a kitchen and bathroom. It proved an excellent arrangement for each young couple to start married life independently, and apart from Ross, the other three all lived there initially, before moving on.

Ross married Irene, a northern girl, living and working as a wages clerk locally. They were both twenty. Two years later, Gerry also married at twenty, a young girl, Joanne, whom he had met at one of the holiday camps when both were young teenagers. She, too was a local girl.

When Jacqueline was seventeen, Penny arranged for her to take a trip to New Zealand to stay with her brother, Lenny, and family. While there, she met a young man, Warren, who followed her back to England, where he worked for some time, and they eventually married when Jacqueline was twenty. They stayed a year in the flatlet, and then went first to Australia to work and make money before settling in New Zealand.

Georgina married at eighteen. Penny tried to dissuade her, as she knew that the young man, Richard, and her daughter were not suited. He was such a meek, mild and placid lad, and so obviously besotted with Georgina. She was a lively extrovert girl, very way-out, with different styles and colours of hair almost every month, always out late and going to clubs and concerts and parties. Penny was forever sneaking her in the house late at night, having told Gareth she was already in bed! Possibly, she identified very much with Georgina's way, well, not the hair, but her liveliness and popularity. She often thought that if she had not married so young, she would have been like her.

Well, they did marry, and after a short stay in the flat, they went to California where Georgina had the offer of a hairdressing job. She, of course, loved the life in Hollywood and Los Angeles, but it did not suit Richard. He really could not keep up with the high life style and eventually came home alone, Georgina refusing to do so. Inevitably, divorce followed. She stayed on and worked her way up, finally opening her own hairdressing salon, and becoming highly respected in her field.

The natural progression of the marriages brought grandchildren. When Ross and Irene announced that a baby was on the way, Penny was completely 'over the moon'. She felt almost as if she was the one expecting. The couple's first child was a girl, and three years later they produced a boy. Penny and Gareth loved them, and they looked after the children wherever possible. It was such a happy time for them all. Little did they know that yet another tragedy was to come, that would change the lifestyle of them all.

Irene was suddenly diagnosed as having cancer. The family could not believe it to be true. She had always been such a fit woman. The little boy was only nine months old, and his sister just four years. There ensued weeks and then months of hospital visits, and stays for surgery and treatment. Irene's family were living in the north of England and could only make occasional visits, although she had a sister nearer.

Penny and family helped as much as they could, to enable Ross to continue with his work. They took the children every weekend, and if Irene's family were not visiting, much of the week as well, while their mother was hospitalised or unwell at home. Lavinia was a great source of support also, but now into her eighties, Penny tried not to impose on her too much.

Katrina, the little girl, was in the nursery class at school, and on the week days when the children were with Penny, she would rush to drop her off on her way to her own school, and take Martin, the little boy with her. Luckily, working in a special school, there was a very free and easy atmosphere. Martin was so good, and the children loved having him in with them, and fortunately the hours were shorter than normal school. At the end of morning session, Penny would dash home with him, give him a meal, and then put him in his cot for an afternoon sleep. Lavinia would be in charge while Penny returned to school for the short afternoon session. Then she would collect Katrina from school and return home just in time for Martin awaking from his nap.

They all managed like this for some time, but only nine months after her diagnosis, Irene died. Everyone was devastated. The two children now only eighteen months and under five moved in with Penny and Gareth permanently. Ross shut up his own house, and spent most of the time with them and the children.

When Irene died, there were only three weeks of school term time left before the school summer holidays. Penny arranged for her sister Rosamund to stay for those three weeks, to help out until the end of term. Rosamund had split up from Morris, and was in the process of getting divorced. She was not working, so agreed to stay. It was all a very traumatic time for the whole family, but they survived the crisis, and arrangements were made for little Martin to attend a day nursery from the start of the term in September.

Penny managed to drop off the two children at their respective schools, and continue with her own teaching, picking them up again afterwards. Penny loved the children and thought of them as her own. Martin did not remember his mother and thought of Penny as his mumma.

It was hard work yet again, but they were such good children, and with Lavinia's help, Penny and Gareth were able to still get out for an occasional evening or weekend, so that they could continue with their social life. For the past few years they had been taking holidays abroad, mainly in Spain, during the autumn and spring school breaks. So, for the next couple of years, they took the youngsters with them. It amused Penny how people were never sure what the set–up was with her, Gareth and the little ones. Most seemed to assume they were their own, and probably thought they had been 'caught out' later in life.

Eventually, Ross took up with a colleague from work, and they bought another house together, and the children moved back with them. Pleased as Penny and Gareth were to see the new family situation, they missed the children terribly. They really did feel they were their own. But they saw plenty of them, still, having them stay when Ross and Karen, his new lady, wished to go out, and collecting them of a Friday for a regular stopover.

And then more grandchildren came along. Gerry and Joanne had a girl and boy, Jacqueline and Warren in New Zealand had two girls, and Georgina had a daughter in America with her new boy friend - one of a string of several she had gone through. But she did not marry him, having found out he was cheating on her, just as they were about to do so. Some years later, she did re-marry, and had two more daughters. She was now a much more placid individual, having settled down and given up her extrovert life style. She had her own salon, had married an established career man, and moved into a lovely mountain home above Malibu.

Ross and Karen also married, and had a son. Karen was a high-flying career woman and held an executive post in local government, and Ross started up his own advisory business. Gerry was now a free-lance photographer and doing well. And Gareth took early retirement at the age of fifty-seven, followed by Penny two years later at the age of fifty.

Lavinia was now in her nineties, and Penny looked forward to giving her more attention now that she would not have to go to work. She planned the trips and outings she would take with her. But Lavinia had a stroke. Penny and her sisters nursed her, but after only five days she died peacefully, aged ninety-three. She had been a wonderful gentle woman loved by all.

Her death left a great void in Penny's life, but now with her gone, and all the children away from home, Gareth announced that he no longer wanted to live in London. He wanted to sell the house, buy elsewhere cheaper, invest the difference, and settle down to retirement. It really would be the end of an era. But now they had to decide where to go.

PART THREE

FULL CIRCLE

CHAPTER THIRTY-THREE
1987

They really did not know where to re-settle. Gareth was adamant that they should move from London. Penny agreed that their particular area had certainly changed over the thirty-three years they had lived there. But she really wanted to stay near to the boys and their families, who were still local. The girls, of course, lived abroad. They had already made several trips to America, and one to New Zealand, where they spent three months of English winter in the Antipodean summer.

They planned to look around various areas of England to see where to re-locate. Penny said she would like a brand new detached house with at least four bedrooms, so that they still had room for family visits. She had always lived in a large house. Gareth would have liked a small bungalow with a little garden, and so less work.

Penny did not feel she could move into a small village, having always been in a London suburb, and she did not want to go to Wales. She and Gareth now had a very stable loving relationship. He did not go out every day drinking the way he used to in the earlier years, and they did so much more together. He told her over and over how he felt he loved her even more than before, if that were possible, and regretted the time he had wasted apart from her. But only when they went to Wales did he seem to slip back into his old ways, and Penny knew it would be fatal to live there.

They began their search around new building sites of central England towards the Welsh border, but nothing really appealed to them. Then one week-end on such a venture, they stopped over at Gareth's home, and took a different route home, passing through Hereford, a town they had never before visited. They saw a sign for new four-bedroomed, detached houses, stopped to look, and immediately knew they had found the right spot.

They chose the largest site, and the house was to be completed within a few months, and, compared to London, the price was extremely cheap. On selling, they would have a good sum to invest. They loved the town; not too small, but large enough to contain the well-known chain stores. They could walk to town along the river, and were surrounded by beautiful countryside, offering plenty of walks, which they enjoyed. And they would be near enough to visit family and friends in Wales, as a day trip, and only three hours drive to the children in London. Yes, they agreed, this was the spot.

They moved in the September. Penny was completely smitten with the house, and loved the idea that no one had lived there before them. Every little touch about the property was only hers and Gareth's. She collected hearts, and each room had evidence of a heart in some form. But she didn't draw them any more with their arrows and initials. She often thought back to her youth when she did so, and was still very much a romantic. Sometimes she even thought of Matt, and wondered what had become of him. Strange, that all those years she had lived in London they had never crossed paths again. She really had believed they were made for each other, but it was not to be. She hoped he had found someone worthy of him. And still in her fantasies she would think of the young girl and boy in the Blue Lagoon – was it her and Matt? Then she would cuddle up to Gareth and feel guilty. She hoped she had been a good wife, and she knew he loved her, and yes, she loved him.

They had pleasant neighbours in the small cul-de-sac, and the whole pace of the area was less stressful than that of London. There were beautiful places to visit and explore, and they were very much involved with each other. But they could not deny that they missed the close proximity of their family and friends, with the numerous, unannounced visits it had always brought. But then it was now a bonus when they came to stay. However, they made a new circle of friends, but not so intensive as that in London.

That winter they made their second visit to New Zealand, and it became a regular trip every other English winter. With visits to Georgina in America, annual trips to Spain and other Mediterranean spots, they were well travelled. And as their retirement years slipped by, Penny felt their love became deeper and deeper.

They were still very physically involved with each other, and were surprised how many people of their age said they had 'finished with all that!' Penny had to feel 'in love' and 'be loved', and every night they would have some contact with each other. Day times often saw them kissing and cuddling somewhere about the house, making love on the settee, retiring to the bedroom, or taking a shower together. They sometimes stopped for a cuddle in the car, or on a country walk, and had once made love in the sand dunes on a deserted beach in New Zealand. It was all still great fun.

CHAPTER THIRTY-FOUR
1996

Yes, they were very happy years, taking Gareth into his seventies, and Penny into her sixties. All the family were settled in good jobs and homes, and businesses were doing well with those of them in England and abroad. Georgina was re-married and very much more stable in America. Jacqueline's husband was building his own, very large house in New Zealand, a venture he had always worked for. Gerry had built his own studio and dark room onto the new house, and was undertaking many photographic assignments abroad through his freelance business, and Ross and Karen now had a son of their own. Karen continued with her executive job, and Ross had ventured out to set up his own advisory business.

Everything seemed fine, except that Gareth had some arthritis problems, which caused some discomfort, but Penny kept well. They were still able to take their walks, although not so adventurous and strenuous, and continued to travel abroad. Penny was never very happy just sitting around, and she began to amuse herself by writing poems and short stories. She entered one or two minor competitions she heard of, on the radio or in the local paper and the national papers. She did achieve a little success, and found it amusing to hear her poem read out on the radio. She also wrote poems for friends and family for special days, such as birthdays and anniversaries, and presented a number for events in the local social club where they were both members. It gave her considerable satisfaction to stand up and deliver her offering, usually amusing, to an audience. Maybe it compensated for her dance creativity, which she certainly did miss.

Gareth was quite amused by Penny's new interest, and would ask her, "What is it this time?" She told him, "One day I will write a poem for you. I think it will be for our Golden Wedding, when we will get all the family together and have a big party for them and our friends from Hereford, London and Wales." Never before had they managed to get the whole family together since the girls moved abroad. "And maybe one day I will write a book," she added.

And then things began to go wrong. In '97 tragedy was to strike once again. Penny and Gareth were coming to the end of one of their winter three month visits to New Zealand and America. She had a feeling something was not right back home, then Joanne telephoned to say that Karen had been rushed into hospital with internal problems, and had had a major operation. They found her still poorly on their return, but she insisted on going back to her job as soon as she could, maintaining she was well again. Not long after, she was diagnosed with cancer, and now began a long-term series of treatment. Poor Karen said that if the disease was painful, then the treatment was worse, but she endured months of it, followed by remission, but then another 'rearing of its ugly head', followed by more treatment and its awful side effects. It was so pitiful to see her at these times, but she was such a fighter, and determined to still hold down her job. Everyone helped as much as possible, Penny and Gareth taking the children, especially the little boy, when things were bad. Ross's business folded, and he went back to local government work. It seemed so unfair that this should have happened to him twice.

Gareth, also, was not as well as before. It seemed his arthritis was spreading, with a lot of pain in his hips and leg, and his usual tablets did not help. He and Penny hardly ever went for the long walks now. The doctor sent him for further blood tests and X-rays, and then a bone scan.

It was summer time, '98, and Georgina and family had been to visit, and travelled on for a two week stay in a villa in Tuscany. They invited Penny and Gareth to join them. Gareth did not want to go, but told Penny to go alone. She did go for just one week, and Karen and her little boy Ieuan, went also.

Penny was not happy about leaving Gareth, especially as he was having hospital tests. The trip was pleasant enough until she received two phone calls from him. His first bad news was that he had been told he had prostatic cancer, which had got into the bones. Penny was so upset that she had not been at his side when being given such terrible news. Then two days later he phoned to say his mother had died. This meant he had to make all the arrangements alone.

Penny was home in time for the funeral. She could not believe Gareth's bad news. The family had suffered this disease enough, and were still having to watch its effects on Karen, who was now fighting a losing battle. Was this to be Gareth's fate also!

He was put on hormone treatment, which the specialist said was the less stressful of the options. Initially, the side effects were not too extreme, apart from his feeling very tired and lethargic. They both adapted to a less energetic life-style. No longer did they undertake the long, country walks, and Gareth was even less able to help with any of the heavy tasks around the house and garden. But they managed reasonably well for the first year, Gareth having regular hospital check-ups and hormone injections with their doctor.

Possibly the most disturbing effect of his treatment, was his loss of libido and ability to maintain a physical love life. It had previously been such an important part of their life. Penny tried to tell him that it did not matter that they could not make love. "We can still kiss and cuddle and have fun," she told him. But Gareth found it very distressing.

"I do still love you, Penny. But I just have no drive or feeling," he replied. And one night, as he held her naked body close to him in bed, he cried, saying, "Oh Penny, if only I could make love to you just one more time. You've always been so loveable." But it wasn't to be.

Penny needed some distraction from their mounting worries. She had for some time wished that she could meet her old school friends Belinda and Joyce. She had lost touch with Joyce very early, but had kept in touch with Belinda for some years. She last saw her soon after starting her teaching career, and then some years later she received a letter, saying that they were moving to the south coast. Penny mislaid the letter, and so did not have the address to follow up.

So often she said that she wished she could re-new acquaintance with 'the girls'. She then heard of the Old Scholars Association for their secondary school, and that a reunion evening was held every two years. This seemed the opportunity to maybe trace her friends, so she attended the one in '98'. It was a wonderful evening, and although neither Belinda nor Joyce were present, several others of her year were. It was so good to re-new acquaintances, but no one knew anything about her two close buddies or where they might be.

Just before leaving the party, one of the old boys who had been in Penny's year came to talk to her. He revived many memories for her, and commented that it was unusual for Matthew Oliver not to be present, as he had been a regular patron previously. At the sound of his name, Penny's heart gave a jump. Why did it do that? She felt disturbed talking about Matt, and being reminded of the 'Item' they had been for so long in school. "You wait 'til I tell Matt that you were here," he said.

"Well, give him my love. I'll see him in two years time," Penny replied, and she left the hall, going to meet Gareth who had gone for a drink with his brother.

As she drove to the nearby pub, she suddenly felt disturbed. To think that Matt could have been there! She felt fluttery. Just to hear his name mentioned had a profound effect on her. And all the memories came flooding back. She had always wondered how she would feel if she ever met him again, and this was only the thought of it. But then, she knew she could only ever think of him with love. Suddenly, two years seemed a long time to wait, and she felt very guilty when she collected Gareth from the pub.

"Was your old boyfriend there?" he asked. She told him no, but said she had sent her love to him through an old classmate. And they both laughed.

"It was good to see so many old friends, but no-one knew anything about Belinda and Joyce," she continued. "Maybe we will meet up in two years time." But that night it was not her girlfriends she was thinking of. It was Matt. Would he be there in the year 2000? And now she felt extra guilty as she nestled against Gareth.

CHAPTER THIRTY-FIVE
2000

The Millennium was not a good year for Penny and family. She and Gareth were in New Zealand on their usual English winter trip. Gareth was now very lethargic with his illness and treatment, but they bought a car there for the duration of their three month stay, and so were able to drive where they had previously walked. It was to prove their last trip together to Jacqueline and family.

On their return, they found Karen extremely ill after enduring more agonising treatment. They tried to help out, having Ieuan to stay for most of the school holidays. Gareth got extremely upset watching Karen fighting her battle, and Penny noticed a change in the control of his condition. She knew she had to keep calm and able for them all to manage.

That spring, it was very obvious how little energy Gareth had. Previously he had always prepared his beloved bean patch in the garden, and Penny performed the delicate task of planting the seedlings. However, this year, Penny had to undertake the digging, and although they erected the cane frames together, Gareth was exhausted afterwards.

But he looked quite well in appearance, and possibly people did not realise the extent of his illness. Even Penny intimated to him sometimes that he should try to do more.

“Please try, Gareth, or you will become an invalid.”

He would reply, “You don’t know what an effort it is,” and then she would feel sorry for what she had said.

There were no long walks now, but they would go for short drives, and regularly still went to Wales to visit Gareth’s relatives and friends. Gareth loved Wales and would enjoy speaking his natural language and experiencing the whole atmosphere of Welsh life again. Each visit would finish with a couple of hours in the village social club where he still held his membership, enjoying some pints with old friends. Then Penny would drive the one and a half-hours’ journey home, and he would always be very emotional at this time.

Some of the family came to visit during the summer, and although it was enjoyable to see them, Gareth could not join in activities with the grandchildren. Penny would go off swimming with them all, as she loved to do, but she was not happy leaving him alone. But he insisted he was okay. And they still hoped to visit the girls abroad, if possible

And then it was that in September 2000 she once more found herself getting ready to attend the Old Scholars’ Reunion evening. She and Gareth had returned from a visit to Georgina and family in California. They had returned to their home in Hereford, but had now come to stay with Ross and Karen and family for a few days, enabling Penny to attend the evening. It was also convenient for them to fly off yet again for their annual two weeks holiday in Spain.

Penny was ready, and, as before, she drove Gareth to the pub, where he was to meet his brother. Then she made her way to the reunion hall. She felt especially awkward making her entrance. The list of those attending was spread out on the reception table. She gave in her name, and then received her label bearing her maiden name, as was the procedure. Penny Saunders was affixed to her chest. She scanned the list quickly, and the name Matthew Oliver stared out at her! Her tummy lurched. What would she say to him? What would he look like? What did she look like? Would he recognise her? Possibly not!

For some time she could not make the final entrance into the hall. She hovered in the powder room. She was already hot, and felt she had put on all the wrong clothes. She looked at herself in the mirror. She was bronzed, and her hair streaked blonde from the recent Californian sunshine. But she certainly didn't look like the sixteen-year-old of nearly fifty years ago! But then, no one else at the gathering would either. She would have to make her entrance.

She was still feeling hot, and fought her way through the mêlée to the bar, where she asked for a Martini and ice. Leaving the bar, she met the classmate who had spoken to her of Matt at the meeting two years previous. He greeted her warmly. "Nice to see you here again. Matt is here this time"

"Oh, is he?" Penny tried to sound passive. "Where is he then?" He turned, searching the crowd. "There he is. Matt," he called, "Look who's here!"

Penny looked. She didn't recognise anyone. A man was walking towards them, smiling, and then stopped in front of her. He looked at her name label.

"Hello Penny." She looked at his label, Matt Oliver!

"Hi, Matt," she replied quietly, and then lay her cheek gently next to his as he momentarily held her.

"Well, what a surprise," he continued, "I heard you were here two years ago."

Some of the other old boys joined them and they all indulged in greetings and reminiscences, including Penny in the jovial conversation, consisting mainly of remember this and remember that. Penny was looking at Matt. Gone was the thick brown, wavy hair. In its place shining light grey hair, almost white, back waves, but now sparse on top, and a moustache! Penny remembered him taller, but then realised she was wearing high heels. No, if she had passed him in the street, she would not have recognised him, and she assumed it would have been likewise if he had passed her.

One of the 'boys' was saying something about "you and Matt," and she joined in the conversation, and Matt was asking her about herself, and then she of him. And the more she listened to him, and looked at him, yes, the same twinkling eyes and without the moustache, it could be Matt. Memories were flooding back, and she was reminding him of how devastated she had been when they split up. She recalled the dreadful scene she had made at the local dance all those years ago, when she believed the young girl, Susan, was taking her place in his affections.

Penny was trying to laugh and sound flippant about it all, but the memories were tugging at her heartstrings. "I adored you, Matt," still trying to sound detached, "and I used to plan each night what I would say to you next morning if we met on the paper round, and how you would still be madly in love with me. But I'm sure you avoided me." And again she laughed falseley about it.

It was time to be seated for the meal. Penny had not, as yet, found her year group of girl friends, and should have been seated with them. But she had not made a note of their assigned table. For a moment she felt lost. But Matt took her arm, and said, "come and sit with us." And, as she sat close to him, she felt an affinity between them. Yes, they were Penny and Matt, the Item of fifty years ago. She might never see him again. This might be her only opportunity to discover what really had happened to cause the break up. And she talked, and probed, and reminded him of so many instances, and asked why?

Many things Matt did not remember, or he had a different account of an event. But he remembered the love seat in the hall of Penny's old house, and then they laughed at other simple memories of their time together. They moved on to the present. He was married with two sons, and still lived locally. He seemed surprised that she had five children. "Good job you didn't marry me then!" she told him.

The meal finished, and she moved across to the girls of her year, apologising for not sitting with them. One of the girls said she often visited relatives not far from Hereford, where Penny lived, and they arranged to meet up for a shopping trip and lunch one day. It was so enjoyable to catch up on news, and also reminisce on school days, but no one knew anything about the whereabouts of Belinda and Joyce.

Penny looked at her watch. It was time for her to collect Gareth from the pub, and so she said her goodbyes. Leaving the girls, she looked for Matt. He was standing, talking and laughing with some 'old boys'. She made her way over towards them. "I'm leaving now, Matt. It was nice seeing you."

"Yes, it was great, Penny. Sorry you're going so soon," and they brushed cheeks in a quick embrace.

She hurried from the hall and out to her car. There was a lump in her throat, and she felt disturbed. She was glad she had seen Matt. She would probably never see him again, and there were so many things that she now wished she had asked him. She wondered what he had thought about her! She called for Gareth and his brother, and as they drove back to Ross's house where they were stopping, Gareth asked her "Did you see the old boyfriend then?"

"Yes, I did. I didn't recognise him. He looked older than you Gareth," was her only comment. "It was good seeing some of the girls. I'm going to meet one of them for a day out in Gloucester. But no-one knows anything about Belinda and Joyce." As they drew up at the house, Penny had that awful guilty feeling again.

CHAPTER THIRTY-SIX

They flew off for the usual two weeks in Spain, but Penny felt uneasy and felt they should not be going. Karen was terribly ill, and Penny thought they should stay to help. But their daughter-in-law was so independent and refused help, but was now continually in and out of hospital. It seemed wrong to go jetting off on holiday again.

Gareth, too, was tired and weak, and it upset him that he was unable to help Penny with the luggage. They received wheelchair assistance at the airports, as they had on the trips to the U.S. and New Zealand, and although it was a great help with some of the long airport treks, Penny knew it hurt Gareth's pride. They had previously enjoyed many trips to Spain, but sitting on the plane, en-route for Alicante, she just knew this was to be their last.

They collected the hire car at the airport, and she drove the hour to the resort, settling them into the apartments which had always given them such enjoyable times. They tried to do some of their usual things, but it was not the same. They sat more than they walked now as Gareth got exhausted. But the hot sun was lovely, and they sat on the balcony playing cards, as before, and sipping a glass of Pymms, which Penny made. Their friends were around, but gone were the late night liaisons at the bars, of previous years.

Then at the start of their second week, Penny suddenly put her back out. She had a weakness there, and regularly suffered pain and incapacity for several days. But this really was the worst it had ever been. Trying to get out of bed, she had ended up on the floor in agony, and could not get up. For three hours she tried. Gareth was so upset that he was too weak to help her, and the situation brought home to them how ill he was.

She eventually spent the second week almost immobile. She wondered how she would drive them back to the airport, but with the help of several cushions, she made it. Reaching home, they agreed that it had been their last trip abroad.

On their return, they were greeted by a pile of two weeks mail. Gareth handed half to Penny and they started scanning through. They had always opened any mail, no matter which of them it was addressed to. This lot proved to be mainly bills and rubbish mail. Penny looked at one addressed to her, typed and with a London postmark. She pushed it into a drawer without opening it. Why, she did not know, but it gave her a strange feeling.

Later that evening, she retrieved it from the drawer. The letter inside was also typed, but signed in pen by Matt! He explained that he was prompted to write due to a strange coincidence. The day following the Old Scholars evening, he and his wife had attended a private party, where he spoke to a complete stranger. It transpired that this person lived in Penny's old house – the very one where Matt had courted her, and when he enquired after the little fixed love seat in the hall, he was told it was still there! He thought it so strange a meeting after their own reunion the previous night, that he was prompted to write.

He also said that he had some written material she might be interested in seeing. Copies of school magazines and sports days and prize givings, which included her name and many of her associates. Would she like to have them? Also, some other written words which he thought she should see. What that could be, Penny could not think. He had old friends near Gloucester he sometimes visited, and would she be interested in meeting for lunch there one day, when he could hand over the material.

Putting back the letter, what did she feel? Intrigued! Surprised! Disturbed! Having first hidden the letter, she could not now show it to Gareth. How could she explain hiding it? And it was a very innocent letter, but she was now feeling deceitful. Yes, she was interested ... what could the written material be that it might interest her? She toyed between whether she should write or phone in reply. He would not know she had been away for the past two weeks, so must assume she had ignored his letter. She hadn't given her address to him, so he had obviously obtained it from the Old Scholars' register. Well she would have to explain why she had not answered. She would write the next day.

Penny did write in reply, and said she would like to meet for lunch, and wondered what written matter he could have that could possibly interest her. She pondered over what to tell Gareth. She wanted to be honest with him, but having already been underhand about the letter, it made it all seem wrong. Strange that she had already told him of the old girlfriend suggesting a shopping trip to Gloucester some time. Well, Matt was an old school friend, so she could use the shopping day out as an excuse. She wouldn't want to have Gareth cast doubt on her.

A few days after sending her letter, Matt telephoned one

afternoon. Penny was completely taken aback to hear him say 'this is Matt.' They arranged a day for the following week, and he asked her to suggest a hotel where they could meet for lunch. Penny said she would think of one and then phone with directions.

Putting down the phone, she went to Gareth, who was watching television. "Well, that was my old school friend. We're going to meet in Gloucester next week," Penny truthfully announced. Next day she phoned Matt to say she knew of a large hotel on the main ring road which would be easy to find, and they settled on the day and time.

She was uneasy the day before the meeting, and wished that she could have been honest with Gareth, but she could not bear to upset his feelings with him not being well. No one would understand how, to Penny, it seemed quite natural that she should wish to meet Matt again, and anyhow, what could it be that he wanted to show her.

She had bought various items to stow in the boot of the car, to give credibility to a shopping trip, and set off in the car, after leaving sandwiches and snacks for Gareth, saying she would be back late afternoon. At one point on the journey, she almost turned back, feeling she wanted to cuddle and kiss Gareth and let him know how much she loved him, and that she would never do anything to hurt his feelings. But it was too late to back out now. Matt would be well on his way from London.

She turned into the hotel car park, and made her way to the entrance hall, heading straight for the Ladies Room. She had worn a trouser suit, hoping she looked casual yet smart. After tidying herself, she returned through the foyer. Someone was sitting in the lounge area reading a paper, and as she drew near, he dropped the paper, looked up, and said, "It's me." He stood up, and they brushed cheeks.

"You beat me here, then," was all Penny could say.

They moved to a table and he had coffee brought up. After general awkward chat, they re-called the Old Scholars' evening, and he re-told the story of meeting the new owners of Penny's old home. And then he brought out copies of the old school literature. Penny was delighted to read her name, and especially proud to see: School Prize for P.E. 1951 Penny Saunders. Then they read over other entries and discussed and laughed over the memories of various boys and girls. Penny began to relax, and it suddenly dawned on her that here she was sitting, laughing and chatting with Matt again. It had been almost fifty years.

They moved to the restaurant for lunch, and sitting with their coffee after the meal, Matt suddenly took out some sheets of paper. "Now, this is what I really want to put right between us," he said. Penny was mystified.

"After meeting you those few weeks ago at the school evening, I was quite disturbed by the picture you painted of me, telling me how I ignored you, avoided you, and was generally indifferent to your feelings. Well when I got home, I thought over how I remembered it otherwise. I have always kept a diary, and have stored them away over the years. So I sorted out the one for 1951, when you said I gave you up. Reading that, I seem to have been as devastated as you say you were. I have copied out some entries that I want you to have, to show that I was not as uncaring as you thought."

He pushed the sheets over to her, and Penny read. And what she read, she could not believe. There were entries on several days of every month right through 1951, such as

'Haven't seen Penny for 3 days', then 4 days, 5 days etc.

'Danced with Penny at school.'

'Round at Penny's. Showed me her diary and her feelings, what am I to do?'

'Saw Penny on paper round.'

'Disagreement with Penny – she wants to call it off.'

Penny could not believe this entry, and did not recall ever saying such a thing. She remembered it all the other way round.

'Danced with Penny, are we back together?'

'Lovely evening at school opera, walked home with Penny.'

'Sat on field with Penny at school.'

'Sat with Penny again.'

And then coming to the summer months at school when Penny would have been going out with Gareth.

'Penny where are you?'

'Penny I miss you.'

'Met Penny. Jenkins has gone back to Wales.'

'Met Penny. Chatted. Didn't walk her home. What a fool.'

'Met Penny. Walked her home. Wish I'd asked her out. Will have to soon or it will be too late.'

'Missed Penny.'

'Heard Penny's gone away with Jenkins. What a fool to let her go. Still, will keep trying!'

'Wish I could go out with Penny again.'

'Saw Penny at school. Said she's leaving. Wish she would go out with me again.'

'Met Penny after school. Talked awhile, but got no response.' THE END!

Penny sat quietly after reading the notes, and she felt a lump in her throat. She could not believe what she had just read. Who would believe that first of all, a young boy of sixteen would have kept such a diary, and also that he still had it after all these years? And how had they misunderstood one another so. She had believed that it was he who was disinterested, and now it appeared that he had thought the same of her. There was no answer to this.

"Well, we sure got it all wrong, didn't we?" she remarked, "And I thought you had gone cold on me for that girl Susan."

"Yes, well the diary frightened me off for a while. I couldn't cope with it," he replied.

Penny looked puzzled. "Diary! What diary?"

"Your diary, the one you gave me to keep," he answered.

"I gave you my diary?" she queried, "I don't remember anything about a diary. I expect I would have kept one, but I have no recollection of ever giving it to you."

He then pointed out one of the entries he had put before her. "Well, you did, and I, as a sixteen-year-old lad just could not cope with the sentiments written there"

Penny looked back at the entry. 'Round at Penny's. Showed me her diary and her feelings. What am I to do!"

"I don't believe it. I would never give a diary away," she stated.

But if the revelations of his diary notes had shocked her, his next words stunned her even more. "Well, you did, Penny, and I still have it."

"You still have my diary after fifty years! You can't have!"
"I do, Penny, and I have looked into it many times, and wondered over your thoughts there. It has been very precious to me all these years."

"Well, I want it," she continued. "I have no recollection

of it whatsoever. I must see it."

"I'll send it to you Penny, but I want it back, having been its custodian for fifty years," was his answer.

Penny felt confused and drained after all these revelations. They had spent several hours together. She would have to return home, and he had a long journey back. "I thought you were going to your friend nearby," Penny queried.

"No, I came to see you," he answered, "I wanted to put right the misunderstandings of that year so long ago."

He walked with her to the car. Strange, they found that both their cars were parked next to one another. He held her momentarily as they brushed cheeks. "I've really enjoyed talking to you again Penny. Perhaps we can do it again."

"Yes, I've enjoyed it too, Matt. Thanks for showing me your notes. And please let me have my diary back. I can't believe such a thing exists."

"I will. I promise," he answered. Penny got into her car, and looked up at him, seeing him now, as Matt, of old. "Drive carefully," he called as she started up the engine.

It was raining as she drove home. She was unsettled. The day's revelations had confused her. All these years she had believed that he had finished with her. Why hadn't he shown his feelings to her then? Why hadn't they been the boy and girl in the Blue Lagoon. But then she would not have gone with Gareth. Tears rolled down her cheeks as she drove. Gareth! She loved Gareth, she really did, and she loved the children they had, and the grandchildren, and …. and.... Now she was getting all sentimental.

She pulled herself together. It had been very interesting seeing Matt again, and now she would look forward to receiving the diary. Arriving home, she put the car in the garage, and carried the parcels into the house. "You bought enough," Gareth greeted her. "Yes, we had a busy time, and it was interesting talking over old times," she answered him.

"Are you meeting again?" he asked.

"Possibly," was her only reply, and she knelt in front of him, lifting her face to be kissed. He looked so weary. "It was very lonely without you, Penny," he said, and she felt the tears welling up again.

CHAPTER THIRTY-SEVEN

Matt did send Penny the diary. She still could not remember ever having given it to him. She could not remember even writing it, but it would have been the kind of thing she would have done. And she read and read.

Here was a whole year of her life. A year when she was completely obsessed with her love for the boy. Every single day started with 'saw Matt', or 'did not see Matt' – a reference to their meetings on the paper rounds. And then there would be notes as to whether they had met, dated, or not, as the case may be. The final statement was always 'I love Matt so much' – or similar. Any other occurrence in her life was incidental. It was a year which showed the development of their relationship. On the final page she had written a beautiful tribute to the boy for giving her such a wonderful time.

Penny felt quite exhausted and traumatised as she closed the little red book. She had just re-lived a very important year of her life. Here was a love story, and the adult sentiments found there would certainly have frightened off a sixteen-year-old boy. But to think that he had kept it for almost fifty years, and he said he had often re-read it. How strange!

Opening the diary once more, she noticed that several pages had black felt crossings out across the tops. Why would she have done that, she wondered. Scanning them closer, she could just make out that there had been words beneath. They were all well scrubbed over, but just one on the inside cover revealed the word 'Bighead'. Why would she have written such a thing in her own diary? Suddenly it came to her that Matt must have written these things – about her, no doubt, and then erased them on its return. But she couldn't read any of the others, Well, she would tackle him over it!

The revelation of the diary had a profound effect on Penny. She knew she must return it as promised. But it was such a lovely piece of writing, that she felt it should never be lost or destroyed. She would like it passed on to her daughters and granddaughters. Maybe he would let her keep it, but initially, she would return it as promised. This she did, but put her thoughts on what should happen to it in the future.

And so began a time of correspondence between Penny and Matt. Occasionally he would telephone, and she found it comforting to have an old friend to talk to. They would talk about old times, and it made a pleasant distraction from the family worries.

Karen was now fighting her last, and she died the first week of December. Penny and Gareth travelled to London for the funeral. It seemed incredible that this should have happened twice to Ross, and yet another young child was left without a mother. It also brought home to Penny the fact that Gareth too was fighting the same disease. He was very much affected by Karen's death. That Christmas was a sad time for all the family, and as the New Year dawned, Penny had an awful feeling of foreboding.

CHAPTER THIRTY-EIGHT
2001

Penny and Matt continued to correspond, and sometimes he would telephone for a chat. Both of them used another outlet for their incoming post, so as to avoid an embarrassing confrontation with their respective spouses. It seemed such a natural thing to Penny, to enjoy this friendship for what it was. But she knew she would not be able to explain to anyone how it was, so was best to stay quiet about it. Matt said, he, too, felt it to be likewise.

They did have a second meeting in the spring. Penny used the same excuse of meeting her old school friend and Matt said he was playing in an away Bowls match for his County. He did play Bowls, and played for his local club, and did in fact sometimes play for the County.

They met at the same hotel, but moved on to a smaller, more intimate inn. Penny had previously sent back her diary to him, but said how she would like it passed on to her family when the time came to dispose of it. But, to her joy, Matt handed it over to her at the hotel, telling her to keep it.

She tackled him over the many black smudges in the diary, as if words had been concealed. He owned up that he had been so annoyed over their break-up, that he had indeed written cruel words about her on several pages. In fact, he had once thrown it in the bin, in frustration, but later retrieved it. And he was pleased he had, reading it over and over throughout the past fifty years.

She had asked him to bring his diary for that same year, 1950, and they had great fun comparing notes on days when they had dated. Penny had brought with her a reel of pink cotton, placing it in front of him and saying, "what does this remind you of?"

"Oh the party at your house," he answered. "Well I'll never forget that!" and he put the reel in his pocket. Then they looked up the entries for the day of the party. They laughed and giggled like two teenagers of that time. And as they left one another at their cars, he brushing her cheek in goodbye, she turned and kissed him. It just seemed the natural thing to do!

Their letters continued, and they sent little things to one another. He sent her a tape of significant songs and the video of The Blue Lagoon. She wrote him a poem, and also a synopsis of what she had done with her life, with some photos of the times. This she did in response to his request, so she then asked that he do the same for her. It was all innocent, good fun, filling in what they had both been up to for the past fifty years.

And it all made an escape for Penny. An escape from the worry that things were not going well for Gareth. He still had his regular check-ups with the doctor and specialist, but it was found that the hormone treatment was now not working, and he was put on another form of medication.

Georgina wanted them to pay a visit to the U.S. to see her and her daughter in a musical show. They had both taken up this new venture the past year. Penny thought it would be something for Gareth to look forward to, and the specialist said he could go. Penny booked their flights to travel in April when the show would be on. Georgina said that during their visit, she would be taking her father to see a specialist in America to see if there was a more advanced treatment for his condition not available in the U.K.

But they never made the trip! Gareth was very ill, and at the next consultation, Penny asked the specialist, "Are we talking of a time, now. Do we have years?"

She and Gareth were stunned when his reply was 'months'! Left alone Penny tried to comfort him. She was so sorry for having asked in his presence as he had always said he would not want to know. But shocked as she was, she was glad they knew. There was so much she needed to ask him, and things to sort out. He had always undertaken their financial matters, so they had to clarify it all for Penny.

Gareth, now on Morphine medication, was changing drastically. At the next hospital check-up, Penny asked, privately, this time, and was told 'weeks'. She could not believe this was happening. Gareth was seventy-five in May. The boys and their families came from London, and it was really a sad birthday for them all, knowing the inevitable outcome.

She called the girls abroad to say they should come soon if they wished to see their father. Georgina arrived first, for one week. She had to leave her little ones behind, so could not stay longer. The day she returned, Jacqueline arrived. In fact the sisters met together at the airport for a few hours.

Complications were setting in with Gareth's condition, and it was becoming very distressing to see him. He had been in and out of hospital a few times, but now they were preparing for the end at home. Penny found it extra disturbing. She tried to talk to him, telling him how much she had loved him and that she still did. But he hardly spoke to her. She asked him if he had things he wished to say to her, but he said not. She would kneel at his side wanting to cling to him in bed at night, but he said it hurt to have her touch or lean on him. And he just seemed too tired to talk.

Eventually he was admitted to the Hospice, where Penny hoped they would sort out his pain and then return him home. On his second day there, Penny told him, "It's Derby Day today, Gareth. Do you remember? It was Derby Day, fifty years ago, that you first spoke to me in school, and asked me out. So we have made our fifty years, Gareth, and I love you for them."

She leaned to hold him and kiss him and his tired and Morphine-doped eyes brightened for one moment, and he squeezed her hand. He did not come home, but died peacefully on the third night, with Penny and Jacqueline at his side.

Penny arranged for the burial to take place in the small country parish church cemetery, in the lane they had so often walked. It was surrounded by fields, and he was laid facing towards Wales. He had always been so proud of being Welsh. She booked a double plot ready for her to join him when ready.

And so it was that the whole family were gathered together for his funeral, not for the Golden Wedding which had been the plans for nine months hence. As a family, they took part in the funeral ceremony. One granddaughter wrote and read a poem, Ross and Gerry both paid tributes to their father, his cousin spoke of him in Welsh and Georgina sang for her father. She had insisted that she wished to do this, so Penny requested she sing 'The Way We Were'. And Penny had got up at dawn a couple of days previous, and written her poem for Gareth. She felt she owed it to him, having promised it for their Golden Wedding. She composed herself throughout the service to deliver her personal tribute to her husband. Yes, she loved Gareth, and on her heart of flowers lying on top of his coffin, she had written, ‘Thank you for loving me’.

CHAPTER THIRTY-NINE

The weeks around the funeral had been such a busy time for Penny, first with the arrangements, and then having so much form filling, letter writing, and business with banks, building societies and such places. But suddenly it began to sink in just how alone she was.

Penny had never really been alone. She was from a large family, and she had a sizeable family of her own, and she and Gareth had been together since the children moved on. She had plenty to do during the day. The garden was enough to keep one occupied, and she visited the cemetery every day she was at home. She would sit on the wooden seat near Gareth's grave, and remember times they had together. Each week she brought the floral heart back, and re-set it with flowers and greenery from the garden.

But at night it was different. To think, that ever since she was seventeen, she had always had Gareth beside her, apart from the very few times one or other of them had been away. They had cuddled every night, and that was what she missed. She had loved to have her back tickled and Gareth usually obliged. He had once told her she was like a kitten curled up beside him, waiting to be stroked, and joked that he didn't know he would have to do that every night when he married her!

Oh, how she missed him. Yes, he had his faults, but then that was Gareth. They had some hard times, but they had also had such fun. They could say or do anything to one another, quite adventurous at times, but Penny was earthy, and he loved her for it. And she knew he had loved her. She had loved Gareth so much and still did.

Lying there, alone, in the bed they had shared, her thoughts drifted back over their life together. And it was the good times that revealed themselves as pictures in her mind.

There was the young girl running through the school hall on the errand for the German master to find out the winner of the Derby. Colliding with Gareth, whose first words to her had been, "Don't run in school," and, later, "My friends call me Gareth," and then, "Would you like to come out one day." Once again she felt the thrill and weakness of her whole body after he had spoken to her, and then the scene on her return to the classroom, unable to answer Mr. Rogers, and forgetting which horse had won!

The first date. The first kiss, which she gave to him. The spooning! How that term amused her. His words of love, and that accent that first intrigued her, but which she came to adore. Being called Cariad. The first trip to Wales, and how she had nearly backed out at the last minute. That week had really sealed their relationship, and she was transformed from the schoolgirl to the young woman.

The first time she had 'gone all the way', and made love in the alley. The dog looking on. She giggled to herself now with the scene before her eyes. And all the lovemaking that had followed right through their years together. The fun and enjoyment it had given them. All the unusual places they had done it. The coach, the golf course, in the sand dunes, the little chalet in the park, and the escapades when they used to go touring in the car and then the caravanette, when the children were older and they could go off alone on their weekends or longer trips.

She smiled to herself when she remembered one little saga as they were touring in the Yorkshire Dales in their Maxi car, which converted to a bed. One lovely sunny day, sitting by a stream, Gareth had started his advances. "Not here," Penny had said, and they strolled on through a little churchyard onto a grass slope surrounded by shrubbery. Getting amorous once more, they were disturbed by a dog barking at them from the nearest house. "It's no good," she had exclaimed. So they walked back to the car and drove on, looking for a suitable place.

"Stop here," Penny said, seeing a pull-in by a stretch of field within which was a very beautiful display of Rhododendron trees. They climbed the gate, and proceeded to the floral area. It was ideal. Within, a grass centre, and the colourful trees around three sides, and before them a wonderful vista of the Dales. "This is a lovely spot," Penny exclaimed, "very romantic."

She had soon divested herself of the skimpy shorts, sun top and undies, but once more they were interrupted. This time it was a swarm of flies, which found the perspiring couple very attractive. Yet again they had to move on. Driving up a lane, which Gareth assured her was completely deserted, in the middle of nowhere, and where he had guaranteed no one would bother them, they pulled into an area beside a gate looking across the sweeping fields to the valley below.

This time they stayed in the car, away from any flies! They converted the seats to make the bed, and once more Penny had stripped off. Indulging once more in their lovemaking, they suddenly heard a steady clip-clop sound. Looking through the side windows, Penny saw a lady riding a huge horse just about to pass the car. There was no time to re-position themselves, and she whispered to Gareth, "Keep still!"

There was no doubt that the lady would have had an excellent view of them from her mount, and Penny felt so embarrassed, all she had been able to do was to bury her face in Gareth's chest. Fortunately she had pulled a rug over themselves beforehand. "I'm not listening to you, anymore," she gasped out, "you saying no-one will come by here!"

"Well, there can't possibly be anyone else," he assured her, and persuaded her to resume their little game.

But it was not to be! Gareth, on top of Penny, and facing the rear window, suddenly saw two men approaching. They wore wellington boots, shooting jackets and carried rifles. Warning Penny, he rolled off her, and lay on his back under the rug, closing his eyes as if having a nap. Penny had jumped up, couldn't get the rug over herself, and grabbed the pillow, holding it to her chest, naked as she was, and trying to sit there nonchalantly as if that was how she always relaxed in the car. The two huntsmen had to squeeze themselves beside the car, to climb the gate, and make their way across the field. It was obvious they would have seen them, and as they descended the hill, they let off a volley of shots!

"That's it," Penny exclaimed. "I'm not saying yes any more. No-one will see us, indeed!" They tidied themselves quickly, their ardour now dampened, put the car straight again, and drove on. But then the funny side of the whole afternoon trying unsuccessfully to make love struck them. Penny could not stop giggling.

"Don't laugh, Penny. You don't know how frustrating it all was," Gareth told her.

"It will make a lovely short story Gareth. Maybe I will write it one day," she answered him.

"Never mind, we'll find a quiet, secluded dark spot tonight somewhere," she added. And they did!

And then there were the tales and jokes that Gareth told. He was a wonderful raconteur, as most Welsh people are. He could hold his audience with stories of the valleys, and his jokes enhanced the many parties they had held. Mind you the same ones were always coming out, but it was a laugh just to hear him tell them.

Penny, too, was known for her teasing and joking. And she recalled what she considered the best joke she had ever played on Gareth. It was April Fool's Day. Gareth was already retired from teaching, but Penny had not yet done so. Waking that morning, she realised what special day it was, and knew Gareth would not realise the significance.

The alarm went off, and she stopped it. She lay there awhile, then turned to Gareth stirring beside her. He was facing away from her, lying on his side. She sidled up behind him, putting her arm around him and nestling herself closer. He stirred again, and said, "The alarm went off, Penny." She wriggled against him.

"Oh, I'm not going to school today. Let's have a day in bed, Gareth!" He turned to face her.

"That sounds a good idea. Nothing could be nicer."

They began their kissing and caressing, and just as they were getting extra-involved, Penny suddenly broke away, flung back the covers, and leapt out of bed, shouting "April Fool," and proceeded to get herself ready for school. She laughed so much but when she looked back at Gareth, he was devastated and cursed her for it.

Coming back from the bathroom she said, "Sorry, Gareth. That was a bit mean of me. It nearly backfired, too, because I was so tempted to stay. But school calls, I'll make it up to you tonight, I promise." And she did!

Yes, they had a lot of fun. She thought of the holidays they had taken, especially when they became financially more secure, and were able to travel abroad. The first time was when they took the whole family as teenagers, plus the boys' friends and Penny's sister Rosamund and her husband Morris asked to join them. They all had a short break in Majorca one school half term. Gareth had always said he would not fly, and for the first time Penny had encouraged him to drink, so that he was quite merry, and they led him to the plane like a lamb to the slaughter.

Since then, they had travelled regularly, and much further afield around the world. Penny had always organised everything, and Gareth left it to her, quite happy to go along with her suggestions and arrangements. Well, now it seemed she would be going alone. But they had been good times.

Her thoughts drifted to the family. She had so enjoyed having the children, and Gareth had loved them all, especially enjoying the first years of each one. She knew he had not coped very well with the later teenage problems, but inwardly he was very concerned for them all. And then there were the grandchildren. What a joy they had all been to them both. They called Gareth, Dadcu, the welsh for Granddad. He so loved being called Dadcu. Well, at least he would not have to cope with the teenage problems with them. He had now gone before most of them had reached that time.

Penny snapped out of her thoughts. Yes, Gareth had gone. He had once told her, "When I'm gone, you will still be nearly a decade younger. Best thing you can do is find someone else to look after you. I would like you to find happiness again, and as long as I'm not there to see it, it's okay."

She was horrified and said she could never do that, but he had said, "You deserve more happiness, Penny."

She lay there now, looking at his photo beside the bed, feeling the empty space beside her, and crying.

CHAPTER THIRTY-NINE

Penny sat in the garden one day, several weeks after Gareth's death, deep in thought. She was looking back over her life, and thought of Matt again. She suddenly realised that she had not heard from him by letter or phone since weeks before the funeral. Last time she had written was when Gareth was very, very ill. In fact, Matt would not know he had died, so she better write to tell him. There would be no need for him to address his reply elsewhere any more.

Some days later, Matt phoned. Penny was surprised to hear him, and he explained how he knew things were bad from previous letters, and he did not like to intrude on her privacy. But he told her he had said a prayer for her in Church. They talked a long while, and gradually Penny brightened up, and they were giggling at silly things once more. "Perhaps we can meet again, when you feel up to it," he said.

"I'd like that, Matt," she replied.

The following month she received a letter to say that he was going to watch a County game just outside Gloucester. Maybe they could meet once more, if possible. Penny thought she would like him to see where she lived. She had written to him previously of Hereford and the beautiful surrounding countryside. Yes, she would like to entertain him at home, and wrote to him with her thoughts. Maybe he could come on after the game, and she would prepare a meal for them.

Matt phoned soon afterwards, accepted her offer and said he would hope to arrive late morning. He might only look in at the Bowls venue. He would be coming the next week, and hoped he wouldn't be an embarrassment to her with neighbours, etc. "Of course not," she answered, "I can have who I like to visit. We're old friends."

Penny thought over her action during the following days. She hadn't really pondered that people might think it was 'not the done thing'. Well, she couldn't just shut herself off from society. And as the day drew nearer, she began to feel excited at the prospect of welcoming Matt to her home.

She planned what she would prepare for lunch, and then wondered how long he would stay. What could they do? She decided that she would take him for a short drive around the lanes, possibly look at a couple of beautiful views of the river and the hills of Wales in the background, maybe take a short walk, then drive through the town. Or they could sit out in the garden, look at old photos, etc. Penny had only visualised a beautiful, sunny day.

Going to bed the previous night, she felt jittery and excited that Matt was coming, but also nervous. She hardly slept, and was up early. Drawing the curtains, she discovered a black sky and heavy rain, and she knew by that sky it would be a whole day of it. They couldn't possibly play bowls in that. Maybe he wouldn't come. But he did!

He arrived on time, and said her directions were fine. He was very smart in his County Bowls gear, and said the team would have set off whatever the weather, but he did not now intend joining them. Penny served coffee in the sun lounge, and the rain was pouring down outside. Matt had brought more old school material with him. Penny had sent some team photos to the organiser of the school web site, and these were returned to her via Matt.

She showed him over the house and he perused the many photos on display, asking about each one. Then they had lunch, and retired to the lounge. Penny suggested a short drive in her car. It was still raining, but they were both agreeable.

She set off down the lanes, a quick look at the Abbey, there's the church where Gareth is buried, here's the Golf Club with its wonderful vista, but it's too wet to get out and see it, higher up a lovely view of the river and mountains, all covered in cloud. Oh, it was ridiculous! And Penny felt she was driving at her worst. What was the matter with her! All she was conscious of was the close proximity of Matt beside her, and she suddenly remembered the first time she had ever gone out with him alone, when he had asked her to go to the big football ground where one of the boys at school was being given a trial. They had travelled on the bus, and she had felt him sitting so close to her. Yes, this was it!

She ploughed on through the wet, muddy lanes, and then drove on for a quick look at the town, finally heading back home. What a futile task it had been! Back in the house, she asked him when he would have to leave, and between them they decided that he should wait until the big towns en–route would have finished with the rush hour.

He was looking at some of her music tapes, and she put them on. They sat together, listening and discussing them. Penny felt strange and was suddenly aware that here she was, with Matt, completely alone, and she thought back to the little love seat in the hall of her old home. It would be more than fifty years since they had been together like this.

She jumped up, saying she would put the kettle on for a cup of tea, as time was now getting late. She put on another tape and went to the kitchen. As she was returning, Matt was coming out of the lounge, maybe he was going to the 'loo', but they collided in the hall, and as she put out her hand, she laughed, "Oh, shall we dance," and suddenly they were dancing to the strains of Frank Sinatra . Matt laughed, too, "Dancing in the hall again." A reference to the lunchtime sessions back at school. Penny giggled, "Oh, yes."

But as they swayed together, with their arms around each other, Penny felt waves and waves of sensations surging through her whole body, and Matt was burying his head in her, and then he was sighing loudly.

Penny was so overcome with her feelings, she came over all weak, and almost thought she would faint. But then she turned her face to him, and they were kissing, and the passion was overwhelming her whole being. It was now a wonderful release from the tension that had been building up between them throughout the day.

Penny tried to think what she was doing. Was it wrong? But no, this was Penny and Matt, the Item of fifty years ago just carrying on where they had left off, and heading where they had always known they were meant to go. They broke apart, she whispering his name, and he hers. Penny felt she was at fault, had led him on, and said she was sorry, but he was saying he didn't know what had come over him, but then they were clinging again and the waves swept through them both, and she whispered to him, "Oh, Matt, it's just like fifty years ago. What are we going to do?"

"Penny, I haven't felt like this for so long," and he was holding her tight and sighing into her again.

Penny pulled slightly away. “What do you want to do Matt?” He knew what she meant.

“I’d better go,” he said, but as they looked at each other, both knew they didn’t want him to leave.

“You don’t have to, Matt. We can go upstairs,” and she led the way.

Reaching the top of the stairs, she turned along the landing into her bedroom, and sat waiting on her big double bed. Her heart was pounding, and for a moment she shut her eyes. She was Penny Saunders again, fifteen, waiting for the young boy to follow the pink cotton.

Matt had paused at the foot of the stairs. He was torn between his desire to follow Penny, and his conscience telling him it was wrong. He saw her turn at the top of the stairs, and suddenly he was the lad of sixteen, following the pink cotton to the unknown.

Mounting the top stair, he heard her call, “I’m in here Matt,” and in his head those words from more than fifty years ago, “Where have you been!” But this time there were no other young party goers getting in a muddle of tangled cottons, only the young and innocent boy finding his young and nubile girl.

He closed the door behind him, and joined her on the bed, pushing her back beneath him. They resumed their passionate kissing and caressing. Both were feeling those same sensations of half a century previous. But this time there were no noisy friends downstairs calling out, ‘Penny, Matt, where are you?’ They were just the girl and the boy about to find their Blue Lagoon.

“Oh Matt. It’s the end of the cotton reel game at last,” she whispered, and he told her over and over that it had been so long since he had felt so wonderful. But although they shared intimate moments, they never made love. Later, lying in his arms, Penny told him it had been a beautiful session of lovemaking, and she guessed their problem was a guilty conscience. And then he told her of the unusual relationship he shared with his wife. Penny listened sympathetically, then looked at the clock, and Matt said he had better leave.

After tidying themselves, they returned downstairs, and saying goodbye, both of them tried to explain what had overtaken them. Each tried to take the blame but finally agreed it had been mutual, a true release of something that had lain dormant for fifty years, but which had always been there. They kissed goodbye, and Penny said, "Don't think badly of me, Matt, please. I would have run a mile if anyone else had done that. But it's just you, Matt. And I didn't plan this, I promise you. I hope you'll come again. Please Matt."

CHAPTER FORTY

There was no sleep for Penny that night. She thought over and over the day's happening. She still tingled from their embraces. She tried to feel disgusted with herself. But it did not seem wrong. How could she explain to anyone that this was she and Matt of old, renewing their relationship, and continuing in a more adult way. No way could she have behaved like that with anyone else. What had happened had been explosive, like a time bomb waiting to go off.

What would her family think of her, and the neighbours and friends? They would all say it had been far too soon after Gareth's death. And as she lay there, she looked at Gareth's photo and whispered, "Sorry, Gareth. Please don't be cross with me. I still love you, but the memory of Matt has always been in me. You told me to find happiness again." And as she lay tossing and turning, she suddenly felt that perhaps Gareth had been there, engineering the past meetings and today's reunion.

Officially she had done nothing wrong. She was now a widow, but most people would say she had not been a widow long enough. What would seem wrong, would be the fact that Matt was a married man. She would never want to be the 'other woman' in a marriage. She knew how she would have felt if it had happened to her. But having heard Matt's story, she felt no shame.

He had not married until he was thirty-eight. He had previously enjoyed many relationships, but none had been long-standing. His main interest was his sport. He met his wife within work. She was in an unhappy marriage and they both seemed to hit it off together, and, on her divorce, they married. Matt was doing well at work, and they set up a very substantial home over the years, plus a holiday bungalow. And they had two sons.

Their relationship had seemed satisfactory until the latter years when he felt things were not quite the same for Veronica, his wife. Their physical activities became uneasy for her, and, gradually, their love-making waned, until it became almost non-existent, and had remained like that for several years now. Matt assumed this to be the normal situation.

They both devoted their energy to their passionate interests. He pursued his bowls, bridge clubs, the opera and music which he liked intensely. Veronica involved herself in local activities connected mainly with the church. Now that the boys were adult, she had devoted herself to missionary and overseas aid work, very often spending lengthy stays abroad.

They were well respected in the community and to all appearances a happy family. They entertained at home, and visited friends and family as a couple. They were, in fact, satisfied with their domestic set-up. But it was now a marriage of friendship, devoid of any physical lovemaking.

Matt said he had just accepted the situation. Yes, he had missed making love, but having experienced the difficulties for so long, he had accepted the outcome. Penny had queried whether he had not strayed elsewhere, but he said not. No wonder he had murmured to her that it had been so long since he had 'felt like that'. She could not comprehend how you could live with someone so close, and not have some form of physical association. It would not have done for her! But now that she knew his story, she did not feel guilty that she was involved with a married man when that man was Matt. He deserved some happiness.

And as she finally lapsed into a half sleep, she had convinced herself that what had happened, not only that day, but over the past months since that meeting at the reunion evening, was fate. It was meant to be! Was this to be the love story that she had believed in so earnestly as a young virgin? Well, she was no longer that, but maybe the Blue Lagoon was still within her grasp.

Matt phoned next morning. He asked how she felt, and she poured out her heart to him with her feelings on what had happened between them. He endorsed almost all she said, and they agreed that he should make a return visit some time. Later that week Penny received a sensitive letter from him in reply to hers, which she just had to send him. She had written, trying to describe the spontaneous beautiful feelings she had experienced as they held each other in the hall. He, too, emphasised the tremendous intensity of their liaison. "I never knew dancing in such a confined space could be so delightful, and lead to such a wonderful embrace," he wrote.

Two weeks later they arranged the second visit. "Do you know what I would really like to do, Penny? I would like us to go for a swim in the pool, just as we used to all those years ago." Penny thought it was a wonderful idea. She went most weeks by herself.

He arrived as before, and after greeting him with a tender kiss, they had a coffee, and then left for the leisure centre pool. It was school holidays and so there were plenty of young people there. They swam a few lengths together, and Penny was remembering how she used to gaze with adoration at Matt diving. But he said he didn't dive now. They changed quickly and returned home. It was another awful rain-sodden day. "You're doomed with the weather when you come here," she told him.

"Yes, and I'm supposed to be at County Bowls again!" he answered.

Entering the house, Penny was going to set about getting the lunch, but he said he would rather eat later, just before he left. They both knew what each other was thinking, and once more Penny turned on the music. They moved together for a moment, and Penny remarked that they both smelled of chlorine. "Shall we rinse it off then?" he said.

"Yes, use the shower in my room if you want, Matt." They both went upstairs, and Penny turned on the shower for him, and went to get fresh towels.

Going back to the bedroom she found he was already in the shower cubicle. She sat on the bed wondering! "Is it hot enough?" she called.

"Yes, lovely! Aren't you showering too?" And she stripped to join him. Now they were truly the boy and girl under the waterfall of the Blue Lagoon. And later her bed served as the white sands. Afterwards, as she lay quietly in his arms, he whispered, "So that's where the pink cotton ended up."

"That's right, Matt, but you sure did take a long time getting to the end of it. It's taken you fifty years."

"It was worth waiting for, Penny. So many times I read

over your diary, and wondered, ‘what if?’ But now I know.

And when Penny received his next letter, it read, ‘That was the finest Bowls match I have played for years. I never knew a game could be so enjoyable!

CHAPTER FORTY-ONE

There now began a time of intense phone calls and letters. Penny was busy with various family and friends coming to stay, and so the lovers could not meet. In fact, Matt had told Penny he had not felt it right, making love to her in her marital bed.

She made some visits to the boys in London, and they were able to meet for a pub lunch or an evening drink, but with a kiss and cuddle in the car, it was very frustrating. Both agreed that they were now very much involved and felt like the sixteen-year-olds of way back. It was certainly as lovely a feeling, but it hurt when they were apart.

They arranged to meet at a hotel, convenient for both, and spend a day together. It was wonderful to be alone for so long, and indulge in their passion. And it was all good fun, too. They swam in the hotel pool, took a Jacuzzi together, played their music tapes that they had given each other, and made love over and over. And they held hands across thc table when dining afterwards. "What a couple of sillies we are," Matt remarked. "Are we really in our sixties!"

"No, Matt, we're sixteen!"

Penny was to pay a visit to Georgina and family in the U.S., hopefully to see Georgina's show. She arranged to go for three weeks. But it meant three weeks apart for the 'teenage' lovers. They met at the hotel for a day together, shortly before she left. At the back of Penny's mind, from the start of their relationship, had been the thought that maybe this was just a 'bit of fun' for Matt, finding her 'available'. Inwardly, she did not think it was so, but the whole scenario of them discovering each other again, and finding love still there, seemed too incredible to be true. Something out of a B grade novel. But the more they spoke or met, she could feel such a tenderness and care from him, that she now believed that he, too, was experiencing the same feelings.

The day before she was to leave for the U.S. they met at lunchtime near to Ross's home where she was staying. Matt said if she didn't mind, he had arranged for them to pay a quick visit to their mutual school-friend who organised the school web site, at his home nearby. He had team photos to pass on. It happened that Derek was the one who had originally spoken to her about Matt, that first Old Scholars' Reunion night, the year that Matt had not attended. Also, his partner, June, would be there, and she and Penny had once been teaching colleagues.

They drove to the house, set in a pretty country village, and spent a very enjoyable two hours. Matt had not divulged his true involvement with Penny, and they were both trying to appear detached from one another. But it was hard to do so. So hard! Tomorrow Penny would be on her way to the U.S. At one point they all strolled around the extensive grounds. Their friends were ahead of them, and Matt took her hand. It was such a special gesture for Penny, and flashbacks of those years ago formed in her mind. Too soon, it was time to leave, but it had been a very special few hours. It was the first time they had been together in the company of friends. Penny was sure their feelings had been sensed by their friends, but she felt that they, as the Item, had been accepted and sanctioned.

Driving back to where Penny had left her car, she asked Matt to pull into a field lay-by for their last few minutes together. They kissed and cuddled, and both promised to write while she was away. Too soon, Penny got in her own car, and they drove their respective ways. Three weeks seemed such a long while.

Penny started her first letter while in the Departure Lounge at the airport, and continued it on the ten-hour flight. She always enjoyed letter writing, and was known for her style. She wrote as she spoke, and could be very amusing and cheeky! And so she wrote to Matt, full of fun and fantasy.

In fact, this was a very important factor in their relationship. They both had such an innocent, amusing side to their characters. Indeed, it had always been so, even back in their school days. It was why they had been such a couple for so long, compared to the short boy and girl relationships most of their peers enjoyed. Possibly this was also a factor in how they had resumed their friendship, seemingly where they had left off.

Penny enjoyed her time with Georgina and family, but her thoughts continually drifted back to Matt. She felt she wanted to tell her daughter of her new relationship, but knew she would not be able to convey her feelings and the circumstances of their new–found association. No onc would appreciate how special it all was, and would think it too soon. And Penny did not want that criticism of her, especially by her family. Possibly in a year or so, they would be happy for her to have found a friend again. But no, for now she must keep it to herself.

She wrote several letters to Matt, and received two from

him, but it was obvious he had not received hers, as yet. Then one morning, Georgina answered the phone, and called to Penny, "It's for you, Mum. Someone called Matt!" Penny was surprised, and thrilled. She was conscious of her daughter in the room, and wondered how to talk to him. He said he had not received her letters yet, and wondered if all was well. She spent most of the time on the call, giggling nervously. As she put the phone down, she knew that the inquisition from her daughter would follow.

"Well, who's that then?" Georgina asked.

"Oh, one of the Old Scholars. We met up at the last reunion. We go back a long way. Used to go out together. The only other real love of my life," she tried to jest.

"We've been corresponding lately." Georgina smiled at her mother. "Well, he must be pretty keen to ring America."

"He's just so considerate," was Penny's stupid answer.

"Now I know why you've been watching for the mail every day," Georgina continued.

"Yes, well there's one problem. I'm afraid he's married," Penny rambled on.

"It can't be a very good relationship if he's corresponding with you. Or do you see him sometimes?" the probing continued.

"We've met for lunch or a drink a few times when I've been up with the boys. He's been good for me since Dadda died. And he says I've been good for him."

"Oh, good luck then, but you better watch out if there's a wife around," Georgina warned. But Penny did not elaborate.

Upon returning home to England, Penny found that Georgina had already passed word around to the other siblings about their mother's new-found friend. Penny expected she would have, and so each one tackled her about it. She could not deny it, but felt Georgina had elaborated on the story. Anyway, she didn't really care any more. It was her life, and she would let things develop as they would.

She had a wonderful reunion with Matt on returning home. But they had still never spent a night together, but she hoped one day they might. Eventually they did manage three days away together. It was wonderful. There were so many incidental gestures that added to the total enjoyment. Walking hand in hand, sitting together in the car, calling in at McDonalds and sitting by the fountain in the shopping mall, making a cup of tea for each other, waking in the night and finding him still beside her, listening to his breathing, taking breakfast together, and of course, enjoying each other in every way without the thought of leaving, and talking, and saying over and over how unbelievable it was that they were together again.

Then the hardship of parting once more and always the fact that Matt was officially a married man. Penny knew he put so much 'on the line' for her. He had his position in the community, and was a prominent member of his club and such groups, and of course there were his family and friends. Yes, Matt had a lot to lose!

CHAPTER FORTY-TWO
2002

Penny was planning a winter trip to her girls, visiting the U.S. first, and then moving on to New Zealand to visit Jacqueline and family in their summer time. She was to leave mid-January, and not return until almost the end of March. She wanted to see the children and grandchildren very much, and she also had several nieces and nephews there, the result of two of her brothers having emigrated there. They had now both died. But it would mean being two months apart from Matt!

Matt had once told her that their old school pal, Jack Stewart, lived in New Zealand. They had corresponded over the years and always telephoned each other on birthdays. Jack and Matt had always been such staunch friends, and Penny remembered how jealous she had been of the time the two boys spent together, in their youth. She had often blamed Jack for the break-up of her and Matt, believing he teased him about sticking to her for so long. But Matt now assured her it was not true. Jack had always 'played the field'.

"Why don't you come to New Zealand while I am there, and visit Jack?" she asked. Matt knew it would be a lovely solution to their parting, but he did not do so.

"Well give me Jack's address any way, and I'll make a point of seeing him," she promised.

They managed a few liaisons in hotels before and after the last Christmas season, and then the time arrived for Penny to leave. Two months really would be the test of time!

Penny enjoyed being with her overseas families again, but found it very sad. She had always had Gareth with her before, and he had particularly enjoyed visiting New Zealand, and they had made many friends there. It meant that his name was constantly being brought up, with people saying how sorry they were, and how she must miss him. She could not deny that, but there was no way that he could be brought back. She still had her memories, but life had to go on.

The lovers corresponded frequently, and Matt telephoned several times. His words were full of missing her, and how he could not wait for her return. Penny's sentiments echoed his. She did manage to meet up with Jack, and realised that Matt had told him some of their story, possibly not saying how intense they had become, but implying they were now more than just good friends. "Yes, you two always were meant for each other," he told her over dinner at his home where she had visited. Jack was on his third wife! Well, he always did go for quantity in women.

Penny returned home. She was sad at leaving her family yet again, but excited at the prospect of a reunion with Matt. He had arranged to meet her, and would take her to Ross's home, where she intended stopping a few days to see the boys and their families, before returning to her own home.

He had said in one of his letters that he had something important to discuss with her on her return. He met her at the station and, seeing him again, she felt all the old feelings surging through her, and as he held her close to him, she caught his vibes, too. "Oh, how I've missed you Penny. I thought when you last went away for three weeks it was a long time, but two months was endless."

"Me, too," she murmured.

They managed to meet briefly of a lunchtime while she was at Ross's, but booked a hotel the day she intended to return home. Matt had said he had to talk to her. Reaching their hotel room, they hardly got through the door before they started their intense lovemaking, and afterwards, as Penny nestled against his chest, she said, "Thanks for the birthday card you sent to New Zealand. I'm now seventeen! It's still the feeling," she teased him.

"I know, Penny, I can't believe we're getting nearer the seventies. Let's hope we have some more years to enjoy each other. Now I want to talk to you, seriously. I've decided to divorce Veronica."

Penny could not believe what he had just said.

"No, you mustn't, Matt. You have too much to lose; the lovely home you worked for, your family, your friends, your standing in the community. You can't give all that up for me. You may regret it. I have nothing to lose, Matt. I'm grateful for the time we can be together, however small, and just your phone calls mean so much."

"No, Penny, I've discussed it with Veronica. We've worked it out between us. I'll keep the house, and she will have the country bungalow plus a good settlement. The boys have both left home now, but the house is there if they wish to return. We both feel now that our circumstances should come into the open. Anyway, we think a lot of our friends have suspected for some time. The divorce will be a mere formality. And then, Penny, I want you to marry me."

For one moment, she didn't think she had heard right.

Matt was asking her to marry him! Oh how she had dreamed of that as a young girl, and to hear him say those words now was incredible. She turned towards him. "Matt, you don't have to do that for me. You don't have to give up so much."

"I'm not giving anything up, Penny. I'm hoping to get the girl I always loved to marry me, and spend whatever years we have left, together. So come on, what's the answer."

"Well it's yes, Matt. It always would have been."

After kissing and cuddling and Penny having a cry, he then said, "and now, young lady, I have something else exciting to tell you." Penny couldn't think what it could be. "We have found the whereabouts of your friends Belinda and Joyce."

Penny was stunned. "How? When? Where?"

"Well, Belinda got logged onto the Old Scholars' web site, and from snippets she passed on, Derek has traced Joyce. Belinda lives on the south coast, and Joyce is only about a mile from where your Ross lives."

When they had sorted themselves out to part, yet again, he gave her the girls' addresses and phone numbers. And the first thing Penny did when she reached home was to phone them both. It eased the pressure of having to leave Matt.

In the following months, she had met up with both girls. There was so much to catch up on. They both still had their husbands, and of course, children and grandchildren. Penny was able to meet up with Joyce each visit to the boys, and she had visited Belinda, and also entertained both girls in her home in Hereford. They were pleased for her when she intimated that she had met up with Matt again.

"Well, I guess that's the way it should have been," Belinda commented.

"Maybe it's better the second time around," Penny replied,

"but I don't think I would have changed my life. I loved Gareth, and still do. But I always felt I loved the two of them – if that is possible. I don't think anyone would understand. So much has happened since I went to the Old Scholars' reunion, and yet, I feel it was all meant to happen. And now I've met my two best friends again. It's Kismet!"

CHAPTER FORTY-THREE

The divorce was finalised by early summer. Matt and Veronica had an agreeable separation and there were no hard feelings. In fact, they both seemed relieved to have finally made the break, got it all in the open, and allowed to get on with their new lives.

Matt and Penny were married in London, with just their immediate families present. Derek was best man and Penny insisted on inviting Belinda and Joyce. Penny's daughters did not come over, as, after the wedding, the newlyweds were going on a trip to visit Georgina and family in the U.S. and then on to New Zealand to see Jacqueline and family, and also Jack Stewart. Derek told them he had put out an item of news on the school web site: 'Penny Saunders and Matthew Oliver have finally tied the knot. Good Luck to them both'.

After a family dinner at a local French restaurant, they spent their first night at the hotel where they had previously enjoyed their days of lovemaking. "I really am Mrs Oliver now," she told Matt, as they checked in. "To think how I dreamed of being called that all those years ago."

Then it was on to Heathrow for their flight to the U.S. They were hiring a car, and were to have a short tour of California, also spending a few days with Georgina. They were then going to move on to New Zealand. Matt had undertaken all the arrangements, and Penny had asked him why they had to go via Fiji to change planes. He said that was what they were offered at the best price, so Penny hadn't argued, as she and Gareth had once taken that route.

Arriving in Fiji, he led the way out of the airport. "I thought we only had to change planes," she queried.

"Well, no, we have a night's stop-over," he answered, then led her to a taxi, saying something to the driver. Off they sped, and indeed had a long drive.

"Well it's a long way for a night's stopover," Penny said, "but it's nice to see around." Finally they stopped, got out, and were then taken to a small boat, the driver carrying the luggage for them. "They include a little boat trip on this sight-seeing," Matt explained. It was a short ride across the clear water, and were then landed on a small island. As they stepped off, the sign read, 'Welcome to the Blue Lagoon Resort'.

Penny looked at Matt. "We've got a whole week here, Mrs Oliver. Will you join me?" Penny could not believe that she had been so naïve in not suspecting what the plans really were. "Oh Matt, you absolute darling. What a softie you are! I have dreamed of this."

It was a beautiful place. There were just fourteen little houses for the couples that were staying there. All the others seemed young, but Penny and Matt weren't bothered. The island was picturesque, and the resort centre had a restaurant and facilities for intimate entertainment. They could sit out on the balcony of their little rush-roofed house built on stilts. There were palm trees all around affording shade from the hot sun, and the white sand led down to the clear crystal, warm sea, with its rocks at either end of the curving bay. There were beautiful flowers with pungent perfumes that filled the air, and they could follow little paths into the centre of the island. At one point, they came upon the waterfall shown in the film, and Penny and Matt stood under it just as the boy and girl had. Yes, this really was where they had filmed the Blue Lagoon, the book that Penny had found so inspiring.

They swam in the sea, and Matt even dived off the rocks, while Penny sat under the palm trees, gazing at him in adoration. He was that young boy, and then he came to join the young girl lying on the sand.

And as they lay together under the palms, Penny whispered, "Matt, we are the couple in the Blue Lagoon. But I'm sorry we weren't each other's first lover as we should have been. It meant so much to me. But I love you Matt as if we were." He leaned over to kiss her.

"Penny, don't you realise that we are each other's last lover, and that is just as special. And I love you for it."

END

APPENDIX

Penny did eventually write her book as she had once told Gareth she would.

She called it, *'Penny's Tale'*.